GOODBYE GIRL

ALSO BY JAMES GRIPPANDO

* A Jack Swyteck novel

GOODBYE GIRL

A JACK SWYTECK NOVEL

JAMES GRIPPANDO

HARPER

An Imprint of HarperCollinsPublishers

HarperCollins books may be purchased for educational, business, or sales promotional use. For information, please email the Special Markets Department at SPsales @harpercollins.com.

FIRST EDITION

Library of Congress Cataloging-in-Publication Data has been applied for.

ISBN 978-0-06-322384-4

23 24 25 26 27 LBC 5 4 3 2 1

For Tiffany.
Thirty years, three kids, and three goldens later,
you are still the LOML.

GOODBYE GIRL

PROLOGUE

Swarms of no-see-ums, millions of tiny insects, hovered over the mangrove-covered coastline, glistening like dust mites in the orange-and-magenta twilight. Nearly all of the 173,000 acres that made up Biscayne Bay National Park lie in shallow waters warmed by the Gulf Stream and subtropical climate. FBI Special Agent Andie Henning was north of the Florida Keys, where fresh water from the Florida Everglades flowed into the bay to create an estuary-like mix of fresh and salt water. Her flats boat cruised at the deliberate speed of a hungry but patient crocodile eyeing an egret. Along the shore, hundreds of pink flamingos, ankle deep in the shallows, stood on one leg and watched the passing boat, as if to wonder what the FBI was doing there.

"This is starting to feel like the proverbial needle in a haystack," said Andie.

Fellow agent Grace Kennedy had one hand on the throttle. At such a slow speed, the outboard engine purred like a sewing machine.

"It's a million-to-one shot that we find anything before dark," said Grace.

Andie peered through her binoculars, her gaze sweeping the tangled, exposed root system of a shadowy mangrove forest.

Homicides were not typically within the jurisdiction of the FBI, but a dead body in a national park was not strictly a matter for local law enforcement. The circumstances surrounding this apparent homicide were of keen interest to Agent Henning. A man identifying himself as the killer had called a local reporter to say his victim could be found at low tide in Biscayne Bay National Park. As a rookie agent, Andie had made a name for herself infiltrating a cult in Washington's Yakima Valley, and by the time she'd transferred to south Florida, she had more experience in the multijurisdictional tracking of serial killers, domestic terrorists, and other homicidal maniacs than anyone in the Miami office.

"How was your date with Perry Mason?" asked Grace. It was an abrupt change of subject, but after two hours of swatting mosquitos a diversion was a good thing.

Andie lowered her binoculars. "You mean the lawyer who asked me out? His name's Jack. Jack Swyteck."

"Swyteck? Any relation to the former Governor Swyteck?"

"He's Jack's father."

"A criminal defense lawyer and son of a politician. What's the third strike against him?"

Andie laughed. "He doesn't have *any* strikes against him."

"Does that mean you're going to say yes if he asks for a second date?"

"He's not going to ask for a second date."

"How do you know?"

"Because I already asked him for a second date. And he said yes."

Grace smiled and shook her head. "A criminal defense lawyer and an FBI agent. I hear wedding bells already."

Andie's cellphone rang, which was weird, even if it did sound more like a xylophone than approaching nuptials. She answered and put the call on speaker so Grace could listen. It was Gustavo Cruz, a homicide detective with the Miami-Dade Police Department.

"We found the body," he said and then quickly shared the coordinates.

Andie checked the map on her cellphone. "That's outside the park."

"Yes. Well north of it."

"The caller said the body was in the park," said Andie.

"I'll note that in my report: anonymous tipster sucks at geography. The point here is that it's outside FBI jurisdiction. We won't be needing your assistance."

Turf wars between the FBI and local law enforcement were as old as the oolitic limestone that formed the Florida Keys. Andie was getting the sense that Detective Cruz had sent the feds on a proverbial wild-flamingo chase as MDPD followed better leads to the actual disposal site.

"I thought you were above these games, Gustavo."

"No games. We got this," he said, and the call ended.

"Jackass," said Andie as she put away her phone.

"It's fine. Let MDPD have it," said Grace.

Andie was not so easily blown off. "The caller said 'in the park.' If the murder was in the park, we still have jurisdiction, even if the body drifted somewhere else."

Grace agreed. The outboard engine roared, the bow rose, and they were suddenly speeding across the glasslike waters, throwing a wake that sent flamingos scattering. Twilight was upon them as they motored away from the mainland and headed north into slightly choppier waters. Andie's long, dark hair whipped in the breeze as they sped past her favorite view of Miami's famous cityscape, which sparkled with one brightly lit high-rise after another. A fleet of Caribbean-bound cruise ships lined the port like floating hotels. To the east was Miami Beach, which—as Andie had learned only after her transfer from Seattle—was actually a barrier island between the bay and the Atlantic Ocean, the mainland's first defense to hurricanes and tropical storms. Their destination was beyond Venetian Islands, a chain of man-made islands that dotted the bay and connected the peninsula to Miami Beach like giant stepping-stones straight out of *Gulliver's Travels*.

"That way," Andie shouted over the noisy outboard. She was pointing to the flashing beacons from a circle of marine patrol boats ahead. Grace cut their speed to "no-wake" as they approached the floating crime scene.

An artificial island that never came to be, Isola di Lolando was supposed to be the next Venetian Island, expanding the availability of pricey waterfront properties in the bay. The seawall for the planned island was under construction when the Great Miami Hurricane of 1926 made landfall and left only destruction in its wake. The market crash of 1929 and the Great Depression that followed sealed the project's fate, forever abandoned, leaving behind only the pilings, which were visible depending on the tide.

"Bizarre," said Grace.

It was low tide. Andie and her partner had a full view of a no-longer-submerged body chained to a concrete piling.

"Even by Miami standards," said Andie.

Darkness had fallen, but the scene was amply lit by forensic lights from a nearby marine patrol boat. Beneath the surface, an underwater recovery team was at work, the sweep of their dive lights setting the submerged half of the piling aglow. Andie kept the FBI's boat on the perimeter, so as not to interfere, but she was close enough to absorb key details. The body was wet but fully clothed. Caucasian male. Probably in his twenties. Warm water hastened decomposition, making it harder to estimate a time of death. Even in the subtropics, however, it could take a week for the skin to peel away from underlying tissues and invite fish, crabs, and sea lice to nibble away at the flesh. Andie guessed it had been a day, at most two, since the killer had put his work on display.

Marine patrol motored up beside Andie's boat and idled its engine. Detective Cruz was onboard. At the risk of sounding defensive, Andie spoke first.

"We may be outside the federal park," said Andie, "but I wouldn't be so quick to rule out FBI jurisdiction over this homicide."

"I agree," said Cruz.

The detective's sudden shift in position caught her by surprise. "What changed?"

"The body has a message on the torso."

"A message or a tattoo?"

"Definitely a message. From the killer, I suspect. It's written in some kind of marker pen. The ink is partly washed away, which tells me the body has been here at least one tide cycle. But you can still read it."

"What does it say?"

"Looks like 'goodbye girl.'"

Andie glanced at the body, then back, confused. "On first look, I thought we had a male victim."

"Definitely male."

Andie quickly caught up to his thinking. "So, is he gay or trans?"

"Don't have an ID yet, so can't say for sure. But given his killer's message . . ."

"You're thinking federal hate crime based on sexual orientation or gender identity," said Andie, filling in the blank.

"About the size of it," said Cruz.

Andie was on the same page. "Looking forward to working with you, Detective."

"I look forward to working with you, as well," said Cruz, and his boat pulled away.

"No, you don't," Andie said quietly. Then she and her partner exchanged glances.

"What do you make of it?" asked Grace.

"Hard to say. A lot depends on whether the victim was chained to the piling alive and left to drown with the rising tide, or if the murder took place somewhere else and the body was brought here purely for display."

"Either way, we're dealing with one sick fuck."

Andie's gaze drifted back to the victim. "You got that right."

CHAPTER 1

Twelve Years Later

Saturday night was date night. Not to be confused with sex night. "One date, one sex night—minimum, per week." Such was the "professional" advice Jack and Andie got as devoted parents of a seven-year-old daughter who were desperate to inject a little romance into the balance between family and career.

Jack jumped behind the wheel and started the car. They were running late, partly the fault of the babysitter, but mostly because they were always running late. Late for drop-off at Righley's school. Late for work. Late for pickup. Late for dinner. Late for the airport. Late for parties. Jack had even missed his chance to see one of David Letterman's final performances because they were late to the *Late Show*.

Andie was still brushing her hair as she climbed into the passenger seat. Jack backed out of the driveway, a crunchy swatch of crushed seashells that was big enough for just one car, which was typical of older homes on the smallest of lots on Key Biscayne. As they pulled away, Andie reached behind his neck and ripped the price tag from his shirt collar.

"Good Lord, I'm turning into my father."

"Better you did it on date night than sex night," said Andie.

Jack smiled, but the truth was, they were just three weeks into "date night/sex night," and he was already tired of it. Rules were a burden— none more so than the one they'd lived under since day one of their relationship. Jack seemed drawn to the most controversial cases, whether it meant using DNA evidence to prove death-row inmates innocent or defending an accused terrorist. Andie's most fulfilling work with the FBI was done undercover. Hence, Rule Number One: no talking about active cases and assignments.

"Can you please go a little faster?" said Andie.

Key Biscayne was notorious for speed traps, and Jack was already doing sixty over the arching bridge that connected their home on Key Biscayne to the mainland. Always late meant always in a hurry, a fact of married life with Andie that Jack had learned to accept, except when it came to leaving their island paradise for the hustle and bustle of downtown Miami. He glanced south, toward Biscayne Bay National Park, where wind surfers and kite surfers enjoyed one last run before sunset, gliding across the flat, blue-green waters. It was the same group of guys every day. They lived in bathing suits, drove open-air Jeeps, drank beer out of coolers, and hung with their bikini-clad girlfriends on the beach. Jack wondered what they did for a living. He wanted their job.

Directly below the bridge, a yacht almost too big for the shallow bay waters was cruising north, perhaps toward their destination in the Venetian Islands.

"Do you really want to go to this party?" asked Jack.

Andie's mouth was agape. "Jack, it's a private party for *Imani*."

"It's not *for* Imani. It's a private party thrown by a sixty-year-old billionaire for his wife's twenty-fifth birthday, and Imani is performing."

"Let me just say 'gross' to the first part of that sentence, and then repeat the operative words: 'Imani is performing.' I love her. You got invited. We're going."

"I honestly can't even name one of her hits," said Jack.

"Please don't say that outside of this car."

Jack made surprisingly good time through downtown Miami before the jaunt back over the bridges to the waterfront estates on the Venetian Islands. Jack handed the car keys over to the valet attendant, and they hurried up the coral-stone driveway. The two-story, modern estate stretched the entire width of the lushly landscaped lot. A grand staircase led to the main entrance, which was actually on the second floor. The glass entrance doors were fourteen feet high, and the back of the house was completely glass, so Jack could see all the way through to the party by the pool and, beyond that, a drop-dead view of Biscayne Bay and the Miami skyline. Jack estimated fewer than a hundred guests, which he surmised was an artist-imposed limit to keep private events manageable.

"We're on the guest list," said Andie, speaking before Jack could.

"Just need to check," said the bouncer, and he quickly snapped a photograph of each of them.

"What gives?" asked Jack.

"We use a facial recognition app."

He uploaded Andie's photograph first. In a few seconds, he had an assortment of matching photos from the internet. The first one was from a website called "Hot Green-eyed MILFs."

"Is that you?" he asked, surprised.

"I do not recognize that position," said Jack.

"It's not me. I'm an FBI agent."

"FBI?"

"Is that a problem?"

His expression turned even more serious. "I'm sorry. You can't come in."

"What?"

"No law enforcement is allowed. Not that there's anything illegal going on here. It's a private party, and guests just feel uncomfortable knowing the cops are here."

Andie was speechless for a moment, then looked at Jack. "Honey, this has to be some kind of violation of my constitutional rights. You're the lawyer. Say something."

"Are you Jack Swyteck?" the bouncer asked. "The lawyer who got Mr. Garcia acquitted?"

Enrique Garcia would have spent the rest of his life in federal prison for violation of the Foreign Corrupt Practices Act had it not been for Jack's trial skills. Jack presumed that was how he'd landed on the invitation list.

"That's me," said Jack.

"You're a VIP. You can come. But not her."

"Bullshit," said Andie. "He's a VIP, but his wife can't get through the front door?"

"We obviously didn't know you were FBI when the invitations went out. No cellphones, no cameras, no recording devices, and absolutely no law enforcement. Those are the rules."

Rules, rules, rules. Jack was sick of them. "Andie, it's fine. Let's just go somewhere on South Beach for dinner."

"No way. You're staying. You missed Letterman because I made you late. I'm not going to make you miss Imani, too."

"The difference is I actually cared who David Letterman is."

The bouncer laughed. "You're a funny guy," he said, but Jack wasn't joking.

Jack took Andie by the hand and started toward the steps, but she stopped him.

"Go inside, Jack. You can't insult a client by being a no-show, even if he does belong behind bars."

"What makes you say he belongs behind bars?"

"You didn't make the A-list because Mr. Garcia was innocent. But that's beside the point. Stay and have fun. That's an order."

Jack knew better than to argue the matter. He walked her back to the valet, kissed her good night, and headed back to the party. The bouncer gave him a claim check for his surrendered cellphone, and there was one more requirement: a nondisclosure agreement. Basically, once Jack left the premises, the event had never happened. He couldn't tell anyone he'd been there, much less what he'd seen or heard.

"Standard at Imani's private events," the bouncer told him.

The lights dimmed, the band started, and guests cheered just as Jack stepped into the backyard. Colored lights bathed the stage, and Imani made her entrance. It was a younger crowd, and it struck Jack that the twentysomethings seemed lost without their phones. A few were still making kissy lips and taking imaginary selfies. Jack felt out of place—not as out of place as he might have felt with a price tag hanging from his shirt collar, but still the odd duck. He stood off to the side leaning against the trunk of a royal palm tree. A couple of Imani's songs sounded familiar, but only because they included riffs taken note for note from older hits by Queen and David Bowie, which seemed to be the industry standard for the making of "new" music. The performance lasted forty-five minutes. At the end, she said the strangest thing.

"My name's Imani, and remember: if you want my early stuff, 'go pirate'!"

The crowd cheered, and she hurried offstage.

Jack was at a loss. One of the hottest pop stars in the world had just told her fans to steal her own music. Jack was a criminal defense lawyer. He was an expert in discerning motive and explaining why people did the things they did.

He was coming up empty on this one.

Jack was home by eleven, out on the back patio with Andie, deflecting questions about the concert that he couldn't answer without violating his NDA.

Their house on Key Biscayne had virtually no front yard. The back wasn't much, either, except that they were on the water, which meant that the entire bay was their backyard. Jack felt lucky to live there. Real estate was priced way beyond his means, but years earlier, before he'd even met Andie, he'd cut a steal of a deal on one of the last remaining Mackle homes, basically a twelve-hundred-square-foot shoebox built right after World War II as affordable housing for returning GIs. Those had to be some of the happiest veterans in the history of warfare.

"Did she sing 'Truly, Madly'?" asked Andie.

"I'm sure she did," said Jack.

"It's her biggest hit. You really don't know it?"

"Of course I know the song. It's just that I was singing along so loudly, you know, that I can't actually swear I heard *her* singing it."

"Uh-huh. I see."

Jack spotted a seventy-foot yacht cutting through the night, running lights aglow—which wasn't unusual, except that this one seemed to be heading straight for his dock. He rose and went to the seawall to investigate. The boat stopped less than fifty feet away from him. A man appeared on deck and called to him from the bow.

"Ahoy, Swyteck!"

Jack recognized the voice right away, not to mention the six-foot-three frame. "Theo?"

Theo Knight was Jack's best friend, bartender, therapist, confidant, and sometime investigator. He was also a former client, a onetime gangbanger who easily could have ended up dead on the streets of Overtown or Liberty City. Instead, he landed on death row for a murder he didn't commit. Theo was the one innocent client Jack had represented during his stint at the Freedom Institute, where Jack spent the first four years of his law career specializing in "death cases."

"Permission to run aground, sir?"

Jack was certain he meant "come ashore," but it was the weekend, which meant the tequila was doing the talking.

"Don't come any closer, or you will run aground," shouted Jack.

Andie walked up beside him. "Whose boat is that?"

"Definitely not Theo's. Unless he won the Lotto and forgot to tell me."

Theo disappeared inside the main cabin, and Jack's cell rang. It was Theo.

"Hey, Jack. Imani wants to talk to you."

"Very funny."

"I'm serious. We sailed over from the Garcias' house on Venetian Island."

Jack did a double take. It looked exactly like the boat docked behind the party.

"Theo, what's going on?"

"I've known Imani since she was an eighteen-year-old nobody fresh out of Miami Senior High playing shithole bars all over south Florida. She even played my place a few times."

Theo owned Cy's Place in Coconut Grove, a nightclub he'd purchased with the settlement money Jack got him from the state of Florida for his wrongful conviction and incarceration.

"Are you seriously telling me Imani is on that boat with you?"

Andie's eyes lit up, and Jack had to fight off her attempt to snatch the phone from his hand.

"Dude, she's right here next to me, and she wants to meet you," said Theo.

"Why?"

"Because you left the party too soon. The reason you got invited was she needs to talk to you."

"About what?"

"Shit, Jack. Do I need to spell it out? She needs a lawyer," he said, his voice turning very serious. "A fucking good lawyer."

Jack glanced at Andie, then back at the yacht, which was way too big for his dock. "Stay right where you are. I'll get in my boat and come to you."

CHAPTER 2

Jack felt like a shark sucker latching onto a great white as he rafted up his little fishing boat alongside Imani's sleek yacht. Theo helped him aboard and took him to the main salon, which was bigger than Jack's living room and definitely more luxurious. An abundance of chrome, leather, and glass, with a mix of direct and indirect lighting of various hues and intensities, made the cabin glow like a South Beach nightclub.

Imani was not quite as tall as she had appeared on stage, but she walked toward Jack and shook hands with a confidence that said, *Don't bullshit me.*

"I hear you're the best," she said.

Jack had expected his prospective client to be a walking advertisement for designer clothes and accessories, but she wore faded, cutoff blue jeans, a yellow top with a scalloped neckline, and flip-flops. The only jewelry was a diamond stud on the right side of her nose and a gold ring on her left-middle toe. Jack found her more beautiful without the stage glitter and makeup. She looked less like a pop star and more like one of the young mothers at morning drop-off at Righley's elementary school.

"That's very kind of you to say," said Jack. "But you don't want any lawyer who claims to be the best. You want the lawyer who's best for you and your case."

"I like you already."

At her invitation, Jack took a seat beside her on a pedestal-style barstool. Theo stood behind the bar, his go-to spot, having tended his own bar at Cy's Place for years.

"I'm being sued by my ex-husband," she said. "He made me sign a nondisclosure and nondisparagement agreement when I was really young, before we got married. It was in the prenup, so it became part of the final order of divorce when we split."

"I'm sure Theo has told you I don't do domestic relations law."

"It's not that kind of case. Theo said you defended a couple of rappers on racketeering charges. It's more like that."

Prosecutors were increasingly using song lyrics as evidence of gang membership to convict rappers of criminal racketeering. Occasionally, the target was a big name, like Jeffrey Williams, aka Young Thug, the alleged founder of the vicious Atlanta street gang YSL, aka Young Slime Life. Jack's case was more typical—a pair of no-name rappers from Liberty City who followed the old adage "write what you know," which prosecutors then used as road maps for indictments.

"That was a criminal case," said Jack. "Which is mostly what I do."

"It involved the First Amendment, and so does mine," said Imani. "My ex says I breached the nondisparagement agreement by saying bad things about him after the divorce. It's really a defamation case based on things that happened in the last month or so."

Theo poured a round of tequila—force of habit. "It would probably help if you told Jack who your ex is," said Theo.

"Shaky Nichols," she said.

Nichols was closer in age to Jack than Imani, so finally there was someone Jack had heard of. "The music mogul?"

"The musician killer," said Imani.

Jack sensed whence the defamation claims had sprung. "What do you mean by that?"

"In the music industry, the big money doesn't necessarily flow to the artist. It goes to whoever owns the rights to the artist's master recordings. When I signed my first recording contract, I was like every other emerging artist—powerless. That means I had no ownership rights to the master recordings of any of my early hits. Those rights belonged to my first record label. After I made it big, I tried to buy them."

"Was the label willing to sell?"

"Yeah. Until another buyer came along."

"Let me guess: Shaky."

"Yes! So, not only did I get nothing in the divorce, thanks to the pre-nup, but now my ex owns my master recordings and collects royalties on *my* songs that launched *my* career. I get the same peanuts I got under my contract with my first record label, back when I was a nobody. Shaky is a fucking scumbag thief."

Imani didn't mince words. Jack could only imagine the Tweets that had triggered the defamation lawsuit.

"Didn't Taylor Swift have a similar problem?" asked Theo.

"Yeah," she said. "Scooter Braun owned the master recordings of every song before her *Lover* album. That's why she re-recorded every one of her old albums and created 'Taylor's version.' Scooter Braun gets nothing from Taylor's version."

"Have you thought about re-recording yours—'Imani's version'?" asked Jack.

"I don't have that kind of time."

Jack arched an eyebrow. "And Taylor Swift does?"

"Taylor did it during Covid when no one was touring. If she had to do it now, she couldn't. I'm in the same boat, recording new material, touring, or doing private gigs like the Garcia party."

"Do you do a lot of these private parties?" Jack asked.

"As many as I can. It's the easiest money in the business. If you're Bruno Mars, you can get four million for a forty-minute gig at a wedding. But you have to be careful. J.Lo caught shit for going all the way to Turkmenistan to sing 'Happy Birthday' to one of the most repressive dictators in central Asia. Oops. Big apology followed, but I'm pretty sure she kept the money, honey."

"I'm sure," said Theo.

"Getting back to the lawsuit," said Jack. "I heard you shout something to the crowd at the end of tonight's performance that left me scratching my head. You said, 'If you want my early stuff—'"

"Go pirate!" she said, finishing for him. "I deliver that message every chance I get. I literally call it my 'go pirate' campaign."

"Why do you want your fans to visit a piracy website and get your music illegally?"

"I only want them to steal my *old* music—the songs tied to the master recordings that are owned by Shaky Nichols."

Jack paused. "Let me make sure I understand. If the songs are purchased lawfully, you get a little piece of the pie, but Shaky gets more."

"A lot more. Almost everything. My share is a joke."

"If your fans go pirate, you get nothing, but Shaky also gets nothing."

"Exactly."

"You prefer the scenario under which Shaky gets nothing, even if it costs you a few bucks."

"You bet I do."

Jack didn't necessarily agree with the reasoning, but he definitely got it, especially when dealing with an ex-spouse.

"Okay. You described this as a defamation lawsuit, which I'm guessing stems from your calling him a thief and probably worse. But my instinct tells me this is really about the 'go pirate' campaign. I'd like to read the actual complaint Shaky filed with the court."

Imani reached for her phone. "I can email it to you right now."

"I don't need it that fast."

"Actually, you do," said Imani. "There's a court hearing set for Monday at nine a.m."

Jack was taken aback. "You have a court hearing in less than thirty-six hours, and you're just now looking for a lawyer?"

"A new lawyer. My old one quit this morning."

"Why?"

"She's an entertainment lawyer. Ninety-five percent of her clients come from inside the industry. If Shaky Nichols calls and tells you that you'll never work in the music industry again unless you dump Imani, you dump Imani."

"Shaky threatened your lawyer?"

"I can't say for sure," said Imani. "But she's the second entertainment lawyer to quit on me with no explanation. That's why Theo recommended you. And he's right. You're an outsider. You can rip Shaky a new asshole and not have to worry about ruffling industry feathers."

"That could be the nicest thing Theo has ever said about me," said Jack, smiling.

"You're welcome," said Theo.

Jack turned serious again. "All right. Lots of work between now and Monday morning. I'll need a retainer right away."

"My business manager will take care of that."

"You didn't ask how much."

"I'm sure we'll work that out, as long as you sign my NDA."

"One hundred K. And no NDA."

"I don't buy a pair of shoes without an NDA."

"I'm not a pair of shoes. I signed one to get into your concert, but I won't sign one to be your lawyer. That's my one non-negotiable rule."

Imani paused, and Jack thought it might be a deal breaker.

"Probably a good rule," she said finally.

"Yeah," said Jack, thinking of how this "date night" had played out. "Every now and then, you run across a rule that actually makes sense."

CHAPTER 3

On Monday morning, Imani's black limo stopped outside the south entrance to the Miami-Dade County Courthouse on Flagler Street. Jack stepped onto the sidewalk—alone, to the disappointment of the adoring fans of his client and a flock of microphone-thrusting members of the media.

"Is Imani a no-show?" a reporter asked him.

"I waited five hours to see her," a random fan griped.

Jack offered no response. He continued up the granite steps to the revolving entrance doors. If all were going according to plan, Imani would be unrecognizable in her floppy sunhat, cheap sunglasses, and plain-Jane attire, as Theo escorted her inside through the north entrance on the opposite side of the building, where hundreds of registered voters who'd been tagged for jury duty funneled through security and into the lobby like herded cattle.

"Go Imani, go pirate!" someone in the crowd shouted. Others hoisted hand-drawn posters, some with words to the same effect, others that simply proclaimed "I ♥ Imani." The ring of onlookers was at least ten deep, and those in the back were too far away to notice that Imani wasn't with her lawyer.

The wait for an elevator was too long, so Jack bailed and took the stairs to Judge Stevens's courtroom on the fifth floor. Another mob of Imani worshipers filled the lobby outside the courtroom. Some were standing on the benches for a better view, and courtroom deputies made repeated requests for them to get down and keep quiet. Jack pushed his way through the noise and commotion and entered the courtroom through the rear double doors. There were only eight rows of public seating, the first of which was "media only." Spectators were shoulder to shoulder, not an open seat available. Jack hurried up the center aisle, pushed through the swinging gate, and joined his client at the rectangular table on the other side of the polished mahogany rail that separated observers from participants in the courtroom drama that was about to unfold.

"All rise!" the bailiff called.

All complied as the side door to Judge Stevens's chambers opened and the silver-haired judge ascended to the bench. Imani's ex-husband was the plaintiff, so he and his lawyer were at the table nearest to the jury box, which was empty, since there was no jury for this preliminary hearing. Jack had never been on the opposite side of Jennifer Ellis, but she was a skilled trial lawyer with a "take no prisoners" reputation.

The bailiff called the case—"Evan 'Shaky' Nichols versus Imani Nichols"—which, for Jack, seemed to shrink things down to size, reducing Imani the pop star to Imani the litigant. For a few, however, the courtroom was not the great equalizer where all players were treated the same, as someone in the audience said in a voice too loud, "I never knew her last name was Nichols." Judge Stevens immediately gaveled it down.

"Please, folks," he said, gavel in hand. "I understand that this case is of public interest, but I can't have two hundred spectators acting like they're sitting at home on their sofa watching Court TV. If you can't keep your comments to yourself, the door is right behind you."

Stevens wasn't a surly old judge, but he did run a tight courtroom. After three decades of service on the bench, the word around the courthouse was that he'd reached the point in his career of saying whatever he felt like saying.

"Mr. Swyteck, how's your daddy?"

As the son of the former governor, Jack was used to it. "Playing a lot of golf."

"Good for him. In the interest of full disclosure, I wanted to point out that the judicial nominating committee put my name forward three times for appointment to the Florida Supreme Court, and three times Governor Swyteck picked someone else. So here I am, all these years later, the longest-serving trial court judge in the state of Florida."

"I was not aware of that," said Jack.

"No reason you should be. I just want you to rest assured that none of that ancient history will in any way affect my impartiality in this case. I'm as evenhanded as they come. 'Even Stevens,' they call me," he said, directing his comments to the row of reporters in the gallery. "In that spirit, Ms. Ellis, how's *your* daddy?"

"My father died twenty-two years ago, Your Honor."

"Well, all right. We all gotta go sometime. Let the record reflect that I asked both sides, at least. Now, the first order of business is a motion filed yesterday by Mr. Swyteck, which seeks to continue this hearing to a later date."

Shaky's lawyer was back on her feet. "We oppose any delay, Your Honor."

"I'm sure you do. But seeing as how Mr. Swyteck was just retained this past weekend, let me check with my assistant to see how long that delay would be. Barbara, what's the next two-day opening on my calendar?"

The assistant checked the computer screen in front of her. "That would be the sixteenth of October."

Jack rose. "Judge, a two-week continuance would be plenty of time for me to come up to speed."

"Actually, I meant October of *next* year," said the judicial assistant.

Such was the reality of the civil docket in Miami-Dade County.

Ellis spoke up immediately. "Judge, this is not a complicated case. My client has brought suit under a nondisparagement clause. Ms. Nichols has disparaged my client by claiming that he is a 'thief' who 'stole' her master recordings. That's a lie. She has compounded the injury to my client by telling her fans to 'go pirate' and purchase her songs illegally, depriving my client of any revenue from the master recordings he rightfully owns."

Jack spoke. "Judge, if by 'not complicated' my opposing counsel means 'frivolous,' I agree with her characterization. If we are given the time to properly prepare for this hearing, the evidence will show that when my client stated that Mr. Nichols 'stole' her master recordings, she simply meant he underpaid for them. That's hardly disparagement."

"Let's keep this simple," said the judge. "Ms. Ellis, what exactly does your client hope to accomplish at today's hearing?"

"We want a preliminary injunction that orders Imani to do three things. First, we want a gag order forbidding her from making any further statements or social media posts encouraging her fans to 'go pirate.' Second, we want an order directing her to take down and delete all previous social media posts encouraging her fans to 'go pirate.' Third, we want a mandatory injunction requiring her to retract her previous statements and to issue a formal statement telling her fans to stop going pirate."

"Understood. Mr. Swyteck, while I don't like the idea of forcing you to proceed before you and your client are ready, I can't in good conscience make Mr. Nichols wait a year to be heard. Ms. Ellis, call your first witness."

Jack didn't like to attribute ill motives to any jurist, but it seemed that Judge Stevens had yet to get over Governor Swyteck's appointment of those three other judges to the Florida Supreme Court.

"The plaintiff calls Imani Nichols," announced opposing counsel.

It was not the norm for a plaintiff to call the defendant as the first witness, but it was a clever tactical move in this case. Jack was a latecomer, and his opposing counsel wanted to land a few punches before Jack could come fully up to speed and prepare his client for everything that was coming. Imani raised her right hand, swore the familiar oath, and took her place on the witness stand.

"Ms. Nichols," the questioning began, but Imani stopped her.

"I prefer Imani."

"All right. Imani it is," said Ellis, and then she took a step closer to the witness. "This case isn't about free speech, is it, Imani."

It wasn't really a question, which prompted an objection from Jack.

"Overruled," said the judge. "There's no jury in this case, so as a word of caution to all counsel, please keep your objections to a minimum. The witness may answer."

"I don't know how to answer that question," said Imani. "I'm not a lawyer."

"I'll go about it a different way," said Ellis. "Your 'go pirate' campaign isn't about free speech at all. It's really just a petty and personal vendetta against your ex-husband."

"Judge, I have to object," said Jack, rising.

"Sustained. Ms. Ellis, when I instructed counsel to keep objections to a minimum, I wasn't inviting you to argue with the witness. Let's stick to the facts."

"Yes, Your Honor," said Ellis. "Ms. Imani—"

"Just Imani."

"Imani," she said, losing patience. "Isn't it a fact that you were a founding member of an organization called MAP?"

"I was."

"What does 'MAP' stand for?"

"Musicians Against Piracy."

"What was the core mission of MAP?"

Imani looked at the judge and answered. "The idea was to educate the public about piracy. Specifically, the way it hurts artists, especially new artists, who already get the short end of the stick in their contracts with record labels."

With the court's permission, Ellis projected an exhibit on the big screen on the wall, which could be seen by everyone in the courtroom.

"Imani, this is a copy of an interview you did for *Rolling Stone* magazine two years ago. I call your attention to the language highlighted in yellow. You said: 'The real mission of MAP was to make life miserable for pirates.' Those were your words, correct?"

"I suppose so. I really don't know what I meant by that."

"Let's get specific. You were a co-founder of MAP, along with a young rapper who called himself Amongus Sicario, right?"

"Yes."

"You go on to say in the *Rolling Stone* interview that the two of you were sick and tired of having your music ripped off by piracy, right?"

Imani checked the exhibit. "It says that."

"You were so sick and tired of piracy that you actually engaged in criminal conduct to stop it."

The judge overruled Jack's objection. All Jack could do was watch as his opposing counsel led the witness into territory unknown to Imani's new lawyer.

"I don't really know what you mean," said Imani.

"MAP hired tech specialists to hack piracy websites, did it not?"

She hesitated. "On occasion."

"Hacking somebody else's website is a crime, is it not?"

"There are laws against it."

"MAP implanted malware in dummy files on piracy websites, so that anyone who visited the website and downloaded pirated music would damage their computer."

"I believe that was also done on occasion."

"That was a crime."

"Again, I think there may be some laws on that."

"You don't have much respect for the law, do you, miss?"

"Objection."

"Withdrawn," said Ellis. "I want to talk now about this apparent epiphany you experienced recently. Specifically, how the old Imani, who went so far as to break the law to stop piracy, became the 'new Imani,' the one who tells her fans to 'go pirate.'"

"Is there a question?" asked Jack.

"My question is this," said Ellis, and she took a step closer to the witness. "Isn't it true that the piracy websites pay you a kickback for every Imani song illegally downloaded from the piracy sites?"

The courtroom erupted, and reporters were on the edge of their seats. Jack's objection could barely be heard over the commotion.

"Order!" the judge shouted, banging his gavel until silence was restored.

Jack continued with his objection. "Judge, there is absolutely no basis for opposing counsel to make such a wild accusation against my client. I move that it be stricken from the record."

"The question calls for a simple yes or no answer," said Ellis. "We are entitled to know if piracy websites are paying Imani more for illegal downloads than her record label pays her for legal downloads. This question goes straight to her defense that her 'go pirate' campaign is protected by lofty notions of free speech."

The judge was noticeably red in the face. "Ms. Ellis, I'll not allow witnesses to be called to the stand simply so that the lawyers can make baseless accusations to grab headlines. You can recall the witness and continue this line of questioning only after you've introduced evidence and laid some foundation for the accusation. And let me add this much: some evidence had better be forthcoming to support the accusation you've already made. Am I understood?"

"Yes, Your Honor," said Ellis.

"Good, now move on."

"Judge, that's all I have for now. I reserve the right to cross-examine the witness if Mr. Swyteck calls her to the stand as part of the defense case."

"Fine," said the judge. "Mr. Swyteck, do you have any questions for your client at this time?"

"Briefly," said Jack, and he approached the witness. He could have deferred until later, but this war was being fought both in the courtroom and in the court of public opinion. He couldn't let the explosive accusation stand without some rebuttal.

"Imani, please tell the court why you started your 'go pirate' campaign."

"Things have changed since I formed MAP. Piracy isn't the existential threat to the industry it used to be. In my opinion, music publishers, not pirates, are the real threat to artists."

"What do you mean by that?"

"Here's a good example. The royalties that streaming services and publishers are conspiring to enforce against songwriters are worse than in the days of piracy. I'm leading a charge for legislative reform. I started the 'go pirate' campaign simply to counter the millions of lobbying dollars the music industry spends on Capitol Hill to oppose any legislative change."

"Is it fair to say that since your divorce from Shaky Nichols, your political action has been a thorn in the side of the music industry?"

"A 'pain in the ass' is what Shaky calls it."

The judge leaned over the bench. "Ms. Nichols, please."

"Sorry, Judge."

Jack continued. "When asking you about MAP, Ms. Ellis described cyberattacks MAP launched to deter piracy. My question to you is this: Did you, personally, launch any cyberattacks against any websites?"

"No."

"Do you even know how to create or launch computer malware?"

"I don't know the first thing about it."

"What did you do when you found out that MAP was fighting piracy by itself committing cybercrimes?"

"I resigned as president."

"Did you maintain any ties at all with MAP?"

"I remained a dues-paying member for a while. But I gave that up when I found out MAP's new leadership was planning something even more radical than just cyberattacks."

"Do you know what this more radical action was?"

"I don't have specifics."

"Were you married to Mr. Nichols at the time you gave up your membership?"

"Yes."

"Did he ask you to resign?"

"To the contrary, he told me to stay active with MAP."

"Did he say why he wanted you to stay active?"

"Shaky was president of my record label, EML. You have to understand that MAP and the music industry were aligned in their fight against piracy."

"So, as president of EML Records, Shaky Nichols wanted to stop piracy."

"Of course."

"And to that end, he actually supported MAP's criminal conduct."

"Objection," said Ellis. "There's no evidence that my client was aware of MAP's criminal conduct."

"I can fix that," said Jack. He was getting out over his figurative skis a bit, and he could only hope his client's answers in the courtroom would match what she'd told him over the break. "Imani, did you ever tell your husband that MAP committed cybercrimes in the fight against piracy?"

"Yes, I did."

"Did you tell him that MAP was considering something even more radical than cybercrimes?"

"Yes."

"To your knowledge, did Shaky Nichols ever ask you or anyone else at MAP to stop all illegal activity?"

"No. Like I said, he told me to stay involved in MAP."

"Would it be accurate to say that to the extent MAP engaged in criminal conduct to stop piracy, you did not condone it?"

"Yes, that's why I quit."

"Can you say the same about your husband?"

"Objection, speculation," said Ellis.

"Sustained," said the judge. "Mr. Swyteck, you promised you would be brief. If you plan to re-call this witness to the stand later in the case as part of your defense, I suggest you wrap this up and allow the plaintiff to proceed with his case in chief."

"Just one more question: Imani, have you received any kickbacks from piracy websites for illegally downloaded songs?"

"Absolutely not. That's ridiculous."

Jack had made his essential points. Not a bad morning, all things considered.

"That's all for now," he said, and he returned to his seat.

The judge directed the witness to step down. She did, with shoulders back and hips moving, more like a Grammy Award winner exiting the stage than a witness leaving the stand. As she walked toward the defense table, her gaze fixed tightly on her lawyer. At first, Jack wondered what silent client-to-attorney communication she might be sending, but as it lingered, the look in her eyes made him feel, in a word, uncomfortable.

"Do you see the way she looks at him?" whispered one reporter to another. They were in the first row of press seating on the other side of the rail, behind the defense table, speaking just loud enough for Jack to hear.

One immediate thought came to Jack's mind. It was fake. Imani was putting on a show. The fact that he knew it was phony wouldn't make it any easier to nip this rumor in the bud, before it splashed all over the internet rag sheets. But one thing was certain.

Whatever her explanation, Imani was about to get an earful from her lawyer.

CHAPTER 4

Judge Stevens announced a lunch break, and Jack whisked Imani from the courtroom. They hurried down the hallway to the only private space available, an empty jury deliberation room. Members of the media were in hot pursuit. Jack closed them out and left Theo outside the door to stand guard. Then he unloaded.

"What the hell did you just do in there?"

Imani took a seat in one of the twelve empty chairs at the table. "What are you talking about?"

"That 'let's get a hotel room' look you threw me."

"When?"

"Just now! When you stepped down from the witness stand. Don't act like it didn't happen. I wasn't the only one who noticed. Two reporters sitting right behind me were talking about it. In about five minutes, it will be all over the internet."

She smiled, and checked her phone, surfing. "Looks like it worked."

"What do you mean, 'it worked'?"

She laid her phone aside. "Here's the deal, Jack. It's your job to handle what happens inside the courtroom. But I control the narrative in the court of public opinion. Outside of this courthouse, I don't want people talking about the evidence. I want them wondering if the hand some Miami trial lawyer is fucking his superhot client."

"I'm not okay with that. I'm a married man. How is my wife supposed to react to that?"

"Your wife is smart enough to know it isn't real."

"That doesn't cut it. I won't allow it."

"You won't allow it?" she said, sounding exactly like a pop star who lived by her own rules, no one else's.

"Let me tell you something," said Jack. "When I was with the Freedom Institute, most of my clients were guilty. I told them, 'If we win in the courtroom, don't hug me. I'm doing a job here.' Sometimes they broke the rule. They were so happy they weren't going to be executed, they had to hug someone. At least they were genuine. But you . . . you're using me as a prop. Let me say it again: I will *not* allow it."

Imani clearly didn't like it. "Fine. I'll have to talk to my public relations manager."

"And rely on the evidence," he said. "Which has been good for you so far."

"So far. But don't kid yourself, Jack. Not all the evidence is going to be good for me. In fact, some of it is going to be bad. Very bad."

Jack's cellphone rang. He wanted to hear more about the "very bad" evidence, but it was Jennifer Ellis on the line, so he answered.

"I want to talk settlement, lawyer to lawyer," she said.

"What do you have I mind?" asked Jack.

"Not on the phone. Take a walk with me down the stairwell. I'll meet you there in two minutes."

It seemed like a scene out of a spy movie, but in a celebrity court battle, a healthy fear of hackers listening to their cellphone conversations made sense.

"I'll meet you there," said Jack, and the call ended. Then he brought Theo inside and laid out the new plan: "Call for the limo, take Imani down the service elevator, and I'll meet you in the car at the Flagler Street entrance in ten minutes."

"Got it," said Theo. He stepped out with Imani and, as Jack had expected, every reporter waiting outside the room followed them to the elevator.

Jack hurried down the hallway in the opposite direction and pushed open the metal door to the stairwell, where Jennifer Ellis was waiting for him.

"Let's walk," she said, and Jack started down the stairs with her.

"What's your offer?" asked Jack.

"Simple. Imani stops her 'go pirate' campaign, she removes all past posts on social media, and she issues a statement of apology telling her fans to buy her musically lawfully."

They continued down another flight. "That sounds like surrender, not settlement," said Jack.

"There's something in it for Imani."

"I'm listening."

A janitor was walking up the stairwell. They let him pass and continued down two more flights until they were completely alone.

Ellis continued, "Tell Imani that if she agrees to everything, Shaky will not press charges."

Jack nearly tripped down the stairs. "Press charges for what?"

"Imani will know."

They'd reached the ground floor. Ellis stopped at the exit door but didn't open it.

"What kind of a bullshit settlement offer is this?" said Jack.

"It's no bullshit. When you tell your client that Shaky won't press charges, she'll know exactly what that means. And if we don't go back into that courtroom after the lunch break and tell Judge Stevens the case is settled, you'll hear it all—including the parts your client is too much of a manipulative little liar to tell you. Trust me, it won't be pretty."

Ellis exited the stairwell to the lobby, making hers the last word.

Imani's warning—some of the evidence would be "very bad"—came rushing back to him. Jack wasn't one to shy away from clients with big problems. In some cases, the "very bad" evidence hadn't even been the worst of it. But this exchange with Shaky's lawyer only stiffened his resolve to slap down Imani's courtroom stunt.

He gave Ellis a minute of separation, and then entered the lobby, hurried out of the building, and continued down the granite stairs. Imani's limo pulled up at the curb and, before the crowd could surround it, Jack jumped in the backseat. Imani and Theo were waiting inside. Jack quickly summarized as they pulled away.

"Shaky says that if we give him what he wants, he won't press charges," said Jack.

Imani laughed.

"His lawyer said you'd know what that means."

"I do."

"You want to tell me what it means?"

Imani's smile faded. "It means you need to hear my side of the story."

Jack's office was just a five-minute ride from the courthouse. Imani talked, and Jack listened, all the way there.

CHAPTER 5

C ourt was back in session. Jack and his client sat side by side at the defense table, watching as the plaintiff's second witness took the stand.

Shaky Nichols was a handsome man, fast approaching the age at which the trendy facial stubble that made younger men look stylish and cool made older men look lazy and unkempt. Based on the photographs Jack had pulled from the internet, Shaky spent most of his time in T-shirts and baseball caps. His lawyer had apparently won the courtroom fashion debate. His conservative dark business suit and baby-blue dress shirt looked brand-new, just delivered from Armani. Jack wondered if the tags were still on.

"Mr. Nichols," his lawyer began, "let's walk through your background for the court's benefit."

Shaky clearly loved talking about himself. He'd never finished college, having dropped out to take a job in marketing at a small record label, which basically made him the party planner in chief. He'd met a number of up-and-coming musicians in various states of late-night inebriation and convinced a few of them that he should be their manager. Still, his career was going nowhere, until he invested every penny of his inheritance in an unknown tech company, and cashed out to the tune of an eight-figure profit right before the dot-com bubble burst. At age thirty-two, he formed an investment company that teamed up with a private equity firm to buy EML Records on the cheap, at a time when the major record labels, EML included, were losing $750 billion a year to piracy and illegal music downloads.

"Let's talk now about your relationship with the defendant," said Ellis.

Over the next twenty minutes, guided by the questioning of his counsel, the witness laid out a selective history of his professional and personal relationship with Imani, emphasizing the positive. His discovery of Imani in a Miami nightclub. Signing her to a record label. Her Best New Artist Grammy. Their friendship that became a romance. A happy marriage—for a few months, anyway.

The focus then shifted to the issue at hand.

"Mr. Nichols, did there come a time when you acquired ownership of the master recordings to Imani's first four albums?"

"Yes. Through my company, Clover Investments."

"From whom did you and Clover Investments acquire those master recordings?"

"Her record label, EML Records."

"Did you hold any position with EML at the time?"

Shaky looked at the judge and explained. "You have to understand that I was wearing three hats. First, I owned Clover Investments, which bought a minority interest in EML Records. Second, I became CEO of EML Records, which owned the master recordings to Imani's songs. Finally, I became Imani's husband."

"What kind of arrangement did Imani have with EML?" his lawyer asked.

"Until Imani became a star, she had the same contract EML gives all new artists. She didn't own the master recordings. Most of the revenue from those songs went to EML. Imani got a small royalty."

"Even smaller than his dick," Imani whispered to Jack.

It was in the category of "too much information," and Jack chose not to respond.

Shaky's lawyer continued. "What prompted you to buy those master recordings from EML?"

"This is where I started thinking like Imani's husband. I knew the arrangement with EML made her unhappy. I wanted to make her happy. So, when I resigned as CEO of EML Records, I bought the rights to her master recordings."

Imani's nails dug into the back of Jack's hand. "Give me a break," she muttered.

"Did you tell Imani about this?" Ellis asked the witness.

"No. It was going to be a surprise. My plan was to give them to her at her thirtieth birthday party."

"Did you follow through with that plan?"

"Obviously not."

"Why not?"

"She filed for divorce two weeks before her thirtieth birthday."

"When did Imani find out you owned her master recordings?"

Shaky glanced in his ex-wife's direction, unable to hide the smirk of satisfaction. "During the divorce proceedings."

His lawyer went to the computer and brought up an image on the screen. Some in the audience had to crane their necks to see, but it was plainly visible to most. It never ceased to amaze Jack how things that didn't look so bad in a little screenshot could make your skin crawl when blown up on a big projection screen in a courtroom.

"Mr. Nichols, I'm showing you now a copy of a Tweet posted by your ex-wife three weeks ago. It reads as follows:

"'Shaky Nichols is a thief and abuser who uses bully tactics and worse to keep artists and musicians under his thumb. I know, because he did it to me. He stole my master recordings, and now my life's work makes him—and only him—a rich man. Go pirate!'"

Shaky's lawyer returned to the podium but left the Tweet burning on the projection screen. "My first question, sir, is this: Did you steal Imani's master recordings?"

"Absolutely not. Clover Investments negotiated at arm's length and paid EML a lot of money for those rights."

"Were you ever an 'abuser' toward Imani?"

"Definitely not. If anything, she was the abuser."

A rumbling of salacious curiosity coursed through the courtroom. Jack rose. "Move to strike the witness's reference to my client as an abuser, Your Honor."

It was the kind of motion that was rarely granted, especially without a jury, but the judge seemed to be considering it.

"Overruled," he said finally, and Shaky's lawyer ran with the judicial green light.

"How was Imani abusive toward you?"

The witness seemed a little too eager to unload, which only reinforced Jack's instinct that it was probably a lie.

"Your Honor, I object," said Jack, rising once again. "The witness's effort to paint himself as a victim of spousal abuse is far beyond the scope of relevant evidence in this hearing."

"It's entirely relevant," said Ellis. "It directly relates to Imani's defense. She claims her 'go pirate' campaign is political speech protected by the First Amendment. We contend that it is a continuing pattern of vindictive abuse on her part."

It was clear from his sour expression that Judge Stevens wasn't happy about this turn in the narrative. "I'll allow this line of questioning to a point," he said, begrudgingly. "But counsel is instructed to proceed with caution. I'm going to keep a tight leash on this."

"Thank you," said Ellis. "Mr. Nichols, how did Imani's abuse start?"

"It began after we got married, when Imani told me that she didn't believe in a conventional marriage."

"Did she explain what she meant by that?"

"She wanted an open marriage," said Shaky.

"Do you mean 'open' in the sense that she wanted sexual partners other than you?"

"Yes," he said, coming across as slightly embarrassed, toning down some of that overeagerness Jack had detected earlier. "Or in addition to me."

"How did you feel about that?"

"I hated it. If I wanted that kind of openness, I never would have gotten married."

"Did you go along with the open marriage?"

He glanced in Imani's direction, this time not with satisfaction but with a hint of anger. "What choice did I have?"

"How did this open marriage work?" his lawyer asked.

"At first, it was just Imani seeing other men. The less I knew, the better. Then we'd have our time together. I would get my hopes up, thinking it would stay normal. But then she'd go away again, always someone new."

"Did that pattern change over time?"

"Yeah. For the worse. It got to the point that if I ever wanted sexual relations with my wife, there had to be more than just the two of us involved."

More prurient rumblings from the crowd. Ellis continued: "Mr. Nichols, I know it must be difficult to talk about this in open court, but did you ever speak to anyone professionally about this?"

"I started seeing a psychiatrist."

It surprised Jack that a man like Shaky was willing to admit in open court that he'd seen a psychiatrist. It surprised him even more that Imani had neglected to tell him.

"Did your psychiatrist ever diagnose you with any psychological or emotional condition?"

"Objection," said Jack. "The clear implication here is that my client caused some kind of psychological injury."

"Exactly what is your objection, Mr. Swyteck?" the judge asked.

The real "objection" was that Jack wanted to know more about his client—and fully understand what he'd gotten himself into—before going down this road of alleged psychological abuse. He found a legal hook.

"Any diagnosis should be presented through medical records or the testimony of Mr. Nichols's psychiatrist," said Jack.

The judge grumbled, as if he didn't like the fact that Jack was right. "We're not bringing a psychiatrist into this hearing. The objection is overruled. But Ms. Ellis, keep this short."

"Yes, Your Honor. Mr. Nichols, what diagnosis did you receive?"

"I was suffering from post-traumatic stress disorder as a victim of what is called forced penetration."

It just kept getting worse. Jack had seen "forced penetration" charges only against women who had sex with boys too young to consent to sex, but the definition was broader. These were undoubtedly the sexual assault "charges" that Shaky's lawyer had offered not to press in their "settlement" discussions. It was red meat to the media. An entire row of reporters were on the edge of their seats.

Ellis continued, "Exactly what was the nature of this forced penetration?"

He sighed heavily, playing the part of the reluctant witness. "I was forced to penetrate Imani's other partners against my will."

"Did these 'other partners' include both women and men?"

"Ooooo-kay," said the judge, stretching out the word. "We get the picture. Counsel, I told you I would keep a tight rein on this."

"Your Honor, please. We have sixteen text messages in which Imani apologizes to my client for incidents involving forced penetration. This will prove that this isn't a case about free speech. We are dealing with an abuser who is dead set on inflicting more pain on her victim."

Jack's client had left him ill-prepared to argue over spousal abuse and forced penetration, let alone sixteen apologies. He had to shut this down and get Imani alone in a room with him. Appealing to the judge's discomfort was his best strategy.

"Judge, we have gone way off the rails here."

The judge breathed in and out. "Ms. Ellis, I take your point. But I agree with Mr. Swyteck. I'm not going to turn this hearing into yet another case of a self-destructive celebrity couple who seem determined to air their dirty laundry in a courtroom."

Ellis would not back down. "It is critical that the court review these text messages."

"Your Honor, the defense has not even seen this evidence," said Jack.

"All right," said the judge. "A short break is in order. *I* sure need a break. Ms. Ellis, give copies of the text messages to my judicial assistant. I will review them in chambers and return with my ruling. This court's in recess until three o'clock," he said, ending it with a bang of his gavel.

All rose at the bailiff's command, and the silence lasted not a nano-second longer than it took the judge to exit through the side door to his chambers. Reporters rushed to the rail and fired questions at the pop star and her lawyer.

"Imani, is it true you had an open marriage?"

"How many other partners did you force your husband to have sex with?"

"Are you sleeping with your lawyer?"

Jack cringed at the questions, especially the last one, especially since he hadn't spoken to Andie yet. They needed privacy until the hearing resumed, and the empty jury room was the only place that came to Jack's mind. He told Theo to lead the way, which was like following an NFL all-pro lineman through the defense. The reporters trailed them down the hallway, and the questions kept coming. Jack and Imani disappeared into the room, and Theo took his place as sentry.

In a criminal case, Jack didn't always want to know if his client was guilty. But there was no presumption of innocence and no Fifth Amendment right against self-incrimination in a civil case.

"Is any of what I just heard in that courtroom true?" asked Jack.

"Not a word! Shaky was the one always pushing for threesomes and an open marriage. That's why I divorced him!"

"What about the sixteen apology messages?"

"I was always apologizing for something. 'I'm sorry I didn't give you enough credit for my success in my last interview.' 'I'm sorry I gained two pounds.' It doesn't matter what his lawyer says now. I wasn't apologizing for forced—" She halted at the word "penetration," then finished in her own way. "For forced *anything*."

Imani fell angrily into a chair. Jack gave her a moment to regain her composure. Finally, she looked at him and spoke, her voice laden with bitterness.

"That Jennifer Ellis is a pick-me girl."

"A what?" asked Jack.

"You should know that term. You have a daughter."

"Righley is only seven."

"How do I explain this?" she asked herself, massaging between her eyes. Then it came to her. "There's an old Janis Ian song about girls with ravaged faces lacking in the social graces. You know it?"

"'At Seventeen.' It's a classic. Of course I know it. But I'm kind of surprised you do."

"She's actually one of my idols. Anyway, that song has a perfect line about the girls whose names are never called when choosing sides for basketball. Jennifer Ellis was never one of those girls. She was always picked, and she did whatever it took to get picked."

"What does that have to do with this hearing?"

"Once a pick-me girl, always a pick-me girl. She lives for validation and approval by men, and she will do whatever it takes to get it, even if it means throwing other women under the bus. Men never see it, but believe me, other women do. 'The world is out to get you, Shaky. You're the victim, Shaky. Women use sex as a weapon. Imani is the abuser.' 'Pick me, Shaky! Pick me!'"

Jack had never seen his client this angry, but she was far from irrational. "I can't say you're wrong," he said.

"That's because I'm right."

Silence hung between them. The reporters arguing with Theo on the other side of the door to the jury room were just white noise, unnoticeable.

"What do we do now?" asked Imani.

"We fight back," said Jack. "With everything we've got."

CHAPTER 6

At three o'clock, Jack and his client were back in the courtroom. The gallery seemed to swell beyond capacity, the buzz about "forced penetration" apparently having sparked even greater interest in the growing public spectacle. Imani sat in silence beside her lawyer, but Jack noticed that her leg was in high gear below the table, bouncing up and down with restless leg syndrome in nervous anticipation of the judge's evidentiary ruling.

"I've reviewed the text messages submitted by the plaintiff," the judge said from the bench. "There is nothing in any of those communications about forced penetration or any other sexual misconduct. They are apologies, but they could be apologies about anything. For that reason, I will exclude them from evidence."

It was a setback for the prurient interests, and the disappointment among spectators was palpable. Jack took the win and pressed forward, emboldened by the reassurance that his client had told him the truth.

"May I cross-examine the witness?" asked Jack, rising.

"Proceed," said the judge.

Jack knew he had his hands full with Shaky. The key was to ask the right questions. Not questions that might elicit the answer a lawyer hoped for, but questions that could be answered only one way. Baked into this calculation was the sad reality that when the case was on the line, a witness like Shaky Nichols told the truth only when the lawyer left no alternative.

Jack approached the witness and faced him squarely, with feet planted firmly at shoulders width—his position of control.

"Mr. Nichols, you testified that you purchased Imani's master recordings through your company, Clover Investments. Do I have that right?"

"That's right."

"I understand that Clover borrowed three hundred million dollars to make that purchase."

"Yes."

"Even though Clover is the borrower, you, personally, guaranteed repayment of that loan, correct?"

"Correct."

"Ultimately, it is you, Shaky Nichols, who is on the hook for the full three hundred million. Right?"

"That's what a personal guaranty means."

"Yes. I can see you're a smart businessman. And as a smart businessman, surely you did your homework before purchasing Imani's master recordings."

"No one spends three hundred million without due diligence, if that's what you mean."

"Naturally, you researched other acquisitions of master recordings."

"Naturally."

Jack retrieved a folded newspaper from his table, then resumed his place before the witness. "I'm looking at the *Financial Times* of London. The sale of Taylor Swift's master recordings was quite a public affair. According to the *Times*, her master recordings sold for two hundred fifty million dollars. You knew that, right?"

"I was made aware."

"The article says her master recordings earned about fifteen million dollars a year. If my math is correct, the two-hundred-fifty-million-dollar price tag worked out to a multiple of about sixteen or seventeen times her annual earnings. Does that sound right?"

He paused to do the math in his head. "Roughly, yes."

Jack put the newspaper aside, then pointed in the direction of his client. "Now look over there, Mr. Nichols. I see the singer Imani. Agreed?"

"Objection," said Ellis.

"What's the objection?" the judge asked.

"It's just condescending," said Ellis.

"I'll rephrase," said Jack. "When you look to the other side of the courtroom, you don't see mega-star Taylor Swift sitting there, do you?"

"No, that's definitely Imani."

That drew a few muted chuckles from the handful of Shaky supporters in the audience.

Jack continued. "The fact is, Imani's catalog earns less than half of Taylor Swift's catalog. Am I right?"

"Roughly."

"But you paid three hundred million dollars for Imani's master recordings—fifty million more than the buyer paid for Taylor Swift's catalog."

"Every deal is different."

"Taylor Swift's catalog went for sixteen times annual revenues. You purchased Imani's master recordings at a multiple of more than *forty* times earnings."

"Like I said, different deals are different."

"But business metrics are business metrics," said Jack.

"I don't understand the question."

"Isn't it true, Mr. Nichols, that on a multiple-of-earnings basis, the three hundred million dollars you paid for Imani's catalog is more than *anyone* has *ever* paid for an artist's master recordings?"

Shaky shifted uncomfortably in his chair. "It could be."

"The truth is, you overpaid."

"I wouldn't say that."

"Can you name one person in the industry who would tell me you didn't overpay? Just one."

He paused, stewing in the uncomfortable silence. "I'd have to get back to you on that."

Jack had him.

"You overpaid because owning Imani's master recordings wasn't just about money."

"Not every deal is about dollars and cents."

"Right. For you, owning Imani's recordings was about control."

"Objection," said Ellis.

"Overruled. The witness can answer."

The witness shot a look at the judge that was less than respectful, and then he looked at Jack. "I have no idea what you mean, counselor."

"Owning Imani's master recordings wasn't a matter of money to you," said Jack, his cadence quickening, affording the witness no wiggle room. "It was about control over Imani—at any price."

"That's not true."

Jack spoke even faster. "What really makes you angry is that Imani's 'go pirate' campaign has taken that control away. You can't control her the way you've always wanted to control her—which makes you the abuser, not her."

His lawyer jumped to her feet. "Objection. Your Honor, Mr. Swyteck objected to my questions about abuse, and now he's speeding straight down that road."

"Sustained. Let's wrap this up, Mr. Swyteck."

"Final point," said Jack. "Mr. Nichols, it was suggested during your direct examination that my client is getting kickbacks from piracy websites. You don't have a shred of evidence to support that accusation, do you?"

"Objection."

Jack didn't really want an answer. "I withdraw the question. Nothing further, Your Honor."

Ellis approached the bench. "Your Honor, given Mr. Swyteck's insinuation that my client is an abuser, I'd like brief redirect examination."

"No," the judge said sharply.

The response surprised even Jack.

"Excuse me?" said Ellis.

"We're done here," the judge said. "I have no appetite for presiding over two celebrities who are hell-bent on trotting out their dysfunctional marriage for the world's entertainment. I'm a judge, not a marriage counselor for the rich and famous. I've heard enough, and I'm ready to rule."

He looked at Jack, then at plaintiff's counsel, and then spoke directly to the media.

"The plaintiff's request for an injunction is denied without prejudice. Mr. Nichols is free to refile his request for injunctive relief if and when he has evidence that the defendant is receiving kickbacks or other remuneration from piracy websites for her 'go pirate' campaign."

Imani's fans cheered. The judge demanded order and gaveled down the outburst to churchlike silence.

"We're adjourned," he said with a final bang of the gavel.

All rose on command, and the entire courtroom waited with anticipation until the side door to Judge Stevens's chambers closed with a thud. Instantly, the crowd erupted with pro-Imani cheers and applause. Shaky Nichols and his lawyer made a quick exit, no congratulatory handshake with the opposition. Theo came barreling through the gate, singing Queen's "We Are the Champions." Imani jumped into his arms and planted a kiss on the lips that was so spontaneous, it seemed to shock and embarrass both of them. Jack, too, was surprised, though on the upside it should have put an end to any "sleeping with her lawyer" rumors.

Maybe that was her angle—she was using Theo, too, albeit to Jack's benefit.

"Let's celebrate!" said Theo.

"The media will expect a press conference," Jack told his client.

"Here's my press conference!" Imani said. Then she turned, faced the gallery, and shouted at the top of her voice: "Go pirate! Woo-hoo!"

The crowd cheered. Reporters jotted down her exact words.

Jack smiled cautiously, hoping to God there were, in fact, no kickbacks to his client from piracy websites.

CHAPTER 7

Theo poured Imani another shot of tequila and set it on the bar in front of her.

"This time without training wheels," he said. "No lemon, no salt."

A small group of Imani's old friends from Miami was with them at the bar, and they let out a collective "ooooh" in response to Theo's challenge.

"Challenge accepted," said Imani.

Theo had closed down one side of the bar for the celebration. Drinks were flowing and, as always, Cy's Place was oozing that certain vibe of a jazz-loving crowd. Creaky wood floors, redbrick walls, and high ceilings were the perfect bones for Theo's club. Art nouveau chandeliers cast just the right mood lighting. Crowded café tables fronted a small stage for live music, where Imani had once performed—too young to drink, but talented enough to grab a microphone and sing the blues in ways that conjured up the likes of Billie Holiday and Ella Fitzgerald. Theo had accompanied her on the saxophone, blowing an old Buescher 400 that had passed down from one of the most talented musicians ever to play in Miami's "Little Harlem" during its mid-twentieth-century heyday—his great-uncle Cy, the club's namesake.

"Take that!" she shouted as she slammed down the empty glass on the bar top. Her friends cheered. Theo kept his word and matched her shot, two-for-one, which roughly evened the playing field in terms of body mass. Another round followed and, before long, Theo was standing on the bar leading the entire club in singing, "Yo-ho, yo-ho, a pirate's life for me!"

Imani was laughing so hard she nearly fell off her stool. Then her expression changed suddenly. Theo climbed down from the bar.

"What's wrong?" he asked.

Imani didn't answer. Theo followed her line of sight across the club, toward the entrance doors, and his gaze landed on the man wearing a flat-brim fedora who had locked eyes with Imani. Theo had never met him in person, but he knew his music and his reputation, and he'd seen his image countless times in the media.

"Amongus is here," Imani said softly.

Before Shaky, Imani had been a celebrity couple with a Latino rapper who called himself Amongus. The press called it "Imani's bad-girl stage." His full street name was reversed as "Sicario Amongus," the Spanglish translation of which was simply "hit man among us."

"Should I tell him to leave?" asked Theo.

Amongus's story was well known to Theo and anyone else who followed Imani's career. He and his brother were deep into the drug trade in Mexico, until they stupidly made a sale to a DEA agent. His brother was beaten to death in a Mexican jail. Amongus was extradited and spent three years in a U.S. prison. From his cell, he wrote violent and angry rap music. His cop-killing, anarchistic, and strongly anti-American message made him popular with young people all over the world who rejected any form of authority. His core followers believed that, by purchasing music through legitimate channels, they were only benefiting the billionaire pigs who ran American corporations. They worshiped Amongus but felt totally justified in ripping off his music from the internet. With that kind of fan base, no record label ever got behind him, and without the support of a label, it didn't take long for him and his posse to blow through every penny he made from performances and selling branded merch. Despite millions of downloads, Amongus was broke. When he met Imani, he did the math and realized he wasn't quite as anti-capitalist as he had once thought. Together, they started the anti-piracy movement that became MAP.

"Let him stay," said Imani. "If MAP sent him, there's a conversation that needs to be had."

Amongus walked straight toward the bar. Two men were with him. Both ex-cons, in Theo's expert judgment. Theo knew the walk—the "I got eyes behind my head" swagger that only prison could cultivate. Theo stepped between him and Imani as he reached the bar, a full head taller than the rapper.

"Wassup?" asked Theo.

"Here to talk to the lady," he said.

Theo glanced at Imani, knowing better than to speak for her.

"It's okay," she said. "Join us."

Amongus pulled up the barstool beside her. Imani asked her friends to give her a minute, and they drifted away from the bar toward the billiard table. Theo walked around to the other side of the bar.

"Whattaya drinking?" he asked.

"Club soda," said Amongus.

"Club soda and what?"

"Ice."

Imani looked at him, not comprehending. "Dude, I'm buying. Have a drink."

"Don't drink. Don't do drugs."

"Since when?" asked Imani.

"Since it stopped being fun."

Theo filled a glass and set it on the bar. "One club soda with ice."

"Thank you," said Amongus.

Theo did a double take, then smiled and wagged his finger, as if he were on to him. "You're fucking with us, right? Amongus Sicario is suddenly Mr. Straight and Mr. Manners? You had me going there for a second."

"People change," he said, deadly serious. Then he looked at Imani. "Once upon a time, a person might be president of Musicians Against Piracy. Next thing you know, they're telling their fans to 'go pirate.'"

Imani sighed deeply. "Come on, man. I'm celebrating here."

"Telling people to steal music is fucked up," said Amongus.

"I'm telling them to steal *my* music."

"That's not what people are hearing. Check out any piracy website you want. You can watch it happen in real time. Piracy is way up for everyone, not just your music."

"That wasn't my intent," said Imani.

"Then do something about it, girl. Come back to MAP. Come back to the organization you and me founded."

"And do what?"

"Retracting your 'go pirate' message would be a good start."

"Say what? I just went through courtroom hell to defend my right to deliver that message."

"And you made your point. You embarrassed your ex-husband, who deserves all the indigestion you can give him. *Felicidades.*"

"That's not what this was about."

"Oh, cut the bullshit, Imani. Can't you see the damage you're doing? Half the fucking world under the age of twenty-five thinks there's nothing wrong with stealing in cyberspace. If they can figure out a way to get my shit online without paying for it, it's not their fault for stealing it, it's *my* fault for not protecting it. You, me, and everyone at MAP worked so hard to make people understand that piracy hurts artists. Now you're telling them it's okay."

"How many times do I have to say this, Amongus? I'm telling them it's okay to pirate *my* songs."

"That's like telling a recovering junkie it's okay to do just one more hit. You think they're gonna stop at just one?"

She didn't answer.

Amongus opened his wallet and placed a ten-dollar bill on the bar. "MAP wants you back, Imani."

She shook her head. "I left because MAP was doing some sketchy shit. Shaky's lawyer asked me about it at the hearing today—about MAP breaking the law. I didn't tell her the half of it. People had some batshit crazy ideas on how to stop piracy."

"That's why we need you back," said Amongus. "You're making that crazy shit sound like our only option. There's people who think the answer is to do something drastic."

"Like what?"

"Nothing's off the table. Use your imagination." Amongus grabbed a napkin from the bar, jotted his personal cell number on it, and gave it to Imani. "Call me. We need you."

Theo and Imani watched as Amongus and his two bodyguards walked to the exit. Then Imani glanced at Theo.

"Didn't see that coming," she said.

"The unlikely prophet," said Theo.

"Good title for a song."

Theo wiped down the bar top. Imani was retreating into her own thoughts, which was not necessarily wise after losing count of tequila shots.

"Hey, there's something I've been wanting to show you," he said, drawing her back. He walked around to the other side of the bar, took a framed black-and-white photograph off the wall, and laid it on the bar top in front of her.

Imani's eyes widened. "Is this—"

"Josephine Baker. The jazz singer."

"More than that," said Imani. "A singer, a dancer, first Black woman ever to star in a major motion picture. Served in the French Resistance during World War Two."

"She performed here in Miami. All the big-name Black performers played the Overtown clubs after their shows on Miami Beach. Couldn't spend the night in the beach hotels. Whites only. The after-hours shows started 'round midnight at the Knight Beat, the Cotton Club, the Clover Club, the Rockland Palace Hotel. Overtown was 'the swingingest place in the South.' My uncle Cy played for all of them. Josephine Baker signed this picture for him."

"Oooh," she said in a playful voice, "'To Cy, *with love.*'"

"Yeah. You're not the first to tease about that."

Imani admired it. "She was so beautiful."

Theo leaned closer, forearms on the bar top. "You look a lot like her, I think."

"Yeah, after how many shots of tequila have you had?"

He laughed, then reached for the bottle. "One more?" he asked.

"No, no, no. I need to go to bed." She reached across the bar and laid her hand on his. "Thank you again, Theo."

"For introducing you to Jack?"

"No. Well, yeah. But mostly, just for being there."

He smiled. "No problem."

She started away, then stopped. "Hey, about that kiss in the courtroom.

I was all excited about winning the case, and I guess I got a little carried away, so—"

"No worries. It surprised me as much as you."

"You know, it's funny. When I met you, I was nineteen. You seemed so much older than me."

"Because I was."

"But now. Shit, I'm not even in my twenties anymore. You don't seem that much older."

"Because I'm not," he said, and then he glanced at the old black-and-white photograph behind the cash register, his uncle Cy, circa 1956. "And I'm still such a handsome devil in my Norfolk suit and natty tweeds."

She smiled. "Good night, handsome."

"Good night, Josephine. And do me a favor?"

"What?"

"Call your lawyer before you call Amongus."

"Sure thing."

Her car was waiting behind the club at the service door. Theo watched as she walked out of Cy's club. But for the ever-present bodyguard trailing behind her, she really could have been the starlet who Uncle Cy had spent the rest of his life telling everyone was "the one who got away."

CHAPTER 8

Thursday morning, Jack was in Manhattan. He and his client had a 9:00 a.m. meeting with prosecutors from the United States Attorney's Office, Southern District of New York. Imani met him downtown outside the federal courthouse at Foley Square.

"Let me do all the talking," said Jack. "Even if the prosecutors speak to you directly, don't say a word unless I ask you to."

"Got it," said Imani.

Jack had thought Imani and the pirates were behind him, at least for a while. Then everything changed when he received a phone call from the head of the U.S. attorney's cybercrime unit in Manhattan telling him that federal prosecutors wanted to meet with Imani and her lawyer. This wasn't the kind of invitation you could RSVP no to.

"This has to be a mistake," said Imani as they stepped into the elevator.

"We'll see," said Jack.

The meeting was in the basement of the Thurgood Marshall United States Courthouse. Prosecutors had proposed their offices, which Jack had nixed. An "Imani sighting" at the U.S. Attorney's Office would have triggered rumors that she was somehow connected to a criminal investigation. The federal courthouse wasn't exactly neutral ground, but prosecutors were loath to give up the inherent power of "you come to us," so Jack agreed. It was surely no coincidence that they were in a windowless conference room near the underground tunnel that connected the courthouse to the detention center. A steady stream of inmates on their way to arraignment served to remind Jack and his client how important it was that this meeting go well.

"We know your client perjured herself at the hearing in Miami," said the senior prosecutor.

Apart from the fact that he was head of the cybercrime unit, Edwin Miles had the markings of a formidable adversary: midforties, perpetual bags under the eyes from not enough sleep, and the vaguely athletic build of a former jock who could no longer find time to exercise. It all added up to a career prosecutor who was married to his job.

"Since when is the U.S. attorney in New York concerned about what goes on in civil cases in Florida state court?" asked Jack.

"Your client testified under oath that she derives no economic benefit from her 'go pirate' campaign. We know that's false."

"What kind of economic benefit do you believe she's getting?"

"Kickbacks," said Miles. "By our calculation, the pirates are paying her more for every illegal download of her songs than her record label pays her for legal downloads."

"That's not true!" said Imani.

Jack hand signaled her, a reminder to let him do the talking.

"Mr. Miles, there are so many things wrong with what you're telling me," said Jack. "First, even if Imani were getting kickbacks, which she's not, doesn't your office have bigger fish to fry than a musician who simply wants to be paid what she deserves for her own music?"

"We set our priorities, Mr. Swyteck, not you."

"Do you? Or does Shaky Nichols?"

"Please, don't insult me," the prosecutor said.

"I'm just stating the obvious," said Jack. "Under Judge Stevens's ruling, Shaky's case against his ex-wife is dead in the water unless and until he can prove she is getting kickbacks from pirates. Lo and behold, three days later, you've summoned us to New York to tell us that federal prosecutors have plugged the hole."

"I'm not going to dignify that accusation with a response," said Miles. Then he glanced at the junior prosecutor beside him and said, "Show him."

The younger lawyer removed a spreadsheet from her file and placed it on the table.

"What's that?" asked Jack.

"Wire transfers from a Latvian bank account to a numbered bank account in the Cayman Islands," said Miles. "We've connected the Cayman Islands account to your client."

Imani gasped. "I don't have a—"

Jack gave her the hand signal again, and she stopped talking.

"Who controls the Latvian bank account?" asked Jack.

"Nominally, the same shell company that controls the largest piracy websites on the planet."

"Sounds to me like you don't know who controls the Latvian account," said Jack.

"We can't *prove* who controls the Latvian account," said Miles. "We're all but certain that it's a Russian oligarch and his son, both deep into cybercrime. I'm not prepared to disclose the family name to you, but I will tell you this. The son has a preteen granddaughter who lives in London. And she's a huge fan of Imani."

Jack could see where this was heading. "What are you asking us to do?"

"A private concert for a young girl."

Jack glanced in his client's direction, keeping her reaction in check.

"Seriously?" said Jack. "You want Imani to perform at a private event for the granddaughter of a Russian oligarch?"

"Spare me the indignation," said Miles. "Even J.Lo played for the president of Turkmenistan."

Imani couldn't contain herself. "Her publicist said it was because she didn't know how evil he was."

"I'm sure that was it," said Miles, sarcasm dripping.

"Please direct your remarks to me, not my client," said Jack.

The prosecutor continued. "This would be just like the dozens of other private events Imani has done in the past. Except this time, she can't leave the party until she has a one-on-one conversation with the girl's father. And she has to wear a wire."

"What information do you expect her to gather from the son of a Russian oligarch?" asked Jack.

"It's premature to discuss those details. As a threshold matter, we need to know if you're on board with the concept."

"No way," said Imani. "I won't do a concert for a Russian oligarch's family."

The prosecutor scoffed. "But you'll accept wire transfers from the family-owned piracy websites?"

"Stop," said Jack. "For the last time: don't speak directly to my client. Imani, we're here to listen, remember?"

"Sorry," said Imani.

Jack leveled his gaze at the prosecutor, knowing that they were entering the critical stage of the negotiation. "Let's say we're not open to 'the concept,' as you describe it. What's the consequence for Imani?"

"One count of perjury for her false testimony in Florida. Multiple counts of wire fraud for the illicit transfer of piracy proceeds to her offshore account. Multiple counts of aiding and abetting copyright infringement for the kickbacks she received for telling her fans to 'go pirate.' All told, ten-to-twenty years in federal prison, I would estimate."

"And if we *are* open to the concept, what's the picture?"

"Complete immunity from prosecution, all charges dropped."

"Charges have to be brought before they can be dropped," said Jack. "Are you taking this to a grand jury?"

"No. The charges are by criminal information."

Not all charges required a grand jury indictment.

"*Are?*" said Jack. "You make it sound as though you already have signed affidavits from the federal agents on the investigation and the charges are ready to be filed with the court."

"Our office plans to make an announcement today at a press conference."

"What time today?" asked Jack.

"Eleven a.m."

Jack didn't hide his disapproval of the hardball tactics. "You're giving us one hour to consider your offer? You can't be serious."

Miles checked his watch. "Actually, I'm giving you ten minutes. You can have the room to yourselves to discuss it. Feel free to review the wire transfer spreadsheet. This is a generous offer," he added, looking directly at Imani. "You'd be a fool not to take it."

The prosecutors rose and left the room, closing the door behind them. Jack's client didn't need the ten minutes.

"I'm not playing for an oligarch's granddaughter," she said firmly.

"I'm impressed," said Jack. "Most of my clients would have said, 'no way am I wearing a wire.'"

"Then I'm not like most of your clients."

Jack didn't show it, but he was smiling on the inside. "Let's hope not."

CHAPTER 9

Jack and Imani left the courthouse and walked across the street into Columbus Park.

Chinese opera singers were performing along the walkway, a reminder that the imposing complex of government buildings was technically in Chinatown. A small audience had gathered in the spotty shade of a tall maple tree that was just starting to show some fall color in its leaves. A few New Yorkers were on the lawn, taking one last shot at sunbathing before autumn started to feel more like winter. As a native Miamian, Jack wanted to hand out coats and scarves, even with the sunshine. Jack found a park bench away from the crowd where he and his client could sit and talk alone.

"What happens now?" asked Imani.

Jack's "thanks, but no thanks" message to the prosecutors had prompted a predictable if unimaginative, "See you in court."

"The U.S. attorney will file charges by criminal complaint today. You don't have to worry about the FBI beating down your door to arrest you and put you in handcuffs. Miles and I agreed that you will surrender voluntarily tomorrow morning. You'll be arraigned before a federal magistrate, who will set bail."

"Any chance he won't let me out on bail?"

"No. You're not a danger to society, and no one could seriously argue that you're a flight risk. Where on earth do they think you could go without being recognized?"

Imani glanced back at the courthouse, but the look in her eyes was distant, as if she were somewhere else. "Funny thing is, I *could* probably play for an oligarch's granddaughter, and no one would ever find out.

Get the right security, take away cellphones, enforce the nondisclosure agreements—it's doable."

"Like the event I went to on Venetian Island?"

"That was amateur hour compared to what I'm talking about. Anyone could have sailed by in a boat, or the media could have sent helicopters, and boom—the cat's out of the bag. I'm talking about the kind of uber-precautions taken when nobody—I mean *nobody*—can ever find out about it."

"For example?"

She laughed. "If I told you, Jack, they wouldn't be top secret, would they?"

A skateboarder whizzed past them. Imani seemed ready to change the subject.

"Amongus Sicario came to see me Monday night," she said.

"Theo told me."

"Really? Do you two lovebirds tell each other everything?"

"He just mentioned that Amongus wants you to come back to MAP."

"No, Amongus doesn't want me back at MAP. Amongus *said* he wants me back at MAP."

"I see the distinction, but what are you getting at?" asked Jack.

"I believe the same ex-husband who got these prosecutors breathing down my neck got Amongus to invite me back to MAP. The end result is the same in both cases: the end of the 'go pirate' campaign."

"Interesting theory. But it presupposes Shaky has rather extreme power and influence on multiple levels."

She gave Jack a very serious look. "Never underestimate the power and influence of my ex."

"I'll keep that in mind," said Jack. His gaze drifted toward a couple of pigeons fighting over what was left of a giant pretzel.

"Tell me about the kickbacks," said Jack.

"The theory makes absolutely no sense. Do you know how many piracy sites there are on the dark web? I couldn't possibly have a kickback arrangement with all of them."

"The prosecutor doesn't have to prove you took kickbacks from all of them. Just the ones owned by the Russian oligarch who's in the prosecutor's crosshairs."

"I'm not taking kickbacks from a Russian oligarch."

"What about the bank accounts?"

"Isn't it obvious to you that I'm being set up? Shaky has all my personal information—Social Security number, passport, driver's license. What more do you need to open a bank account in the Cayman Islands?"

Jack smiled.

"Why are you smiling?" she asked.

"Long time ago, I had a case involving a Cayman account. I flew to Grand Cayman to talk to the manager. I was young and honestly didn't know much about offshore banking, so I was expecting see an actual bank—granite floors, teller windows, the usual things. Turned out the 'bank' was nothing more than a table at a Jamaican jerk restaurant in a strip mall by the beach. The table next to it was reserved for 'Joe's Bank of the Caribbean.'"

"Do you think I would do business with a bank like that?"

"The Cayman Islands have cleaned up their act a lot since those days. But I take your point. If Shaky wanted to set you up and connect you to wire transfers from Latvia to the Cayman Islands, it wouldn't be difficult."

A clock tower chimed from somewhere around the block. It was eleven a.m. Jack pulled up the livestream of the press conference on his cellphone. The U.S. attorney was standing at a podium that bore the great seal of the Department of Justice. A team of prosecutors was behind him. Draped on a pole beside them was the American flag. Jack and Imani listened as the charges were announced.

"On behalf of the criminal division of the U.S. Department of Justice and the U.S. Attorney's Office for the Southern District of New York, it gives me great pride to announce that today marks the end of the most-visited worldwide digital piracy website in the world. Criminal charges have been filed against thirty-six different defendants in five different countries. Collectively, these defendants and their criminal enterprise stole more than a billion dollars in profits from the U.S. entertainment industry by enabling website visitors to reproduce and distribute hundreds of millions of copyrighted motion pictures, video games, television programs, musical recordings, and other electronic media."

"This is not right," said Jack. "No way should you be lumped together in the same charging document as these crooks."

"I guess it gives their case more sex appeal," said Imani.

"It's more than that," said Jack. "They want the judge and jury to see you as part of one big criminal enterprise."

"Shaky must be having an orgasm," said Imani.

The prosecutor continued, "The job is far from over. Our cybercrimes unit will continue to work with our law enforcement partners around the globe to identify, investigate, and prosecute those who attempt to illegally profit from the innovation of others. Today's announcement sends a clear message that cybercriminals can run, but they cannot hide from justice."

"That's it," Imani said angrily. "We're holding our own press conference."

"I'm on board with that," said Jack. "But I don't want you talking publicly about criminal charges against you. The government can use anything you say against you. I'll speak as your lawyer with you at my side."

"We can do it right across the street on the courthouse steps."

"I like it. But I'll need time to read the actual criminal complaint and prepare."

"I'll give you fifteen minutes," she said.

Jack had already downloaded the pdf from the DOJ website. "The complaint is over fifty pages. I need more time."

"We can't wait any longer than that. News goes viral in real time. Fifteen minutes with no rebuttal is an eternity in cyberspace. I can't have my name associated with cybercriminals for one minute, let alone fifteen."

Jack couldn't disagree. "I'll keep it short. We can do a more fulsome response later."

Imani dialed her publicist. A Tweet immediately went out to millions of Imani followers: "Meet me on the courthouse steps at 11:30 a.m."

Jack took ten minutes to jot down his thoughts. Imani made phone calls.

It was a two-minute walk from the park to the federal courthouse. Crossing the street, Jack witnessed the power of social media in real time. An impromptu social-media blast from Imani had turned the granite steps outside the old Roman Revival–style building into the most crowded public space in Manhattan. Hundreds of fans, bloggers, reporters, and onlookers drawn to the sudden excitement had all gathered in less than fifteen minutes.

"Imani!" someone shouted, spotting her.

Imani took Jack's arm, and suddenly he was both lawyer and bodyguard as the crowd rushed toward them. They reached the sidewalk, but the crowd would let them go no farther.

"We love you, Imani!" was the message heard over and again, but it was mob-style love, which could take a turn for the worse at any moment.

"Please, let us through!" Imani shouted.

It wasn't nearly enough to part the Red Sea, but those directly in front of them did back away just enough for Jack and his client to climb up as far as the third step. Jack stopped and turned around. Reporters and their crews did their part and pushed the crowd back far enough to allow the cameras to capture useful video. Jack raised his arms and called for quiet, and for the most part the crowd cooperated and listened. He dispensed with his notes and spoke directly to the cameras.

"My client has done nothing wrong. She is not a cybercriminal. She's not any kind of criminal. She's Imani."

It was the easiest and loudest applause Jack had ever drawn from a crowd.

"Telling her fans to 'go pirate' and download her own songs is not aiding and abetting copyright infringement. It is not a crime. It is free speech, and we will vigorously defend Imani's First Amendment right of expression."

More cheering from the crowd. Jack was feeling the energy, and it was tempting to say more, but he checked his personal ego and held true to his professional judgment. He wrapped it up.

"Imani thanks each and every one of her fans for their love and support, and we look forward to her total vindication. Thank you."

Imani took her lawyer's arm. A black SUV pulled up to the curb, which Imani's publicist had hired to take them to a hotel for the night. Jack took a step forward, but a wall of reporters stopped him and his client in their tracks.

"Imani, are you a criminal?"

"Imani, don't your fans deserve to hear from you?"

"Imani, does this mean Shaky wins?"

Jack tried to continue forward, but the resistance seemed to be coming as much from Imani at his side as the reporters in front of them. Jack suspected that it was the last question that had really landed.

Then Imani spoke.

"I'm outraged," she said. "As everyone knows, these charges come on the heels of my complete victory in the civil lawsuit brought by my ex-husband, who couldn't prove I got any financial benefit from my 'go pirate' campaign. It's despicable that the U.S. Department of Justice would succumb to the pressure of Shaky Nichols. Our government should protect victims of abuse, not roll over and do the bidding of bullies who flex their political muscle to make life miserable for their exes."

She took tight hold of Jack's arm, and the two of them pushed forward to the waiting SUV. Jack opened the rear door. Cameras flashed and questions kept coming even after they were safely inside.

"We agreed that you were not going to speak," said Jack, as the SUV slowly tried to pull away from the crowd. It was delicate work, as some supporters seemed to be hugging the SUV, their noses pressing against the window.

"Do you have a problem with anything I said?" asked Imani.

"I generally advise my clients against making the entire Department of Justice their enemy."

"I didn't say anything you didn't say in our meeting with the prosecutors."

"That was a private negotiation. Saying it at a public press conference is a declaration of war."

The SUV finally broke away from the crowd. Imani fell quiet, seemingly contrite. "I'm not intentionally trying to make your job harder. I'm just not used to an advisor who has a problem with anything I say or do. I kind of like it. I don't feel so alone."

Jack looked out the passenger-side window. A few fans were sprinting along on the sidewalk, keeping pace with the SUV.

"Are you ever really alone?" asked Jack.

CHAPTER 10

Friday morning's arraignment went exactly as Jack had promised: release on $200,000 bail, which for a pop star who claimed a nine-figure net worth—not even *Forbes* knew for sure—was effectively no bail at all. Afterward, Jack spoke to the prosecutor in the hallway outside the courtroom.

"I assume the government will file a pretrial motion to stop Imani from telling her fans to 'go pirate,'" said Jack. "When can I expect to see it?"

"You assume wrong," said Miles. "Contrary to what your client said yesterday on the courthouse steps, the Justice Department is not doing her ex-husband's bidding. If Shaky Nichols wants an immediate order telling Imani she can't say 'go pirate,' he has to get it himself from the judge in Florida."

Jack tried not to show too much surprise. "It sounds to me like you're not very confident in your case."

"Wrong again. We're solid on the wire transfers from Latvia to Imani's Cayman bank account. But to be honest, we don't want her to stop saying 'go pirate' just yet. It gives her common ground to talk about when she puts on the wire and talks to the oligarch's son."

"My client already told you she won't do a private concert for the grandchild of an oligarch."

"She'll come around," said the prosecutor. "Call me as soon as she does."

Jack and Imani's flight landed in Miami late Friday afternoon. At 4:50 p.m., Jack was back in state court before Judge Stevens. Jennifer Ellis was again appearing on behalf of Shaky Nichols. The clients weren't needed. The judge limited each side to five minutes of argument, no testimony from any witnesses allowed. Like many short hearings in state court practice, this one was in chambers rather than the courtroom. Judge Stevens was seated behind an imposing antique desk that was in even greater disrepair than the century-old courthouse. A simple rectangular table jutted out from the front of his desk in T-shaped fashion, with opposing counsel facing each other from opposite sides. It was the plaintiff's motion, so Ellis went first.

"Your Honor, earlier this week you ruled that Mr. Nichols could reassert his challenge to Imani's 'go pirate' campaign when we have evidence that she derived a financial gain from telling her fans to 'go pirate.' We now have such evidence."

"I presume you're referring to the criminal charges filed in New York," said the judge.

Jack interrupted. "Judge, criminal charges are an accusation, not evidence."

"Not so fast," Ellis countered. "This criminal information filed by the U.S. attorney sets forth in detail a series of wire transfers to an offshore account owned and controlled by Imani. To me, that's evidence."

"Let me ask this question," said the judge. "Why isn't the government seeking this order in New York? Why should I be dealing with this request in a civil lawsuit brought by her ex-husband?"

"Respectfully, you shouldn't be," said Jack.

"We disagree," said Ellis. "There is plenty of precedent for civil lawsuits and criminal cases to proceed simultaneously on parallel tracks."

"The only action this court should take today is to stay this case until after the jury has reached a verdict in New York," said Jack.

"That will be months from now," said Ellis.

The judge held up his hand like a traffic cop, stopping the back-and-forth between counsel. "Here's my concern. The defendant has a Fifth Amendment right not to testify in the criminal case. Imani has no right against self-incrimination in this civil case. That's a thorny issue."

"That's not an issue here," said Ellis. "Less than fifteen minutes after the charges were announced, Imani stood on the courthouse steps and said that she's done nothing wrong, that she didn't benefit financially from her 'go pirate' campaign, and that the government has essentially teamed up with her ex-husband to bring trumped-up charges against her."

"I saw that," said the judge, and Jack detected a hint of disapproval.

"The whole world saw it," said Ellis. "Clearly, Imani has no intention of invoking her right to remain silent in the criminal court, in civil court, or in the court of public opinion."

The judge nodded in agreement. "I have to tell you something, Mr. Swyteck. It rubs me the wrong way to see criminal defense lawyers standing on the courthouse steps and proclaiming their clients' innocence only to hide behind the right to remain silent at trial."

"It's called the presumption of innocence, Your Honor."

"I know what it's called," he said, annoyed. "I'm not here to argue the Constitution with you. I'm just saying that as an officer of the court—which is what all lawyers are—if you're going to rely on the right to remain silent at trial, the more professional thing to do is to keep your mouth shut before trial."

"I will keep that in mind," said Jack.

The judge continued, clearly wanting to press his point. "It's especially bothersome when it's not just the criminal defense lawyer declaring his client's innocence. But here, it's Imani herself accusing the entire Department of Justice of essentially conspiring with her ex-husband to bring false charges against her."

Jack had expressed this fear to his client, but he hadn't expected it to actualize so quickly. Again, Jack had to wonder if Judge Stevens had truly forgiven Governor Swyteck for choosing not to elevate him to the Florida Supreme Court.

"Judge, I couldn't agree with you more," said Ellis.

"Here's my ruling," the judge said. "I'm going to allow the civil case to reopen. My docket is jammed, but I will reschedule a hearing upon the first cancellation I receive in one of my other cases. Mr. Nichols will have the opportunity to present evidence of the bank account transfers, and if that evidence shows that Imani benefited financially from her 'go pirate' campaign, I will rule accordingly."

"Thank you, Judge," said Ellis.

"Have I made it clear where I stand, Mr. Swyteck?"

"You have, Your Honor. Very clear."

Jack left the courthouse quickly—too fast for his opposing counsel to keep pace and gloat all the way to the parking lot. He called Imani from the car with the news. She took it better than he'd expected.

"Only one way to make this better," she said.

"What?"

"Sing."

They agreed to talk over the weekend, and the call ended.

Traffic out of downtown Miami was the usual Friday-at-rush-hour nightmare. Jack stopped by Cy's Place before going home. Happy hour was in full swing. Theo was working the bar. He poured Jack a draft beer but was too busy to talk. It was too loud to have a conversation, anyway.

"Who's that playing?" asked Jack, nearly shouting to be heard.

"Drake."

"Ah," said Jack, as if he knew him.

"You don't like it?"

"The music's good. A few too many words that rhyme with U-C-K for my taste on the lyrics."

Theo shook the mixer and poured a couple of cocktails into stemmed glasses. "Like the world needs another fucking song about taking a little chance, doing a little dance, and finding a little romance," he said, and then went to the other side of the bar and delivered the cocktails to customers who were about half Jack's age.

The man could have a point, thought Jack.

Jack drank his beer. His cellphone rang. He didn't recognize the incoming number, and he might have let it go to voicemail if he hadn't just spoken to Imani. Pop stars had more phone numbers than drug dealers.

Jack answered, but it wasn't Imani's voice on the line. It was someone speaking through a voice-distortion advice.

"Judge Stevens screwed you."

Jack didn't hang up. The ruling had been announced in chambers and was less than an hour old. Not that many people on the planet were even aware of it yet.

Jack closed one ear with the press of his fingertip so he could hear. "Who is this?"

The distorted, mechanical-sounding voice continued. "Tell Shaky's lawyer that if he reopens the hearing, you'll call Shaky back to the witness stand and ask him about Tyler McCormick."

"Who is Tyler McCormick?"

There was a pause on the line and then, finally, a response. "He died twelve years ago."

"How?" asked Jack, but the caller was gone.

Jack's gaze swept the club. It was a long shot, but maybe someone had called him from inside Cy's Place. He saw only the usual happy hour gatherings. He swallowed the last of his beer and dialed Imani on the same number he'd used from the car.

"Hi, Jack, what's up?" she answered.

Jack inserted his earbuds so he could hear more clearly. "What can you tell me about Tyler McCormick?" he asked.

"Never heard of him," she said. "Why do you ask?"

Jack told her, and he was searching the internet while speaking. A twelve-year-old headline from the local section of the *Miami Tribune* popped onto his screen.

BODY FOUND IN BISCAYNE BAY RULED HOMICIDE, the headline read. Jack froze as he skimmed ahead:

The victim has been identified as twenty-three-year-old Tyler McCormick, a resident of the Bahamas who was enrolled as a student at Miami-Dade College. According to MDPD homicide detective Gustavo Cruz, Mr. McCormick's body was found at low tide in approximately nine feet of water, fastened to a concrete piling. Investigators have yet to determine the motive for the murder and the unusual display of the victim's body, said Cruz.

"Jack, are you still there?" asked Imani.

"Yes," he said, his mind still processing. "Imani, you and I need to talk."

"We are talking."

Jack wanted to see Imani's reaction—not just hear her words—when he told her. "No. I mean a sit-down, face-to-face, lawyer-to-client talk."

"Shit, Jack. You make it sound like somebody died."

"Funny you should say that," said Jack.

CHAPTER 11

Imani glistened with sweat, her damp running shirt and shorts clinging to her toned body. Her only available time to meet with Jack was early Saturday morning, after a two-hour run. She was renting an estate on Star Island, one of the artificial islands dredged up by the Army Corps of Engineers in the 1920s and now home to multimillion-dollar estates, just south of the Venetian Islands. They sat poolside in her backyard, alone at a table beneath the shade of an umbrella. Jack had worked late into the night scouring the internet, and he told her what he'd found.

"The Miami-Dade Police Department has a cold-case website," said Jack. "Tyler McCormick is there. Which means that whoever called me is suggesting that your ex-husband is connected to a murder that was never solved."

"That's crazy," said Imani.

"Is it?" asked Jack.

Imani drank water through a plastic straw. It was an enormous clear plastic jug, an entire day's supply with hourly milestones marked along the side, along with words of encouragement to ensure proper hydration. *Good start! Keep drinking! Don't give up! Just a little more!* It was probably healthy, but it made Jack want to add, *Take a pee!*

"I've said a lot of things about my ex," said Imani. "But he's not a murderer."

"No one said he is. But maybe he knows something."

"You mean like a cover-up?"

"It doesn't have to be anything incriminating. It could be just something Shaky wouldn't want the world to know about his connection to a young man who was the victim of a brutal murder whose body was put on display in the bay."

"Connected how?"

"It's speculation on my part. But I'd like your reaction to one possibility."

"Sure."

"There were a few more newspaper articles written about the crime before the victim was identified as Tyler McCormick. The first one reported that there was a message left on the victim's body. It said 'goodbye girl.'"

"I thought you said Tyler McCormick was a man."

"He was. But with a message like 'goodbye girl' . . ."

"Maybe gay or trans," said Imani, following him.

"Which leads me back to Shaky. Any possibility that there's something he wouldn't want the world to know about his connection to Tyler McCormick?"

"You do realize that Shaky and I were married at the time this happened, right?"

"All the more reason for him not to want anyone to know."

Imani drank more water. By Jack's estimate, only fifty-six more ounces to go!

"Shaky is borderline homophobic," she said. "There's no way he was having an affair with a man."

"I'm just floating the possibility," said Jack.

"Why?"

"Frankly, we need a silver bullet to make Shaky's lawsuit go away. I'm nervous about moving forward in front of a trial judge who apparently never got over the fact that Governor Swyteck thought someone else was more deserving of an appointment to the Supreme Court. I have no idea who called to plant this bug in my ear about Tyler McCormick. But if I can get Shaky nervous about questions I might ask him on the witness stand that could connect him to a homicide victim, I might be able to convince his lawyer to drop the case."

"If your theory is that Shaky is in the closet and trying to hide a relationship he had with another man, I think you're going down a rabbit hole."

"Maybe there's another angle. What else can you tell me about this time period? What was going on in Shaky's life?"

"Twelve years ago? Some bad shit."

"Bad in what way?"

"Shaky was CEO of EML Records. They were bleeding money, like everyone else in the industry. This was before the streaming services helped get music piracy under control. People were downloading everything, and there was no end in sight."

"Did Shaky have an answer?"

"Nobody did, until streaming came along. He got fired. Our marriage was never the same afterward."

A four-foot green iguana crawled out from the hibiscus bush, stopped on the pool deck, and stared at Jack. Imani jumped from her chair, and the reptile darted away.

"Welcome to Jurassic Park," said Jack.

Imani smiled nervously, then checked her sports watch. "I have a full-body massage at nine a.m. Anything more we need to talk about?"

"I want your permission to talk to MDPD about the Tyler McCormick case."

"Are you going to tell the police about the call you got?"

"No. If I tell them, they'll start running down Shaky as a possible lead. Then the cat's out of the bag. We want Shaky to be in a position where he'd rather drop his civil case than face questions from me or anyone else about Tyler McCormick."

"So what's the purpose of your meeting with MDPD?"

"Learn as much as I can. If this is a powder keg, I want to be prepared."

"I guess the worst-case scenario is that Shaky knows something about the murder of Tyler McCormick. That's his problem, not mine."

"No," said Jack. "The worst-case scenario is that he knows something, and so do you. That makes it your problem."

"I see what you're getting at. Is this why we're having this conversation in person, just you, me, and the iguana?"

"Do I have your permission to talk to MDPD?" asked Jack. It was another way of asking if she knew something about the murder of Tyler McCormick.

She grabbed her water bottle, then looked her lawyer in the eye. "Yes. You have my full permission."

CHAPTER 12

Detective Cruz's name was no longer on the MDPD website, but Jack found him on Facebook, where all retirees went. Jack messaged him, and they agreed to meet at 10:30 a.m. at a Cuban coffee shop that, according to Cruz, served Doral's best breakfast empanadas.

Doral was not only home to the famous Blue Monster golf course and a plethora of retirement communities, but it was also the main headquarters of the Miami-Dade Police Department. Cruz had arranged for Detective Wallace Green from the cold-case unit to join them. The three men found a booth near the window, with Jack sitting opposite the detectives.

Cruz broke his empanada in half and took a bite. "The investigation hit a dead end long before I sent it to the cold-case unit," he said.

"Were there ever any suspects?"

It wasn't the kind of question that Jack would have asked a detective in an active homicide investigation and expected an answer. But cold cases were different. Information flowed more freely after every possible avenue had been explored and investigators were hoping for any information that might solve an unsolved crime.

"None while I worked the case," said Cruz. "I can't speak for Wallace and what's happened in the cold-case unit since I left."

Green was younger than Cruz but looked older, the weight of too many unsolved crimes having taken its toll. He cleared his throat, then spoke. "Mr. Swyteck, you have to understand that MDPD has thousands of unsolved cases. Up until last year, I was one of two detectives assigned to the cold-case unit. Now I'm one of three."

"I'm casting no aspersions here," said Jack. "Just wondering if there were ever any suspects."

"We solved fifty-nine cases last year," he continued. "One of them was a homicide dated back to the 1980s. Unfortunately, we can't provide answers for every family. So, no. We've identified no suspects in the Tyler McCormick homicide."

Jack turned his attention back to the original detective on the case. "There must have been leads you followed, even if they never led to an actual suspect."

Cruz started on his second empanada. "The cause of death was asphyxiation—a rope around the neck. The body was then moved and put on display in the bay. We had no motive for that kind of violence and apparent anger. No evidence of any threats against the victim. No enemies. We couldn't find a single person who even mildly disliked him. Nothing added up."

"Any possible connection to drug trafficking?" asked Jack.

"A narco-style execution was my first impression. But Mr. McCormick had absolutely no connection to that world."

"So, what theories were you left with? A gang ritual? Maybe a cult of some sort?"

"We looked at both of those angles. More dead ends."

"What about a serial killer?"

"That theory actually showed some promise because of the signature."

Jack had read about it in the first newspaper article. "You mean the message on the body, 'goodbye girl.'"

"Right," said Cruz. "But that was a dead end, too. The VICAP database turned up nothing even remotely similar."

VICAP stood for Violent Criminal Apprehension Program, a unit of the FBI responsible for the analysis of serial violent and sexual crimes. The VICAP database allowed a local law enforcement agency to input the details of its investigation and determine whether a seemingly random crime might be connected to a larger pattern of similar criminal behavior in other jurisdictions.

Detective Green chimed in. "If there's something you can tell us to steer us in the right direction, we're all ears, Mr. Swyteck."

Jack hesitated, measuring his response. "I'm in a delicate situation here. As a criminal defense lawyer, I hear things all the time. Of course,

I would never run to law enforcement with information that would implicate my own client, so that's not my concern here. But even when the information relates to someone who is not my client, I'd like to know it's reliable before I share it. Rumors and wild accusations help no one."

"You'd be surprised," said Green. "The cold-case unit will happily take anything you're willing to give us."

Jack had still heard nothing to lend any credibility to the anonymous tip about Shaky Nichols and a possible connection to Tyler McCormick.

"Is there anything else you can tell me?" asked Jack. "Any other theories about the case?"

"I did have one that was very short-lived," said Cruz. "It ties in with the signature I mentioned, 'goodbye girl.'"

"Tell me about that," said Jack.

Cruz explained his initial theory that the homicide might be a hate crime based on sexual orientation or gender orientation. "I called in the FBI, since a hate crime triggers federal jurisdiction."

Jack's interest was piqued. It fit nicely with his theory that Shaky might have been hiding something about his relationship with the victim.

"Why was that theory 'short-lived,' as you say?"

"The FBI ruled it out almost immediately."

"Why?" asked Jack.

"I assume it was because McCormick wasn't gay or transgender. We established that fact right away. But I can't speak for the FBI. You'd have to ask them why they did what they did."

"Who was your contact over there?"

"Andrea something. Henner, maybe?"

Jack's pulse quickened. "Andie Henning?"

"Yeah. You know her?"

"She's my wife."

The detective smiled. "Well, isn't that convenient?"

Jack took a breath. "'Convenient' isn't exactly the word that comes to mind."

Their coffee cups were empty, and Jack had nothing more to say. They exchanged business cards—the title on Cruz's read *Currently Unsupervised and Loving It*—and promised to keep in touch.

Jack took his time pulling out of the parking lot. He did some of his best thinking behind the wheel, but he didn't necessarily do his best driving while doing his best thinking. The issue at hand, and the trickiest step in the process, was how to communicate the settlement demand to Shaky's lawyer. Technically, settlement discussions were confidential, not to be repeated to the court or anyone else—unless the lawyer crossed the line and the settlement demands amounted to outright blackmail. Jennifer Ellis struck Jack as someone who wouldn't hesitate to distort his words, paint him as an extortionist, and seek his immediate disbarment. Jack needed a witness to the conversation.

He used the car's hands-free system to dial up Theo at Cy's Place. "Hey, I need you on a conference call," said Jack.

"Yeah? You threatening somebody, or are they gonna threaten you?"

Theo knew the drill, and Jack explained quickly. Then he dialed Jennifer Ellis into the conference call and laid out the deal for her. Her antagonistic response was what Jack had expected.

"Seriously, Swyteck? Are you threatening my client with criminal prosecution to gain advantage in a civil lawsuit?"

"Of course not," said Jack. "That would be against the rules of professional conduct. I'm simply stating facts. If this civil case continues, I will get to the bottom of the Tyler McCormick connection. And I have a client who wants me to leave no stone unturned. If that makes your client uncomfortable, he needs to take it into consideration."

"If you don't call that a threat, you're walking a very fine line."

"The practice of law is filled with fine lines."

Ellis hung up without so much as an "up yours and have a nice day." Theo was still on the line.

"Well, that went well," said Jack.

"You probably should have just said 'arrgh' and told her to walk the plank."

"I'd put the odds that she drops the case at about one in ten thousand."

"Add at least two zeroes, dude. About the same odds as Righley's soccer team winning a game this season. Man, this morning was ug-*lee*."

Jack's stomach dropped. He couldn't believe he'd forgotten. "You went?"

"'Course I went. What kind of godfather you think I am?"

The *god*father's qualifications were not at issue. "Was she upset I wasn't there?"

"Nothing that a trip to Disney World and years of therapy won't cure."

The traffic light changed. Jack drove past a Mister Softee ice-cream truck parked along the side of the road, and it didn't help to see the kids in soccer uniforms lining up for a postgame soft swirl.

"I feel like such a fuckup," said Jack.

"That's because you fucked up."

Jack steered onto the expressway ramp, heading home. "The day's only going to get worse."

"What's worse than not seeing the next Mia Hamm pick flowers at midfield?"

"Missing the game," said Jack, "*and* having to ask Andie about Tyler McCormick."

Another Saturday, another date night. They dined downtown at Andie's favorite Japanese restaurant, and then went for cocktails at a rooftop bar in the East Hotel called Sugar. From forty stories up, a seat inside at the Balinese-style bar or outside in the garden offered the best views of the Miami skyline. A full moon rising over the bay was a bonus.

"Mmm, watermelon margarita," said Andie. She ordered one for each of them.

Jack had procrastinated all afternoon and throughout dinner, waiting without success for the perfect moment to broach the subject of a homicide that Andie may have investigated on some level when she and Jack had barely known each other. It was obvious that such a moment would never arise. He was just going to have to dive in.

The server brought the cocktails to their table in the garden. Andie drank her margarita, as Jack told her about his meeting with the MDPD detectives. He stopped short of mentioning the phone call from an anonymous tipster and the possible connection to Shaky Nichols.

"Why are we talking about Tyler McCormick?" asked Andie.

"We've always known that when an FBI agent marries a criminal defense lawyer, there's at least a theoretical possibility of some overlap between our work. It looks like Tyler McCormick could be a point of intersection."

"How?"

"I can't tell you how. It's not in my client's best interest to be telling anyone in law enforcement why I'm asking questions about Tyler McCormick. I just wanted to make you aware, in case it circles back to you."

"Okay. But one word of advice. If you don't want anyone to know which client has you meeting with MDPD homicide detectives on a Saturday morning, Imani shouldn't be tweeting about a Saturday-morning meeting with her lawyer."

"She tweeted about that?"

"Yes, Jack. She lives on social media. Life is only worth living if you can post about it." Her voice had that *joking, but not joking* tone to it.

"I'm not saying this has anything to do with Imani," said Jack.

Andie laughed. "Well, can you at least confirm or deny that she looked hot in her super-short running shorts?"

"How do you know she was wearing running shorts?"

Andie pulled up the tweet on her phone and read aloud. "'Looking hot, hot, hot in my sprinter shorts for meeting with super-lawyer Jack Swyteck. Watch out, Shaky. We got a surprise for you.'"

Jack felt a headache coming on. "Why are you even following Imani on Twitter?"

"I don't. My sister texts me this crap."

"Your sister slept with your fiancé. You can't stand her."

"Yes, and it's mutual, which is why she sends this stuff to me. And it's not just her. The jokes are nonstop at the field office. 'Hey, Andie, did you read the *Daily Mail*? Jack and Imani are planning a double wedding with Johnny Depp and that lawyer who helped him sue the shit out of Amber Heard.'"

"I'm sorry about the crazy rumors, but Imani said you would be quick to see it for what it was."

"Of course I see it. Imani is playing you, Jack."

"She *tried* to play me. She said it was better for the media to be talking about a possible romance between a lawyer and his client than to be focused on what the client actually did. I shut it down. I should have talked to you about it, and I'm sorry I didn't." She seemed inclined to forgive him, but Jack didn't always leave well enough alone. "And, for the record, you look hotter than she does in running shorts."

"Oh, please. Imani has probably spent a half-million dollars cool-sculpting her body. And I can assure you, she's never even heard of the eighth day of the week."

"Eight? As in the Beatles song?"

"No. As in the book of Genesis."

"There's no eighth day in the book of Genesis."

"On the eighth day, God said, 'Let there be cellulite.' And there was cellulite. And God said, 'Damn, that was a mistake.'"

"Honey, you're sounding a little tipsy."

She finished the last of her margarita, which had gone down way too quickly.

"Maybe I am. And you know what that means."

"Either I'm going to get kissed or you're going to get something off your chest."

"Or maybe both," she said, and she gave him a quick one on the lips. Then she turned serious, or at least as serious as she could look with a little tequila buzz.

"I was really mad at you today. Saturday mornings are family time. You never miss Righley's soccer games, but this morning you were out the door before she or I were even awake."

"I had to—"

"No," she said, shutting him down. "You didn't *have* to. Was it really so urgent that you rush out and speak to Imani? Or are you a little star-struck yourself?"

"Come on, Andie. A week ago, I hardly knew who Imani was."

"What a difference the eighth day makes."

Jack's cell rang. He checked the number and said, "I have to take this."

"Let me guess," she said, pointing a finger in the air to make her point. "Imani!"

It was actually Shaky's lawyer, but that would have been a distinction without a difference.

"I'll ignore it if you want me to," he said.

"No, no, it's fine," she said, moving his margarita to her side of the table. "If you have to take it, take it. And if it matters, I had very little to do with the Tyler McCormick case. The FBI was out of that investigation almost as soon as we got in."

That jibed with what Detective Cruz had told him. "Thanks for sharing that," he said. "I'll make this quick."

The call had gone to voicemail. Jack walked to the other end of the garden terrace, where he could talk in private, and dialed her back.

"I spoke to my client," said Ellis.

"And?"

"Shaky has decided not to pursue the civil case in Florida until after the criminal case against Imani is concluded in New York."

Jack tried not to convey his surprise—shock, actually. By the time the criminal case played out in New York, the civil suit would be moot. Shaky was effectively dropping his lawsuit.

"That's good news," said Jack.

"Just to be clear, this is purely a strategy decision. It has nothing to do with Tyler McCormick."

"Understood," said Jack.

"And don't get cocky," she said. "As soon as this case goes back to court, your client will be on the ropes with her knees wobbling. Just to make sure you understand, I had another batch of text messages couriered to your office today. Take a gander. Judge Stevens didn't think much of the sixteen messages we showed him, but these are another ball game."

Had he downed his watermelon margarita the way Andie had inhaled hers, Jack probably would have said something like, "Ooh, I'm scared."

"Good night," was all he said, and the call ended.

Jack's gaze drifted toward the bay. Through the narrow, vertical slats between high-rises, he could see almost as far as Isola di Lolando, the island that never was, where the body had been found twelve years earlier. Then he turned away from the railing and started back toward his wife, the first FBI agent to arrive on the crime scene.

Nothing to do with Tyler McCormick, thought Jack, tucking his phone away. *Right.*

CHAPTER 13

Theo placed a tall glass on the table before his favorite customer. Great-uncle Cy was in his nineties, but he still came by the club every now and then. Climbing up onto a barstool was difficult at his age, so Theo kept a small table near the stage on permanent reserve for the club's namesake. Saturday was jazz night, but the musicians were on break.

"This ain't right," Cy said.

"Ginger beer, three ice cubes," said Theo.

"Not that," said Cy, pointing to his copy of the *New York Times* on the table. It was open to an article about Imani's "go pirate" campaign and the criminal charges brought by the U.S. attorney in New York. "Explain *this* to me."

Theo let his other bartender know he was "taking five" and joined his uncle at his favorite table, the one that still had a matchbook from the long-gone Cotton Club under one of the legs to keep it from wobbling.

"It's a complicated thing," said Theo.

"Nothin' complicated about telling people to steal someone else's property. It's just wrong."

"It's her music."

"It ain't her music," said Cy. "If I build you a car, and then I sell that car to you, can I still drive that car? No! I have to build a new car."

"I hear what you're saying," said Theo. "Taylor Swift re-recorded her masters to get around her contract."

"I was talking about Frank Sinatra. He did it first. But good for Taylor. Your friend Imani needs to get her butt in the studio, stop whining, and do the work."

"It's not whining. A lot of artists agree with her."

"Like who?"

The answer was in the article, and it concerned Theo to think the old man had forgotten what he'd just read. Or maybe he just didn't believe the *New York Times* when it reported that hundreds of artists were retweeting Imani's "go pirate" message. Some, like Imani, were trapped in onerous contracts with their first label. But even artists who opposed piracy under any circumstances stood in support of Imani's First Amendment right to free speech. The most influential supporters of all were the world's richest and most visible musicians, who made their real money not from music, but from clothing lines, perfume, jewelry, and the like. The royalties they might lose to an uptick in music piracy was chump change compared to the earnings from a joint venture with a French luxury goods conglomerate or a sponsorship with a cosmetic company. In fact, "standing in solidarity" with Imani's "go pirate" campaign made them all the more controversial and interesting to their fans.

Theo's gaze was drawn toward the club entrance.

"Well, look what the cat dragged in," said Theo. "Amongus Sicario is back."

"Who?"

"Amongus. Rhymes with 'fungus.'"

"Who's that?"

Theo told him as the rapper approached from across the room. He stopped at the table and, at Theo's invitation, he pulled up a chair.

"Where's Imani?" asked Amongus.

"She's not here."

"She said the three of us was meeting here."

"News to me," said Theo.

"There she is," he said, pointing with a jerk of his head toward the entrance. A blonde woman entered in the company of two very muscular men and went straight to Theo's table.

"Don't mind the wig," she said. "Sometimes it's easier to be someone else when I go out in public."

It seemed odd that she'd planned a meeting with Amongus without telling him. "The wig ain't what's got me confused," he said.

"Sorry I didn't loop you in, but until I walked through the doors, I wasn't sure this meeting was going to happen. I wasn't looking forward to more badgering about going pirate."

Her words caught Cy's attention. "Are you the singer in this article?" asked Cy, pointing to the *Times*.

Theo introduced him to Imani and Amongus, hoping to change the subject, but it didn't deter Cy. "That's *you*, telling everyone to 'go pirate'?"

"That's me," said Imani.

Cy shook his head with disapproval. "You're playing with fire, telling your fans to 'go pirate.' Piracy almost killed our business. You need to stop this shit."

Amongus seemed happy to have a new friend. "She knows all that. That's why I asked her to come back to MAP and fight piracy."

"MAP's a good organization," said Cy.

Theo made a face at his uncle. "What do you know about MAP?"

"I know enough to fight my enemies, not join 'em."

"Amen to that," said Amongus. "Traffic on piracy websites is up twenty-five percent since Imani started saying 'go pirate.' The message is going viral now. We're getting close to the point where nothing can stop it."

"All Shaky has to do is tear up the contract, and I'll stop," said Imani.

"He paid three hundred million dollars for your masters. He can't just tear up the contract."

"I'm not backing down," said Imani. "You called and said you wanted to meet. I came. But unless you have something to say besides 'give up,' I'm leaving."

"There's a local chapter of MAP in London. Lots of musicians like me. Our fans don't need much encouragement to steal. So when you and a hundred other big names say 'go pirate' and hit Shaky Nichols and all the other music executives where it hurts, our fans are all-in. We're getting killed."

"I'm sorry about that," said Imani. "I never said anyone should steal *your* music."

"Saying 'I'm sorry' isn't fucking good enough."

"Then what do you want from me?"

Amongus leaned in closer to the table. "I read about your testimony at the hearing. You said you left MAP because they did some questionable things. Things much worse than hacking websites and spreading computer viruses."

"It was true."

"That's my point," said Amongus. "The London group is desperate. I hear something 'much worse' is coming."

"Like what?" asked Imani. "Blocking traffic until Parliament does something about piracy?"

"*Much* worse," said Amongus. "MAP will cease to exist if these guys haul off and do the crazy shit they're talking about."

"You mean violence?" asked Theo.

"I mean nothing's off the table," said Amongus.

"Do you mean violence against *me*?" asked Imani.

Amongus didn't answer directly. "People remember what it was like ten, fifteen years ago, when piracy was out of control. They don't want to go back to the bad old days."

It sounded like a bluff to Theo. "Come on, dude. Now you're just trying to scare her."

"I'm just saying she's been living in a penthouse apartment too long. It wouldn't hurt to reconnect with the musicians on the street. Tell them this 'go pirate' campaign isn't going to last forever. Convince them to wait it out."

"I couldn't go if I wanted to," said Imani. "I surrendered my passport as a condition of bail."

"Theo should go," said Cy.

It was like the sage voice of the wise elder. No one spoke for a moment until Cy continued.

"Theo can handle himself better than anyone Imani knows. He can go in her place. But only if he has full authority to tell these boys that the end is in sight."

Theo looked at Imani. "Amongus is right. This can't go on forever."

"You don't have to get in the middle of this," said Imani.

"I want to," said Theo. "If I have your blessing."

Imani glanced at Cy, who nodded his approval.

Imani extended her arm as straight as a sword, placed her hand on

Theo's right shoulder, and spoke like the queen of England: "I hereby knight thee Sir Theo Knight," she said, moving her hand to his other shoulder, "ambassador of Imani."

"I happily accept," said Theo.

I think.

Jack and Andie were home by eleven thirty. Jack paid the babysitter, who apparently was no match for a seven-year-old. Righley was in their bed to greet them.

"I had a bad dream," she said.

Jack looked at Andie and said, "I got this."

She gave him a quick kiss and whispered, "I'm going to shower."

Jack wasn't sure if this was "date night" morphing into "sex night" or, even better, the complete abandonment of any rules about which night it was. Either way, he was happy. He gathered Righley in his arms, carried her back to her room, and tucked her into bed. She asked him to stay a little while, so he kicked off his shoes and lay beside her.

"I had a bad dream about pirates," she said softly.

"Why were you dreaming about pirates?"

"Mommy said you missed my soccer game this morning because you were with a pirate."

"No, honey. I was with a client."

"Is your client a pirate?"

"No. She's accused of helping pirates. But not the kind of pirates who were in your dream."

"Aren't all pirates bad?"

"Well, yes."

"Aren't all pirates scary?"

"They can be."

"Is your client helping bad, scary pirates?"

Jack had to think about that one. "I'm not sure she understands exactly who she is helping."

"Your client doesn't sound very smart."

Food for thought, but Jack changed the subject. Righley selected a chapter book from the stack on her nightstand, and Jack listened to her read aloud. In five minutes, her eyes closed, and she was fast asleep. Jack quietly slid out of bed and returned to the master bedroom. Andie was still in the shower. He turned on the television. Since Imani's arraignment on charges of piracy, one entertainment industry expert after another had appeared on cable news. Jack caught the tail end of the interview of a Hollywood executive.

"The list of streaming services goes on and on," the expert said. "Netflix, Disney Plus, Amazon Prime Video, Hulu, Apple TV Plus. Each one has its own subscription fee, and they are all trying to lure new subscribers by pumping out exclusive content. But exclusive content means that unless you pay a subscription fee to every streaming service, you're going to miss something. Who can afford that? No one. That's why we are seeing the highest levels of piracy since the early 2000s. Even people who are basically honest have had enough, and they can rationalize it by saying, 'Well, at least I don't pirate *everything*.'"

A cellphone vibrated on the dresser. Jack glanced over, thinking it was his, but it was Andie's. He didn't intend to read the message, but the preview bubble popped right up on the screen. The fact that it was from Detective Wallace Green from the MDPD cold-case unit and written in all caps made it impossible for him to disengage quickly enough to avoid reading it.

BREAK IN TM CASE. SAY NOTHING TO YOUR HUSBAND. CALL ME IN A.M.

Jack looked away. He should not have seen it, but there was no erasing it from his brain. Obviously, "TM" stood for Tyler McCormick. According to Andie, she'd had virtually no involvement in the McCormick investigation. If that were true, why was she getting a text message from the cold-case detective—someone she would never have even met if, in her words, "the FBI was out of that investigation almost as soon as we got in," years before the case was transferred to the cold-case unit?

An unsettling feeling came over him. The one rule that made sense in their marriage was "no discussing active cases," which was their way of avoiding a compromising situation between law enforcement and a criminal defense attorney. But not talking about active cases and lying about them were two different things. Jack had never thought deception was part of the arrangement. He'd apparently thought wrong.

The bathroom door opened. Andie stepped out, wrapped in a bath towel.

"Smooth leg alert," she said, eyebrows dancing.

Jack still wasn't sure what to do about her lie. One thing for sure: he was in no hurry to explain how he'd seen a work-related message on her cellphone, which was, arguably, the bigger sin. This could wait.

"Come to bed," he said with a smile.

CHAPTER 14

Theo's nonstop from Miami left Sunday night and landed at Heathrow on Monday morning. At one point in his life, he would have embraced without qualification Jack's legal arguments that the execution of an innocent man is "cruel and unusual punishment" in its most egregious form. Flying coach overseas had him rethinking things.

At least Amongus had arranged for a limo. The driver met him at the end of the immigration chute and led him to a black SUV in the parking garage. His name was Benjamin.

"First time in London?" asked Benjamin.

Theo wondered how he'd guessed right. Did he really look that out of place? Then it hit him. He'd walked around to the wrong side of the car. The preferred backseat with more leg room was never directly behind the driver, and in the United States that seat was on the right. Benjamin was standing on the other side, holding open the rear door for him. Theo walked around and climbed into the backseat.

"Never gonna get used to this," he said.

Theo listened to music on the drive into the city. To show her appreciation, Imani had shared a studio recording of a track on her album-in-the-making, and Theo was a lucky Beta listener. He wondered how much a pirated version might fetch on the dark web, which made him wonder half-seriously whether he should be traveling with his own bodyguard.

The streets were getting narrower, and the neighborhood was definitely upscale.

"Where are we?" asked Theo.

"Covent Garden."

"Lots of flowers," he said in kneejerk fashion, reacting to the colorful window boxes.

"Perhaps that's why it's called Floral Street," he said dryly.

The SUV stopped halfway down the block. The street was just wide enough for one car to pass and one row of parking. A Thai restaurant was so close that Theo could have practically reached out and touched the plate-glass window. Several stories above street level, a covered walkway stretched from one side of the street to the other, like a twisted ribbon tied between buildings. It reminded him of the modern version of the Bridge of Sighs in Venice, pictures of which he'd come across in his macabre research on capital punishment while on death row.

"What is that?" he asked, pointing.

"The Bridge of Aspirations," Benjamin said.

"Aspirations of what?"

"The building on the left is the Royal Ballet School. Across the street is the Royal Opera House. All student dancers who pass through that tunnel in the sky aspire to greatness with the Royal Ballet."

That sounded a whole lot better than the Bridge of Sighs and a prisoner's last view of the Venice canals before execution.

"Why are we at a ballet school?"

Benjamin chuckled. "*A* ballet school? You mean *the* ballet school."

"Okay, why are we at *the* ballet school?"

"This is where Amongus Sicario wants us to meet him."

Theo would have expected a guy like Amongus to pick an East End strip club, but he could go with the flow.

A motor scooter passed. A pigeon landed on the hood of the SUV. The driver cursed and shooed it away with the honk of his horn, and then he fixed his gaze on the entrance to the ballet school, which was four stories below the Bridge of Aspirations. After several more minutes, the glass door swung open. A man dressed in a business suit walked out. He was holding the hand of a preteen girl whose hair was in the classic ballet bun. They acted like father and daughter, and there was enough physical resemble to lead Theo to believe that they were. Behind them was another man dressed in a suit. He rivaled Theo in stature. Clearly a bodyguard.

"There they are," said Benjamin.

"Who?"

"We're sharing a ride."

"With them?"

Benjamin glanced over his shoulder at Theo, his voice taking on an edge. "Don't ask questions."

Benjamin climbed out and closed his door. As Theo watched him walk around the front of the SUV, the locks clicked inside. Benjamin had locked all doors with the keyless remote. Theo tried his door, but the child-lock system had him trapped.

Don't ask questions. It wasn't just a change in Benjamin's tone. Theo thought he'd detected a slight change in the accent, too.

Theo watched through the windshield as Benjamin stepped onto the sidewalk to meet the man and the girl. They clearly knew each other. Benjamin led them to the passenger side of the SUV, tapped on Theo's window, and said, "Scoot over."

Definitely a change in the accent. Less British. A hint of Russian.

"Move *over*," he said again, more firmly.

Theo had been in bad situations before, and his antennae were on high alert. But his options were limited. He was locked inside the vehicle and unarmed. He glanced through the window at the girl's face. She was smiling, which seemed to weigh against his suspicions of funny business. He slid across the bench seat until he was directly behind the driver's seat. Benjamin manually unlocked the rear door on the passenger side only, but not Theo's door. The passenger-side door swung open, and Theo's fears became reality.

Benjamin pivoted with the precision of Baryshnikov and thrust a metal probe of some sort into the bodyguard's arm. The huge man shrieked like a wounded animal and collapsed to the sidewalk, writhing like a Taser-gun victim. As the girl screamed, another man launched from behind a parked vehicle, broadsided the girl's father, and pushed him into the backseat. He kept pushing until the man was nearly in Theo's lap. Then he jumped in the car and pulled the door closed, sandwiching the girl's father between him and Theo and leaving the girl alone with the writhing bodyguard on the sidewalk. Benjamin jumped into the front passenger seat, never unlocking the doors on the driver's side, and climbed over the console to get behind the wheel.

"Go!" his accomplice shouted. He was wearing a black ski mask and pressing a gun to the hostage's head and, at that moment, Theo realized who it was.

Fungus Amongus.

The tires squealed as the SUV launched from the parking space and barreled down Floral Street, passing several restaurants and a pub at the corner. They entered a large, multilane roundabout, and Benjamin steered his way through traffic like a Formula 1 driver, the SUV weaving between vehicles at ever-increasing speed. A siren blasted behind them.

"Police!" said Benjamin.

"Get out!" Amongus shouted, and Theo realized he was speaking to him.

They were halfway around the roundabout, with traffic flowing like a giant wheel around a granite monument at the axis. At such high speed, the centrifugal force created by the SUV's circular path had shifted the other passengers to the left, their weight pressing Theo against the door.

"Say what?" said Theo.

"Jump, or I'll blow your head off!"

Benjamin unlocked the door from the driver's control panel, but the vehicle didn't slow down a bit. Jumping out of a speeding SUV was Theo's first worry, but rolling across two lanes of traffic to the sidewalk was an even bigger concern.

"Now!" shouted Amongus. He reached across, yanked the handle, and pushed Theo out the door.

Theo tucked and catapulted like a human cannonball from the vehicle, landing feet-first and fighting to roll—not skid—toward the perimeter. The pavement ripped through his leather jacket at the elbow, and somewhere in the tumble he lost a shoe. Cars swerved and horns blasted, but somehow he found daylight between bumpers like an urban cat with nine lives. It was a blur but, to his amazement, he was alive and fully conscious as he rolled up the curb and onto the sidewalk.

The SUV continued through the roundabout without him, exiting on the other side of the monument. A police car raced toward Theo, hopped the curb, and screeched to a halt so suddenly that the front bumper nearly kissed the sidewalk. Two officers jumped out.

"Hands up!" they shouted.

Theo couldn't even begin to explain. A trail of blood ran down his forehead to the bridge of his nose, but he didn't dare make a false move and wipe it away. He raised his arms in the air, hoping Jack knew a good lawyer in London.

"Don't shoot!" he said. "You've got the wrong guy."

CHAPTER 15

Jack's phone rang on the nightstand. His cellphone was set to silence incoming calls during bedtime hours, with the exception of Andie and his closest friends and relatives. He reached across his mattress, grabbed the phone from the charging stand, and checked the screen: THEO.

Jack was tempted to ignore it and go back to sleep. But the last time Theo had called him at 5:00 a.m. was to tell his lawyer that the prison barber had shaved his head and ankles for placement of the electrodes so that "Old Sparky"—the affectionate name for the electric chair at Florida State Prison—could do its work. Jack picked up.

"What's up, Theo?"

"I'm in jail."

Jack sat up in bed, his mind still cloudy. "Nobody calls from their own cellphone in jail."

"You do if your 'one phone call' is to a lawyer overseas. I tried calling you collect from the phone here, but you didn't answer. The custody officer said I could have three minutes."

Jack was suddenly wide awake, and his thoughts cleared enough to recall Theo's telling him that Imani had put him on a plane to London.

"You're in jail in *London*?"

"They call it a custody suite. One of the other guys in the pen said they can hold me at the station for twenty-four hours before charging me."

Andie grumbled in her sleep and stirred beside him. Jack quickly climbed out of bed, hurried to the master bathroom, and closed the door.

"Listen to me carefully," he said into the phone. "As much as I'd like you to tell me what happened, I'm not going to ask because I have no idea who else can hear us. Do you understand me?"

"Uh-huh."

"Answer my question yes or no. Have the police mentioned or threatened you with any specific charge?"

"Yes."

"What?"

"Kidnapping."

Jack was expecting something on the order of a bar fight. "Are you sure about this? They're threatening to charge you with kidnapping another human being?"

"Not by myself, but with—"

"Stop right there. Not another word. Here's the plan. I'm going to find you a lawyer in London. They're called solicitors."

"Fitting. I knew a prostitute who called herself a solicitor."

"This is no time to joke. Actually, it might be a barrister. I don't know. I don't practice law in England, and it's five o'clock in the fucking morning. I'll get you a lawyer with a British accent, and then I'm flying over there as soon as I can. You got it?"

"Yeah."

"Don't talk to anyone. Not to the police, not to another detainee, not even to yourself."

Jail messed with the mind, and Jack had known inmates to incriminate themselves by talking aloud to no one.

"I don't talk to myself," said Theo.

"And now would be a terrible time to start. The next person you hear from will be your London lawyer. Do you know what police station you're in?"

"Charing Cross."

"Okay. Just sit tight."

"I'm definitely not going anywhere."

Jack said goodbye and ended the call. He took a seat on the rim of the bathtub to try to remember exactly what Theo had told him about London. Meet up with Amongus. Spread some love from Imani to some guys in MAP. "Kidnapping" didn't make any sense.

He opened a travel app on his phone and booked the first available nonstop to London, departing Miami at 4:55 p.m. He was scrolling through his contacts, looking for the friend or colleague most likely to have the name of a London lawyer, when his phone vibrated with an incoming email. It was from his assistant. The subject line read, "Call me as soon as you get up!" He dialed her cell.

"Bonnie, are you in the office already?"

"Been here all night for the Freedom Institute. Last-minute death appeal."

Jack recalled those days. "I saw your email. Is this about Theo?"

"No. A package came by courier for Saturday delivery. It's from Jennifer Ellis, marked 'urgent.' I scanned the documents for you. They're attached to the email I sent."

"I'll read them later."

"But it says 'urgent.'"

"Bonnie, I'll look at them later. Jennifer sent them right before she called and told me the case is on hold."

"Jack, I don't trust her. I've been up all night. I'm on my tenth cup of coffee, and I don't need another fire drill today because there's something in there that you didn't see until it's too late. Look at the documents!"

About once a year, Bonnie hit the breaking point. She was there.

Jack gave the electronic file about ten seconds of his attention, scanning through copies of text messages between Imani and Shaky. "Sex, sex, and sex. More of the salacious nonsense Judge Stevens doesn't want to hear about, and that for some reason Shaky's lawyer thinks is more embarrassing to my client than hers. Done. I looked."

"What should I do?"

"File it away and get a shot of penicillin. I'll call you from London."

"London?"

"Long story." He said a quick goodbye, and there was an immediate tap on the bathroom door.

"Jack, is everything okay?" asked Andie.

With parents of a certain age, Andie was one of those people who thought a phone call before dawn could only be horrible news. Jack opened the door and said, "Nobody died."

"Thank God. Who were you talking to?"

He was about to tell her, but another call came up on his phone. This one didn't ring but vibrated in his hand. The incoming number was international, which meant either that his car warranty was about to expire or that Theo was calling back on another number. He answered.

"This is Amongus," the caller said.

"I just heard from Theo," said Jack.

"That boy's in deep shit," said Amongus.

Jack's golden retriever waddled into the room, half asleep, but carrying a slipper in his mouth. With Andie still in the doorway, it was officially a team meeting.

"This is business," he whispered to Andie, and then he retreated into the bathroom and closed the door.

"Tell me what's going on," Jack said into the phone.

"Looks like Theo tried to kidnap the son of a Russian oligarch."

The morning just kept getting wilder. "What are you talking about?"

"I'd say about twenty-five years in prison."

"Theo is not a kidnapper."

"I'm sure that's what he'll say. Probably try and blame me. But the fact is, he's the one sitting in jail right now. Not me."

Jack gripped the phone tighter. "What kind of shit are you trying to pull here, Amongus?"

"I'm offering a solution to a very serious problem that your friend Theo has gotten himself into."

"Don't play games with me."

"No game. A simple business offer. Imani drops all this 'go pirate' bullshit. Theo gets his 'get out of jail free' card."

"That's not an offer. That's extortion."

"It's an offer where I come from."

"You couldn't even keep yourself out of jail. How are you going to get Theo out?"

He chuckled over the line. "I'm not that kid anymore who went to prison, Swyteck. I'm a man of international power and influence. Don't you know that?"

Jack's anger rose. "Listen to me, you punk. I'm coming to London, and I'm going to find you. If you set up Theo to be arrested just so you could leverage a deal with Imani, I will make you pay for it. Do you hear me?"

There was a crackling on the line.

"Do you hear me?" Jack said.

The crackling got louder. Then it sounded like a scuffle, followed by indecipherable shouting in the background.

"Amongus?"

The unmistakable crack of gunshot pierced the conversation. Then silence.

"Amongus, what just happened?" Jack said with urgency.

Jack waited, but there was no response.

"Amongus, are you all right?"

"I'm . . . hit," he said in a voice that faded.

"Amongus, tell me where you are!"

No reply.

"Amongus!"

More silence, and Amongus's words—*kidnap the son of a Russian oligarch*—echoed in his mind. Oligarchs didn't mess around. Jack caught a glimpse of himself in the vanity mirror over the sink. His hand was shaking as he lowered the phone.

"Holy shit," he said to his reflection.

CHAPTER 16

Vladimir Kava spent the afternoon relaxing on the deck of his superyacht, eighty-five meters of luxury that he loved so much he'd named it the *Dilber*, after his late mother. Built and launched in Germany, the elegant yacht seemed to change colors in the sunlight as it glided across the Indian Ocean at a cruise speed of up to 14.4 knots. The *Dilber* accommodated twelve guests and twenty-eight crew. Two heliports made it easy for guests to come and go, and once onboard, they were sure to enjoy themselves with three swimming pools, a spa with two Jacuzzis, a smaller speedboat, jet skis, and a movie theater.

Kava was sixty-two years old, which actually exceeded the combined ages of the three beautiful, bikini-clad women in his company. They were in the Maldives Islands, southwest of Sri Lanka, a favorite destination of Russian oligarchs and their superyachts. The allure was much more than warm waters and scenic archipelagic islands. At the outset of Russia's war with Ukraine, international sanctions triggered government seizure of Russian superyachts worth in excess of $200 billion. The Republic of Maldives had proven to be a friendly refuge for oligarchs. The bribes from Kava had been especially generous.

A porter approached with a satellite phone on a silver tray. "You have a call, sir," he said.

Kava raised his sunglasses up over his eyes, but otherwise didn't move from his relaxed, prone position in the chaise lounge. "Who is it?"

The porter leaned closer and whispered, "It's Utkin, sir."

A call from Utkin was always cause for utmost discretion. For so many reasons, his role in the Kremlin didn't officially exist. Mercenaries are illegal in Russia, but over the years, Utkin, a lieutenant colonel in the armed forces, had received numerous medals for his "leadership," all secretly tied to Wagner, a group of special-force mercenaries that had proven itself indispensable to the federation. Wagner mercenaries had a bloodthirsty reputation for fighting battles that Russia's organized military could not undertake without violating international law. Under Utkin's leadership, thousands of mercenaries had carried out operations in Ukraine, South America, the Middle East, Syria, Libya, Mozambique, the Central African Republic, and other war zones. Prisoners were regarded as an unwelcome mouth to feed. Countless shallow graves marked the group's trail of massacres, rapes, torture, and indiscriminate killings along their way. The Wagner Group eventually became so dangerous that even the Russian government refused to pay them directly. An oligarch was needed to finance and control the group. Moscow tapped Vladimir Kava, a close ally of the Kremlin who was once dubbed "Putin's chef." The official position was that Wagner didn't exist, and that Kava provided only catering services to the Russian government.

With a dismissive wave of the hand, Kava shooed away the sunbathers and the three women gathered up their bikini tops and moved to the other side of the swimming pool.

The two men spoke in their native Russian.

"London's Metropolitan Police Service has your son in custody," said Utkin.

"For what?"

"Our London solicitor tells us that the Department of Justice is seeking extradition to New York to face charges under U.S. law."

"What charges?"

"A criminal case was just filed in Manhattan. It involves piracy. The U.S. attorney is dragging in everybody he can get in his crosshairs. Even that singer, Imani, is one of the defendants."

Kava had first entered the piracy business in the days of peer-to-peer file sharing, when his network of platforms provided access to websites where total strangers could exchange pirated material in peer-to-peer file transfers. In its first year alone, Kava's network facilitated the exchange of 132 billion music files and 11 billion movies. Even though the pirated files were free, other forms of revenue—advertising, links to

gaming websites, and data mining—were off the charts. P2P file sharing was no longer the business model, and frankly, the modern piracy
model in the streaming world was beyond Kava's technical comprehen-
sion. His son, Sergei, ran that part of the organization.

"This is not possible," said Kava. "Is this the same solicitor who told
us that if the U.S. sought extradition, we would know about it in time
to get him out of the UK before he could be arrested?"

"Yes. And under normal circumstances, that would be the case. The
U.S. makes the extradition request. The UK secretary of state has to
certify the request and send the case to court. The judge has to issue a
warrant for arrest, and by the time the police go out to make the arrest,
Sergei would be long gone. But there was a quirk."

"I don't accept quirks."

"This was not foreseeable. Sergei's driver betrayed us."

"How?"

"Every man has his price. He was supposed to pick up Sergei in
Covent Garden. There was an ambush, and Sergei was kidnapped."

"I heard nothing about a ransom demand."

"There was none. The kidnappers held him just long enough for the
arrest warrant to issue. They dropped him off right at the fucking police
station the minute the judge issued the warrant. No chance for us to get
Sergei out."

"Obviously, this was no coincidence. Who did this?"

"We'll find out. I'm told one of the kidnappers is also in custody. An
American. Theo Knight is his name."

"Get all the information you need from him. The Americans will
deny it, but clearly there has been very precise coordination between the
authorities and these kidnappers."

"I will get to the bottom of it."

"Good. And once you do, deal with this Theo Knight appropriately."

Utkin chuckled. "Who shall I send?"

Kava considered the question. "Someone who will make this American wish he'd never been born."

"I have just the right operative in mind."

"You always do," said Kava, and he ended the call.

CHAPTER 17

British Airways Flight 208 from Miami landed at Heathrow as scheduled. Jack had done all the right things to avoid jet lag. His wristwatch was set to London time before boarding. Plenty of water, no alcohol on the flight. He even managed to sleep a few winks before landing. Still, he was having a hard time accepting that it was time for breakfast, Wednesday.

"Charing Cross police station," Jack said as he climbed into the taxi.

"Not one of our top tourist destinations," said the driver.

The phone call from Amongus had put Jack in the unusual posture of "ear witness" to a crime. He'd immediately told Andie, who'd connected him to the FBI's legal attaché at the U.S. embassy in London. Amongus was their problem. Theo was Jack's.

The taxi took him straight to the police station. Oddly enough, it struck Jack as the kind of place that actually could have been a tourist destination, at least for fans of British noir or Agatha Christie who wanted to step back in time to a station house of another era. The four-story building was triangular in shape, conforming to streets that were laid out long before surveyors with precision instruments platted the emerging cities of the New World into grid systems. An iron fence ran the length of the building, the black pickets standing like prison bars against the white stone façade. An old red phone booth punctuated the street corner at the narrow end of the triangle. Four fluted columns with Doric capitals marked the main entrance, and the globe-shaped lanterns on either side of the mahogany doors were straight out of Dick Tracy.

Jack entered the lobby, where the criminal defense solicitor he'd retained for Theo had agreed to meet him. Instead, he was met by a woman who was dressed like a lawyer but spoke with a decidedly American accent.

"Madeline Coffey," she said, shaking Jack's hand.

"You don't sound very British," said Jack.

"That's because I'm from Detroit," said Coffey. "I'm the FBI's legal attaché for the U.S. embassy here in London."

"Where's Mr. Carlisle, the solicitor I hired?"

"I sent him back to his office."

"Why?"

"Can we go for a short walk around the block," she said as she stepped toward the door. Jack followed her out of the station house and down the front steps.

"You hired a very fine lawyer in Mr. Carlisle," she said as they started down the sidewalk. "As a Crown prosecutor, he handled dozens of extradition cases involving U.S. citizens. That international experience has served him well as the go-to criminal defense solicitor for foreigners charged in the UK."

They passed Bright's Bakery on the corner. Jack wondered if London police craved doughnuts as badly as their American counterparts. Probably preferred scones. Or crumpets, whatever the hell those were.

"He came highly recommended," said Jack.

"Fortunately, Mr. Knight will not be in need of his services."

"Why not?"

"There will be no charges brought against him."

Jack stopped on the sidewalk. "Then let's go back and get him. He should be released. Now."

"He's no longer there."

"Where is he?"

"He was taken to the U.S. embassy this morning. The plan is to put him on a flight back to Miami just as soon as we can."

It was great news, but Jack couldn't help feeling annoyed. Then a thought came to him. "Did my wife have anything to do with this?"

"No, sir. Agent Henning is about as straight an arrow as we have. This was not about any favors being called in."

Jack reached for his cellphone. "I need to call Theo."

"He won't answer," said Coffey. "He no longer has his cellphone."

Jack put his phone away. "You said he was released. He's entitled to the return of his property."

"It's for his own safety. We don't want the wrong people tracking his movements by GPS locator."

Jack's annoyance turned to concern. "I flew across the ocean because Theo was arrested on suspicion of kidnapping. Now you're telling me no charges will be brought, and he's being moved around in covert fashion for his own safety. I need a full explanation of what's going on here."

"Absolutely," she said, and she continued down the sidewalk. Jack walked with her. They left the sunshine and entered the shade as they rounded the corner, and it was like stepping from summer into winter.

"You did the right thing by telling the FBI about the phone call from Amongus Sicario."

"What came of that?"

"I can't tell you."

"What *can* you tell me?"

"Nothing, really. But since you did the right thing, and in no small measure due to the fact that you are married to an FBI agent, I'm going to keep talking. But just so you are aware, I will deny ever having said what I'm about to tell you."

"I'm listening," said Jack.

"Have you ever heard of an extraction kidnapping, Mr. Swyteck?"

"Only in spy movies."

"Then you get the general idea of how it might work in this situation."

"What situation are you talking about?"

"The fight against piracy."

"I don't follow."

A woman pushing a jogging stroller ran past them. Coffey continued.

"When piracy was at its peak, going back ten years or more, MAP and other private organizations got 'creative,' shall we say, in finding ways to fight back. Some of these organizations, MAP included, would adopt rather questionable practices, some even going so far as thefts and break-ins to gather evidence. MAP would then pass along these leads to law enforcement agencies in whatever country the pirate was operating."

"And law enforcement used this information, even though it was obtained illegally?"

She paused to measure her words. "Hypothetically speaking, law enforcement might use some of that information from MAP to build a case for the extradition of foreign-based pirates for prosecution in U.S. courts under U.S. law."

Jack knew she wasn't talking in hypotheticals, and it was clear now why she would deny ever having shared any of this information with Jack.

"Gathering information is one thing," he said. "But you said kidnapping."

"Yes. Extraction kidnappings. This is where MAP set itself apart from some of the more cautious organizations. Extradition can be painfully slow. The U.S. is a Category Two country for extradition purposes."

"Meaning what?"

"Meaning it can be difficult to initiate the process without tipping off the target. The U.S. has to make the request to the UK. The national extradition unit has to certify the request and send the case to court. The judge has to decide whether to issue a warrant for arrest. By the time the local police go out to make the arrest, the target could be long gone. It's sometimes possible to make an arrest without a warrant, but that's risky business."

"Are you saying MAP kidnapped someone and held him until he could be arrested?"

"Not just someone. Sergei Kava, son of a Russian oligarch. Sergei runs the largest piracy platform in the world."

Jack suddenly connected the dots. "Does Sergei have a nine-year-old daughter?"

"Yes."

"They live here in London?"

"Londongrad, some call it."

"Is this nine-year-old girl a fan of Imani, by any chance?"

Coffey smiled. "My, you do put two plus two together quickly, Mr. Swyteck."

Jack finished the "equation," leaving the attaché no wiggle room. "It sounds like the FBI no longer needs Imani to perform for the grand-daughter of a certain oligarch."

"That would be awkward. Sergei Kava is currently in the high-security unit of one of Her Majesty's prisons, Belmarsh, awaiting an extradition hearing."

They stopped on the corner at the red light. A double-decker bus rushed past them.

"Are you telling me that Theo participated in the extraction kidnapping of Sergei Kava?"

"He denies it."

"Do you believe him?"

"The more important question is whether Sergei's father, Vladimir Kava, will believe him. I think not. Which puts your friend in serious danger."

The light turned green, but Jack didn't move. "Are you talking about the Witness Security Program?"

"That could be an option. We'll monitor the situation."

"Does Theo know this yet? That this could lead to life in witness protection?"

"Not yet. I'll explain all of that before he leaves London."

Jack glanced back toward the station house. It was hard to say whether Theo would be better off on an airplane home. "Theo's my best friend. I need to speak to him about this."

"That's not possible while he's in London."

"Why?"

"As long as he's here, his safety is my responsibility. I'll pass along any message you want to give him, and I'll convey any message he wants to send to you."

"That seems a bit extreme," said Jack.

"Vladimir Kava controls one of the most sophisticated internet platforms in cyberspace. He makes billions from piracy, but he makes even more by stealing personal information from anyone who is stupid enough to visit his piracy websites. Any electronic communication between you and Theo could lead Kava directly to him."

"Then let us talk face-to-face. I can go to the embassy right now."

"Brilliant. That way whoever is tailing you on Kava's orders can follow you straight to Theo's precise location."

It was frustrating, but Jack saw her point.

"Do you have a message you want me to give Theo?" she asked.

Jack appreciated the offer, but strangely, his search for the right message harkened back to the darkest of times, when Jack struggled to find words of encouragement for an innocent man on death row.

"Tell him I'll take care of Uncle Cy and the club until he's ready. Tell him not to worry about anything but himself."

"Anything else?"

It felt like something was missing, but a sloppy "I love you, man" was not it. "Tell him Righley needs her uncle Theo," said Jack.

CHAPTER 18

At 9:00 a.m. Miami time, Shaky Nichols was in a windowless room in the criminal courthouse, seated in the witness chair, waiting for the state prosecutor's show to begin. Eighteen grand jurors, three rows of six, sat facing him. Their expectations were high, no doubt. They, like Shaky, had seen the flock of reporters perched outside the grand jury room.

By law, grand jury proceedings were secret, no one allowed in the room but the jurors, the prosecutor, and a court reporter. Not even the witness's legal counsel was allowed inside, though a witness was free to invoke his or her right against self-incrimination in response to any questions. The constitutional theory was that the grand jury would serve as a check on the prosecutor's power, but Shaky's lawyer had been painfully blunt in advising her client: the prosecutor always got the indictment he wanted.

"Good morning," the prosecutor said, greeting his captive audience of eighteen.

Owens was smiling, and Shaky could see it was genuine. It wasn't exactly clear what case the State Attorney's Office was trying to build, but whatever it was, Owens surely had stars in his eyes. A beautiful, smart pop star and her music mogul husband in the crosshairs, each hell-bent on destroying the other. Imani was already facing federal charges. Perhaps the state attorney was cooking up similar piracy charges under state law. Whatever the indictment might bring, Shaky's lawyer had warned him that Owens would treat this case as his breakout trial, his ticket to the cable news talking head circuit. And he'd been waiting a long time. Owens was a twenty-year veteran of major crimes with plenty of ability, hundreds of victories, and not much publicity. He worked for a district attorney who was a veritable media hound. Owens had brought the office some of its most impressive wins, but at the press conferences he somehow always found himself positioned just far enough away from the state attorney to be off-screen on the evening news. He did the work, the state attorney took the bows.

Shaky just hoped this "breakout case" had nothing to do with Tyler McCormick.

"Please swear the witness," Owens told the court reporter.

Shaky swore the oath and settled into the chair. He was expecting a few introductory questions about his background and other benign matters, but the prosecutor went straight for the witness's discomfort zone.

"Mr. Nichols, during the time that you were married to Imani, was she ever unfaithful to you?"

Nichols shifted in his chair. "You should probably be asking her that question."

"I'm asking *you*, sir. You understand you were commanded to be here by a court-issued subpoena, and you are required to answer my questions, right?"

"I understand."

"And you understand that you're under oath?"

"Yes."

"So let me ask again: Was she ever unfaithful?"

He hesitated. His lawyer wasn't in the room with him, but she'd advised him to answer with a simple yes or no whenever possible.

"Yes."

"In fact, your wife had sexual relations with several other men during your marriage, did she not, sir?"

It was only the second question, and Shaky already wanted out of the room, which was not an option. "I don't know the exact number."

"I'll accept that. But she's admitted to multiple affairs in numerous media interviews. You agree there was more than one, correct?"

"Yes."

"Did that make you angry?"

He glared back at the prosecutor. "I wasn't happy about it."

The prosecutor tightened his gaze. "You were more than unhappy. You were humiliated."

"I don't know how to answer that."

"At times, you were furious."

Shaky imagined that if his lawyer were in the room, she would be on her feet, objecting. But there was no judge to referee the fight, and a witness without legal counsel was no match for a prosecutor. He bit back his anger and answered. "Like I said: I wasn't happy."

"Did you ever threaten to harm any of the men with whom she was having sexual relations?"

"That's ridiculous. No. I never threatened anyone."

Owens retrieved a file from the table behind him and faced the grand jurors. "I bring to the grand jury's attention the sworn testimony of Ms. Beatriz Alonso, who is testifying by affidavit."

Shaky's lawyer had warned him that in a grand jury proceeding, unlike a trial, the prosecutor could stop and explain things at any time, or even submit hearsay affidavits from witnesses who failed to appear. It was his show.

"Mr. Nichols, Beatriz Alonso was your live-in housekeeper throughout your marriage to Imani. Is that correct?"

Shaky swallowed hard. Beatriz knew the good, the bad, and the ugly, and it seemed safe to assume that this was not going to be good. "That's correct."

"In her affidavit, Ms. Alonso recounts an argument that you had with your wife about one of her indiscretions. Her testimony is as follows: 'One night, Mr. Nichols was very mad. He was screaming at Imani. He shouted, "If I catch you two together, I'll shoot him in the balls and you in the head." And he kept saying it, over and over again. "Him in the balls, and you in the head." He was like a madman.'

"End of quote." The prosecutor looked up from the affidavit and locked eyes with the witness. "Did you say that to your wife, Mr. Nichols?"

"If I did, it was hyperbole. I didn't mean it literally."

"Did Imani have any response?"

Shaky paused. There was no point in lying. It was obvious that the prosecutor already had the answer in the sworn affidavit from their housekeeper. It would only hurt his credibility with the grand jurors to feign no recollection.

"She said something like—"

Shaky stopped himself. His anger was rising, and he needed to check it before saying more.

The prosecutor stepped closer, prodding him with his proximity. "Mr. Nichols, when you said that if you caught Imani and her lover in the act, you'd shoot him in the balls and her in the head, what did your wife say?"

Nichols was seething. "She said, 'If you catch us, you'll only need one bullet.'"

The old woman in the front row gasped, made the sign of the cross, and whispered something to Jesús in Spanish.

The prosecutor laid the sworn affidavit aside. "Thank you, Mr. Nichols. I have no further questions at this time. You are reminded that grand jury proceedings are secret, and you are not allowed to speak publicly about anything that transpired here, except for your own testimony. You may step down and leave the room."

Shaky rose and started toward the door. The fact that he was in and out so quickly gave him no comfort. It told him only that the prosecutor already had the evidence he needed to get the indictment he wanted. It told him that this grand jury investigation was not about music piracy.

This was all about Tyler McCormick.

Jack called Andie from his hotel room. The next available flight was not until the following morning. He was staying at the Tower, a business hotel north of the Thames and about a ten-minute taxi ride to the Old Bailey, the criminal courthouse where Theo's first court appearance would have occurred. Should have occurred, but for the fact that law enforcement was apparently willing to look the other way when it came to the extraction kidnapping of a Russian oligarch's son. The more Jack thought about it, the more it made sense that the FBI would have a vested interest in keeping the extradition pipeline flowing. Jack imagined that many of the pirates extradited on copyright charges were charged with even more serious crimes once they were in the United States.

"How's Righley?" he asked into the phone.

"She was fine this morning," said Andie. "I haven't picked her up from school yet."

Jack forced himself up from the bed. He'd powered through the day to avoid Miami-to-London jet lag, and he was tired enough to fall asleep in his clothes on a made-up bed. Andie had just reminded him that he now had to power through another four hours, at least, to avoid London-to-Miami jet lag.

"Give her a kiss for me."

"I will."

Jack walked to the window. He had a nighttime view of the famous Tower Bridge, and the reflection of its lights twinkled on the river.

"I have a confession," said Jack.

"That sounds kind of scary."

"I glanced at your phone when I shouldn't have. I saw a text I should never have seen."

"Shit. I swear, that Bradley Cooper just won't leave me alone."

"I'm serious," Jack said. "It was work-related."

The line was silent.

"You have every right to be angry," said Jack.

"What was the text?"

"The one from Detective Green at MDPD. About the Tyler Mc-Cormick cold case."

"Why would you read that, Jack?"

"It just popped up on your screen in preview, and I saw it. Then you came out of the shower wrapped in a towel, and I got a bit distracted. I've been meaning to tell you. I'm sorry."

"I'm not sure what to say," Andie said stiffly.

"We can talk more about it when I get home."

"No," she said. "We can't ever talk about this. After all the jokes we've gotten about an FBI agent married to a criminal defense lawyer, this is about as close as we've come to a serious conflict of interest."

Jack considered his words. "So, were you not completely truthful when you told me that you had only brief involvement in the Tyler McCormick case?"

"You're accusing *me* of being dishonest?"

"It's just that Green didn't take over the Tyler McCormick case until after Cruz retired. Why would Green be texting you about a break in the 'TM case' if, like you told me, the FBI's involvement was over almost as soon as it started?"

"My God, you actually are accusing me," she said, her disbelief tilting more toward anger.

"No. I'm just saying it seems strange that Green would text you out of the blue."

Her cadence quickened, the way it did when she was really angry. "Maybe it's because you went to see him and Cruz to ask about the case. Which, by the way, you didn't tell me about until after it happened."

"I didn't know you were on the case until Cruz told me."

"And even though he told you I used to be on the case, you looked at my phone and read the text from Detective Green."

"Your phone was right there."

"Oh, good defense, counselor. I can't wait to hear your explanation as to why it took you two days to tell me about this."

"I was meaning to—"

"Stop already. You were meaning to talk to me about Imani's stunt in the courtroom. You were meaning to tell me you met with the cold-case detectives. It's starting to sound like the same old song."

Jack took a breath. "Can we stop talking about this?"

"No. Not yet. Did you tell your client what was in Detective Green's text message?"

"I can't tell you what I tell my client, honey."

"Don't call me 'honey,' when what you really mean is 'dumbshit.'"

"I'm not calling you a dumbshit."

"That's exactly what you're doing. 'I can't tell you what I tell my client, *dumbshit.*' Fuck, Jack! This makes so much trouble for me, and you just don't get it."

"I do get it."

"No, you don't!"

She wasn't screaming at him, but it was close. "That's fine," said Jack. "I don't need to get it. It's none of my business."

"None. I agree."

"Great. It's good to be in agreement. I'll see you when I get home tomorrow."

"See you," she said, and the call ended.

Andie was pissed, no question about it. Making things better, fast, was not exactly Jack's specialty. An argument with his father had once lasted a decade. He would be up all night trying to figure out this one.

He turned on the television, but nothing caught his interest. He wasn't hungry, and ordering something to eat just to have something to do was a terrible idea. Rather than lie in bed staring at the ceiling, he put on his workout clothes and went outside for a run. The jogging map on the hotel's app came with a tourist guide's audio. Jack listened through his earbuds.

. . . concentric stone walls along the bank of the Thames River, the oldest of which date back almost a millennium.

It was a cool night, perfect for a run along the river. Jack was feeling strong. Maybe too strong. Thirty minutes into his run, the audio descriptions no longer matched Jack's surroundings. He was off the guided path, having hung a right when he should have gone left. Or was it the other way around? It was Jack's firsthand introduction to the fact that London streets could change names three times in the span of three blocks. He was in a business district, but all of the shops were closed, and Jack was alone on the street. He was tired, and his run became a walk. He was headed somewhere in the general direction of his hotel, checking the street signs carefully, when he noticed the clap of footsteps behind him. They had the rhythm of his own footfalls, seeming to match his pace and direction. It suddenly occurred to him that Theo was landing in Miami at that very moment, and the words of the FBI attaché replayed in his mind:

"Russian oligarchs don't mess around."

Jack saw no one, but he walked a little faster. A car passed, then more silence. Uncomfortable urban silence. He passed the darkened storefront windows of a "chemist" and continued around the corner. Jack quickened his pace when, all of a sudden, it felt as though he'd been broadsided by a rugby player. The force knocked him off his feet and sent him tumbling into a narrow alley. He landed facedown on the pavement. The attacker was on him immediately.

"What the—"

Before Jack could finish his sentence, much less react, the man rolled him over and grabbed Jack by the throat.

"Don't move, just listen," the man said.

He had the fingers of a mountain climber, and the pressure around Jack's neck made it difficult to focus on what he was saying. The thick, slurred speech didn't make things any clearer.

"Where is Theo Knight?"

Where ish . . . It wasn't that he was drunk. Something was in his mouth—a wad of cotton or some spy toy to make his voice unrecognizable.

Jack could barely breathe, let alone talk. "I don't know where Theo—"

"If you lie, you die."

Jack was having trouble following even that simple line of logic. The pressure around his neck had his head pounding and lungs burning as he struggled to breathe. Jack couldn't see the man's face, couldn't see much of anything. His attacker, like everything else, was a blur.

"I got a message for you to deliver to your friend. You listening?"

"Uh-huh."

The grip was atomic. The burning sensation in Jack's lungs was unbearable. A hint of blood flavored his mouth, the pressure somehow having triggered it. Jack fought for air, but his attacker was in complete control.

"If Sergei Kava is extradited to the States, your friend Theo is a dead man. Understand?"

"Mmm-hmm."

It was the most audible response Jack could muster. The vise grip at Jack's throat rose higher around Jack's neck and closed even tighter. Jack had one final burst of resistance left in his body, and then nothing more. The pounding in his head seemed to explode into his ears, and then the night went from black to blacker. He was on the verge of unconsciousness when the vise grip released.

Jack lay on his back, gasping for air, as the footfalls of his attacker faded into the night.

CHAPTER 19

Jack found his way back to the hotel. His first call was to the FBI's legal attaché, Madeline Coffey. She'd already left the embassy for the evening, but it was a ten-minute drive across the river from her house to the hotel, where Jack met her in the lobby. They found a table in the lounge near the window.

"Are you sure you don't want to see a doctor?" she asked.

"No. I thought about going to an emergency room, but once I caught my breath, I recovered pretty quickly."

"That's definitely going to bruise," she said, nodding at his neck.

"I'm sure. But it was as if the guy knew how to shut off my air supply without serious injury to my throat or neck."

"Probably not his first rodeo," said Coffey.

"Which only makes this creepier—the fact that he's developed such a well-honed skill with that level of control."

"Nobody has perfect control. Cemeteries hold plenty of teenagers who watched videos on the internet on how to strangle yourself until you pass out."

Jack sighed. One more thing for the parent of a curious seven-year-old to worry about.

"The most important thing is to put Theo on notice," said Jack. "That's why I called you first. The threat was directed toward him."

"I put the message through as soon as you called," she said.

"Thank you. What's the plan?"

"Theo needs to lay low."

"Hopefully, only for a few weeks," said Jack.

"What do you mean?"

"My attacker said Theo is a dead man *if* Sergei Kava is extradited. Extradition is a process. There has to be a hearing, and that won't be for a few weeks."

"Correct."

"And there's no guarantee Kava will be extradited. I presume Sergei's lawyers are smart enough to argue that the extraction kidnapping was illegal and makes extradition improper. If the request for extradition is denied, Theo has nothing to worry about."

The legal attaché didn't seem amused by the criminal defense lawyer's suggestion that extradition might not occur. "We should operate under the assumption that Sergei Kava will be extradited. And you should take precautions to protect your own safety. Not to be an alarmist, but with Theo in hiding, they could come after you again."

"I appreciate your concern," said Jack. "But when it comes to a situation like this, the best advice I got was from my mentor, Neil Goderich. Neil hired me right out of law school to work for the Freedom Institute."

"Yes, where you defended death row's finest. I'm fully briefed on your background."

"My point is, threats came with the turf. I got plenty of them from cops, clients, witnesses, and some very creepy anonymous sources. Neil always said that any criminal defense lawyer who couldn't handle a dose of intimidation needed to find a new career."

She smiled knowingly. "You didn't have a family when you worked for this Neil Goderich, did you?"

"No. My first marriage wasn't until after I left the Freedom Institute. I was divorced and well into private practice by the time I met Andie."

"I thought so. Because it doesn't sound like something a man with a wife and young daughter would say."

Jack didn't have a quick response, and Coffey didn't seem to expect one. She rose, Jack followed suit, and they shook hands.

"Put some ice on that neck before you go to bed," she said.

"We haven't talked about a police report," said Jack.

"I suppose we could do that," she said.

"Don't we want to give the local police everything to find the guy who threatened me?"

"If they find him, there will be another to replace him."

"You make it sound hopeless."

Coffey settled back into her chair and invited Jack to sit for a few more minutes. "Let me tell you about the Kava family," she said.

Over the next thirty minutes, Jack got the complete download, from the Wagner Group mercenaries to the superyachts. The legal attaché did most of the talking. Jack listened, all ears.

Jack caught the morning flight from Heathrow. He slept the entire flight.

Pointless as it might have been, he was at the station house until after midnight filling out a police report. By the time he'd finished with the Metro Police, his neck was so sore that he'd presented himself at the ER for pain medication. The physician had warned him not to take it until he was on the plane, or he would surely oversleep and miss his flight. The pain kept him awake until he was in his seat, then he popped two pills. The flight attendant had to wake him once to buckle his seat belt for landing, and then wake him again to deplane in Miami. He wanted to text Andie to let her know he'd landed, but his cellphone battery was completely dead, drained by hours of streaming inflight entertainment, even though Jack had slept through every minute of it. By the time he got through customs, it was late afternoon.

A mob of reporters surrounded him the moment he left the restricted area and stepped through the sliding glass doors to the main terminal. An "Action News" television reporter pushed her way forward and thrust a microphone toward his face.

"Mr. Swyteck, what is your reaction to the indictment?" she asked.

Jack suddenly felt like Rip Van Winkle. "Indictment?"

More questions followed, and Jack picked up bits and pieces of information.

"Is it true that Tyler McCormick was Imani's lover?"

"Why is the charge second-degree murder and not first?"

"Will you be defending both Imani and her husband at trial?"

Both charged? Jack took Mark Twain's advice—"Better to keep your mouth shut and appear ignorant than to open it and remove all doubt"—and forged ahead toward the exit. He spotted a limo driver holding a sign with his name on it. Jack hadn't ordered a limo, but he quickly realized that someone had planned ahead for him. The driver handed him a handwritten note. It was from Imani.

Why don't you answer your fucking phone. I need you NOW!!!

The flock of reporters followed him and the driver out of the terminal and all the way to the waiting car at the curb. Cameras rolled, and reporters continued to fire questions, as Jack climbed into the backseat and the driver pulled away.

"Somebody really needs your help," the driver said, clearly meaning Imani.

Jack plugged his cell into the USB port in the center console. It slowly came back to life. "Yeah," said Jack, thinking of Theo. "That makes two."

CHAPTER 20

The bridge to Star Island is a stubby finger that projects north from the busy east-west causeway that connects Miami to Miami Beach. As Jack's limo approached the guarded entrance to the island, about a dozen reporters were waiting right outside the gate. Jack looked straight ahead, not pandering to the barrage of cameras aimed at the passenger-side window, as one photographer after another snapped soon-to-go-viral images of Imani's lawyer arriving at her waterfront estate. Jack was pretty sure he recognized Gloria and Emilio Estefan's house on his way to Imani's place. Nice, but not quite what Imani had. According to the media coverage, the house Imani had rented was a truly unique property on 1.4 acres at the tip of the island, offering unobstructed views of both sunrise and sunset, a ballroom-sized living room, and a wine cellar for a thousand bottles, all with enough dock space for a 250-foot superyacht.

The wrought-iron gate at the end of the driveway swung open, and the limo driver dropped Jack at the front entrance. One of the servants brought Jack inside. Imani was in the kitchen, baking chocolate chip cookies. Over the years, Jack had seen clients invoke a variety of strategies to cope with an indictment, most of which landed on Jack's list of "don'ts." The smell of Toll House cookies was now officially at the top of the "do" list.

"Thank God you're here," she said, and she hugged him, but not in the way that had made him uncomfortable in front of the cameras in the courtroom. This one simply felt like someone who needed a hug.

"Where's Theo?" she asked. "I thought he would come with you." She removed a sheet of cookies from the oven and placed them on the countertop to cool. "I made cookies," she said with a shrug.

As if that would make up for the hell he was going through. "We won't be hearing from Theo until he feels it's safe."

She seemed to appreciate the import of his words. They sat on the barstools at the island, facing each other from opposite sides of the polished granite slab, as Jack gave her the two-minute version of the great adventures of Theo Knight.

Imani held her head in her hands, elbows on the counter. "I should never have trusted Amongus. But how could I have known he was going to try to pull off something like that?"

"The goal now is to make sure Theo doesn't end up like Amongus."

"Do you think he's dead?"

"I don't know. But I'll deal with that and Theo's situation. Let's focus on you."

She breathed in and out, regaining her focus. And her anger. "First off, what kind of games is this prosecutor playing, announcing an indictment at three o'clock in the afternoon while my lawyer is on an airplane?"

Jack had seen it before. "It's a holdover strategy from the days when people used to catch up on the entire day by watching the evening news on one of the networks. Prosecutors would hold the press conference in the afternoon so the defense couldn't get in a response in time for the evening news broadcast."

"So, where's this prosecutor from, 1985?"

"Fair point. There's always time to respond in the modern world of social media and real-time news, twenty-four/seven."

"We need to get a response out ASAP," said Imani.

"I ginned up a draft on the ride over here," said Jack.

"Give it to my publicist. She's in the living room with her team." Imani called to the next room—"Carla!"—and a frazzled young woman hurried into the kitchen. Jack gave his notes to her, Imani told her to "make it work," and Carla left pronto, leaving Jack and his client alone in the kitchen.

"I assume you've read the indictment by now," Imani said.

"Online, in the limo," said Jack. "It's a two-count indictment. You and Shaky are charged with the same crimes. Count one is second-degree murder."

"Second degree sounds better than first, right?"

"It's still punishable by life in prison."

"Great. I can pick up my career when I'm as old as Madonna and a free woman."

Madonna as "old" didn't make Jack feel any younger. He could remember when she was "striking a pose" and showing love to Bette Davis.

"Count two is gross abuse of a dead human body," said Jack. "Obviously, that relates to the depraved manner in which the body was displayed on the piling in the bay."

Imani grimaced at the thought. "Why would I do something so sick?"

"Technically, it doesn't matter why. It's a common misunderstanding to think that if there's no motive, there's no crime. A prosecutor doesn't have to prove motive to get a conviction. Not even for first-degree murder."

"Then why is the charge here second degree and not first?"

"Good question. Let me just say this is a very strange indictment."

"I'll say. Last week Shaky and I were suing the pants off each other. Now we're going to be joint defendants in a criminal trial."

"It's not just that. The technical legal distinction between first- and second-degree murder boils down to premeditation and deliberation. Did you have time to reflect before the murder of Tyler McCormick?"

"I didn't commit murder, let alone plan it."

"I get that," said Jack. "But what I find strange is that the prosecutor probably could have asked the grand jury for a first-degree murder indictment and let second-degree murder be a fallback position for the jury, just in case the evidence on premeditation and deliberation doesn't play out at trial."

"So he's being kind to us?"

"No. He's being clever."

"In what way?"

"If he had charged you with murder in the first degree, you would have no right to bail. You and Shaky would be locked in jail until trial."

Imani shook her head, confused. "Again, that sounds like he's being kind to us for some reason."

"It's part of his strategy."

"I don't understand."

"He doesn't want the two of you sitting in separate jail cells awaiting trial. He wants you on your cellphones all day long, taking shots at each other on social media, blaming each other for the murder."

"It sounds like you want control of my posts."

"Everything you or your publicity team puts out needs my advance approval. Unless you want to help the prosecutor build his case."

"Exactly what *is* 'his case'?"

"The indictment is bare bones. Basically, it alleges that Shaky, 'with the active aid and assistance of Imani Nichols,' strangled Tyler McCormick."

"What is 'active aid and assistance' supposed to mean?"

"The State Attorney's Office will have to send us the grand jury materials soon, which will flesh that out. But based on what I can tell so far, the first piece in the prosecutor's puzzle is that you were having an affair with Tyler McCormick."

"Which isn't true."

"We'll get to that," said Jack. "The indictment charges that Shaky confronted Tyler and killed him. The way I read the rest of the indictment, you helped him cover up the crime."

"How is a cover-up second-degree murder?"

"It's not," said Jack. "At most, it would make you an accessory after the fact, but the law says you can't be charged as an accessory after the fact when your spouse is the killer. It's called the related person exception. Instead, the prosecutor charged you with mutilation of a dead body."

"Why would he also charge me with second-degree murder if you're saying he doesn't have the evidence?"

"He shouldn't. But prosecutors usually have a strategic reason for everything they do."

"What's the strategy here?"

Imani's publicist returned to the kitchen. "Are the cookies ready?" she asked. "Sorry, but that smell has my whole team salivating."

Imani handed her the tray, and Carla hurried away with the goodies. Imani apologized to Jack, then smiled wistfully as she returned to her seat.

"I was raised by my grandma," she said. "When I was little, if something bad happened, Grams would always make cookies."

"I get it," said Jack. "My abuela's go-to medicine is tres leches."

"Is she Nicaraguan?"

"No. Cuban."

"Isn't tres leches a Nicaraguan dessert?"

"Conventional wisdom says it is. But Abuela nearly started a civil war, Miami style, when she called in to Hispanic talk radio claiming she invented tres leches and that the Nicaraguans stole the recipe."

Imani laughed. "Thank you. I needed that."

Laughter was good, Jack agreed, but there was nothing funny about what he needed to say next.

"Don't take this the wrong way," he began, but before he could say another word, Imani's publicist returned with Jack's draft press release in one hand and a red pen in the other.

"I have some helpful suggestions," she said, but Imani shut her down.

"Carla, now is not a good time."

It was a tone Jack hadn't heard from her before. Obviously, Carla had. She withdrew without another word.

"You were saying?" said Imani.

Jack needed absolute privacy, no interruptions, for what he was about to discuss, and he sensed that Carla hadn't gone very far. "Can we step outside?"

"Sure," said Imani, and she led him out to the terrace, which was like a fully furnished living room in the garden.

"This is purely my instincts talking," said Jack. "But I think the prosecutor charged you with second-degree murder simply to put added pressure on you to turn against Shaky."

"You mean he wants me to turn state's evidence?"

"Exactly," said Jack. "You provide the testimony to convict Shaky of murder in the second degree. In exchange, the prosecution drops the murder charge against you and lets you plead to the lesser charge of gross abuse of a dead body."

"But I still go to jail on the lesser charge?"

"Probation is possible."

"The sentence doesn't matter. I would never cut a deal on these charges."

"Never say never."

"I won't admit to allegations that aren't true. As Theo's best friend, you of all persons should respect that."

Jack didn't always ask if his client was guilty and didn't always need or want to know. But any client who put herself in the same category as Theo Knight had a few questions to answer.

"Nothing in this indictment is true? Is that what you're saying?"

"None of it."

"Not even your alleged extramarital affair with Tyler McCormick?"

Imani drew a breath but didn't answer.

"You want to tell me about that?" said Jack.

"I was a twenty-year-old spoiled brat when I married Shaky. He's eleven years older than me. He controlled everything. My career. My record contract. My finances. My image. My social media. Even the clothes I wore. The one thing he couldn't control was whoever I randomly hooked up with. So I did it. I did it to spite him. And I did it *a lot*."

It wasn't Jack's job to judge. "Men and women? Or only men?"

"What makes you ask that question?"

"Shaky's claim at the court hearing about forced penetration. You said he wasn't bisexual, but he claims you forced him to have sex with your partners."

"Yeah, he wishes. That's Shaky's way of protecting his own masculinity. He's not the weak man who stays with a wife who sleeps with other men. He's a poor victim forced to have sex with two women. What misery."

"Was Tyler McCormick one of your random hookups?"

"No. Absolutely not."

"Then how does he fit into the picture, if he wasn't your lover?"

"He fits in because he was the farthest thing from it."

"What does that mean?"

Imani looked away, then back. "Tyler McCormick was stalking me."

Her response seemed to hang in the air between them.

"Oh," said Jack.

Imani locked eyes with her lawyer, the expression on her face deadly serious. "Yeah," she said. "Oh."

CHAPTER 21

Sixteen days after his client's indictment, Jack burned an entire tank of gas driving north to the state's most secure correctional facility for men, located in Raiford, Florida.

Imani's arraignment had gone as expected. Both defendants entered pleas of "not guilty" and were released on bail. The rules of discovery required the prosecution to turn over all grand jury materials to the defense, but it had taken more than two weeks for the boxes to land in Jack's office. Only after reviewing the grand jury transcripts was Jack able to identify the state's key witnesses. Stop number one on his list of pretrial priorities was Florida State Prison, which housed some of the state's most dangerous convicted felons. Among them was the prosecution's star witness against Imani.

Jack checked in at the visitors' entrance. "I'm here for the deposition of Douglas Paxton," he told the guard behind the glass.

Jack had been to FSP dozens of time before to see clients—including Theo and others on Florida's death row. Andie had never warmed up to it. "Off to defend the guilty," she'd say on his way out the door. He'd always thought it was good-natured ribbing on her part, and that, on some level, she respected him for what he did. Jack wasn't sure if there was something different about the Imani case, or if it was the cumulative effect over the years. But that blowup on the call from London seemed to drive home that Andie was able to love him *only* by separating who he was from what he did. Jack was starting to wonder if that was even possible.

"Follow the guard down the hallway," the corrections officer said.

This time, Jack wasn't a lawyer for an inmate. Paxton had refused to talk to the defense, which was his right. Jack's only option was to subpoena him to appear for deposition and force him to answer questions under oath.

The deposition was in a windowless conference room in the attorney visitation center. At 1:00 p.m., the secure doors unlocked, and two corrections officers brought the prisoner inside. Jack and the prosecutor were opposite each other on the long sides of a rectangular table in the center of the room. The guards unshackled the witness, ankles and wrists, and seated him at the short end of the table to Jack's right. The court reporter sat close enough to the witness to hear his testimony, but a little farther away than she might otherwise have positioned herself for the deposition of a less dangerous man.

Paxton was six-feet-four and two hundred and fifty pounds of badass. His pecs and biceps bulged beneath his prison jumpsuit. Jack surmised that he spent his "free time" evenly divided between lifting weights and intimidating other inmates.

The witness was sworn, and Jack asked the questions.

"Mr. Paxton, what crime are you currently serving time for?"

"Armed robbery."

"What was your sentence?"

"Twenty years."

"How much time have you served so far?"

"Five years, eight months, and twelve days. But who's counting?"

"I'm guessing you are," said Jack. "Which leads to my next question: How much time did the state attorney promise to shave off your sentence in exchange for your testimony?"

"Objection," said the prosecutor, grumbling. "Let me just state clearly on the record that there have been no promises made to Mr. Paxton for his cooperation in this matter. Any reduction in his sentence is completely in the hands of the parole board."

Objections at depositions were literally "for the record," as there was no judge or magistrate to make a ruling. Jack moved on.

"Mr. Paxton, when is your next hearing before the parole board?"

"Four months and two days. But again, who's counting?"

"Sounds like the timing of your cooperation in this case works out quite nicely, doesn't it."

"Objection," said the prosecutor.

"Timing is everything, they say."

Jack left it at that, then turned to the substance of the witness's testimony. "Mr. Paxton, I read the transcript of your testimony to the grand jury. I understand that you once worked as a bodyguard for Mr. Shaky Nichols."

"Right. For two years."

"Was Mr. Nichols married to Imani Nichols during that time?"

"Yup."

"I can understand why a celebrity like Imani needed a bodyguard. But why did Mr. Nichols have a bodyguard?"

He chuckled. "Shaky fancies himself a pretty important guy. It was like a competition between those two. If Imani had a bodyguard, Shaky needed one, too."

"While you were Mr. Nichols's bodyguard, did you have any contact with the victim in this case, Tyler McCormick?"

"Not while he was alive."

The answer was not unexpected, but Jack still found it unsettling. "When did you first hear the name Tyler McCormick?"

"Not sure. Best I can remember, Shaky just called him 'the body.'"

"And what did you understand 'the body' to mean?"

"A dead guy."

Jack showed him a picture of Tyler McCormick. "Is this the 'dead guy'?"

"Yeah. That's him."

"Did Mr. Nichols tell you anything about the dead guy?"

"Yeah. He said, 'Get rid of him.'"

"Did he tell you how Mr. McCormick became the dead guy?"

"Nope."

"Did you ask him?"

"Nope."

"Why didn't you ask?"

The witness shrugged, as if Jack's question were stupid. "If he wanted me to know, he would've told me."

"Where were you when Mr. Nichols told you to get rid of the body?"

"In his house."

"Where in the house?"

"In the garage."

"Was Imani Nichols there?"

"No."

It was Jack's first score, and it came as a relief. "Was Imani Nichols in the house?"

"No idea. I just know she wasn't in the garage."

Jack would take that much and use it at trial. "What was the condition of the body when Mr. Nichols told you to get rid of it?"

"Dead."

"Let me be more specific. Was there any blood?"

"No?"

"Any cuts or wounds?"

"None that I saw."

"Was the body clothed?"

"Nope. Naked."

"Completely naked?"

"Yeah," he said, and then he smiled. "And he had a boner."

A postmortem erection was rare, but Jack had heard of it before. "You're saying that you observed an erection?" asked Jack.

"Yeah," he said, on the verge of laughter. "Never seen a dead guy with a boner before. I guess he died happy."

"I don't want to hear your 'guess,'" Jack said firmly. "I just want you to answer my questions. Understand?"

Paxton glared at him. Like most bullies, he clearly wasn't keen on being put in his place. "What's your question?" he fired back.

"You testified that you were in the garage with Mr. Nichols and a naked corpse. What did you do after Mr. Nichols told you to get rid of the body? Did you have a plan?"

"I think I said I could dump the body in the Everglades."

The Florida Everglades were the dumping ground of choice, a murderer's best friend. The warm waters hastened decomposition. Sawgrass, muck, and flora seemed to swallow cadavers. Alligators, pythons, and other wildlife feasted on whatever remained.

"But you didn't dump the body in the Everglades, did you?"

"No."

"Why not?"

"Mr. Nichols gave me very specific instructions on what to do."

"What were those instructions?"

"Take the boat. Go out in the bay to Isola di Lolando. Tie him to the concrete piling and leave him there."

"Did Mr. Nichols tell you why he wanted Mr. McCormick's body displayed in this way?"

"No."

"Do you have any information at all as to why he told you to put the body on display like this?"

"All I can tell you is what Shaky said."

"What did he say?" asked Jack.

"He said it was Imani's idea."

There it was—the testimony that had gotten Imani indicted. At trial, Jack would of course challenge the credibility of a convicted felon, and he would attack whatever deal the witness had cut with the prosecutor for a reduction of his sentence in exchange for his testimony.

The prosecutor pushed away from the table and stretched, as if morning had just broken. "Is now a good time for a break, Mr. Swyteck?"

Jack had promised to call Imani as soon as anything "important" happened. This was definitely in that category, as evidenced by the hint of a smug smile from the prosecutor.

"Let's take ten," said Jack.

CHAPTER 22

It was a cloudy night in southeast London, typical for late October. Light rain started to fall as Theo reached the Underground station at Bethnal Green. He hurried down the stairs and caught the train just before the doors closed.

Theo had never actually left London after his release from the station house in Covent Gardens. He was fully aware that Jack and others had been led to believe that the FBI had put him on a flight back to the States, but a death threat from a Russian oligarch made travel too dangerous. The safest course was for Theo to stay in London and cast confusion to the world with a false narrative as to his whereabouts.

"Stay in London," of course, could mean many different things. When a six-foot-six Black man with an American accent needs to keep a low profile, he doesn't exactly disappear by moving to Cherry Tree Lane and hiding out with Mary Poppins and the Banks family. Theo chose Bethnal Green and rented a studio apartment in one of the typical three-story redbrick buildings that defined the beaten-down neighborhood. Some said the area wasn't safe, and to their point, plenty of gang graffiti on walls, billboards, and fences marked the territory of Money Squad, African Nations Crew, and other thugs who ruled the night. But in the morning, the shops opened, buses ran, and sidewalks were lined with commuters. Theo had even seen children playing and parents pushing baby strollers. Bethnal Green was not as bad as its reputation. But Theo had chosen it precisely because of its reputation, betting that he would feel more comfortable there than anyone sent by a Russian oligarch to find him.

Still, it wasn't Kensington. While Theo could protect himself in a bad situation, not everyone could. The teenage girl standing at the front of the car, holding tightly to the safety pole, had no business catching a train alone after dark at the Bethnal Green Underground station. Theo kept one eye on the girl and the other on a "dodgy bloke," as the locals would have called him, who was rubbing his crotch and sizing her up. Theo had him pegged for one of the many creeps who rode the train all day begging for money, bumming cigarettes, talking nonstop to strangers, asking women if they're "selling," and, more than anything else, looking for teenage runaways who bit their fingernails and tugged at their hair in ways that signaled they were ripe for appropriation. "Those are just the flavors of London's northern lines," people liked to say. Theo didn't like it one bit. So, when the self-aroused creep rose from his seat and started toward the front of the car, Theo couldn't just sit in silence and do nothing, the way so many commuters did, as a pathetic excuse for a human being rubbed himself up against a defenseless teenager. Even if he was trying to avoid trouble and keep a low profile, it wasn't in his blood to be a bystander.

"Back off, asshole," said Theo.

The creep stopped and faced Theo. "This your girl?"

"Definitely not yours," said Theo.

"Says who?"

Theo rose. In general, he'd found it helpful to stand in situations such as these. As it became apparent that he was about a foot taller than this punk, the situation quickly de-escalated.

The man laughed nervously. "Take it easy there, mate. No problem at all here."

The train stopped. The doors opened. The creep scurried onto the platform like a startled cockroach. The doors closed, and the train pulled away with just Theo and the girl in the car.

"That was very kind of you," she said.

The voice was definitely that of a girl. Sixteen, maybe seventeen. "No problem," said Theo, as he returned to his seat.

Commuters came and went at the next few stops along the Central Line into the city. Theo exited at Oxford station to pick up the Victoria line. He hadn't noticed her on the platform, but once on the train, he saw that the girl had also transferred to the Victoria line. She was standing at what was apparently her preferred spot, clinging to the safety pole at the front of the car. Ten minutes passed. Theo exited at the Vauxhall station. The girl exited, too. Theo had no umbrella, and so he covered his head with a left-behind copy of the *Daily Mail* and started walking toward the river. On the north side of the busy Vauxhall Bridge was the massive SIS headquarters, instantly recognizable to any fan of the more recent James Bond movies. Theo was walking in the opposite direction, toward the U.S. embassy. He heard footfalls behind him on the wet pavement. The girl, apparently, was heading in the same direction.

Theo stopped. The girl kept coming, then stopped about twenty feet away from him. The rain had soaked through his newspaper, so he tossed it in the trash.

"Do you have nowhere to go?"

She shook her head. "My boyfriend kicked me out."

By "boyfriend," he worried she meant pimp. He walked toward her, removed a few bills from his wallet, and handed them to her. "There's a Holiday Inn two blocks that way," he said. "Get yourself a room."

She took the money. "When will you get there?"

"No, no, no. The money is for you to get a room for yourself. I'm not coming."

She looked at him as if he had sprouted a second head. "What?"

"Just go. It's your lucky day."

She smiled. Theo turned and started back toward the river. There was no telling what she might actually do with the money, but there was nothing more he could do. He had a meeting with the FBI's legal attaché at the Riverside Pub, and he was already late.

Madeline Coffey was waiting for him at an umbrella-covered table by the river. Flaming space heaters threw off enough warmth to allow for outdoor seating, but Theo still found it cold by Miami standards. Farther downriver, the embassy was alight and in full view, but Coffey had made it clear that she didn't want this meeting on government property.

"We lost the hearing," Coffey said.

Theo knew what she meant. The court hearing to determine whether

Sergei Kava should be extradited to the United States to face charges on piracy-related crimes was scheduled for that afternoon.

"Sergei Kava is not being extradited?"

"No. The judge just issued her ruling."

"How did you lose?"

The server brought a couple lagers, a pint for each of them. Coffey waited for her to leave, then continued.

"Kava retained top-notch counsel. They convinced the judge that it is unlawful for the UK to fulfill extradition requests that relied on private vigilantes like MAP to carry out extraction kidnappings against people like Mr. Kava."

"How were they able to prove there was an extraction kidnapping? Did Kava's daughter testify?"

"Even Kava has enough sense not to put his granddaughter through that. Their witness was the bodyguard who was tasered and left behind with Kava's daughter." She took a long drink from her pint glass, then shook her head. "This extraction kidnapping was not well planned. Too many witnesses."

"You're barking up the wrong tree. I had nothing to do with the kidnapping or the planning of it."

"Maybe you did. Maybe you didn't."

"There's no maybe," said Theo.

"Lucky for you, the bodyguard only mentioned two kidnappers in his testimony. Sergei Kava's driver, who obviously betrayed him. And another guy who fits the description of Amongus Sicario."

"That means I don't have to worry about the Metro Police coming out to arrest me on kidnapping charges."

"Correct," she said.

Theo connected the remaining dots. "And since Kava is not being extradited, I shouldn't have to worry about the death threat Jack passed along to us."

"Not correct," said Coffey.

"Why do you say that?"

"The fact that the bodyguard made no mention of you in his testimony tells me something very different. Kava wants to deal with you himself, outside the legal process."

"But the threat was clearly stated: *if* Kava is extradited, Theo Knight is a dead man. He's not being extradited."

"Let's look at reality. There's no sign of the driver who betrayed Kava. The last we heard from Amongus Sicario, Jack was speaking to him on the phone, heard a gunshot, and heard Amongus say he was hit. But there are no hospital records anywhere in the city showing that Amongus ever showed up at the ER for treatment, and his body has never been found."

"You're thinking the oligarch took care of both of them."

"Don't you?"

"That doesn't mean they'll come after me. I'll say it again: Sergei Kava is *not* being extradited."

She looked off toward the river, then back at Theo. "Have you ever heard the old saying 'All's well that ends well'?"

"Sure."

Her expression turned very serious. "That's not a creed that Russian oligarchs live by. They don't just let bygones be bygones. You kidnapped Vladimir Kava's son with the intent to put him behind bars. The fact that he's not being extradited doesn't make that okay."

Theo considered it. He'd grown up with countless dudes who had the same mind-set. "What would you do if you were me?"

"I can't advise you on that. What I can tell you is that now that the extradition case is lost, I can't offer you any protection. And I can no longer pass messages between you and Jack or your uncle Cy. You'll need to find some other safe way to communicate that doesn't give up your position to Kava's thugs."

"Sounds like I should just go back to Miami."

"It's up to you to decide when you feel safe traveling under your own name. I can't guarantee you that a man with Kava's resources isn't somehow monitoring the passenger lists on international flights out of Heathrow."

"What's the alternative?"

"Continue making yourself invisible in Bethnal Green for a while longer. Maybe take the Chunnel or the ferry over to the Continent when you're ready. Fly out of Paris or Amsterdam."

She finished the rest of her pint and set the glass down heavily, signaling that their meeting was over. "Any final message you want me to pass along to your lawyer or your uncle?"

"Tell them to sit tight. I'll reach out when I get back to Florida."

"Done. I wish you luck, Mr. Knight."

They rose and shook hands. Coffey said it was best that they not leave together. Theo gave her a head start and finished his pint. The large umbrella over the table had kept them dry during their talk, but it was still raining as Theo left the pub and started walking back to the Vauxhall Underground station. A woman was standing on the corner, and Theo quickly recognized her as the girl from the train. He called to her.

"What are you doing out here?"

"What does it look like I'm doing?"

"I told you to get a room."

"I couldn't find that hotel you said was around here."

The rain started falling harder. "Don't stand out here getting wet." She didn't answer.

"I can walk you to the hotel," he said.

She smiled and walked with him up the sidewalk.

"You're new to this, aren't you," said Theo.

"How can you tell?"

"Man, is that a long story," he said, more to himself than to her. His uncle Cy had done everything in his power to shield Theo and his brother Tatum from their mother's work on the street, eventually raising the boys himself.

Theo changed the subject. "What's your name?"

"Any name you like."

"What do people call you?"

"Depends on which people you're talking about."

"What does your mother call you?"

"My mother's dead."

"What does the rest of your family call you?"

"Whore."

They stopped at the traffic light. The rain continued to fall, the wet pavement glistening in the glowing streetlamps.

"What do you like to be called?" asked Theo.

"My boyfriend was a jerk. But I kind of like what he called me."

"Yeah? What did he call you?"

"Goodbye Girl."

The light for the crosswalk changed. Theo started across the street, and the girl went with him.

"We'll have to find something better than that," he said. "Goodbye Girl. G-G. Gigi! How's that?"

Her legs were long but still much shorter than Theo's, and she had to hurry to keep up. "Gigi it is," she said.

CHAPTER 23

Halloween morning was their first court appearance since Imani's plea of "not guilty" at the arraignment. Jack and his client were before the Honorable Cleveland Cookson, the circuit court judge who would preside over all pretrial matters and the jury trial in the case of *State of Florida v. Nichols*.

Owens and another assistant state attorney were seated at the table for the prosecution, closest to the empty jury box. The defendants and their counsel shared the rectangular table on the other side of the courtroom, but there was considerable space between them: Imani and Jack sat at one end; Shaky and his lawyer, Jennifer Ellis, at the other. The gallery was packed with spectators, as expected, though the entire row of Imani look-alikes—young woman dressed in costume to honor their pop star idol—was a bit unnerving. It was especially weird after Sunday evening's clash over Righley's costume.

Jack and Andie had managed to go the entire weekend without talking about Imani or Tyler McCormick. They'd been a normal family, focused on pumpkin carving, baking cookies, and hanging spooky decorations—until Righley's announcement that she no longer wanted to be Elsa the *Frozen* princess for Halloween.

"I want to go as Imani."

With a slip of the carving knife, Jack had robbed their pumpkin of its only tooth. "That's probably not a good idea, sweetie."

"Why?"

Jack hadn't even tried to explain. But the mere injection of Imani's name into their nice family weekend had seemed to spoil it all, triggering

Andie and Jack to take mental note of all the reasons Righley's idea was a bad one.

"Good morning, all," Judge Cookson said, bringing the hearing to order. Counsel announced their appearances, and the judge then turned straight to business, which was not his usual style. Cookson had a reputation around the criminal courthouse as a bit of a jokester.

"We're here on the joint motion of the defendants, Imani Nichols and Evan Nichols. Is that correct, counsel?"

"Yes, Your Honor," the lawyers said in unison.

Judge Cookson was a former prosecutor, and was generally regarded as straight down the middle, neither pro-defense nor pro-prosecution. He put on his reading glasses, opened the file before him, and pretended to read aloud from the filed papers.

"The motion is styled the 'Joint Motion of Defendants to Make the Judge and Jury Do Twice the Amount of Work.' Do I have that right?"

The sharp wit was more like the Judge Cookson Jack knew, and his characterization of the motion did not bode well for the defense. Jack rose to address the court.

"Your Honor, in all seriousness, the defendants have filed a motion to sever their cases. Although my client and Mr. Nichols are named together in the same indictment, each defendant wants a separate trial. They do not wish to be tried jointly."

"Isn't that what I just said, Mr. Swyteck? You want to empanel two separate juries to hear the same evidence, and you want me to try this case twice."

Shaky's lawyer rose. "Judge, the defendants in this case are divorced, and that divorce was anything but amicable. In fact, they recently sued each other in civil court. In a word, they are antagonistic. The law allows for separate trials where joint defendants are antagonistic."

Owens rose for the prosecution. "That's not exactly right, Judge. The law does not require separate trials just because the joint defendants don't like each other."

"Mr. Owens is correct," the judge said. "Separate trials are needed only when the *defenses* are antagonistic. Not the *defendants*. My understanding is that defenses are antagonistic where one defendant intends to defend himself by blaming the other defendant."

"That's correct," said the prosecutor.

The judge looked straight at defense counsel. "Is that the situation here? Mr. Swyteck, does your client intend to defend herself by presenting evidence or argument that her ex-husband, alone, murdered Tyler McCormick and disposed of the body?"

Jack and Imani had been over it many times. As much as she disliked Shaky, it was her position that he was no murderer.

"That is not our present intention," said Jack. "But in light of the deposition testimony I elicited recently from Mr. Nichols's former bodyguard, it is possible that we may pursue such a defense at trial."

"Ms. Ellis? How 'bout it? Does your client intend to defend himself by presenting evidence or argument that his ex-wife, alone, murdered Tyler McCormick and disposed of the body?"

Jack had warned his client before the hearing that, if she filed this motion and made it public that she *might* say something to incriminate her ex, Shaky could push back even harder.

"Judge, may Mr. Nichols and I have a minute to confer in private?" asked Ellis.

Imani gasped, but only Jack was close enough to hear it.

"You can use the jury room," said the judge. "Let's take a five-minute recess."

The hearing adjourned with the crack of the gavel. At the bailiff's command, all rose, and the judge exited to his chambers. Shaky and his lawyer hurried off to the jury room. Jack and his client remained at the defense table, mindful of their words, as members of the media and the Imani look-alikes rushed from their seats to the rail and called for Imani's attention.

The prosecutor stepped across the courtroom and laid a file folder on the table before Jack.

"What's this?" asked Jack.

"Phone records," said Owens. "We didn't have them in time for the grand jury proceedings, so I'm disclosing them now."

"Can I have some color?" asked Jack.

"We subpoenaed Imani's cellphone carrier," said Owens. "These records show a series of phone calls between your client and Tyler McCormick in the weeks before his murder. The relevant calls are highlighted in yellow for you."

Owens stepped away and returned to his table. Jack opened the envelope and examined the highlighted phone records. He immediately had questions for his client, but the crowd at the rail was only getting more aggressive.

"Swyteck, what's in the envelope?" a reporter asked.

"Imani, don't you love my outfit?"

Jack led his client to the far corner of the courtroom, behind the witness stand, where they could talk in private away from the crowd.

"You never told me you talked to Tyler McCormick," said Jack.

"It was twelve years ago. I must have forgotten."

Jack showed her the records. "You forgot about *twelve* calls?"

"Maybe I blocked them out of my mind. Like PTSD or something. This was traumatic. He was stalking me."

Jack checked the records again. Subpoenaed phone records included not just the list of calls, but also the duration.

"This call was for eleven minutes," said Jack, pointing to the entry. "Who talks to a stalker for eleven minutes?"

"All rise!" called the bailiff, cutting their conversation short.

Shaky and his lawyer emerged from the jury room and hurried back to the defense table. Jack and Imani followed, but without words Jack made it clear that he was not going to let his question go unanswered. Judge Cookson ascended to the bench, settled into his leather chair, and looked across the courtroom.

"Ms. Ellis, do you have a response to my question?"

The courtroom was silent. An announcement from Shaky that he fully intended to implicate his wife in the murder would have been headline news. As Shaky's lawyer rose, Jack felt the same rush of adrenaline he felt when a jury foreperson rose to render a verdict.

"Our answer is the same as Mr. Swyteck's," said Ellis. "It is not our present intention to do so, but it may turn out that Mr. Nichols will pursue an antagonistic defense."

The answer came as a relief to Jack.

The judge was ready to rule. "If this were a capital murder case, I would be required to hold separate trials. But this is second-degree murder. At most, I'm hearing there is some possibility that the defendants may at some point in the future raise defenses that could be antagonistic. That's not enough to justify the added burden on the judicial system, expense to taxpayers, and inconvenience to witnesses and jurors. The motion for separate trials is denied. Anything further?"

Jack was hesitant to make another request in the current climate, but he had to take his shot when it was available. "Your Honor, the defense has requested to take the deposition of Mr. Gustavo Cruz, the homicide detective who led the investigation into Mr. McCormick's death. He is now retired, and the State Attorney's Office has taken the position that only the current cold-case detective will be made available for deposition."

"Mr. Owens, what is your objection to the deposition of Mr. Cruz?"

Owens looked more confident than Jack had ever seen him, clearly feeling momentum. "Delay, delay, delay. First, they want two trials. Now they want to depose two detectives. And once they've caused enough delay, they'll come running into court screaming that their rights to a speedy trial have been violated."

The judge smiled thinly, as if the prosecutor had taken the words right out of his mouth. "The request to depose retired Detective Cruz is denied. We are adjourned."

The crack of the gavel and the bailiff's command brought all to their feet. The silence lasted only as long as it took Judge Cookson to enter his chambers, and then the courtroom sprang into action, starting with a wave of reporters rushing to the rail.

Jack needed a clear and immediate understanding of the "joint defense" arrangement with Shaky and his lawyer. With the bailiff's permission, the defense lawyers and their clients retreated to the jury room to talk behind closed doors.

"Looks like we're stuck with each other," said Imani. She and Jack were seated on one side of the table, and Shaky was with his lawyer on the other.

"I'm no happier about it than you are," said Shaky.

Jack took control. "Let's talk about how we can make this work," he said, and then he laid out the basic rules of joint defense, most importantly that communications among the four of them were just as privileged as attorney-client communications. When Jack was finished, Shaky's lawyer offered her take.

"That's all very nice, Jack. But let's be real. Some joint defense relationships work because there is some level of trust. Not this one. This joint defense will work much in the same way the United States and the Soviet Union survived the Cold War. The threat of mutually assured destruction keeps both sides in line."

"I take your point," said Jack.

"Can I say something?" asked Imani.

"It depends," said Jack. "If it has to do with strategy or procedures, yes. If it has to do with the actual guilt or innocence of anyone in this room, you and I need to discuss it in private first."

"It has to do with what I see as a deal breaker in this whole arrangement. Jack, you seem to have doubts as to whether Tyler McCormick was stalking me. Shaky knows that's the truth. If he can't back me up on that, we have no business being in the same room together."

"Let's discuss this in my office, just the two of us," said Jack.

"No, we're going to discuss it now. The phone records show that Tyler McCormick made a bunch of phone calls to me. I should have told you about those calls. But I didn't. Not because I was hiding my guilt, but because I didn't want to dredge all that up again. He was stalking me, and for twelve years, I put that part of my life behind me."

"Imani, the two of us need to talk first."

"No, Jack. It's fine if the four of us don't trust each other, but you and I sure as hell better. You said the phone records show there were more than a dozen calls. Did it ever occur to you that most of those were voicemail messages that I deleted without even listening to them? You said one of the calls went on for eleven minutes. Yeah. I made the mistake of trying to reason with him and tried to convince him to stop what he was doing. I should never have done that. It only made it worse."

She paused and looked straight across the room at her ex-husband.

"So, I need to hear it from you, Shaky. I know your first instinct is to tell everyone I lie about everything. But am I lying about this?"

Shaky folded his arms, his body language less than conciliatory. "Why should I back you on anything as long as you're still telling the world to 'go pirate' your old songs? I'm bleeding money by the minute."

"I'd rather lose my pitiful share of royalties to pirates than let you keep an even bigger share."

"Then fuck you!" said Shaky, slapping the table. "You're a liar who lies about everything, including Tyler McCormick!"

"Fine," she said, rising. "I didn't back down to the U.S. attorney in New York when he tried to silence me, and I won't back down to you. Let's get out of here, Jack."

Imani started for the door.

"Wait," said Shaky, and Imani froze. Shaky paused, as if preparing himself for what he was about to say, and then looked at Jack.

"She's not lying."

Imani settled back into her chair, casting a look at Jack that said, *I told you so.*

"Progress," said Jack. "That's a good thing. But this version of the truth is not without problems. If Tyler McCormick was a stalker, both of you, as a married couple, had reason to want him dead."

"In other words, you both had motive," said Shaky's lawyer.

"Perhaps even motive enough to want his body chained to a piling for the fish to eat," Jack added. "Depending on how bad the stalking was."

"Then we need to find someone else who had motive," said Imani.

"Sometimes that's a good strategy," said Jack. "Sometimes not. Keep in mind that we don't have to prove that someone else did it in order for the jury to find you not guilty. All we have to do is create 'reasonable doubt.'"

"But won't the jurors ask themselves that question?" said Imani. "If Shaky doesn't try to pin the murder on me, and I don't try to pin the murder on Shaky, that leaves an obvious unanswered question. Who did it? Who killed Tyler McCormick and put his body on display in Biscayne Bay?"

"There's a reason some cases go cold," said Jack. "We don't always get all the answers. We don't live in a perfect world."

"And sometimes innocent people get convicted," said Imani. "Right, Jack?"

She was doing it again, comparing herself to Theo. But this time she seemed to be looping in her ex-husband, and Jack wasn't ready to go that far.

"That won't happen here," he said, keeping his response intentionally ambiguous, offering no explanation whether he meant there would be no conviction, or no conviction of the innocent.

CHAPTER 24

Theo couldn't remember the last time he'd placed a call from a phone booth. He'd seen plenty of London's signature red booths in the movies, but it surprised him to discover that they were actually still functional, not mere relics of the past protected from extinction like some inanimate endangered species. He found one on a street corner near the Holiday Inn Express, where Gigi was staying on his dime. The strange dial tone threw him for a moment. Once he realized it was normal, he dialed the operator and told her he wanted to place a "long-distance" call.

When was the last time I said that?

Theo knew absolutely no one, save Uncle Cy, who still had a landline in his apartment. He'd almost forgotten that there were indeed advantages, including at this moment, to this security. A call on a cellphone could easily be intercepted by anyone with the right gadget sold by countless tech stores on the internet. A call *from* a cellphone could give up the caller's location via GPS locator. These things mattered when a Russian oligarch and his goons were determined to find and kill you.

"Hello?" said Uncle Cy, his aged voice cracking on the line.

"Cy, it's me! Theo!"

"Theo who?" he said, and then he laughed. "So good to hear your voice, boy. Where are you?"

"Still in London."

"When are you coming home?"

"That's what I'm calling about. Could be a little while."

"Somethin' bad happen?"

"No, there's this girl."

"Ah," he said, and Theo could almost see him smiling. "There's always a girl."

"No, it's not like that. I mean, literally, she's a girl. A teenage runaway."

Theo could feel the vibe change.

"Uh-huh," said Cy. "Now, you need to be very careful here, boy."

"There's no funny business. She's in trouble. She's on the street."

"Mmmhmm."

"She's not cut out for this. It's not gonna turn out good, I can tell. I want to help her."

"I see."

A motorcycle pulled up to park on the street outside the booth, engine rumbling. Theo waited for the noise to stop, then spoke into the phone.

"Do you really?" he asked. "Understand, I mean?"

"Sure do. You want to save this girl from herself. Just like I tried savin' yo' mother from herself."

Theo had not done the full psychological self-analysis, but he would never forget that night in Miami, when Cy was a much younger man. When the crowd of onlookers had gathered outside the liquor store on Grand Avenue in the heart of what white folks called the Grove Ghetto. When Theo and his friends had pedaled up on their bicycles to see what was going on. When his uncle Cy had pulled him away, kicking and screaming, a moment too late to keep Theo from seeing that the thirty-year-old woman lying lifeless on the street with her skirt hiked up for all to see was the same teenage runaway who'd given birth to him.

"You're one smart old man," said Theo.

"Yes, I am," said Cy. "You be careful."

"I will. It's just going to make it harder to come home. The safest thing for me is to get out of London and fly home from Paris or someplace like that. But I can't take a teenage runaway out of the country. That's asking for trouble."

"You do what you gotta do," said Cy.

"You don't think this is stupid?"

"I didn't raise no fool."

"Damn straight," said Theo, and he hung up the phone.

Jack settled in at his desk for a zoom conference on his computer. The image on his LCD screen was Madeline Coffey from London. Jack listened as the FBI legal attaché explained how this would be her last update on the extradition of Sergei Kava and the safety of Theo Knight.

"Is there any chance that the judge's decision to deny extradition will be reversed on appeal?" asked Jack.

"An appeal would accomplish nothing. Sergei Kava was released from prison the minute the magistrate judge ruled against extradition. He's probably in Moscow eating caviar as we speak."

"Understood," said Jack. "Even so, is there really nothing you can do to help Theo get home safely?"

"I suppose there would be a few things we could do," said Coffey. "If we were so inclined."

Her implication did not sit well with Jack. "Theo is an innocent American caught in a terrible situation. Why would the embassy be anything but 'so inclined'?"

"The judge at the hearing was swayed by the argument that the extraction kidnapping made extradition illegal. He seemed especially interested in the fact that MAP was behind the kidnapping."

"Theo is not part of MAP."

"Here's the problem. Sergei Kava's bodyguard was the only witness who testified about the kidnapping at the hearing."

"So?"

"He was tasered and incapacitated during the kidnapping. There is no way that bodyguard could have possibly known that Amongus Sicario and MAP were behind the kidnapping. Nonetheless, that was his testimony."

Jack considered what she was saying. "Unless Kava's men found the driver who betrayed him, and he gave up Amongus's name before they put a bullet in his head."

"That's possible," she said. "But we don't know for certain that Kava's men ever caught up with the driver, let alone killed him."

"You let me know when to add him to my list of trusted employees who betrayed an oligarch's family and lived to tell about it."

"Fair point," she said. "But consider another possibility."

"Meaning what?"

"You said it yourself the last time we spoke. The threat against Theo was conditional: *if* Kava is extradited, Theo is a dead man."

Jack saw exactly where she was heading. "Hold on. Are you suggesting that Theo shared details about the kidnapping with Kava's lawyers in order to derail the extradition proceeding?"

"No. I'm saying he did it to save his own skin."

Jack had to check his anger at the suggestion. "That's not who Theo is."

"Says you. But we never really know what people might do when faced with a death threat."

"I represented Theo for four years when he was under constant threat of death. I know what he would and wouldn't do. He would never rat out anyone by name to a Russian oligarch and his henchmen. Not even Amongus Sicario, who fucked him over and made him an unwitting accomplice in the extraction kidnapping. It's not in Theo's DNA."

"But if you're wrong, it could very well have been Theo who got Amongus Sicario killed."

"That's not possible. Theo was still in jail in Covent Garden when I was on the phone with Amongus and heard him get shot."

Coffey seemed to accept his point on the timing, but she wasn't budging on the bigger issue.

"Even if I believed you, there are decision makers here—people much higher up than me—who believe it was Theo Knight who worked behind the scenes and filled in the blanks for Kava's lawyers."

"So, you're saying Theo is completely on his own."

"On his own," said Coffey. "Unless . . ."

Jack waited. It was almost as if her image had frozen on the screen due to technical difficulties, but she was simply waiting for Jack to acknowledge that he was ready to negotiate.

"I'm listening," said Jack.

"The extradition of Sergei Kava would have eliminated the need for

Imani's cooperation in the piracy investigation in New York. Now it seems we need her again."

"You mean the idea that she do a private performance for Sergei Kava's daughter?"

"More specifically, that she tell the Kava family that she will perform only if she can have a private conversation with the grandfather, Vladimir Kava."

"How is she supposed to sell that condition?"

"The FBI will figure that out. We'll coach her on the questions to ask Kava. And, of course, she'll be wearing a wire for us to listen."

"That's a big ask."

"She's in big trouble."

Jack couldn't argue with that. "If she agrees to cooperate, what does she get in return?"

"All federal charges against her in New York are dropped. And her friend Theo gets whatever protection he needs or wants."

"What about her indictment here in Florida?"

"The FBI can't help you with that. But I'm solving two big problems for you, which lets your client focus her energy where it needs to be focused."

"It's an interesting proposal," said Jack. "But it's impossible. She can't go to London to perform. One of the conditions of her release on bail is that she can't leave the state of Florida."

"That's why the conversation will be between Imani and the grandfather, not Imani and Sergei."

"I don't follow you," said Jack.

"Vladimir Kava owns a huge estate on Miami Beach. I'm sure his granddaughter and all her friends would love to fly over on Kava's private jet to see Imani perform at Grandpa's estate. Obviously, Sergei won't be there. He'd be arrested the minute he set foot on American soil. But the FBI is confident that a conversation between Imani and the old man can elicit the information we need for our investigation."

"There are a lot of details to be worked out here," said Jack. "A lot of unknowns."

"As in any deal," said Coffey.

"I'll need some time to sit down with my client and calculate the risks."

"I'll give you three days."

Jack couldn't imagine it would take that long for Imani to decide, one way or the other. It all depended on how genuine her concern was about Theo. Baking him cookies was one thing. Wearing a wire to talk to a Russian oligarch was quite another.

"I'll get back to you," he said, and the video conference ended.

CHAPTER 25

Jack left his office around four o'clock on Friday, early enough to fight rush hour traffic out of the city and still make it to Doral in time for happy hour.

Judge Cookson's ruling had foreclosed any possibility of deposing retired Detective Cruz prior to Imani's trial on murder charges. It did not preclude an interview. The trick was to get the detective to talk without a subpoena commanding his appearance. Had Jack called him cold and tried to set something up, the detective would have surely declined. Jack's best shot was to bump into him somewhere unexpectedly and strike up a conversation. Cruz's Facebook page was filled with Friday happy hour photographs from a popular multilevel driving range called Top Golf in Doral. Jack chose to ambush him—er, bump into him—there.

"Hey, what a coincidence," said Jack as he filled the open space at the bar right beside Detective Cruz.

The Top Golf cocktail bar was on the roof of a three-story complex. The building's façade looked like an enclosed sports entertainment complex. The rear was open to the elements and faced a driving range. At peak hours, hundreds of golfers hit hi-tech golf balls from private bays on the three terrace levels below the rooftop bar. The object of the game was to hit the targets positioned at various places in the range, and the hi-tech golf ball recorded each player's score.

Jack had been waiting on the rooftop for nearly an hour before finally finding his target at the bar.

"Are you a golfer, Swyteck?" asked the detective.

"A hacker, like most of us."

"Well, hack away," he said as he reached for his wallet to pay for his drink.

"Can I get this round?" asked Jack.

He smiled. "You trying to bribe a witness?"

"Just compensating him for his lost time. I only need five minutes."

The detective thought about it for a moment, and for whatever reason—maybe because this wasn't his first scotch on the rocks of the evening—he agreed. Jack left a twenty-dollar bill for the bartender, and the two men found a couple of open club chairs at a cocktail table overlooking the driving range.

"How's your old man?" asked Cruz.

For all the disagreements between Jack and his father over the years, former Governor Swyteck could always be counted on as an icebreaker when it came to conversations with law enforcement. Jack gave the detective the usual update, then turned to the matter at hand.

"I deposed Shaky Nichols's former bodyguard at FSP," said Jack. "His testimony is that it was Imani's idea to tie the body to a concrete piling in Biscayne Bay."

"That's a bad fact for you," said Cruz.

"*If* it is a fact. Paxton wouldn't be the first prison inmate to mold his testimony to the prosecutor's theory of the case in the hope of early release."

"That's a very cynical view you have there, Jack. Your daddy wouldn't approve."

"You're right. He wouldn't. But I have a job to do, and this story came out of the blue. Have you heard it before—that Imani conceived and planned the disposal of the body?"

"Honestly, I have not. But I've been away from the case since my retirement, so I can't tell you when the investigation uncovered her involvement."

It was helpful to know that the case against Imani was a relatively new development, but not a huge score. Jack needed to use the rest of his five minutes wisely. He went to the most perplexing piece of the puzzle.

"Goodbye girl," said Jack.

"Yeah. The message on the body. What about it?"

"I understand it was you who released that information to the public."

"I did."

"Do you think Imani put it there?"

The detective sipped his scotch. "No comment."

"Do you think Shaky Nichols put it there?"

Another sip. "No comment."

Jack was starting to sense that he'd wasted ten bucks on the detective's drink.

"According to the autopsy report, the body was in the water at least thirty-six hours before the killer—or whoever—made an anonymous call to the media and told them where to find the body. We talked a little about this before, but what's your current thinking on the reason for the thirty-six-hour delay?"

"No comment."

"Sounds like the fact that my dad was a cop before he became a politician only gets me so much love."

"Courtesy, I'd call it. Not love."

A gray-haired man dressed in plaid golf knickers approached from the bar, a drink in each hand. "Cruz! Let's go! We're starting another game."

Cruz rose and shook Jack's hand. "Say hi to your dad, Jack. But don't come calling on me again."

Jack watched as the retired detective regrouped with his friends and stepped into the elevator. Getting anything of value from a retired homicide detective had been a long shot, so Jack couldn't be too disappointed in himself. He got a diet soda in a go-cup, took the elevator to the ground floor, and was in the parking lot, walking to his car, when his cellphone rang. It was Imani.

The three-day expiration deadline on the FBI's offer to Imani was fast approaching. Jack and Imani had talked about it several times, considering all angles. If it became public that she performed a private concert for an oligarch, it could affect her trial. The judge might decide to revoke bail and it ran the risk of prejudicing the potential jury pool. Beyond that, if something went wrong and the oligarch found out she was wearing a wire, she'd be on her own without an FBI agent present to protect her.

"It's decision time," Jack said into the phone.

"I think I've made up my mind. There's just one thing."

It was always one more thing. "Talk to me," he said.

"If I'm going to tell Kava's people that I'll do the concert only if I have a face-to-face meeting with Vladimir Kava, I can't have a B.S. reason for a condition like that. It has to be solid."

"The FBI says the explanation they created for you is solid."

"Do you think it rings true?"

Jack got into his car and closed the door. "It is true that pop stars are extra cautious about doing these events ever since J.Lo's concert in Turkmenistan turned into a public relations nightmare."

"Definitely. But insisting on a private meeting with Grandpa Oligarch in order to get his personal assurance that he'll give a million dollars to charity—that just seems lame. There's no way he'll go for it."

"The pretext is that if the public finds out about the event, you have plausible deniability. You can say you did it for charity, not for an oligarch."

"But that doesn't mean I need a one-on-one sit-down meeting with him. He could just donate the money without the meeting."

"I understand your point. But do you have a better idea?"

"I do."

Jack started the car and turned on the A/C, but he stayed parked. "Let's hear it."

"Is it true that Vladimir Kava named his superyacht after his late mother?"

"That's what people say. I guess even a ruthless tyrant can love his mother."

"Then here's my idea. My people talk to Kava's people and tell them Imani is not going on stage until Vladimir Kava looks her in the eye and swears on his dead mother's soul that no one is going to lay a hand on Theo Knight."

Jack's feelings had blown hot and cold on Imani. At that moment, he liked her better than he ever thought he would.

"That's better."

"You think?"

"Definitely better."

"Can you call the FBI and tell them we have a deal?"

"I will," said Jack.

And when they hung up, he did.

CHAPTER 26

Vladimir Kava watched from the beach of his superyacht, as a Sikorsky S-76 helicopter touched down on the helipad. The "beach" was actually a mechanically retractable platform that, upon the push of a button, slid out over the sea from just below the main deck, complete with sand, palm trees, and deck chairs. It was just one of the many extras on what Kava called the most "pimped-out" vessel afloat.

The oligarch's son climbed out of the helicopter, his hair whipping in the wind of the whirring blades overhead. Sergei had returned to Russia after winning his extradition hearing in London. He was dressed casually, having flown by private jet from Moscow to Malé before catching the chopper. A deckhand escorted him past the wave pool and down a flight of stairs. Kava wrapped his handsome son in a bear hug.

"Shoes off," said Kava, and he led a barefoot Sergei across the sugar-white sand to the lounge chairs. A server brought them an ice-cold bottle of vodka and poured each of them a drink, which they enjoyed while talking business in Russian on a makeshift beach in the middle of the Indian Ocean.

"That was a close call you had in London," said Kava.

Sergei sighed deeply, though Kava guessed his exaggerated reaction was more jet lag than anything. The time change from Moscow to the Maldives was just two hours, but the flight took nearly all day.

"Too close," said Sergei.

"You need to be more careful in choosing your staff, son. I've been chauffeured around every country in the world for over forty years. Not once has a driver betrayed me."

"Mine will never betray anyone ever again," said Sergei. "Guaranteed."

Kava nodded approvingly. "How much did MAP pay him to set you up?"

"We never found out."

Kava did a double take, surprised. "Starikova always finds out."

Starikova was among the most vicious mercenaries in the Wagner Group. Kava considered him the go-to contractor for private special-ops.

"My coward of a driver stuck a gun in his mouth the second he found out Starikova was on his heels," said Sergei.

Kava chuckled. "Starikova has that effect. We had to pull him from the Bucha Building interrogations. Too many prisoners took the quick way out after seeing what Starikova did to the defiant ones."

The Soviet-era Bucha Building, located just outside Kiev in the sleepy town of Bucha, was one of the first interrogation sites set up by the Wagner Group to support the Russian invasion. In the dark basement of a four-story office building at 144 Yablunska—a tree-lined lane that translates to "Apple Tree Street"—Wagner's most trusted and ruthless operatives questioned, tortured, and executed in grisly fashion the local politicians and residents rounded up by the Russian army as leaders of the resistance.

"Is Starikova on the trail of that Black guy, too?" asked Kava.

"Yes, Theo Knight is his name," said Sergei. "But there has been a development as to him, which is the reason I came here to talk."

"What sort of development?"

"It turns out that this Theo Knight is friends with Imani, the pop star Natasha is crazy about," he said, meaning his daughter. "I've been trying for months to get her to do a private concert for Natasha and her friends."

"What my granddaughter wants, my granddaughter gets."

"And it finally looks like she will get it. Imani's people reached out this week. Between telling her fans to pirate her music and the legal fees she's racked up lately, I think Imani needs some quick cash."

"How much?"

"Money is not the issue. It's the location. My original plan was to have her perform for Natasha and her friends in London."

"You should avoid going back to London for a while," said Kava.

"Understood. Her people have proposed your estate in Miami Beach."

"That's ridiculous. I just spent three weeks fighting your extradition to America in the London courts. Now you want to show up in Miami Beach at a party for your daughter? Have you lost your mind?"

"You're right," said Sergei. "I can't go. But Natasha can. And so can you."

Kava smiled. One advantage of having passed control of the piracy business to his son was that Vladimir Kava was no longer on the front line of extradition efforts under U.S. law.

"You didn't have to fly all the way out here to ask me to take my granddaughter to a party," he said.

"There's more to it than that," said Sergei. "Imani has a certain condition that must be met before she will go onstage."

"Let me guess. She wants two cases of 1959 Dom Pérignon delivered to her room so she can bathe in it?"

"That would be easier," said Sergei, laughing. Then he turned serious. "She wants a private, face-to-face conversation with you. She wants to hear it straight from your mouth that if she performs the concert, we will rescind the hit order on Theo Knight."

"After this Mr. Knight and his MAP friends kidnapped my son and tried to put him in prison for the rest of his life?"

"That is Imani's demand," said Sergei.

Kava looked out toward the open sea. "Do you want me to make this deal?"

"Natasha wants the concert."

"That was not my question," he said, giving his son an assessing look. "I asked if you want me to make this deal for Theo Knight?"

"Yes. Make it."

"Done," said Kava.

"But . . ."

Sergei finished his glass of vodka and poured both him and his father another from the bottle on ice.

"But what?"

"No one can guarantee that another man will live forever. Accidents happen."

Vladimir smiled widely, raising his glass. "I've taught you well, Sergei."

CHAPTER 27

The rhythmic steel-on-steel clap of a train moving through London's Underground was rocking Theo to sleep in his seat.

The death threat from Kava had been keeping him up at night, so a few moments of shut-eye on the train were "makeup winks." He'd told Uncle Cy he was staying in London to look after Gigi, and that was mostly true. It was also true that, with a Russian hit man looking for a Black American man alone on the run, moving around London with a teenage girl was decent cover.

Theo was also intrigued by the man Gigi called her "ex-boyfriend." She'd mentioned his clothes, his car, his money. His age was perhaps most telling. "Thirtysomething," she'd said. He sounded more like a sex trafficker than a boyfriend, and if there was one thing Theo had carried with him from four years at Florida State Prison, it was an intense hatred for a sex-trafficking pedophile. Theo wasn't sure what he would do if he found this scum. But it wouldn't take more than one encounter with Theo Knight to convince him to leave Gigi alone.

"Our stop is next," said Gigi, nudging him partly awake. The crackle of the conductor's voice over the loudspeaker shook off any remaining slumber:

"King's Cross St. Pancras."

The blur of the platform whizzed past in the train's window, slowing steadily to a stop. He and Gigi were the first riders to exit when the doors parted.

The largest Tube station in central London was so named because it served two rail stations: King's Cross and St. Pancras. Forty million riders coursed through the complex each year. Gigi led him to the suburban building, platforms 9 and 10 to be exact.

"Right there is where I met him," said Gigi, meaning her "boyfriend."

In the *Harry Potter* series, King's Cross is the starting point of the Hogwarts Express. Riders enter secret platform 9 3/4 by passing through the brick-wall barrier between platforms 9 and 10. Real-life muggles capitalized on the phenomenon, erecting a cast-iron PLATFORM 9 3/4 sign on a wall next to the world's first Harry Potter store. Part of a luggage trolley is mounted below the sign, half of it seeming to have disappeared into the wall. It's the ultimate photo op for fans of the series, one after another taking turns at pretending to push the cart through the wall.

Theo's quick take was that, for a guy like Gigi's "ex," this was exactly the right place to find girls of a certain age.

Definitely a fucking trafficker.

"So now you'll take me shopping?" said Gigi.

That was the deal. If she showed him where she first met this boyfriend of hers, Theo would buy her an age-appropriate outfit that didn't make her coltlike legs and still-growing body look for sale. They took the escalator up to the mall level. Gigi made a beeline to the Forever 21 store. Theo wasn't about to go inside with her. He gave her some shopping money, and she was happy to go it alone. Theo found a bench outside the store and put to good use a newspaper someone had left behind. The story above the fold was yet another sex scandal involving a minister of parliament. Theo's eyes were drawn below the fold to a photograph of Imani and Shaky Nichols outside the criminal courthouse in Miami.

IMANI MURDER TRIAL TO BEGIN THIS MONTH, the headline read. Theo continued reading. None of it was news to him, until he got to the part about Jack's unsuccessful efforts to depose the retired homicide detective:

"Judge Cookson's ruling is fundamentally unfair," said Imani's defense lawyer, Jack Swyteck. "Detective Cruz was among the first on the scene. He discovered the message that was written on the victim's body, presumably by the killer. It was his decision to release that message to the media twelve years ago." According to Mr. Swyteck, unless the defense is allowed to depose former Detective Cruz before trial, "we will be cut off from critical evidence that there is no connection between my client and this signature-like message from the real killer, 'goodbye girl.'"

Theo stared at the words a moment longer—*goodbye girl*—and then laid the newspaper aside. Just then, Gigi rushed out of the store, shopping bags in hand and brimming with excitement.

"I got the coolest skirt," she said. "And the top was on sale, two-for-one, so I got both the red one and the black one."

"That's great," said Theo. "Hey, you hungry?"

"I'm always hungry."

Theo coached basketball at the Coconut Grove rec center, and he could spot a kid on the verge of a growth spurt in an instant. Gigi had all the signs.

"How about pizza?" he said.

"Yum."

They started walking toward the exit. "I know I wasn't going to ask any more questions about your old boyfriend."

"But you lied," she said, seeming to know one was coming.

"Yeah, I kinda did. Do you have any idea why he called you 'Goodbye Girl'?"

"Nope. Why do you ask?"

"Just curious," he said. They walked a little farther, pushed through the turnstiles, and exited to the street.

"You think you could show me where your ex lives?" asked Theo.

"No," she said firmly. "He said I should never, ever go back there."

"I'm not saying you should go back. I just want you to show me where it is."

Gigi stopped on the sidewalk. "Theo, no! I don't want to get near

that place! I don't even want to think about that place! Do you understand?"

It was the harshest she'd ever spoken to him, and Theo could see the
fear in her eyes.

"Yeah," he said. "I definitely get it."

CHAPTER 28

I t was early Friday evening, and Jack was inside the operations cabin of an unmarked FBI surveillance van. Two FBI tech agents from the Miami field office were with him. They were parked on a residential street in Miami Beach near Vladimir Kava's estate on scenic Pine Tree Drive. As the name implied, the street was famous for the towering Australian pine trees that divided northbound from southbound traffic, but perhaps it was better known for the speeding ticket Justin Bieber got for seeing how quickly his red Ferrari could get from zero to a hundred.

"Can you hear us?" the tech agent said into his microphone.

"Roger that," came the reply.

Listening remotely, via an encrypted digital audio connection, were the assistant special agent in charge of the Miami office and the FBI's legal attaché from London.

"How is your client going to hold up, Jack?" asked Coffey.

Jack was outfitted with a headset, and her question had come through loud and clear.

"Imani's a performer," said Jack. "She has ice water in her veins."

Jack was slightly overstating things, but the technology had gone a long way to ease Imani's nerves. Had she been forced to strap a bulky tape recorder to her chest, à la an old episode of *The Sopranos*, and heave her breasts into Kava's face to make sure the hidden microphone picked up his every word, Imani would have surely said "*fuggedaboutit*." A "wire" still had the basic mechanics of old—a transmitter, microphone, and battery pack—but the modern device was small enough to hide in Imani's undergarments, light enough to attach by Velcro, and sensitive enough to pick up even whispers.

"How far away is SWAT?" asked Jack.

The risk of detection was real whenever an informant wore a wire. Sending in SWAT was a last resort, but the FBI had to prepare for the worst.

"Less than a minute," said Coffey.

The ASAC spoke up, also remotely. "I won't hesitate to make that call if Imani is in danger," he said.

Jack turned his attention to the A/V equipment. The operations cabin was divided into a seating area, which was directly behind the driver's seat, and the equipment station, which was behind the driver. An image appeared on the center LCD screen.

"I have a visual," said the tech agent.

Like all the residences on the east side of Pine Tree Drive, the back of the Kava estate faced the Intracoastal Waterway and the bay. The FBI had deployed drones over the waterway to capture real-time video of the estate. Imani had been coached to conduct her pre-concert conversation with Kava outdoors, and it appeared that she had managed to follow instructions. She and Vladimir Kava could be seen together, seated at a patio table near the swimming pool. The guests had yet to arrive for the performance, but the stage was fully set, and a dozen or more workers and servants were on the grounds, making final preparations.

"We have audio," said the tech agent.

The surveillance team went silent. Jack watched and listened, pleased that Imani had put first things first. She laid out the condition of her performance: Theo's safety. Kava's reply was given with a heavy Russian accent.

"You have my word that no one will lay a hand on Mr. Knight."

If Jack had been grilling Mr. Kava on the witness stand, he would have pressed harder. "That's all very fine and dandy that no one will lay a hand on him, Mr. Kava. But what about a baseball bat to the side of his head? A dose of Novichok nerve agent in his tequila? A sudden bump from behind that sends him flying off the platform and onto the tracks as a speeding train arrives at the subway station?"

But Imani didn't follow up. "Thank you, Mr. Kava," was her only response.

"Is there anything else I can do for you?" asked Kava.

A pause followed his question, and Jack could almost feel the FBI's anticipation. Coffey and her team had prepared her with key questions about the Kava piracy empire, each designed to strengthen the U.S. case for extradition of Sergei Kava.

"Let's go inside for a minute," said Kava.

The suggestion seemed to suck the oxygen from the van.

"We'll no longer have a visual," said the tech agent. "No cameras inside the house."

"Audio's fine," said Coffey.

Jack watched the LCD monitor, as Kava escorted Imani across the patio and into the lower level of the three-story estate. While other houses dotting the neighborhood had a multistory wall of glass facing the water to exploit the view, Kava's estate put a premium on privacy. The style was more medieval fortress, with heavy landscaping that screened all doors and windows from outside viewers. The video feed from the FBI drone froze on the last captured image of Imani, just as she and Kava disappeared into the house. The audio feed continued in real time, the voices in Jack's headphones.

"Love your art," said Imani.

"That's an original Kandinsky," said Kava. "I was lucky enough to purchase three of his works at—"

The audio crackled and suddenly cut out. Jack heard only the hum of the electric fan that cooled the A/V equipment. The tech agents sprung into high gear, their fingers a flurry of panic across the keyboards. The team communicated internally by headset.

"What's happened?" asked Coffey.

"It's on Imani's end, not ours," said the tech agent. "Her unit has a backup battery, so it's likely either the transmitter or the microphone."

"Can you fix it?"

"Possibly. Unless—"

The tech agent stopped herself, but Jack filled in the blank. "Unless Kava found her device and ripped it off her."

"We have no reason to believe that happened," said Coffey.

"I want her out of there," said Jack.

"Let's not overreact," said Coffey.

"We're dealing with a Russian oligarch, not some high school kid selling pot," said Jack.

"We have time," said Coffey. "Even in a worst-case scenario, Kava wouldn't harm Imani before she performs for his granddaughter. That spoiled little princess would never speak to him again."

Jack actually couldn't argue with that logic. "All right. But we need to be on high alert. Imani's safety has to be our number-one concern."

"Of course," said Coffey. "But a close second is what she and Kava are *really* talking about inside that house, now that they're off microphone."

Jack didn't answer. But Coffey's remark had him wondering.

CHAPTER 29

Theo took Gigi for Saturday breakfast in Flat Iron Square, a gentrified neighborhood south of the Thames filled with popular bars and restaurants that thrived in what were once abandoned railway arches and other disused structures. Theo and Gigi were at a place called Where the Pancakes Are, which was exactly what Gigi had said when Theo asked where she felt like having breakfast. The colt ate like a draft horse. Assuming horses loved Dutch pancakes.

"You look taller to me," said Theo.

She stuffed half a pancake into her mouth. "You just saw me three days ago."

"Four," said Theo.

"You gonna use your butter?"

Definitely growing. "Have at it," said Theo.

She swirled the pat around until it formed of pool of powdered sugar and melted butter. "*Sooooo* good," she said of her next bite.

"I need you to do me a favor," said Theo.

"I thought you'd never ask," she said in a flirtatious voice.

Theo reached across the table and grabbed her by the wrist. "Hey. Don't even joke about that. You hear me?"

"*Sorr-eee,*" she said, shaking his grip.

Theo tasted his hot tea with milk and sugar and made a face.

Gigi laughed. "I was waiting for you to taste that. You don't squeeze lemon into a hot tea with milk. You have a lot to learn, Theo."

"Noted," he said. "Which brings me back to the favor. I want you to show me where your old boyfriend lives."

She stopped chewing. "Are you trying to get me killed?"

"Are you saying he would kill you if he saw you?"

"I don't mean literally killed."

"Are you sure?"

"Yes," she said, then took another bite of her pancake. "Pretty sure."

"What's his name?"

"I don't know his real name. He said to call him Judge."

"Like the sci-fi character Judge Dredd?"

Gigi shrugged. "Just Judge."

"So, you called him 'Judge,' and he called you 'the goodbye girl,' and you have no idea why?"

"You ask like that's strange. And it's not *the* goodbye girl. Just 'Goodbye Girl.'"

"Did you know there's actually an old movie called *The Goodbye Girl*?"

"No."

"Me neither. I had to google it. Marsha Mason and Richard Dreyfuss, the guy from *Jaws*, were in it."

"Never heard of them."

"It was written by a famous playwright named Neil Simon."

"I've heard of Simon and Garfunkel. 'Hello darkness, my old friend.' Speaks to me."

"Different Simon," said Theo.

"Why are we talking such ancient history?"

"Sorry. Back to my point. I want to see where Judge lives."

"So you're bribing me with pancakes?"

Theo smiled. "Seems to be working."

She finished her last bite of pancake. "You really want to see?"

"I really do."

She slung her backpack over her shoulder, rising without enthusiasm. "Then we'll go."

Theo paid the check, and they walked to the Tube. The twenty-minute train ride ended at Bermondsey station, where old photographs on the wall near the exit showed a neighborhood destroyed by World War II bombings. The images explained why nothing Theo saw looked "old" by London standards, virtually every building less than eighty years old.

Gigi led him down the street and around the corner to one of the oldest ones, or at least one of the least well kept.

"That's it," she said.

Theo was standing on the sidewalk and looking across the street at a three-story, redbrick apartment building that, he guessed, dated back to the 1950s.

"Which apartment is his?"

"The basement."

"How many basement units are there?"

"Only one, I think. Who the fuck wants to live in a basement in this area?"

Theo glanced across the street. "Walk with me," he said.

"This is as close as I get," she said.

Theo took her by the hand. She resisted at first, then crossed the street with him. They stopped on the sidewalk and stood in the shade of a London plane tree so big that it might actually have been a survivor of the German bombings. A steep flight of concrete steps led from street level to the basement door.

"Would Judge be home on a Saturday morning?" asked Theo.

"I hope not," said Gigi.

Theo went down the stairs, stopped outside the door, and knocked. Gigi waited on the sidewalk, tugging at her hair nervously. Theo knocked a second time, but there was no answer.

"Not home," said Gigi. "What a shame. Let's get out of here."

Theo opened the letterbox outside the door. It was full. Based on the post dates, it appeared that no one had checked it for some time.

"When was the last time you were here?" asked Theo.

"A while."

Theo knocked again, then waited and listened. This time, he heard something—a thump or a bump of some sort from somewhere inside the apartment. He knocked again, but the noise did not return. One distressing thought came to mind, and it was the reason he'd come. Judge had let Gigi go. Maybe another young runaway had not been so lucky.

"Gigi, do you still have your key?" Theo asked.

"What?"

"Your *key*. Do you still have it?"

"Yeah."

"Give it to me!"

She dug it from her backpack and tossed it to him. Theo grabbed it in midair, turned the lock, and pushed open the door. A cat raced across Theo's feet, as if running for its life. Maybe the cat had made the noise he'd heard. Maybe not. He took a step inside and called out.

"Is there anyone in here?"

No response.

"Gigi, wait right where you are," he said, and then he entered with slow and cautious steps.

The basement apartment was one room with a kitchenette, plus a small bathroom. The lone window was essentially a slit of glass at street level, which had been made translucent with a streaky coat of white paint. Theo took a few more steps and stopped at the small dinette set. A couple of empty beer bottles were on the table. Baltika No. 7, Theo noted. A Russian brewery. Gigi had said nothing about Judge being Russian. In the far corner was a mattress resting directly on the floor, no bed frame. Beside the mattress was a coiled-up length of rope. It made Theo's blood boil to think how Judge might have put it to use, but then he spotted something on a chair beside the mattress that changed his thinking entirely.

It was a black ski mask—like the one Amongus Sicario had worn for the extraction kidnapping.

Theo froze, and then his mind nearly overloaded with images of Amongus Sicario and the unfaithful Russian driver seated at the table, drinking Russian beers, debating what to do with their hostage, as Sergei Kava lay hogtied on the mattress.

And then he saw the dried brown bloodstain on the floor.

Theo raced out of the apartment and up the concrete stairs to where he'd left Gigi waiting on the sidewalk. She wasn't there.

"Gigi!" he called out, but she didn't answer.

He sprinted half a block to the intersection, but there was no sign of her. He ran across the street and called to her again.

"Gigi!"

He looked up the street and down. He checked the alley. He went from one parked vehicle to the next, peering through windows, checking the front seat and back. Nothing.

Gigi had vanished.

He stood at the top of the stairs, looking down at the basement apartment, wondering what Judge and Gigi—"Goodbye Girl"—had to do with MAP. Then he ran to the phone booth at the corner and dialed Madeline Coffey's number. She answered.

"Mr. Knight, I am not your handler anymore. You cannot dial this number."

"Just listen," said Theo, breathless from the run to the booth. "I think I may have found the place where Amongus Sicario got shot."

CHAPTER 30

On Saturday at 9:00 a.m., Jack and Imani were in the FBI's Miami field office for a debriefing. Arnie Greenberg, Miami's assistant agent in charge, and the tech agents from the surveillance van were in the conference room with them, seated on the other side of the long rectangular table. Madeline Coffey from London, and an assistant United States attorney on the New York prosecution team, participated remotely by video conference, their boxed images lighting up the sixty-inch LCD screen on the wall.

Friday night's concert at the Kava estate had gone off without a hitch. Imani had left without incident and, more importantly, without SWAT support. The mystery—and the focus of Saturday's debriefing—was the private conversation between Imani and Kava that had taken place indoors, "without ears."

The ASAC began with his tech team's findings. "Our tech unit has thoroughly examined the device Imani was wearing last night," said Greenberg. "They found absolutely nothing wrong with it."

"Then why did it stop working?" asked Jack.

"Somebody made it stop working," said Greenberg.

"How?" asked Jack.

The ASAC turned very serious. "If I told you, then you and your client would hire a tech expert to concoct an explanation of how it wasn't Imani's fault."

"Are you accusing my client of tampering with the device?"

"Not formally. At least not yet. But the fact remains that the transmission cut out at a very convenient time. Just when Imani was about to make the proposal to Mr. Kava that we scripted for her."

"I don't accept your characterization of 'convenient,'" said Jack. "My client kept her end of the deal. She made the proposal, and Mr. Kava responded. It's unfortunate that the device malfunctioned and failed to pick up the conversation, but that doesn't relieve the government of its obligations under our agreement. All charges in New York must be dropped."

Greenberg shook his head. "The deal was premised on a successful wire transmission of their conversation."

"No," Jack said firmly. "I struck that language from the agreement before signing it. Technical difficulties are the government's problem, not mine. You may prefer a recording of the conversation, but my client can uphold her end of the bargain by testifying as to what was said between her and Kava."

The ASAC seemed surprised. "I didn't approve that modification."

"I did," said Coffey, her voice coming over the speaker. "With New York's approval."

The ASAC's surprise drifted toward annoyance, if not anger. "You didn't think to raise this with me directly, Jack?"

It hadn't been Jack's intention to do an end run on the Miami office, but unfortunately that seemed to be Greenberg's take on the situation.

"I assumed you guys talk to each other," said Jack.

"This isn't productive," said Coffey. "The bottom line is that unless the technical malfunction was an intentional act of sabotage, Ms. Nichols can satisfy the agreement through her testimony. But we need a proffer of what that testimony would be."

The ASAC still seemed put off, but Jack was fully prepared and had a written proffer with him. He forged ahead, though it troubled him on multiple levels to have lost at least some support from Andie's boss.

"Imani and I worked on it this morning," he said. "I'll read it to you."

Jack read aloud, starting with the usual preliminaries of a witness statement, then a description of the setting and circumstances of the conversation. Imani was with Vladimir Kava in the art room, where his private collection was on display. They walked slowly from one painting or sculpture to the next, as Kava described his finest pieces. Classical music was playing in the background. Stravinsky, she believed. The only other person in the room was Kava's bodyguard, who stood at the door, which was closed.

Then Jack read, in Imani's words, the proposal she'd made to the oligarch:

"'I asked Mr. Kava if he had heard about my "go pirate" campaign, and if he was aware that I was telling all of my fans to get my old songs on piracy websites. He said yes, he was aware, and that, from what he had read in the newspapers, I was trying to hurt my husband, Shaky Nichols, who owned my master recordings and stood to lose the most from the pirating of my music. Mr. Kava then asked, "How long do you intend to keep this up?" I told him I could keep it up forever, if he could make it worth my while. He asked what I meant, and I told him I had a business proposal for him: "I'll keep telling my fans to pirate my songs, if you and Sergei will pay me at least double what I make under my record contract."'"

Jack stopped there, taking a moment to address Coffey via videoconference. "I would point out that Imani's proposal is the exact proposal you asked her to make."

"Agreed," said Coffey. "What was Mr. Kava's response?"

"I'll read it to you," Jack said, and then he continued.

"'Mr. Kava said, "What makes you think I profit from your 'go pirate' message to your fans?" I laughed and said, "Let's be honest with each other, Mr. Kava. Everyone knows that your son controls the largest piracy platform in the world." Mr. Kava was obviously insulted and said my words were slanderous. He immediately ended the conversation and told me that he did not care to have any further contact with me once the performance for his granddaughter was over. He left the room, and we did not speak again.'"

Jack laid the written statement on the table and waited for the response.

"That's not helpful," said Coffey. "All you're offering is a flat denial that the Kava family has anything to do with piracy."

"Our agreement requires Imani to provide truthful testimony, not helpful testimony," said Jack.

"Yes," said Coffey. "And that's quite a piece of work you've created to hide the truth."

"Excuse me?" said Jack.

"Here's the truth," said Coffey. "The goal was to wire up Imani and get Kava to admit that his son owns and controls the largest piracy website in the world. To help us get that admission, your client agreed to make a business proposal: she keeps telling her fans to pirate music, and Kava pays her a cut of his profits. But your client had a big problem. She already had that arrangement with Sergei Kava."

"That's not true!" said Imani.

Jack admonished her to stay silent, as the cooperation agreement was clearly going sour.

Coffey continued. "When Imani met with Kava, she couldn't propose to enter into a business relationship that already existed. And she couldn't risk letting Kava say something that would reveal the truth to the FBI. There was only one thing she could do. She had to sabotage the wire. And that's what she did."

"What she *did* was risk her life by talking to a Russian oligarch while wearing a wire," said Jack.

"That's just bullshit, Jack," said Greenberg.

No one liked to be accused of bullshitting the assistant special agent in charge of an FBI field office, but it was especially bothersome when that ASAC was your wife's boss.

Jack rose, and Imani followed his lead. "I'll be filing a motion with the court to enforce our agreement and get the charges dismissed," he said.

"And the U.S. attorney in New York will be filing additional charges against your client for interfering with a government investigation."

Greenberg called for his assistant to escort Jack and his client out of the building. She came quickly, but before Jack could leave the conference room, the ASAC had one more thing to say.

"Jack, I want you to know that I still have the utmost respect for your wife."

Jack knew he wasn't complimenting Andie. It was his way of saying that he'd lost respect for her husband, and it made Jack wonder what, perhaps, Andie had been telling her boss about Jack over the past couple of weeks.

"Couldn't be happier to hear that," said Jack, and then he and his client left the room.

I t was a chilly November night in Boston. Judge was on the prowl.

He'd left London two weeks earlier, right after giving Goodbye Girl the boot. He had no plans to return—ever. His intentionally circuitous flight from Heathrow to Boston Logan—connecting in Amsterdam, Paris, and Madrid—had been under a new name, new passport, and new identity. He was officially a new man. But he was unchanged.

His stakeout position was on the flat roof of an apartment building in Cambridge. His target lived in a studio on the third floor of the redbrick building across the alley. The lone window was oversized, something the landlord undoubtedly touted as a "plus," even though it overlooked a Dumpster. The curtains were parted, affording Judge a clear view inside. His target was a twenty-three-year-old woman who lived alone and served drinks at a tavern until 10:00 p.m. on weeknights. She was alone on the Murphy bed, sitting up against a corduroy husband pillow, her face aglow in the light of an open laptop computer. Judge estimated five steps from the bed to the door. With the aid of binoculars, he was able to make out every essential detail. There was a chain lock, but it was hanging straight down on the door frame, unused.

Can you make it any easier?

Judge lit up a cigarette to settle his nerves. His plan was foolproof, and the anticipation of his next move was no cause for concern. His only worry was Goodbye Girl.

Giving her that name had been a mistake. Letting her go had been downright stupid. As the start date for Imani's murder trial drew closer, the media coverage intensified with each passing day, and not just in the United States. More coverage meant more mention of the killer's signature. Judge could only hope that Goodbye Girl would be true to her stupid self and remain oblivious to what was happening in the world.

Should've strangled the little slut.

Judge crushed out his cigarette and raised his binoculars. Clueless was still on the Murphy bed, staring at the LCD screen, completely unaware that the hard drive was loaded with malware. Like most hacks, it had been a self-inflicted wound, triggered by browsing activity that younger users considered normal, other users regarded as an acceptable risk, and only the tech savvy labeled "reckless." Judge opened his laptop but kept the LCD display on the dimmest setting so as not to draw attention to himself in the darkness. In just a few moments, his screen would display exactly what his target was seeing. The embedded malware was programmed to launch and take control at 11:00 p.m. Judge couldn't wait to see her reaction.

Three . . . two . . . one.

The image appeared on Judge's screen. The malware was performing exactly as programmed, but technology was only half the equation. The key to the entire operation was to elicit a certain human response from his target. Judge raised the binoculars and peered into the studio apartment. Confirmed: Clueless was no longer in control. Her expression showed confusion, then concern. Panic soon followed. The target laptop had become the slave. Judge was the master, and the on-screen image was having the intended effect.

Clueless was freaking out.

Even though Judge was watching through binoculars from across the alley, it was as if he were sitting on the Murphy bed beside his target, close enough to hear the gasp for breath, check the racing pulse, and dab the sweating brow. The next minute was crucial. Some targets just froze, wondering if what they'd just seen was real. Some slapped the laptop shut and quickly pushed it away, as if to pretend they'd seen nothing. Others grabbed their cellphone and texted or called someone who, perhaps, could convince them that it had all been their imagination.

Judge waited and watched. His bet was that Clueless would call someone, and it made him smile with satisfaction to see that he was right. The call on her cellphone lasted just a few minutes. The friend, brother, sister, coworker—whoever had been on the line—seemed to put Clueless at ease, for a moment, at least. She disappeared into the bathroom to get ready for bed, but whatever comfort or courage the caller had imparted was short-lived. Barely enough time to wet a toothbrush passed before the door flew open and Clueless dived beneath the covers, as if the bogeyman himself had appeared in the bathroom mirror.

She hadn't even bothered to turn off the lamp on the nightstand. Judge guessed it would stay on all night. Fine by him. A little light would keep him from stubbing his toe.

Judge lowered his binoculars. He would wait until well after midnight. Maybe as late as 2:00 or 3:00 a.m.

And then he would make his move.

CHAPTER 31

Security at Miami's criminal courthouse was tighter than usual on Monday morning. Squad cars lined the street at the front entrance. Police barricades prevented onlookers from gathering on the steps. It was all for the trial of Imani and Shaky Nichols, day one. Jack had handled high-profile cases before, typically as counsel to the infamous. Imani was his first client to have found fame for the right reasons—and then for the wrong.

"This isn't the red carpet," Jack said as their SUV pulled up to the curb. "Don't wave, don't smile, and, above all, don't say anything."

Imani was looking out the passenger-side window at her supporters, who cheered her arrival. It was a sunny morning and Jack reached for his sunglasses, a cheap plastic pair from next to the checkout line, but Imani handed him a new pair. "Your drugstore specials won't cut it, Jack. Look the part."

Jack tried them on. He suddenly had an appreciation of how his father must have felt after cataract surgery. "Nice," he said.

"Persol 714," said Imani. "Limited edition in honor of Steve McQueen."

"You're on trial for murder, and you're worried about what sunglasses your lawyer is wearing?"

"You do your job. I'll do mine."

Police were able to contain the crowd long enough for Jack and his client to climb out of the SUV, but not much longer. Imani's fans were only half the problem. More than six hundred media passes had been issued. Every major network and entertainment magazine had at least one reporter at the trial. The top cable news networks had constructed a two-story air-conditioned structure across from the courthouse for reporters and crews. In addition to real-time court coverage, Jack knew of at least two prime-time segments in the works, "Inside the Imani Trial" from Dateline, and "Only Imani Knows" from CNN. In the week running up to the trial, Imani's picture had appeared on the cover of everything from *People* in the United States to *Bunte* in Germany. Judge Cookson's courtroom would surely become another Miami tourist destination, like South Beach and the Seaquarium, with spectators coming from all over the world to vie for the fifty seats available to the public. The first altercation among spectators broke out as Jack and Imani entered the building.

"This is my spot!"

"I've been here since five a.m.!"

The police broke it up, Jack and his client shuffled through security, and by 9:00 a.m. they were seated safely in Judge Cookson's courtroom. Jack had expected jury selection to carry over to Tuesday, but by three o'clock they had a jury. Four women and two men, each of whom had assured the judge that they had formed no preconceptions about the case, despite the plethora of pretrial publicity. Judge Cookson kept the freight train rolling.

"Let's proceed with opening statements," he said from the bench. "Mr. Owens, if you please."

The prosecutor stepped to the lectern and faced the jury. He had a notebook with him, but he didn't open it. He spoke without notes.

"A wife cheats on her husband. The husband finds out about it, and he's enraged. The wife is under her husband's thumb. Her career is in her powerful husband's hands. He wants her to get rid of the lover. At her husband's insistence, she coaxes her lover into something kinky in bed. A second male participant is involved. Ropes are definitely involved. Perhaps her lover is blindfolded. Or perhaps the second man is wearing a mask. Either way, her lover is unable to recognize him as the husband. At some point in this frenetic orgy of sex, the rope finds it way around the lover's neck. The lover ends up dead."

The courtroom was utterly silent. For a moment, it seemed as if the prosecutor might return to his seat, having said enough.

"How did Tyler McCormick end up dead? Who strangled him? Was it Shaky Nichols, a disgusted husband who was finally done with other men having their way with his wife?"

Then his gaze drifted across the courtroom, landing squarely on Imani. "Or was it Imani Nichols, the wife who had pushed her husband too far, and who would do anything—*anything*—to redeem herself in his eyes."

The prosecutor's focus returned to the jurors. "We don't know where the murder occurred. Tyler McCormick's body was found sometime after his death on display in Biscayne Bay in an elaborate attempt to make the killing look like something it wasn't. In the coming days, you will hear evidence on all of this. For now, let me share a little irony.

"There's a song by Imani. It was one of her first hits. The name of the song is 'Safe Word.' For those of you who don't know, a safe word is used by couples who engage in rough or even dangerous sex. The safe word is a code from the submissive partner to let the dominant partner know that things have gone far enough. A safe word like 'red light' might mean 'Time to stop. You're really hurting me.' Interestingly, Imani's song has this lyric: 'Ain't no safe word; you ain't safe with me.'"

Jack rose. It was unusual to object during opening statement, but with a celebrity client, it was important to force the prosecution to stick to the evidence. "Your Honor, I object. Is my client on trial here, or her music?"

"Sustained," the judge said. "Mr. Owens, let's confine our opening remarks to what the evidence will show."

"Absolutely," said the prosecutor, tightening his focus on the jurors. "Ladies and gentlemen of the jury, the evidence in this case will show you one thing. For Tyler McCormick, there was no 'safe word.'"

Jack was about to rise, but the judge stopped him.

"Keep your seat, counsel. Mr. Owens, that is the last time I want to hear about song lyrics."

"My apologies, Your Honor. It won't happen again."

Owens returned to his seat, seemingly satisfied that twice being reprimanded by the judge was well worth it, as long as that song stuck in the jurors' heads.

The judge turned his attention to the defense. "Mr. Swyteck? Your opening statement?"

Jack hesitated. For weeks, he had been pushing the prosecutor for a clear articulation of how he intended to prove Imani's active participation in the murder of Tyler McCormick. The answer had come in a song.

Imani grabbed her lawyer by the wrist and whispered, "My songs are not murder plots. You have to say something."

Jack understood her reaction. But the joint defense team had weighed all options before the start of trial, and the agreed-upon plan was for Jack to plant seeds of doubt in his opening statement, to lay out a theme for the defense, not to respond point by point to every theory and every piece of evidence presented by the prosecutor. It was a good strategy, and Jack resisted the urge to change it based on Owens's clever reference to a song.

Jack rose and stepped to the well of the courtroom, that stage-like opening before the bench where lawyers could seemingly step away from the action and speak directly to the jury, as if delivering a Shakespearean soliloquy. He buttoned his suit coat, bid the jurors a good afternoon, and dove straight into his theme.

"A cheating spouse, a dead lover. If it were really that simple, this jury would have the easiest job on the planet.

"But it isn't so easy. Your job is to make the prosecution prove its case against Shaky Nichols and Imani Nichols beyond a reasonable doubt. That standard applies to each of them. They were husband and wife at the time of the victim's death, but the charges against them are separate. Each has been charged with murder in the second degree. Each has been charged with mutilation of a dead body. It's as if the prosecutor wants you to tack a scarlet letter on each of their foreheads and simply conclude that they did it. *They* did it."

Jack shook his head. "The prosecution has it all wrong, folks. There is no *they*. Look carefully at the charges in the indictment. Notice what is missing. They are *not* charged with conspiracy to commit murder. That's not an oversight by the prosecutor. There is no charge of conspiracy because the essence of a conspiracy is an agreement. You will hear no evidence of an agreement to murder Tyler McCormick. No evidence of a plan. The reason? There was no agreement. There was no plan. This all just sort of happened, is what the prosecutor would have you believe.

"To convict my client, the state must prove beyond a reasonable doubt that Imani Nichols did it. To convict Shaky Nichols, the state must prove beyond a reasonable doubt that he did it. It isn't enough that one of them might have had some theoretical desire for Tyler McCormick to go away. Two weak cases do not add up to a conviction.

"I submit that after all the evidence is in, you will conclude that neither of them killed Tyler McCormick. You will most certainly conclude that the prosecution has failed to prove the guilt of anyone in this courtroom beyond and to the exclusion of every reasonable doubt. Your verdict must be 'not guilty.'"

Jack started back to his seat, then stopped. He supposed he owed it to her client to defend her work. "Oh, one other thing before you swallow this life-imitating-art nonsense. Imani composes the music to her songs. She does not write the lyrics. I guess that makes the lyricist from 'Safe Word' a co-conspirator in the murder of Tyler McCormick."

Jack returned to his seat beside his client at the defense table.

"Nice work," Imani whispered.

Judge Cookson looked at Shaky's counsel. "Ms. Ellis, your opening statement, please."

She rose and said, "My client elects to defer his opening statement until the close of the prosecution's case, Your Honor."

Dividing their opening statements in this fashion, Jack first and Ellis later, was a joint defense strategy, but it came as no small relief to Jack that Shaky's lawyer had actually honored the arrangement.

"Very well," said the judge. "Ladies and gentlemen of the jury, Mr. Nichols has elected to save his opening statement until after the state has presented its case. That's his right to do so, and if any defense is necessary, you will be hearing from his lawyer at that time." Judge Cookson checked the clock in the back of the courtroom. "It's almost five o'clock. Let's reconvene tomorrow at nine. The jurors are reminded of their oaths. We're adjourned for the day," he said with the bang of a gavel.

All rose, and as the judge exited to his chambers, Jack noticed Shaky and Imani exchange glances. Though Jack could only guess, he imagined the defendants were thinking the same thing. All this talk about reasonable doubt was nice. But even nicer would have been the one thing Jack couldn't deliver.

A forceful denial that Imani had ever met Tyler McCormick.

CHAPTER 32

Boston Harbor was awash in gray. Seas, sky, and the steady drizzle blended into a monochromatic band on the horizon. It reminded Andie of weathered tin roofs and spent steel bullet casings, as she and two officers from the Boston PD's harbor unit sped across choppy waters at over thirty knots. They were aboard one of the fastest police boats operating out of South Boston's Terminal Road, a sleek thirty-four-foot Intercept with twin 300-horsepower outboard engines.

"How much farther?" Andie asked, shouting over the roar of the engines. Her FBI raincoat kept her dry for the most part. For added measure, she'd positioned herself forward in the cockpit, as close to the windshield as possible, allowing the speed of the boat to take the raindrops and sea spray over her head.

"Just a few more minutes," the BP officer shouted back.

A speck of land appeared on the horizon. "Is that it?" she asked, pointing.

"Yup."

Andie's day had started in Miami with a predawn phone call from her ASAC. The body of a twenty-three-year-old woman had been found chained to a concrete piling in the harbor. An alert Boston homicide detective had immediately noted the similarities to the Tyler McCormick homicide, which had returned to law enforcement's top of mind, thanks to the trial of Imani and Shaky Nichols. FBI Agent Andie Henning was the only still-active law enforcement officer who'd observed the McCormick recovery site firsthand. Andie was in Boston by noon, and twenty minutes later they were headed east-southeast to a tiny island in the harbor.

"This is it," said the boat pilot, throttling down to no-wake speed. "Nixes Mate."

Once a twelve-acre island suitable for farming, Nixes Mate today is just two hundred square feet of uninhabited rock protruding from the harbor, most of the land lost to mining operations and rising sea levels. It essentially serves as a pedestal for a cone-shaped, black-and-white navigation marker for ships entering the harbor.

When Andie arrived, it was an active crime scene. In addition to the Boston Police's harbor unit, responders included the U.S. Coast Guard, Massachusetts State Police, Massachusetts Environmental Police, Boston Fire Department, Massport Fire, and Boston EMS. Several other boats were outside the crime-scene perimeter, from which camera crews were recording footage for the local news.

"Who's in charge?" Andie asked.

The pilot maneuvered his boat alongside a larger police boat on the scene. "Boston Police, homicide," said the pilot. "Lieutenant Wall."

Wall was the detective who had summoned Andie from Miami.

The first mate dropped rubber fenders over the side, and the two vessels rafted up close enough for Andie to hop over to the bigger boat. Lieutenant Wall met her on deck, as the speedboat pulled away. The crime scene was on the leeward side of the island, which afforded just enough protection from the northeast wind to keep the stationary boat from rocking and rolling. The rain had stopped, but Wall was still wearing a bright yellow rain jacket with the Boston Police logo. After a quick introduction, Andie started where she started any investigation.

"What do we know about the victim?" she asked.

"We think her name is Shannon Dwyer. Aspiring model who supports herself by waiting tables. Lives alone in Cambridge. But we're not positive it's her. The only clothing on the body is a nightgown, so no ID."

"What makes you think it's Shannon Dwyer?"

"A girlfriend reported Shannon missing yesterday morning. They were supposed to meet for brunch, and Shannon never showed up. The girlfriend was worried because Shannon called her late Saturday night freaked out about something. When Shannon didn't show up for

Sunday brunch, she went to Shannon's apartment to check on her. The door looked like it had been jimmied open. Shannon was gone."

"Does the victim meet Shannon's description?"

"So far. We'll know more when we bring her up."

"Up?"

Wall pointed with a jerk of his head, indicating the concrete piling at the island's edge. "We're at high tide. Right now, the body is completely underwater."

Andie spotted the scuba divers' bubbles at the surface. "Still chained to the piling?"

"Yeah. I directed the underwater recovery team not to remove the chains until the body is at least partly above the waterline, so we can get a clear look at the killer's work. I want to see the body exactly as it was left here, which I presume was low tide. Then we'll move into recovery mode."

Andie's gaze drifted back toward the piling. "I understand there was a tip to the local newspaper."

"'This morning, to the *Boston Herald*," said Wall. "Anonymous caller. Said exactly where the body could be found. Just like in the McCormick case."

"Actually, even the timing of the tip is like McCormick."

"How do you mean?"

"Once the medical examiner gave us an approximate time of death, we were able to determine that the call came in to the Miami news station about thirty-six hours after the murder. If Shannon went missing after that Saturday night call to her friend, that's pretty close to the same time lag between the time of death and the anonymous tip."

"What do you make of that?" asked Wall. "The time lag, I mean?"

"Too soon to say," said Andie. "But it could mean we have a copycat."

"That's what I was afraid of," said Wall. "Which is why I wanted you here when the tide is out. If there's something inauthentic about this, I want to know if we have a copycat to worry about. On the other hand, if it strikes you as authentic, well . . ."

"You're referring to the signature, I presume," said Andie. "Goodbye girl."

"Yeah," said Wall. "No report yet from the divers whether it's there."

Andie's gaze swept the island, then fixed on the concrete piling. "If it is, then we really have our hands full."

"Either way, our hands are full. Your husband's, too."

"It's best if we don't bring my husband into this."

"Nobody's bringing him in," said Wall. "He's in, whether he likes it or not."

It was a curious remark, especially coming from a cop all the way up in New England. Andie hoped it simply reflected the national interest in the Imani trial. She worried that talk of the tension between Andie and Jack—wife and husband, agent and defense lawyer—was rippling through all levels of law enforcement.

"Is there something specific about this investigation that makes you say that?" she asked.

He smiled a little, as if her question amused him. "You really have no idea why this island is called Nixes Mate, do you?"

"I didn't even know the name of the island until the boat ride out here."

"Would you like a little history lesson?"

Andie could tell he wasn't just offering interesting background. He seemed to have a theory about the case, and it was somehow rooted in the island's history.

"If you think it will help with this investigation," she said.

"Oh, it'll help," he said. "Tremendously."

Andie listened. And over the next five minutes, with the November wind whipping over Nixes Mate, Lieutenant Wall told her.

CHAPTER 33

Tuesday morning came quickly. Jack and Imani were back in Judge Cookson's courtroom at the Criminal Justice Center. To Jack's relief, his client not only was on time but, perhaps more important, had followed his directions on courtroom attire. Dark slacks and blazer. Shoes with at most one-inch heels. Blouse with no cleavage. The only thing more choreographed than an Imani concert was an Imani trial.

"Mr. Owens, the prosecution may call its first witness," said Judge Cookson.

To Jack, the calling of the first witness marked the *real* first day of trial. Everything before that was important but without bloodshed, like a war without casualties.

"The state of Florida calls Dr. Harvey Leed," said Owens.

The decision to make the Miami-Dade medical examiner the first witness came as no surprise to the defense. It was important for the jury to understand the forensic basis for the charge of murder. After letting the witness describe his credentials and other preliminaries, the direct examination moved to the cause of death.

"Asphyxiation due to ligature strangulation," said Dr. Leed.

"In layman's terms, what does that mean?"

"A rope closed around the victim's neck, restricting the airways and flow of blood, and depriving the brain of oxygen."

"You understand that the body was recovered from Biscayne Bay, correct?"

"Yes. Chained to a piling."

"Is it your testimony that the victim did not drown?"

"That is my expert opinion," said the witness.

"How did you come to that conclusion?"

Dr. Leed removed his spectacles and wiped them clean, as if shifting from witness to professor. "The first thing you have to understand is that drowning cannot be proven by autopsy. It is a diagnosis of exclusion, based on the circumstances of death."

"Mr. McCormick's death presents some rather grim circumstances."

"Yes, it does. But a dead body underwater does not always mean a drowning. I've seen victims strangled and then thrown into swimming pools."

"Please tell the jury, Doctor: How did your diagnosis by exclusion proceed in the case of Tyler McCormick?"

The witness seemed to take the prosecutor's cue, turning in his chair to speak more directly to the jurors. "The first thing I look for is some sign of life-threatening trauma. If a body is recovered in a lake but there's a hole in the back of the head as big as a hammer, I pretty much rule out drowning."

"In the case of Mr. McCormick, was there sign of life-threatening trauma?"

"Yes. In addition to horizontal ligature marks around the neck, Mr. McCormick's autopsy showed a fracture on the upper-left horn of the thyroid cartilage."

"Were there any other factors that helped you rule out drowning?"

"Yes. When I dissected the lungs, I found no algae, sand, bits of seaweed, seagrass, or other particles commonly floating in Biscayne Bay."

"Why is that important?"

"It's a critically important fact if you think about what happens when you drown. Your normal reaction when the head goes underwater is to hold your breath. Eventually, you can't do it any longer, and your body is forced to gasp for air. That presents a major problem if you can't reach the surface."

"Or if you are chained alive to a piling and the tide is rising."

"Yes. If the victim were alive in that circumstance, he would start gulping water into the mouth and throat, literally inhaling water into the lungs. This, of course, sends the victim into an even more frenzied panic, and the struggle becomes more desperate. If he can't keep his head above water, the lungs continue to fill, resulting in a vicious cycle of struggling and gasping that can last several minutes, until breathing stops."

"And as the victim breathes in the water, his lungs also fill with whatever else is in the water. Do I have that right, Doctor?"

"Exactly right."

"None of which was found in the lungs of Mr. McCormick."

"Correct," said the witness. "Which leads me to conclude that Mr. McCormick was dead before he was chained to the piling."

"How much longer before?"

The witness paused. "That's difficult to determine when a body is found in water, especially water as warm as Biscayne Bay. Water affects the natural rate of decomposition, which complicates the estimation of the time of death."

"Understood," said the prosecutor. "Let me ask the question this way. If I told you that Mr. McCormick's cellphone records show that he last used his cell thirty-eight hours before the recovery of his body, would it be your opinion that he died more than thirty-eight hours or less than thirty-eight hours before the recovery of his body?"

Jack rose. "Objection, Your Honor. Cellphone records are way outside the scope of this witness's medical and forensic expertise."

"Overruled. The witness can estimate time of death."

"I would say that thirty-six to thirty-eight hours would be consistent with my observations as to the condition of the body."

"Thank you," said Owens. "We've covered cause of death and time of death. What is your professional opinion as to manner of death?"

"My conclusion is that the manner of death is homicide."

"How did you conclude it was a homicide?"

"First of all, suicide by ligature strangulation is extremely rare. So the first step is to rule out the possibility that the asphyxiation was due to hanging, which could raise the possibility of suicide."

"In the case of Mr. McCormick, were you able to rule out hanging?"

"Yes. With hanging, there is typically a classic V-shaped bruise running up the neck and behind the ear. It's easy to visualize if you picture a rope tied to the rafters in the garage and the body hanging straight down with toes pointed to the floor. That rope around the neck will be jerked upward from below the chin and running up both sides of the neck and head, thus causing the V-shaped bruise."

"Did Mr. McCormick's body have the V-shaped bruise?"

"No, he had a straight-line bruise from the front of the throat to the back of the neck."

"What does that tell you?"

"It tells me this was not a suicide by hanging. It was a homicide by ligature strangulation, probably from behind."

"Thank you, Dr. Leed. I have no further questions."

The judge looked toward the defense. "Cross-examination, Mr. Swyteck?"

Jack rose, thanked the judge, and approached the witness. There were times to be an assassin in cross-examination, and times not to be. A seasoned trial lawyer knew the difference. It wasn't Jack's goal to make the medical examiner his enemy. His plan was to use him to his client's own benefit. Dr. Leed could be most useful in blunting the hurtful—and potentially salacious—testimony that Jack knew was coming from the state's star witness, FSP inmate Douglas Paxton.

"Dr. Leed, are you familiar with a condition called postmortem erection?"

A few giggles rose from the public gallery. The judge gaveled the courtroom to order.

"Let's keep this respectful, please," said the judge. "Mr. Swyteck, where are you going with this?"

"Judge, Mr. Paxton testified in his deposition that he saw Mr. McCormick's dead body, and that his penis was erect. I'm sure Mr. Paxton will testify the same way later at trial. I want to explore the pathological reasons for that condition with the medical examiner while he is here in the courtroom."

The media section of the gallery came to life, eating it up. Judge Cookson grumbled.

"Mr. Owens, does the prosecution intend to elicit testimony from Mr. Paxton about the victim's penis?"

More giggles, and this time the judge's gavel cracked with added force. "That's enough! If there is anyone is this courtroom who finds the death of Mr. McCormick funny, please leave now!"

The courtroom was still. "No more outbursts," said the judge. "Mr. Owens? Could you answer my question, please?"

"We do intend to elicit that testimony, Your Honor. As I explained in my opening statement, the prosecution will prove that the murder of Mr. McCormick occurred during the performance of deviant sexual activity. In some ways, that theory rises or falls with the erection."

What a choice of words. Somewhere in the back of the courtroom, Jack imagined, the Imani look-alikes were biting their fists.

The judge replied in a begrudging voice. "All right, then. Mr. Swyteck, proceed."

"Thank you, Your Honor. Dr. Leed, let me rephrase my question. In your thirty-plus years as a medical examiner, you've observed the condition commonly referred to as postmortem erection, have you not?"

"Yes, I have."

"And now, Dr. Leed, I'm going to do something no sane trial lawyer ever does. I'm going to ask you a question without knowing what your answer will be. The cases in which you observed postmortem erection involved death by hanging or strangulation. Am I right?"

The witness made Jack wait a few seconds, but the answer was as expected. "Yes."

"In fact, it's not unusual for death by hanging, whether an execution or a suicide, to result in postmortem erection for men. Right?"

"I wouldn't say it's common. But as you say, it's not unusual to observe a more or less complete state of erection of the penis."

"And the same goes for death by strangulation, correct?"

"Less common. But yes, it happens."

"And this complete state of erection occurs even if the man did not engage in any sexually arousing activity prior to his death."

"That's correct," said the doctor. "This engorgement of the genitals is something we see in both men and women."

"Let's consider this phenomenon in the context of this case," said Jack. "You testified that the cause of death was asphyxiation by ligature strangulation. In such a case, does the fact that Mr. McCormick had a postmortem erection indicate to you that he was engaged in sexual activity?"

"I don't know what he was doing."

"Precisely," said Jack. "So, even though Mr. McCormick had a postmortem erection, you can't say that he was engaged in sexual activity at the time of his death, can you, Dr. Leed?"

"No, medically speaking, I cannot."

"You can't even say that he was sexually aroused, can you, Dr. Leed?"

The witness seemed to know that his answer would be helpful to the defense, but there was no way to avoid it. "No. I cannot."

Jack took the win—small, but it was enough. The postmortem erection was the prosecutor's only "evidence" that the victim died while engaged in sexual activity. Jack had left him with none.

"Thank you, Dr. Leed. No further questions."

The judge shifted his gaze to the other end of the defense table. "Ms. Ellis, any cross-examination on behalf of Mr. Nichols?"

"Yes, Judge," said Ellis.

Jack did a double take. The defense had agreed that Jack alone would cross-examine Dr. Leed. It hadn't taken long for Shaky and his lawyer to breach the joint defense agreement.

Ellis stepped forward and placed her notebook on the lectern.

"Dr. Leed, I'd like to turn now to the subject of autoerotic asphyxiation."

The judge shot Jack a look that said, *You can't be serious*—as if it were somehow Jack's fault for having started down this road.

"A word of caution, counsel," the judge said. "I allowed Mr. Swyteck some leeway here, but let's not get too far off-track."

Off-track it was. Jack had considered the autoerotic asphyxiation line of questioning before trial and rejected it. To his dismay, Shaky's lawyer was pursuing it anyway. Objecting to your own co-counsel's questions in front of the jury was never a bright idea. There was nothing Jack could do.

"Understood, Judge," said Ellis. "Dr. Leed, is that term familiar to you?"

"Yes. Essentially, erotic asphyxiation is the practice of strangling yourself, or allowing someone else to strangle you, while masturbating or having sex. The idea is that by restricting the flow of blood through the veins in his neck, blood congests in the brain. Oxygen levels drop, and carbon dioxide levels increase, producing light-headedness that, for some, intensifies erotic pleasure."

"It sounds dangerous."

"It is. People die from it. Most famously, David Carradine, the actor who starred in the old TV show *Kung Fu*."

Jack had researched it, so he was familiar with the Carradine case. He hoped his co-counsel was, too.

"The medical examiner ruled Mr. Carradine's death accidental, am I right?" asked Ellis.

"That's correct."

"In the case of Mr. McCormick, you ruled out suicide. But as Mr. Carradine's case demonstrates, self-strangulation does not necessarily mean homicide, does it? It could be accidental."

"Objection," said Owens, rising. "This case is about the death of Mr. McCormick, not Mr. Carradine."

"Sustained."

Jack hoped the judge's ruling would discourage his co-counsel from taking his abandoned line of questioning any further. His hope was in vain.

"Dr. Leed, in the case of Mr. McCormick, you didn't even consider the possibility of accidental death in the form of self-strangulation, did you? When you ruled out suicide by hanging, you went straight to homicide."

"Objection," said Owens.

"Overruled," the judge said. "The witness shall answer."

Dr. Leed complied. "As I told Mr. Swyteck, suicide by ligature strangulation is extremely rare. Cases of accidental ligature strangulation are just as rare."

"Rare but not impossible," said Ellis.

Dr. Leed paused. "Not impossible, but I stand by my report."

Jack understood that his co-counsel was trying to inject one more element of reasonable doubt—accidental death—into the prosecution's case. But he was well aware of the dangers of the Carradine comparison, and he prayed she wouldn't push it any further.

"We'll leave it at that," she said to Jack's relief. "I have no further questions."

The judge looked to the prosecutor. "Redirect examination, Mr. Owens?"

"Briefly, Judge."

Ellis returned to her seat, obviously thinking she'd scored. Jack tried not to show how worried he was.

The prosecutor took his place before the witness. "Dr. Leed, I have just one question: If Mr. McCormick's death was from self-inflicted injuries—whether accident or suicide—why would someone go to all the trouble of chaining his body to a concrete piling in Biscayne Bay and make it look like the bizarre work of a deranged serial killer?"

It was the gaping hole in the erotic asphyxiation theory, and it was *the* reason Jack had steered clear of it. But Shaky's lawyer had served up the lob, and the prosecutor had smashed it into the forecourt at the jury's feet. Jack had to do something to minimize the impact.

"Move to strike," said Jack. "That's not a proper question to put to a medical examiner. It's pure argument."

"Sustained," said the judge.

Jack appreciated the ruling, but the prosecutor had made his point to the jury simply by asking the question. In the trial lawyer's parlance, the bell had rung, and no ruling by a judge could unring a bell.

"I withdraw the question," said Owens, seemingly satisfied that the bell was still tolling.

CHAPTER 34

Theo made another pass by Judge's flat—not too close, just to see what was going on. Metro Police were gone, but the flat was padlocked and marked as a crime scene. Madeline Coffey had taken his tip seriously.

Two days had passed since Gigi had spooked and bolted. Filing a missing person's report would have been useless. He didn't even know her real name. What would he say, "A runaway ran away from me?"

"Carpenters Arms," he told the taxi driver.

Theo spent the afternoon doing "research" as only the proprietor of Cy's Place could do research. East End pubs had a colorful history, and Theo found it particularly amusing the way so many establishments claimed a connection to Ronald and Reginald Kray, the East End's kings of organized crime in the 1950s and 1960s. The claim by Carpenters Arms, his fourth stop on the pub crawl, was more credible than most. Once upon a time, it was owned by the Kray twins and run by their dear old mum. Somehow over the years the tiny old pub had avoided conversion to flats, and it stood in refurbished splendor at the corner of Cheshire and St. Matthew's Row.

"Try the Greene King IPA or Staropramen lager on draft," the barkeeper told him when he asked for a recommendation.

Theo tried both.

It was dark by the time Theo left the pub, though not nearly as late as it seemed. There was no such thing as 4:30 p.m. sunsets in Miami, and no matter how long he stayed in London, Theo would never get used to just nine hours of daylight. His flat in Bethnal Green was within walking distance. He zipped up his jacket and breathed in the cool night air. Afternoon air.

Whatever.

The walk took him down the old brick streets of Vyner, past the picnic tables outside the Victory Pub, and past the whitewashed buildings spray-painted with gang graffiti. He wasn't drunk, but a few pints made it harder to recognize his neighborhood landmarks. Then he spotted "Smash the Reds" in big, red graffiti letters on the sidewalk, and he knew his flat was just around the corner. He stepped into the zebra crossing and slammed straight into an oncoming pedestrian. It was Gigi.

"There's a man waiting for you in your flat," she whispered. "Behind the front door."

Before Theo could say a word—before he could even react—she was off and running.

"Gigi, wait!"

Theo sprinted after her, trying his best to keep up. Two minutes into the chase, he was digging for a gear he didn't have. He owned socks older than Gigi and, with legs like a gazelle, she was pulling away, the distance expanding between them.

"Gigi!" he called out.

She never looked back, never broke stride. Theo had never logged a five-minute mile in his life, and Gigi was bettering that pace on a cracked and buckled sidewalk. He pulled up at a zebra crossing to catch his breath. In the glow of the streetlight at the end of the block, he caught one last sighting of Gigi as she turned the corner and disappeared. It was no surprise that a girl on the run could run like the wind. Theo hoped she would keep right on running, at least until she got past Somaal Town, where gangs had been known to crack skulls just to protect their turf. Closer to his flat, up around Wadeson Street, was a slightly better area, where a steady increase of trendy clubs and restaurants like Bistroteque and Bethnal Green Working Men's Club drew crowds from all over the city. Theo turned and started walking.

A man waiting behind your front door.

It had to be Judge. He'd come to reclaim his "property," and make sure Theo stayed clear of her. Theo would have something to say about that.

He had a knife holstered to his ankle, a little self-defense he'd acquired after the death threat. The flat next door had a tiny garden outside the front door, and Theo took the liberty of borrowing the six-foot length of chain that the neighbor had hung between two posts to protect the flowers from trampling. With that, Theo's plan was fully formed. First, he had to make his attacker think he was in no condition to put up a fight. Three concrete steps led to his front door, and as he climbed them, he sang the old drinking song made famous in the movie *Jaws*.

"Show me the way to go home . . ."

He was intentionally clumsy in putting one foot in front of the other, scraping his shoes on each of the steps.

"I'm tired and I want to go to bed."

He unsheathed the knife from his ankle holster and tucked it inside his jacket. He gripped one end of the chain tightly, ready to employ it. With his other hand, he aimed the key at the lock, tapping it several times around the metal cylinder, as if he were too drunk to find the slot.

"I had a little drink about an hour ago . . ."

The key slid across the tumblers, the deadbolt clicked. His attacker was probably waiting for the sound of the key sliding out of the lock, so Theo left it right there, adding to his element of surprise.

"And it went right to my—"

On the final lyric—*"Head!"*—Theo turned the handle and shoved the door open with the force of a battering ram, leading with his shoulder, driving with his legs, and putting the entire mass of his six-foot-six frame into the surge. He kept pushing even after the unsuspecting attacker was pinned against wall, to which the only response was the breathless groan of the man trying to get an elephant off his chest.

Theo released the pressure, but only for an instant. In a quick pull-and-push motion, he slammed the door a second time against his target. This time, he heard a bone crack, followed by a blood-curdling scream. Theo flung the door shut and swung the chain as hard as he possibly could. It snapped like a whip against his attacker, knocking him to the floor, where he landed facedown with a thud. Theo pounced on him immediately, burrowed his knee into his spine, smashed his nose into the hardwood floor, and then pressed the knife to the man's throat.

"Don't move!"

Theo wrapped the chain around his neck, jerked the man's hands behind his back, and then tied the other end around his wrists. In seconds, his attacker was hogtied. Only then did Theo notice the pistol on the floor. With a silencer. Theo had knocked it from his hands with the door by barging in unexpectedly. It seemed his attacker was an assassin.

Theo pulled on the chain like a dog leash, lifting the man's head off the ground, choking him. "You're not Judge, are you?"

He struggled to answer. "Not . . . Judge."

The accent sounded Russian. "Who are you?"

He didn't answer.

"Did Kava send you?"

"Go fuck yourself!"

Definitely a Russian accent and, with the silencer, it was clear that Theo was dealing with a professional who wasn't going to break easy. Theo had to adjust his approach and become someone totally off the wall, someone who was way outside any training this hired assassin had received.

Theo pulled the knife from inside his coat and brought it down with full force, stabbing the wood floor less than an inch from the man's nose. Then he pulled tighter on the chain.

"I'm going to ask you some questions. And you are going to give me some answers. You understand?"

"Go—*fff*—"

Theo cut the cursing short with another jerk of the chain. The man groaned, and then Theo let him breathe.

"Here's what I want to know, tough guy. If it's four thirty in the afternoon, and the sun has set, is it night? Or is it day?"

"What?"

The tip of the knife was still embedded in the floorboard. Theo yanked it free and pressed the steel blade against the man's throat. "Listen to me. This is very important. It gets dark really fucking early here, and it's making me crazy. When I get crazy, I do crazy things. So help me out here. If it's dark before it's evening, is it nighttime? Or is it still daytime?"

"Huh?"

"The evening news doesn't come on until five. How can it be night before the evening news? It's still the day, right?"

"Uhm, I don't know."

"I need an answer!"

His voice shook. "Yeah, you're right! It's day!"

Theo jerked the chain. "It's fucking dark! How can it be day?"

"Oh . . . kay," he said, groaning. "It's night!"

Theo stabbed the floor again, this time even closer to his nose. "It's four thirty! How can it be night!"

"Stop! You're a crazy man! What do you want me to say?"

Theo jerked the chain. "Who sent you?"

The man struggled for air. Theo gave him some slack, which allowed him to speak.

"Did you really think you could kidnap Sergei Kava?" the man said.

Theo wanted answers about the blood he'd seen at Judge's flat—answers he knew he'd never get from Madeline Coffey.

"Did you kill Sergei's driver?"

No answer. Theo choked him with another jerk of the chain, then released the tension just enough for the man to answer.

"The coward stuck a pistol in his mouth. No need to kill him."

"What about Amongus?"

"Who?"

Theo gave the chain another tug. "Amongus Sicario."

Before he could answer, there was a knock at the door, which startled both men. Theo ignored it, but another knock followed and it was more of a pounding.

"Open up! It's the police!"

Theo didn't answer. "Quiet," he whispered to his attacker.

The same officer spoke. "Your neighbor reported a disturbance. Is everything all right?"

Theo had three options. Answer and let them in. Answer and tell them to go away. Ignore them and hope they would just leave.

"The key is in the lock," said the officer.

Theo had left it there.

"If you can hear me, stand away from the door. We are going to open it."

That eliminated option three. If he answered and sent them away, what would he do with the Russian hit man? Kill him in cold blood? Even if he did, Sergei Kava would send a replacement to finish the job.

"I'll be there in one minute," Theo said in a voice loud enough for the police to hear.

He checked to make sure the Russian was securely chained, then rose and stepped toward the door, thinking about how to explain.

"There was an intruder," Theo said through the closed door. "I took care of him, he's still alive, but you'll see him as soon as you open—"

The door flew open. Uniformed police officers charged into the flat and took Theo to the floor. In seconds, Theo was facedown beside the Russian, with hands cuffed behind his waist.

"He brought me here to kill me!" the Russian shouted. "The gun is his!"

"That's a lie!" shouted Theo.

"He's a kidnapper!" said the Russian.

"Quiet!" the officer said. "We need to sort this out. Now, which one of you knobs stole the neighbor's chain?"

Theo could hardly believe his ears. Seriously? They wanted to know about the stupid chain around his neighbor's flower garden?

"That would be me," said Theo.

CHAPTER 35

Wednesday morning. The courtroom was exactly as they had left it. Only the faces in the packed public gallery had changed.

Jack knew what the prosecution's next witness was going to tell the jury, having deposed him. Still, it stuck in his craw to hear Florida Department of Corrections Inmate No. M60795 swear to tell "the truth, the whole truth, and nothing but the truth."

"Good morning, Mr. Paxton," the prosecutor said.

"Mornin'," said the witness.

While criminal defendants have the right to wear civilian clothes for court appearances, inmates do not, so it came as no surprise to Jack that Paxton's testimony began with an explanation of the orange jumpsuit and an acknowledgment that he was a convicted felon. With that baggage out of the way, the prosecutor let Shaky Nichols's former bodyguard tell his story. There was one important detail, however, that Jack was determined to keep out. It came up about twenty minutes into the testimony.

"What did Mr. Nichols tell you to do with Mr. McCormick's body?" asked the prosecutor.

"He wanted me to get rid of it."

"Did he give you any instructions?"

"Yeah. He was real specific like."

"What did he say, specifically?"

"He said put the body in the boat and head out to this spot in Biscayne Bay where there's a bunch of old concrete pilings sticking out of the water."

"Isola di Lolando?"

"I don't know what it's called. Mr. Nichols gave me the GPS coordinates, and I went there."

"Did you do that?"

"Yeah."

"What did he tell you to do once you got there?"

"He said when it was low tide, I should chain the body to one of the pilings."

"Did you do that?"

"Yeah."

"Did he tell you to do anything to the body before you chained it to the piling?"

"Yeah. He gave me a black marker pen and told me to write a message on the stomach."

"What message did he tell you to write?"

"Goodbye girl."

"Did you write the message?"

"Yeah, I did."

The prosecutor stepped away from the lectern, as if he needed more room to set up his big question.

"So Mr. Nichols gave you these detailed instructions: take the body out to the bay, wait for low tide, chain it to a piling, write the message 'goodbye girl' in black marker pen. Did Mr. Nichols tell you *why* he wanted you to do all these things?"

Jack rose. "Your Honor, I'm concerned the question will elicit inadmissible evidence. May we have a sidebar?"

The judge waved the lawyers forward. They gathered at the side of the bench farthest away from the jury so that they could confer without being overheard. Jack explained his objection.

"Judge, when I deposed Mr. Paxton, he testified that he had no idea why Mr. Nichols told him to do those things and that all he could say was what Mr. Nichols told him."

The prosecutor interjected. "If Mr. Swyteck is making a hearsay objection, it's frivolous. Mr. Nichols is a defendant in this case. Any incriminating statements he made to Mr. Paxton are admissible as evidence."

Jack pushed back. "If Mr. Nichols had incriminated *himself* with his own statement, I would not be making this objection. But the testimony here will be that Mr. Nichols told Mr. Paxton that the whole plan was cooked up by my client—that 'it was all her idea.'"

The judge seemed to get it, and Jack continued to press his point.

"I filed a pretrial motion asking for a separate trial for Ms. Nichols. This court denied the motion because the defendants were not presenting inconsistent defenses by pointing the finger at each other. If you allow the prosecution to inject this testimony into evidence, we will have exactly that: one defendant blaming the other. I will have no choice but to move for a mistrial. Then we can start all over again—with separate trials for each defendant."

"Judge, that's a 'sky is falling' argument if I ever heard one," said the prosecutor.

The judge shook his head. "Mr. Owens, we are not going to have two trials, and I have no intention of starting all over again."

"But, Judge—"

"No *buts*. You can withdraw your question and play it safe, or you can live dangerously and let the witness answer. But if the witness volunteers that Mr. Nichols blamed Ms. Nichols for the whole scheme, I am going to declare a mistrial. And I am *not* going to be very happy with you. Proceed accordingly."

The lawyers returned to their places. Jack wasn't entirely sure that his argument was right under the law, or that the judge had made the right ruling, but it had carried the day. On the other hand, Jack was absolutely certain that the witness had been primed to blurt out "it was all Imani's idea," whether or not it was true. The prosecutor was between a rock and hard place.

Owens stood at the lectern, silent, as he weighed his options.

Imani leaned closer to Jack and whispered, "What's happening?"

Jack was suddenly thinking of his old mentor at the Freedom Institute, Neil Goderich, and something Neil used to say about prosecutors who built their case on the testimony of a convicted felon who had cut himself a deal.

Jack whispered back, "When the prosecutor reaches into the sewer, rarely does a swan end up on the witness stand."

"What does that mean?" asked Imani.

"Watch."

The prosecutor closed his notebook. "I withdraw the question. Nothing further for this witness."

Maybe the prosecutor was simply making a tactical decision and playing it safe. Maybe he—like Jack—had come around to the view that 'it was all Imani's idea' was a bald-faced lie offered up by an inmate in hopes of a nice letter from the prosecutor to the parole board. Either way, Jack took the win.

The judge looked toward the defense table. "Any cross-examination, Mr. Swyteck?"

Jack rose. "Yes, Your Honor."

Jack positioned himself in front of the witness, feet apart and shoulders squared, full eye contact. It was the "control posture," the body language of a trial lawyer that denied wiggle room during cross-examination.

"Mr. Paxton, I'm going to ask you a few questions that can be answered yes or no. First, on the night you claim to have met with Mr. Nichols and talked about what to do with the body, you never saw Imani Nichols, did you?"

"No."

"You didn't talk to her on the phone, text her, or communicate with her in any other way. Did you?"

"No."

"Did you speak to Imani Nichols at any time before that night?"

"No."

"Did you speak to Imani Nichols at any time after that night?"

"I probably ran into her at some point as Mr. Nichols's bodyguard. I might have said 'hello' or 'good afternoon.'"

"Other than an occasional 'hello' or 'good afternoon,' have you ever spoken to Imani Nichols about anything?"

"No."

Jack could have ripped into him about his criminal history and the possibility of a deal between him and the prosecutor. But the fact of the matter was, his testimony had implicated only one defendant.

"No further questions," said Jack, and he returned to his seat.

"Ms. Ellis?" the judge said. "Cross-examination?"

"May I have a moment to check my notes?" she asked, and then she dropped her notepad. It fell at Jack's feet, but as she and Jack reached down simultaneously to pick it up, their heads dipping below the table-top, it became apparent that the drop had been intentional.

"If there's a bad guy here, it's your client, not mine," she said. "You're going to regret this."

"Ms. Ellis, last chance," said the judge. "Do you have cross-examination?"

She picked up her notepad, and then rose to address the court. "I have nothing at this time," she said.

She threw one last set of dagger eyes at Jack, as if to underscore the last three words.

At this time.

CHAPTER 36

A white transit van with the blue-and-yellow markings of the London Metropolitan Police stopped outside the Bethnal Green station house in Victoria Park Square. The sign posted at the curb read POLICE VEHICLES ONLY, but the heavy-gauge steel post was bent over at a forty-five-degree angle from an earlier mishap of some sort, and the sign itself was defaced with gang graffiti. It was Theo's second visit to a police station in as many weeks, and from the very first impression, he knew he was no longer in Covent Garden.

"In you go," the sergeant said, and a team of uniformed officers whisked Theo and the Russian up the steps and into the station house.

The lobby was straight out of cop-show classics: uniformed police officers coming and going, a couple of handcuffed gangbangers still seething over an unresolved territorial dispute, a drunk with a handkerchief to his bloody nose, and a homeless guy with vomit all over his shoes sitting on the end of a long wooden bench. Two officers took the Russian down the hall. The sergeant led Theo in the opposite direction, past the nightly circus and around the corner to an interrogation room.

It was just Theo, the sergeant, and another officer in the small, brightly lit room. Theo sat on one side of the rectangular table. The sergeant stood by the window on the other side of the table, and the patrol officer guarded the door. Theo wondered if anyone else was watching or listening from behind the one-way observation mirror on the wall. It wasn't as scary as the time a fifteen-year-old Theo had been hauled in for questioning about the shooting of a convenience store clerk in Miami, but he assumed this wasn't about the theft of a garden chain.

The door opened, and another officer entered with a bag of takeaway food. He handed it to the sergeant and left.

"Hungry?" asked the sergeant as he took a seat at the table opposite Theo.

Theo smiled. "Damn, I almost forgot it was the Brits who invented good-cop/bad-cop."

He laughed. "Nothing to do with that. Just dinnertime."

The sergeant opened the sack and started eating. It smelled like curry. He ate in silence. The guard stood at the door, saying nothing. It was as if they were waiting for Theo to start talking. Theo knew better, and not just because his best friend was a criminal defense lawyer.

They waited for twenty minutes. The sergeant stuffed the paper plates and plastic utensils into the brown sack and pitched the trash into the metal can in the corner.

Theo broke the silence. "At some point, I'll need to use the—whatever you call it here. WC?"

The sergeant checked his watch. "Is it an emergency?"

"Not yet."

"Then hold it. She should be here any minute."

"She who?" asked Theo.

There was a knock, and the door opened. In walked the FBI's legal attaché from the U.S. embassy, Madeline Coffey. She took a seat beside the sergeant and looked across the table at Theo.

"Bet you didn't plan to see me again, did you, Mr. Knight?"

"Nope."

"I have good news and bad news," she said.

"Another British invention," said the sergeant.

"What?" asked the attaché.

"Nothing," said Theo. "Go on."

"The good news is, you're somewhat of a hero, Mr. Knight."

"A hero?"

"Yes. The name of the man taken into custody with you is Starikova. He was known as the Butcher of Bucha in the early stages of Russia's war with Ukraine. Bucha is a small town outside Kiev where the Russians set up an interrogation center for prisoners of war. Starikova is part of a bloodthirsty private militia called Wagner Group. It's run by Vladimir Kava."

"So, killing me was his side job?"

"The point is that Starikova is wanted for war crimes. Thanks to you, he is now in custody and will stand trial."

"Is he also going to stand trial for the murder of Sergei's driver and Amongus Sicario?"

"Those are active investigations. We can't comment."

It was the response Theo had expected. "There's nothing to thank me for. He came here to kill me for kidnapping Sergei Kava—which I had nothing to do with. All I did was fight back."

"Whether thanks are due or not, that is the good news. Self-defense is not a crime in this country. You are free to go."

"Go where?"

"That is the question," she said. "Which leads me to the bad news. You may have shaken the Butcher of Bucha, but you would be foolish to assume that his capture is the end of your troubles."

"I assume the opposite. There will be someone to take his place, and Kava will only be more pissed at me for taking out one of his key men."

"Yes," she said. "Which brings me to the even worse news."

"Ah," said the sergeant. "That must be an American twist on our British invention."

The attaché glanced at the Brit, confused.

"Never mind him," said Theo. "What's the even worse news?"

"Our intelligence sources tell us that Lyudmila Mironov has entered the UK."

"Who?"

The attaché opened a folder and slid a glossy photograph across the table for Theo to see. It was a color headshot.

"A woman?" asked Theo.

"Yes."

Theo took a better look. She had a boyish haircut with bangs down to her large, dark eyes. She seemed smug in the picture, her smile all lips.

"What's her story?" asked Theo.

"Both she and Starikova are highly paid mercenaries in Kava's private militia. Both were recruited from the ranks of the real Russian army. Starikova's specialty is torture. Mironov is a sniper."

"Is that unusual?" asked Theo. "A female sniper in the Russian army?"

"Not really. Russia has a long history of female snipers. They took out twelve thousand German soldiers in the Second World War. Pavilchenko was the most famous. Over three hundred confirmed kills."

"How many kills does this Mironov have?"

"At least forty that we know of. More that we don't."

Theo took another look at the headshot. "What am I supposed to do now?"

The legal attaché was silent. The sergeant had no more jokes.

"That's what I thought you'd say," said Theo.

"I do have one suggestion," said the attaché. "Don't go back to your flat. Get a new one. Better yet, get out of the country. As soon as possible."

"I take it the rules haven't changed. I'm on my own?"

The attaché glanced uneasily at the police officers, as if not entirely comfortable taking this conversation any further in their presence. "Let me walk you out, Mr. Knight."

She rose, and Theo followed her out of the interrogation room and into the indistinct clatter and noise of the station house. She spoke as they walked down the hallway and through the lobby.

"I wish I could tell you that we have an armed escort to take you straight to the airport in a bulletproof SUV, and that we're putting you on a plane tonight. But that's not going to happen."

"Why not?"

"The official position of the U.S. government is that our law enforcement agencies do not tolerate, let alone reward, extraction kidnappings to facilitate extradition. In matters of international affairs, your participation in the extraction kidnapping of Sergei Kava makes you, in a word, toxic. It requires us to keep our distance."

"I didn't participate."

"That may be the reality. That's not the perception. And I don't have to tell you which one matters."

They stopped at the entrance doors, still in the lobby, just short of leaving the station. "I'm going now. Please wait a few minutes before you step outside."

"I got just one favor to ask," said Theo.

"No," she said. "I put my career at risk by getting the kidnapping charges dropped. I further put my career at risk just now by sharing intelligence with you about Mironov's whereabouts. That's all the favors I can do. Take care of yourself."

"The favor isn't for me," said Theo. "It's for a teenage girl. A runaway."

"You're out of favors."

She took a half step closer, so close that it made Theo uncomfortable. And then he felt something slipping into his hand.

"Except this one," she whispered.

Theo took it, then glanced discreetly at her offering. It was a U.S. passport.

"Like I told you," the attaché said. "Take care of yourself. *Ivan*."

The attaché turned and left the station house, hurried down the front steps, and disappeared into the Mercedes waiting at the curb.

Theo checked the passport. Everything about it was authentic, including his photograph. His name was Ivan Walker.

As the Mercedes pulled away, he watched through the glass door, sure of one thing. That was the last he would ever see of Madeline Coffey.

CHAPTER 37

Jack wondered where he stood. With his wife.

Too much time had passed since his trip to London and the heated phone conversation with Andie. He'd been busy. She'd been busy. But everything they'd said to each other was still just "out there," with no resolution.

Things had felt less than perfect, even before his trip to London. Worst of all, Jack couldn't put his finger on what the problem was. With his first marriage, the failings had been obvious. He'd married a pathological liar. This was . . . a fog. Jack knew that the pressures of their careers and parenting led to a different focus in their marriage, but he never thought that he and Andie would be one of those couples whose love story just peters out. "Date night" and "sex night" weren't solutions. They were Band-Aids. So, when Andie proposed "dance night," it caught him off guard.

"Dance night?" asked Jack. He was alone in his office, reviewing documents and preparing his cross-examination of the next witness. Dinner was on its way from Uber Eats.

"Yes," said Andie. "Tonight is dance night."

Jack didn't know quite what to make of it. Was this another Band-Aid, a way of sweeping things under the rug? Or was it her way of waltzing into a much-needed, deeper conversation?

"I know you're in trial, but it's one hour, Jack. It'll be good for you. It'll be good for us."

She wasn't guilting him into it or imposing it on him. It would have taken one colossal jerk to say no.

"Sure. What's the plan?"

The plan was perfect. They met at Cy's Place. Uncle Cy was in on it. He seated them at a little, round table that Cy liked to say was "perfect for lovebirds, big enough for two cocktails and two pair of elbows." Cy's club didn't always have live music on weeknights, but what good was "dance night" without live music? The musicians were older than Theo might have booked, but most of Cy's contacts had gone on to work that great gig in the sky, so he'd done the best he could. They played tunes that were meant for dancing, at least in Cy's book, and after twenty minutes of holding hands and moving across the floor to Gershwin, Jack and Andie needed a break, and the octogenarian orchestra was ready for oxygen. Andie went to the "little girl's room," and Cy brought two fresh cocktails to Jack at their table.

"What do you hear from your nephew?" asked Jack.

"Nothin' since Halloween. Been two weeks now."

"Are you worried?"

"Should I be?"

Jack doubted the old man knew the full extent of the danger. "Theo can take care of himself."

Andie returned, and Cy retreated to bring refreshments to the boys in the band.

"What are you smiling at?" asked Andie.

She'd caught him staring. "It's weird," said Jack.

"What's weird?"

Jack had witnessed a good many "Andie transformations" over the course of their marriage, all connected to her undercover work for the bureau. The blonde and blue-eyed Andie who'd donned a wig and contact lenses to infiltrate a neo-Nazi organization. The henna-tattooed Andie who'd "joined" a cult. But it was the little things, not the huge makeovers, that made him smile—like the way she'd brushed her dance-swept hair into silky perfection.

"Guys go to the bathroom, and they go to the bathroom. Women go to the bathroom, and they come out looking like a million bucks."

"One of the world's great unsolved mysteries. Right up there with 'where is Cleopatra's tomb?'"

Jack tasted his drink. Strong. He'd have to nurse this one. It was back to work after Cy's Place.

"Are we ever going to finish the conversation we started when I was in London?" he asked, choosing the word "conversation" advisedly.

"It's finished."

"It didn't feel finished."

"I figured out the solution."

Jack was taken aback. "Are you going to tell me what it is?"

"Yes. When your trial is over."

"Why are we putting this off?"

"Because the conflict of interest between your trial and my investigation is real. Until that conflict goes away, we can't say the things that need to be said."

"Then what's up with tonight?"

"A reminder."

He waited for her to say more, and if she thought he was enjoying the way she was forcing him to pull it out of her, she was mistaken. "A reminder of what?"

"That we have something worth fighting for. Not just about."

Jack smiled uneasily. It was too Pollyanna for Andie, and it made him worry about the unilateral "solution" she was holding close to the vest. "It's great to hear you say that. Really great. I feel the same way. But—"

"But what?"

"Look, I'll be the first to concede: you're smarter than I am. But that doesn't mean you should figure out all the answers without me."

"When I say I have the solution, it's a proposal, Jack. Not a mandate."

"The 'solution' depends on how you define the 'problem.' I'm just not sure the clash between our careers is the only thing we need to sort out."

"What do you mean?"

She seemed genuinely confused, which wasn't the reaction he'd expected. He was testing the waters, to see if she'd been feeling the same "fog" he was feeling. Apparently not. Jack wished he hadn't raised it.

"Never mind. I like your approach better. Tonight should be about what's right between us."

Andie arched an eyebrow. "Never mind?" she said, having none of his tap dance. "If there's something else wrong, I want to know."

"There's nothing."

"There must be something, or you wouldn't have said it."

Her point was irrefutable, and it put Jack in backpedaling mode. He wasn't prepared to discuss amorphous feelings—or loss of feelings—he couldn't explain, especially if he alone was experiencing them and, now that he'd brought it up, Andie was not going to let it go. He dug deep for a "problem" that wasn't real, just to have something to say.

"I just want to make sure none of this has anything to do with the stunt Imani pulled in the courtroom."

"Imani? Please," she said, groaning. "Like I'm threatened by the ultimate pick-me girl."

"You know that term—'pick-me girl'?"

"Well, yeah. The hashtag has over two billion hits on TikTok. At least that's what the online-bullying bulletin from Righley's school said."

Jack was starting to feel like a social media dinosaur, but he was happy to take the conversation in a different direction. "It's weird you call her that. Imani says my opposing counsel is a pick-me girl."

"If Imani is calling anyone a pick-me girl, all I can say is that it takes one to know one."

"Imani is a pick-me girl?"

"Oh, my God, Jack. Do you know anything at all about your client?"

"Apparently not."

"She was married to Shaky Nichols."

"Well, I know that much."

"Shaky was almost as bad as Harvey Weinstein. He was so gross, and she not only defended him, but she married him. All to advance her career. 'Pick me, Shaky, pick me.'"

"If she was trying to advance her career, it backfired. He screwed her over on the master recordings contract."

"Of course he did. I love Imani's music, and she's an amazing performer. But no one ever said being a pick-me girl was a smart move."

Andie's cellphone vibrated on the table. She glanced at it, and then her eyes met Jack's.

"Go ahead," said Jack. "It's a weeknight."

She took the phone and stepped away from the table. Jack's gaze drifted across the club toward the bar, where Theo should have been. Then his thoughts turned to Shaky, the Harvey Weinstein of the music industry. He tried to fight it off, but he was on the slippery slope back into work mode.

Andie returned, and the glow of her earlier visit to the ladies' room had evaporated.

"I'm so sorry, Jack. I have to go to the field office."

He didn't ask what for. He knew better.

"It's okay. I can Uber. This was fun."

She took the car keys and kissed him goodbye. "So, dance night is a keeper?"

He smiled, but it only masked the guilt he felt for having alluded to problems beyond their clash of careers. "You bet," he said.

She kissed him again, a little longer than just goodbye, and hurried toward the door.

Cy came to the table and took her seat. "My boys are here for another forty-five minutes."

Jack raised his cocktail and clicked glasses with Cy. "Let the band play on," he said, still wondering what Andie's "solution" was.

Andie's meeting was in the first-floor conference room of the Miami field office. The Miami ASAC was with her, along with an IT specialist. A tech agent from the Boston field office and a computer forensic examiner from the FBI's New England Regional Computer Forensics Laboratory joined by video conference. The tech agent's voice was on the speaker, but Andie couldn't see him. He was sharing his computer screen in Boston on the LCD in Miami. On it were the results from the FBI's search of all electronic devices owned by Boston's most recent victim of homicide, Shannon Dwyer.

"At first, we thought Agent Henning's music piracy theory just didn't hold water," said the Boston agent. "We searched the victim's cellphone and tablet. Nothing. We checked the computer she sometimes used at work. Nothing. We even checked her boyfriend's devices. Still nothing."

"And then?" asked Andie, hanging on his opening words "at first."

"Then we discovered that Shannon sometimes visited a certain internet café in Cambridge. And it almost gets funny."

"Funny?" said Andie.

"Yeah, well, funny from a tech standpoint. I can't tell you the number of people who go to an internet café to run searches or send emails 'anonymously' with a temporary username. That can be done, of course. But not if you pay the internet café with a credit card linked to your name. Which is what Shannon did."

"So you were able to link certain internet activity to Shannon based on the credit card records?" said Andie.

"Exactly. And that's when we hit paydirt."

The LCD screen blipped in Miami, and then it changed to a new image shared from Boston. It was line after line of white code against a blue background.

"What am I looking at?" asked Andie.

"Shannon Dwyer's browsing history at the internet café," the agent said. "I presume she didn't want to risk infecting her own devices with malware, or worse, when getting free music, TV shows, and movies."

"These are all piracy websites?" asked Andie.

"Every single one of them," said the tech agent. "It looks like your hunch was right, Henning."

The ASAC looked at Andie. "Right about what?"

The Miami office had more than a hundred agents, but just three ASACs. All three had been hyperfocused on one of the largest sting operations in the history of the Miami office. That left no time to hear every angle Andie was pursuing in a homicide investigation for which, as yet, primary responsibility lay with the Boston police.

"Let me tell you the story of a tiny island in Boston Harbor called Nixes Mate," said Andie.

CHAPTER 38

The trial resumed Thursday morning.

Jack liked the way things were going so far, with the only admissible evidence of guilt pointing to Shaky alone, and even that was "shaky." Despite her "under the table" threat to Jack—"If there's a bad guy here, it's your client, not mine"—Shaky's lawyer had not yet turned against Imani and tried to make her into the bad guy. *Yet*. Jack wondered if she was just keeping her powder dry.

"The state of Florida calls Deacon Betters," announced the prosecutor.

Betters was dressed in a sharply tailored designer suit, a light blue shirt with French cuffs, and a red Hermès necktie. The cost of his gold cuff links alone probably exceeded the average juror's weekly salary. Betters was one of many witnesses whose name was on the state's list, but who had not testified before the grand jury. What Jack knew about him had come from his client.

"Mr. Betters, what do you do for a living?" the prosecutor began.

"I am a senior investment banker in the New York office of Saxton Silvers."

"Have you ever met either of the defendants in this case?"

"I know Mr. Nichols. I have never met his ex-wife."

The response was consistent with what Imani had told Jack, which came as a relief. Jack's quick glance to his right, however, confirmed that Shaky's lawyer was anything but relieved.

"When did you first meet Mr. Nichols?"

"Twelve or thirteen years ago. Mr. Nichols was the chief executive officer of EML Records at the time."

"Was that before or after the death of Mr. Tyler McCormick?"

"Before."

The time frame was right, but Jack still had no idea how the prosecutor intended to establish the relevance of this witness's testimony. For the moment, he held his objections.

"How did you come to meet Mr. Nichols?" asked the prosecutor.

"EML Records was in serious financial distress. Mr. Nichols reached out to Saxton Silvers to explore the possibility of selling the company. I presented a plan to him, and EML Records engaged us."

"Engaged you to do what?" asked the prosecutor.

"I identified several potential buyers. Mostly large private equity firms. Saxton Silvers structured a blind auction. Each potential buyer submitted a sealed bid stating how much over market price they were willing to pay on a per-share basis. The highest bidder would be the winner."

"What does that investment term mean, 'over market price on a per-share basis'?"

"EML Records was listed on the NASDAQ as a publicly traded company. Its shares had a price established by the market. To get control of the company, a buyer would have to pay a premium over market value. So, the bid might be 'two dollars over market value.' Or three dollars. Whatever the buyer was willing to bid after conducting its own due-diligence review of the company's financial records."

The prosecutor turned the page in his notepad. "You mentioned that EML Records was in financial distress at this time. What was the nature of that financial distress?"

"EML shares were down thirty-six percent over the previous fiscal year. Forty-eight percent over the last two years. Mr. Nichols's choice was either sell or file for bankruptcy."

"What was the cause of this precipitous decline in stock value?"

"In a word: piracy."

The word had popped into Jack's head before the witness had answered. This seemingly irrelevant testimony was suddenly hitting closer to home.

"Can you elaborate?" asked the prosecutor.

"Sure. This time period was the height of music piracy. Rather than pay for music, consumers went to piracy websites and got their music for free under the peer-to-peer, or P2P, file-trading platforms. It was illegal, but it was an epidemic. P2P is largely outdated now. But piracy still costs the movie and music industries about two hundred fifty billion dollars each year. Back ten or twelve years ago, it was even worse."

"Was Mr. Nichols's company affected by the piracy epidemic?"

"Absolutely. More than most labels."

"Why was that?"

"Most companies have two major lines of business, licensing and recording. Song licensing for movies, TV shows, and commercials was unaffected by piracy. Only consumer sales for recorded music were down. Most companies stayed profitable because of licensing revenue. But EML's licensing was done by a separate company, EML Licensing, Inc."

"Did Mr. Nichols have any stake in the licensing company?"

"No. Licensing was a completely separate company with its own NASDAQ ticker symbol, its own shareholders, and its own management. Mr. Nichols's compensation was tied strictly to the performance of EML Records, which was very well run, but it was getting killed by piracy."

"Did Saxton Silvers do any valuations of EML Records prior to the auction?"

"Yes."

"What value did Saxton Silvers put on the company?"

"Two-point-three billion dollars."

"And that valuation took into account the ravaging effects of piracy, correct?"

"Yes."

The prosecutor flipped to the next page of his notes. "Mr. Betters, let me ask you now about Mr. Nichols's personal stake in EML Records. Did he own any stock?"

"He held stock options."

"Did he stand to profit from the sale of EML Records?"

"Not at this price," he said, scoffing.

"What do you mean?" the prosecutor asked.

"An option is the right to buy stock at a stated price. Mr. Nichols's option price was set before piracy wiped out almost fifty percent of the company's value. His option price was higher than the market price."

"In other words, his stock options were worthless?"

"That's correct," said the witness.

"But let's say piracy suddenly stopped, and the company regained that forty-eight percent loss in value. How much would Mr. Nichols stand to make in that situation?"

Jack rose. "Objection, Your Honor. Mr. Betters is a fact witness, not an expert. The prosecution cannot put hypothetical questions to a fact witness."

Owens fired back. "Judge, I'm not asking the witness for an expert *opinion*. This is simple math. What would the value of Mr. Nichols's stock options have been if the value of the company had not declined by forty-eight percent due to piracy?"

"The objection is overruled," said the judge. "The witness can answer."

"About a hundred million dollars," said Betters.

Owens stepped away from the lectern and placed his notepad on the table, but he wasn't finished. He returned to the gooseneck microphone, formulating one last question in his head.

"Mr. Betters, would it be fair to say that in this time frame—right before the sale of EML Records and right before the death of Tyler McCormick—Mr. Nichols had every motivation to do *something* to stop piracy? Maybe even something drastic?"

"Objection," the defense lawyers said in unison.

Jack thought the judge might allow the witness to answer, given his prior rulings. But he drew the line here.

"Sustained," the judge said.

The ruling didn't seem to faze the prosecutor in the least. "No further questions, Your Honor."

Owens glanced in Jack's direction as he returned to his seat. Their gaze met and held for a moment, and it was as if they were thinking the same thing: for a second time, the prosecutor had rung the proverbial bell—the one that could not be unrung.

"Mr. Swyteck, cross-examination?" the judge asked.

The prosecutor's entire theory of the case had pivoted from kinky sex to good, old-fashioned greed, and Jack needed to recalibrate.

"Judge, I'd like fifteen minutes to confer with my client, if I may."

Shaky's lawyer was also on her feet. "Same, Judge."

"I think our jurors could use twenty," he said with a smile, and all six nodded in agreement. The judge excused them, and they filed out the side door.

"This court is in recess," he said, and with a final bang of his gavel the twenty-minute clock was ticking.

The bailiff's command brought all to their feet. Judge Cookson exited to his chambers, and the courtroom silence was broken. The media was at the rail, and the clogged center aisle made the rear exit unreachable. Jack and Imani took the side door and hurried toward a small, window-less conference room across the hall from Judge Cookson's chambers. It was slightly larger than a closet, furnished only with a small table and two chairs, which was fine, until Shaky's lawyer knocked on the door and insisted on a joint defense meeting. She was boiling mad, and Jack feared that if he turned her away, she'd vent to the press. There was room for four with the lawyers standing.

"What kind of shit are you and your client feeding the prosecution, Swyteck?"

Calling her paranoid would have been counterproductive. "This is not the time to turn against each other," said Jack.

"You already made that turn. Yesterday, in open court, when you linked Shaky's bodyguard to my client and completely distanced him from yours."

"Those are helpful facts for Imani. You can't expect me to just ignore them."

"I get that. I was angry at you in the courtroom, but I really do under stand. But today's attack on Shaky over the sale of EML Records and music piracy is different. Somebody put that idea in his head."

"And by *somebody*, you mean me?" asked Jack.

"Something is going on behind the scenes," said Ellis. "It's clear enough where Owens is going with this new theory, and one thing is crystal clear. He's going after Shaky, not *her*."

The use of a pronoun in such cramped quarters only emphasized how angry Ellis was—too angry even to say her name.

"Listen to me!" said Imani, and then she looked straight at her ex-husband. "If I wanted to paint a target on your back, Jack would have told the prosecutor that Tyler McCormick was stalking me."

Her words left the tiny room silent. It was as if they had all suddenly realized that they'd lost sight of the forest for the trees.

"Imani makes a good point," said Jack. "It was a relief to me when Owens laid out the rough sex theory in his opening statement. Getting rid of a stalker is a much stronger motive to commit murder and make it look like something it wasn't by disposing of the body in such a bizarre way."

"Except that we didn't kill him because he was stalking Imani," said Shaky.

Jack had heard the denials from his client, but this one left him a little confused. Shaky's lawyer seemed to appreciate the need for clarification.

"I think what Shaky meant is that he and Imani didn't kill Tyler McCormick. Period. For any reason. He wasn't suggesting that they killed him for some other reason."

"I get it," said Jack.

"Good," said Ellis. "It's an important point."

Imani checked her watch. "We have five minutes to get back in the courtroom. What have we accomplished? Nothing."

"I wouldn't say nothing," said Shaky. "We know the prosecutor has dumped the lovers' triangle theory. Instead, he's bringing in music piracy."

"He hasn't dropped anything," said Jack. "There's no reason two motives can't be in play at the same time."

"I don't see how the two relate here," said Shaky.

Jack's response was to the group, but he directed it mostly to Shaky. "You have to remember there are two separate crimes and two different questions. First question: Why did Mr. McCormick end up dead? Owens's answer is that the victim was having sex with your wife in ways that you probably never did. That's enough to make any man angry. If that man is already at the end of his rope, about to lose a hundred million dollars in the sale of EML Records, maybe he snapped. He killed the guy and put his body on a post so the fish can eat it."

"Do you think that's what today's testimony is about?" asked Imani. "Shaky snapped?"

"It could be. But I don't think so."

"Why not?" asked Shaky.

"The prosecutor's last question is key. He isn't painting a picture of a desperate husband who snapped. That last question implied that Shaky had a very clearheaded motive to do *something* to stop piracy."

Shaky scoffed. "How the hell would killing Tyler McCormick stop piracy?"

"Maybe that's not the right question," said Jack. "A better question might be how would putting a dead body on a piling in the bay stop piracy."

"I have no idea what you're talking about, Jack," Imani said.

"The second crime in the indictment is mutilation of a corpse. That raises a separate question: Why did the body end up chained to a concrete piling? The narrative so far is that you staged the body to make it look like the work of a bizarre serial killer or a cult. To make the crime look like something it wasn't. But maybe the point was to make the victim look exactly like *who* he was."

"I still don't get it," said Imani.

"Is it possible that Tyler McCormick was operating a piracy website?" asked Jack.

"Oh, yeah," said Shaky, sarcastic. "He's another Vladimir Kava. In fact, after Imani and I strangled him, we thought about just hanging him off the side of his superyacht, but we went with the concrete piling."

"Fair point," said Jack. "The victim here is no oligarch. But maybe the prosecutor's theory is that Tyler McCormick was a Vladimir Kava wannabe. Or was operating at some middle or low level in the Kava empire."

"Meaning what?"

"Meaning that the murder of Tyler McCormick was a way of sending a threat to Mr. Kava."

"What kind of threat?" asked Imani, adding a nervous chuckle. "That there's a pirate killer on the loose?"

"No," said Jack. "A pirate executioner."

CHAPTER 39

I t's called gibbeting," said Andie.

She was standing behind a lectern at the front of a lecture room inside the J. Edgar Hoover Building in Washington, D.C. Her work on the Boston homicide investigation had led to the first break in the Tyler McCormick cold case in more than a decade. She'd been summoned to FBI headquarters by the National Center for the Analysis of Violent Crime, a specialist FBI department that coordinated investigative and operational support functions of federal, state, local, and foreign law enforcement agencies investigating unusual or repetitive violent crimes. Andie's presentation was to a newly formed multijurisdictional task force that included more than twenty different law enforcement agencies from three different states, as well as INTERPOL. About a dozen men and women were in the room with her. Others participated remotely by videoconference.

On the large projection screen behind her was a grainy reproduction of a nearly three-hundred-year-old sketch depicting the events on Nixes Mate dating back to the early eighteenth century.

"The sketch you are looking at is from 1726," said Andie. "It was drawn by an unknown witness to the execution of William Fry. Mr. Fry led a band of pirates in the waters around Boston Harbor. He was captured, convicted of piracy on the high seas, and sentenced to death by hanging."

Andie clicked ahead to the next slide. "This next sketch is by the same unknown artist. The man in the sketch is once again William Fry, but it is post-execution. The body is clearly lifeless. Yet it is erect, as if the prisoner is standing on the waves that lap at his feet."

Andie zoomed in on the image with her remote control. "If you look closer, it becomes obvious that the prisoner is not standing at all. The body is upright, but only because it is chained tightly to the piling that projects from the shallow waters of the Boston Harbor around Nixes Mate."

Andie clicked to the next slide, which included numerous images like those of William Fry. "In the eighteenth century, gibbeting was part and parcel of the sentence of death by hanging meted out to pirates by a court of law. Gibbeting was the practice of putting the body on public display after execution. Not on display just anywhere, but in a place where it would serve as a warning to other would-be pirates."

She continued to the next slide, which was a map of Boston Harbor. "The tiny island of Nixes Mate was the perfect place for gibbeting the corpses of executed pirates. Its location in Boston Harbor made it virtually certain that sailors on any passing ship would see it on their way in or out of Boston. The intent, of course, was to send a clear warning to any sailor who was even thinking about falling into piracy: 'this is what will happen to you.'"

Andie clicked to the final slide. Whatever "yo-ho-ho-and-a-bottle-of-rum" aura that had attended the first part of her presentation quickly evaporated. On the left side of the screen was a crime-scene photograph from the recovery of the body of Shannon Dwyer at Nixes Mate. On the right was a similar photograph from the recovery of the body of Tyler McCormick in Biscayne Bay.

"The forensic similarities between Shannon Dwyer and Tyler Mc-Cormick are obvious," said Andie. "The cause of death in both cases was asphyxiation—which, but the way, was the same cause of death in the hanging of William Fry. Pirates were hanged with a short rope, to increase suffering, so they did not die instantly with the breaking of the neck that comes with a long rope with a thick noose. Convicted pirates were essentially strangled to death.

"As to both Ms. Dwyer and Mr. McCormick, the manner of death was homicide by ligature strangulation. Both bodies were moved after death and put on display by chaining them to a piling in an open waterway. One was in Biscayne Bay. The other was in Boston Harbor. In other words, both were gibbeted."

Andie paused, interrupted by what sounded like laughter. It had come from the videoconference audience, and it had been more than one participant. The unit chief for the National Center for the Analysis of Violent Crime, the highest-ranking law enforcement officer in the room with Andie, spoke up.

"Something funny about this?" he asked, annoyed.

There was momentary silence, and then one of the remote participants spoke without identifying himself. "I'm sorry. But is she seriously saying that the common thread in these investigations is that the victims are pirates?"

Andie took a breath and tried not to sound defensive. "Here's what we know," she said. "Shannon Dwyer accessed hundreds and hundreds of songs, TV shows, and movies from illegal piracy websites."

"What about Tyler McCormick?" another remote participant asked.

"We are trying to locate Mr. McCormick's data," said Andie. "I understand that Miami-Dade Police captured all of his electronically stored information on a hard drive, which is somewhere in a warehouse in Miami."

"So you don't know if Tyler McCormick ever accessed a piracy website," came the reply by videoconference. "Do I have that right?"

"We don't," said Andie. "But the fact is, virtually everybody in Mr. McCormick's age group and demographic was engaged in piracy of some sort in this period of time around his death. It was an epidemic."

"Okay, fine. Let's say it turns out that Mr. McCormick was the biggest music pirate the world has ever known. A virtual Blackbeard. Let's also say that Shannon Dwyer was the second worst. Let me ask you this question: Did William Fry have the message 'goodbye girl' written anywhere on his body?"

"Obviously not," said Andie.

"Both Shannon Dwyer and Tyler McCormick did, right?"

"Yes."

"Which raises this question: What does 'goodbye girl' have to do with piracy of old or piracy on the internet?"

"That's an important question," said Andie. "The answer is still unknown."

"Which leads me to one conclusion: As interesting as this lesson in pirate history may be to you, we have more important leads to follow. So, can we please move on to the FBI's analysis of the 'goodbye girl' signature? We're all very busy."

Several others seconded the sentiment—even a couple of the agents in the room with Andie. Times had changed, supposedly, but it was all oddly reminiscent of Andie's first presentation ever as an FBI agent, when she was with the Seattle field office, back in the days when she was literally the only woman in the room.

The unit chief rose. "Thanks very much, Agent Henning. I think we've heard enough for now."

"Sure," said Andie.

She switched off the projector and took a seat in a chair off to the side of the room. The unit chief was introducing the FBI handwriting analyst on the team when her phone vibrated in her pocket with a text message. It was from the Miami ASAC.

Onward and upward, it read.

She hadn't even been aware that he was among the remote participants. His words were surely offered as encouragement, but the sting of the insulting laughter from her peers was all the more painful knowing that her boss had heard it.

CHAPTER 40

Late Thursday, Theo got plaits. He'd walked into the barbershop asking for braids, only to discover that, at least in East London, what he actually wanted were plaits. One look in the mirror confirmed that the idea was a bad one by any name. The barber had done his best, but Theo's hair was too short for plaits, and "undoing" them was not an option.

"Shave it," he told the barber.

A clean-shaven head wasn't new for Theo. It had been his look for most of his twenties and into his early thirties, ditching it only because his hair grew faster than the average Charles Barkley, which made maintenance a hassle. On balance, the added trouble would be worthwhile if it made him less recognizable to the Russian sniper on his trail.

"Anything else for you today?" the barber asked.

A Kevlar vest, maybe, thought Theo. "No, that'll do it."

Theo was the last appointment of the day. It was almost seven o'clock, well after dark, as he left the shop and started walking to the Tube station. He had no personal belongings with him. In line with the legal attaché's advice, he'd gone straight to a hotel without returning to his flat to collect his things. He'd spent Wednesday night and all of Thursday's daylight hours in his room. Only after sunset did he venture out to the barbershop for his new look.

His airline tickets were printed and inside his coat pocket. With no cellphone or laptop, he'd used the hotel's business center to book one flight from London to Amsterdam, and a separate flight from Amsterdam to Miami. His thinking was that Kava might have someone monitoring nonstops from Heathrow to Miami. The tickets were under

his new name and passport number. The shaved head might prompt a
few questions from customs agents as to why "Ivan Walker" didn't look
exactly like the photograph in his passport. But one of Kava's assassins
had already found him, and Theo didn't want to risk going to the airport
looking like the man who was, quite literally, in Kava's crosshairs. His
plan was to move to another hotel for the night, closer to Heathrow, and
hole up there until it was time for his morning flight to Amsterdam.

He was a block away from the Tube station when he heard a familiar
voice from behind him.

"I like the new look," she said.

Theo stopped, turned, and saw it was Gigi.

"Your hair was too short for plaits," she added. "It was like somebody
glued a bunch of caterpillars to your head."

Theo went to her quickly, took her by the arm, and continued walking toward the station. "You need to stay away from me."

"Why?"

"Because it's not safe to be around me."

"You're the safest person I know."

"No, I'm not," he said with an empty chuckle. "I'm leaving tomorrow."

"Why?"

"Because tomorrow is the first flight I could get."

"What's the hurry? They caught the guy who was after you. I saw
the cops come."

Theo stopped on the sidewalk. She looked up at him. "You need to
stop spying on me," he said.

"I can't help it. You're so cute with your bald head."

"And stop sayin' shit like that. You're a *kid*."

"Okay, okay. Sorry. You're not cute. But you still make me feel safe."

"You have no idea what's going on with me."

"I know more than you think. I know you were in prison."

Theo stopped. "Who told you that?"

"You booked my hotel room in your name. I googled you. You were in
prison for four years in Florida and got out on a technicality."

"I was innocent. It wasn't a technicality."

"It's okay, Mr. Theo Knight, owner of Cy's Place in Coconut Grove,

Florida. I'm cool with technicalities. Technically speaking, I'm still a virgin, if you don't count the things I've done above the waist."

"Stop talking like that! For your own good, don't follow me. Don't get *near* me." He started away.

"I heard from Judge," she said.

Again, Theo stopped. This time, he didn't turn around right away, but he was fighting the urge.

"He threatened me," she said.

Theo breathed out. Self-preservation—survival—was supposedly the most basic of human instincts. He needed to be on that plane out of Heathrow in less than twenty-four hours, to spend as little time as possible in the same country as Kava's hired assassin. But it was impossible to leave a threatened teen standing alone on the sidewalk.

"I saved your life, you know. When I warned you about that guy waiting for you."

She'd had him at "he threatened me." But it was true. He was alive only because of her. He turned and walked back, then led her to a seat on a bench.

"Tell me what happened."

The tough-kid veneer began to melt away. Theo could see the fear in her eyes as she spoke.

"He called me on my cell."

"When?"

"Today. A few hours ago."

"From where?"

"I don't know."

He paused, realizing that he must have sounded like a drill sergeant with his rapid-fire questions. He softened his tone, knowing the next question might be difficult to answer.

"What did he say?"

She looked away, then back. "If I tell you, can I stay with you?"

Theo hadn't expected this to turn into a negotiation. "No."

"I need a place to stay."

He didn't want her on the street. "I'll get you a room."

"I don't feel safe by myself."

Negotiation was turning to manipulation. "Gigi, tell me what he said to you."

"He said he—" she started to say, then stopped. "Can my room at least be in the same hotel as yours. I'm really scared."

"Okay, fine. Tell me what he said."

She lowered her eyes. And her voice. "He said he's sorry he let me go."

"Gigi, I know he was not your boyfriend. So don't try to tell me he called to say he regrets dumping you."

"No, I meant literally *let me go*. Like, turn me loose."

Theo had thought he'd imagined the worst, but maybe his imagination had fallen short. "Are you afraid he's going to come back?"

She nodded.

"To make you work for him again?" asked Theo.

She shook her head.

"What are you afraid he's going to do?"

She shrugged.

"What did he say?" asked Theo.

She touched Theo's wrist. Her hand was shaking. "He said, 'Goodbye Girl should have kept her mouth shut. Now I need to shut it for her.'"

He was angry at Judge and afraid for her at the same time. "Kept her mouth shut about what?"

She didn't answer. The alone time in his hotel room had given Theo a chance to catch up on the most recent media coverage of Imani's trial, as well as the links to "related stories." He'd read about Shannon Dwyer in Boston Harbor.

"Gigi? Do you know something about the name this guy gave you? Goodbye Girl?"

She seemed flustered. "Should we really be sitting out in the open like this, a couple of sitting ducks?"

It was a valid point, but Theo also knew it was a diversion. He rose and took Gigi by the hand. "Let's go."

"Where?"

"You're coming with me," he said, starting toward the Tube station. "And this conversation is not over."

CHAPTER 41

B y Friday morning, Jack was able to match the faces of certain spectators to specific seats in the public gallery. These were celebrity worshipers, the hardcore observers who arrived before dawn and waited for hours outside the courthouse to be first in line, even ahead of Imani's biggest supporters. Once inside the courtroom, they could take any available seat, but they grabbed the same one, day after day, as if they owned it. Their biggest fear was that they would miss the "big day"—that critical moment when a witness broke down on the stand, the judge lost his shit, or the lawyers nearly came to blows.

"Courtroom rubberneckers," Jack called them, driven as they were by the same morbid curiosity that stopped traffic around a car accident.

Thursday afternoon had surely disappointed the rubberneckers. Cross-examination of the investment banker from Saxton Silvers had been about as riveting as that guy at the cocktail party who thinks the world can't get enough of his nearly verbatim recount of the latest CNBC podcast. Ears had pricked up when the prosecutor called retired MDPD homicide detective Gustavo Cruz to the stand. But that, too, had fizzled. Wisely, the prosecutor had addressed the detective's every vulnerability through direct examination before Jack could land a punch on cross. "Stealing the defense lawyer's thunder," it was called. Cruz forthrightly admitted to the jury that there was not a shred of physical evidence connecting either defendant to the crime. No fingerprints. No DNA. No hair, fibers, or bodily fluid of the victim found at the Nicholses' house. No rope found in the garage that matched the rope around the victim's neck. No chains that matched the chains on the piling. It was all perfectly explainable. The police didn't find those things because they never searched the Nicholses' house. "And," the detective had told the jury, "we didn't search because they weren't suspects until twelve years after the murder."

The prosecutor's clever move had left Jack with essentially one point to make on cross-examination:

"What you're saying, Detective, is that it wasn't *evidence* that made my client a suspect. It was a tip from a former bodyguard twelve years later—a tip from a convicted felon."

One point for the defense. A nice point on which to end the day. The prosecutor seemed intent upon erasing that point from the scoreboard come Friday morning.

"Your Honor, the state of Florida would like to re-call Mr. Paxton to the witness stand."

The judge did a double take. "To quote the late, great Yogi Berra, this feels 'like déjà vu all over again.'"

Calling a prosecution witness to the stand a second time, except to rebut the defense's case, was highly unorthodox. Jack objected, but the prosecutor had an answer.

"The relevance of this additional testimony did not become apparent until yesterday," said Owens. "It will be brief."

"Objection overruled. But do be brief, Mr. Owens."

Paxton entered through the side door, dressed in orange and accompanied by two officers whose job it was to make sure the FSP inmate saw nothing but the inside of the courtroom and the courthouse stockade on his trip to Miami. Again, he swore to tell the truth—*Yeah, right,* thought Jack—and took his seat. The prosecutor bid him good morning and went straight to work.

"Mr. Paxton, during the time you served as Mr. Nichols's bodyguard, did you ever hear him discuss music piracy?"

"Are you kidding? The man never stopped talking about it."

"Can I take that as a yes?"

"Yeah. I heard him many times."

"Did you ever hear him talk about music piracy with his then wife, Imani Nichols?"

He glanced in Imani's direction, then back at the prosecutor. "Yeah. I remember one time I heard them talking about it."

"Were you part of the conversation?" asked the prosecutor.

"No. I was just standing around. Which, you know, was basically my job. That's what bodyguards do."

One of the jurors smiled. Despite himself, Paxton was actually coming across as relatable, a regular guy.

"Where were you when you overheard this conversation?" asked Owens.

"We were on a boat. Somewhere in the Caribbean."

"Was this a pleasure trip?"

"Yeah. A mini vacation. A little time off from the grind."

"Whose boat was it?"

"I don't remember."

"Where in the Caribbean?"

"I don't know. Palm trees. Sand. It's all the fucking same."

The judge glared. "Language, please, Mr. Paxton!"

"Sorry, Judge," said the prosecutor.

"Next time, I'll hold you both in contempt," the judge said.

"Understood," said Owens, and then he addressed the witness. "Let's keep this in the Disney version, shall we, Mr. Paxton?"

"Got it."

"When was this trip to the Caribbean and the conversation you mentioned?"

"I don't remember when."

"Was this conversation you heard Mr. Nichols and his wife having about music piracy before or after the death of Tyler McCormick?"

"Before. Definitely before."

"How long before?"

"I couldn't tell you."

"Was anyone else part of the conversation?"

"Yeah."

"Who?"

"I don't remember."

Jack was jotting down the number of "I don't remember" answers. The prosecutor continued.

"Do you recall how the issue of piracy came up?"

He sighed, as if he were looking back on the good ol' days. "Like I said, we were on a boat in the Caribbean. Naturally, somebody started talking about the new Johnny Depp movie."

"Do you recall which one?"

"I don't know. *Pirates of the Caribbean* number thirty-two, or whatever it was."

The same juror smiled. Paxton was connecting, which made it all the more imperative that Jack break that connection on cross.

"That movie is not about music piracy, is it?"

"No. But I mention the movie because that's when one of the guys who worked on the boat pointed to a place along the shore. He told us they actually used to hang pirates there. In real life."

"In real life. You mean not in the movie."

"Right. In real life. Well, in the movie, too. Hanging pirates was the opening scene in the very first *Pirates of the Caribbean* movie. *Curse of the Black Pearl*, I think it was. Captain Jack sails past a string of hanging corpses. 'Pirates, Be Ye Warned,' the sign says."

"Let's focus on real life. Was this someone on the crew who made this remark?"

"Yeah. He worked on the boat."

"Did he say anything more about these hangings of pirates in real life?"

"Yeah. He pointed to another spot in the harbor. He said—"

"Objection," said Shaky's lawyer. "Hearsay."

Owens had the right response. "Judge, we're not offering this testimony to prove that pirates were actually hanged in this particular spot. It's only offered to show that these statements were made and, true or not, the defendants heard them."

"Overruled," said the judge.

Owens refocused. "Please continue, Mr. Paxton."

"The guy pointed to the harbor. There's hundreds of boats there these days. But there's been pilings and piers there for hundreds of years. According to him, after these pirates were hanged, they chained the bodies to the pilings so sailors coming into the harbor could see them. It was supposed to scare them."

The prosecutor glanced toward the table for the defense. "Did either Mr. Nichols or Ms. Nichols say anything in response?"

"Imani did."

"What did she say?"

Jack wished he had a basis to object, but an out-of-court statement by a defendant was admissible against her.

"She said, 'We should try that with music pirates.'"

"Did Mr. Nichols have any response?"

"Well, he laughed. We all kind of laughed. It sounded like a joke."

"My question was: Did Mr. Nichols say anything?"

"Yeah. After he stopped laughing, he looked over at me. The joke was over, and he looked kind of serious."

"What did he say to you?"

"He said, 'Yeah. We should try that.'"

The prosecutor paused to let the words have their intended effect. Then he looked up to the judge and said, "I have no further questions."

The judge looked toward Jack. "Mr. Swyteck? Cross-examination?"

The testimony fell far short of proving that Imani and Shaky were on a bloodthirsty campaign to rid the world of music pirates. But it did show that they'd heard of a pirate's dreadful punishment prior to the murder of Tyler McCormick, and that they would have fully under-stood the significance of the manner in which the victim's body was put on display.

Jack had to prove the witness was lying.

"Mr. Paxton, you didn't tell your *Pirates of the Caribbean* story when I deposed you at Florida State Prison. Did you?"

"You didn't ask."

"You didn't tell this story two days ago, the first time you testified for the prosecution. Did you?"

"I didn't think it was important."

"But now you do think it's important, is that right?"

"Yeah."

"Because the prosecutor told you it's important," said Jack, his tone more aggressive. "Right?"

"Objection," said the prosecutor.

"Overruled. The witness can testify as to what the prosecution told him."

"Let me ask it this way," said Jack. "After you testified the other day, you went out that side door, got in the elevator, and went straight down to the stockade. Am I right?"

"Yeah."

"And while you were sitting down there in a jail cell, you didn't have an 'Oh my God' moment when it suddenly occurred to you that, 'Holy cow, I forgot to tell Mr. Owens about the pirate conversation.' That didn't happen, did it, Mr. Paxton?"

"No."

"No," said Jack. "What happened is that Mr. Owens came to see you and said, 'I need you back on the stand.' Right?"

"He came, right."

"It was Mr. Owens, not *you*, who first brought up the subject of piracy. Correct?"

"He was the one asking the questions."

"He did more than ask questions," said Jack, his voice a little louder. "He *told* you that piracy was suddenly an important issue in the case, right?"

"Objection," said Owens. "Mr. Swyteck is putting words in my mouth."

"Overruled," said the judge. "This is cross-examination. The witness can tell us what the prosecutor said to him."

"He brought up piracy," said Paxton.

"And after the prosecutor brought it up, only *then* did you remember that Imani and Shaky Nichols had a conversation about hanging pirates and putting their bodies on a piling."

"It's not that I suddenly remembered it," said Paxton. "I just didn't know it was important until Mr. Owens asked me about it."

"I see. Let's talk about how well you remember it. Interestingly, you claim to remember the exact words Imani Nichols said to the group, and the exact words Shaky Nichols said to you. Right?"

"Uh-huh."

"But you don't remember where you were."

"I said we were in the Caribbean."

"It's a big place, Mr. Paxton. It's like saying you were in the United States."

"Objection," said Owens.

"Sustained."

Jack's focus remained on the witness. "You don't remember whose boat it was."

"It was . . . somebody's."

"You don't remember when it happened, except to say that it *definitely* was before the death of Tyler McCormick."

"Definitely before."

"How convenient."

"Objection," said Owens. "Judge, really?"

"Please just ask your questions, Mr. Swyteck," said the judge.

Jack continued without missing a beat. "Other than you and the un-named crewmate, you don't remember who was there, do you?"

"Can't really remember."

Jack paused. He was at the end of his list of "don't remember" an-swers. It was time to drive the point home.

"Mr. Paxton, in your deposition you told me that you were convicted of armed robbery."

"That's right."

"You were sentenced to twenty years in prison."

"Uh-huh."

"So far, you've served less than six years on that twenty-year sentence. Is that right?"

"Thereabouts."

"Let's be honest, sir. Is there *anything* you wouldn't say to this jury if you thought it would shave a few years off your sentence?"

"Objection," said Owens.

"Overruled."

Jack waited. The jurors waited.

"I wouldn't lie," said the witness, "if that's your question."

"Of course you wouldn't," said Jack. "I have no further questions."

Jack returned to his seat at the defense table, having pressed his point as far as he could, at least for the moment. But there were additional ways to discredit the testimony of a lying witness.

He leaned close to Imani and whispered, "I may need your old passport from twelve years ago."

"I don't know if I still have it," she whispered back.

"Find it," said Jack. "But only if you were *not* on that boat in the Caribbean."

CHAPTER 42

Andie was right across the street from Jack, but she couldn't tell him. She and Arnie Greenberg, the assistant special agent in charge of the FBI's Miami office, had a meeting with the state attorney.

The official name for the main facility of the Office of the State Attorney for Miami-Dade County was the Graham Building, but every prosecutor Andie had ever met called it the Boomerang. The building had two wings, and the footprint was angled like a boomerang, but the appellation had more to do with the fact that prosecutors started their day there, spent the next eight hours whirling through one court appearance after another, and at the end of the day landed exactly where they'd started, preparing for the next trip to the courthouse. The boomerang.

"We're here to see Abe Beckham," Andie told the receptionist.

Before Beckham's election as state attorney, Andie had known him only by reputation as senior trial counsel and the go-to prosecutor in the office for homicide cases. He'd never lost a capital case, including two against Jack, both before Andie and Jack were married. She'd never heard Jack say an unkind word about him, and she hoped he would be equally gracious to her. Andie's understanding of the office hierarchy made Beckham the boss of Mr. Owens's boss, which hopefully distanced him enough from the trial of Imani Nichols to not take any of the courtroom jousting personally.

The door to Beckham's office was open, and the receptionist led the FBI agents inside. It was bigger than Andie had expected, bigger even than the ASAC's office in Miami, with top-floor views of the Miami River and the criminal courthouse. Beckham stepped out from behind his desk and greeted the agents cordially. They moved to the more comfortable end of the office, away from the cluttered desk, and seated themselves in the armchairs around a cocktail table, though the state attorney and the ASAC seemed to jockey for position to see who got the only "power seat" available, the one closest to the American flag.

"How can I help you?" asked Beckham.

"We're here to talk about Operation Gibbet," said Greenberg, using the official name of the multijurisdictional task force.

Beckham glanced in Andie's direction. "Isn't that awkward? My office is currently in the middle of the Nichols trial, and so is Agent Henning's husband."

"Jack and I don't speak about the trial," said Andie.

He smiled with skepticism. "Well . . ."

The innuendo surprised her, given Beckham's reputation as a stand-up guy. "*Excuse me?*" she said, but Greenberg interjected before she could bat back the insult.

"Let me be plain," said the ASAC. "We have every reason to believe that whoever killed Shannon Dwyer and put her body on display in Boston Harbor will strike again. The parallels to the Tyler McCormick murder are undeniable. Agent Henning has more knowledge about those two cases than anyone in my office. I'm not going to put the public at risk and pull her off Operation Gibbet over a *perceived* conflict of interest that doesn't exist. Anyone who has a different view and wants to force my hand on this issue can answer to the family of the next victim and explain why we fell one step behind the killer."

Andie couldn't have said it better.

Beckham nodded slowly. "Fair enough," he said. "As long as we're not talking directly about trial strategy, I'm comfortable."

"We're not here to discuss trial strategy," said Andie. "We're here to give you a heads-up."

"About what?"

"Technically, we don't have a serial killer yet. We have two homicides that may or may not be related. We'll have a serial killer when one of two things happens. When we determine that Shannon Dwyer's killer is not a copycat. Or, as we fear, Shannon Dwyer's killer strikes again, copycat or not."

"I follow you," said Beckham.

"If either one of those things happen," said Andie, "we will have an obligation to notify the public that we have an active serial killer on the loose."

Beckham was clearly getting the message, his expression showing concern. "Go on."

"If Shannon Dwyer's killer is a copycat emulating the Tyler McCormick gibbeting, there's no impact on the Nichols trial. But if our investigation determines that Shannon's killer is *not* a copycat . . ."

Andie's voice trailed off, allowing the state attorney to draw his own conclusions.

"I see," said Beckham. "Someone other than Imani and Shaky Nichols killed Tyler McCormick."

"That would appear to be the case," said Andie.

"Understood," said Beckham. "We should stay close on this."

"Agreed," said Andie. "Which leads to my next point."

"I'm listening," said the state attorney.

"Yesterday morning marked an abrupt change in the prosecution's theory of the case in the Nichols trial. That was the first time Mr. Owens presented evidence that Shaky Nichols had strong motive to stop music piracy. We now know that the theory is that Mr. McCormick's body was displayed—gibbeted—in the same way that pirates were gibbeted in the eighteenth century."

"It's his prerogative to change the case theory."

"True," said Andie. "But follow the timeline with me. Later that morning, I made a presentation to the joint task force based on my work with Boston homicide. My presentation was the first time anyone mentioned piracy and gibbeting in connection with the McCormick case."

"So?"

"So, Mr. Owens is somehow out in front of the FBI, the MDPD, Boston homicide, and every other agency on Operation Gibbet."

"Owens is one of my smartest prosecutors. He figures things out."

"Or does he have a source that the task force should know about?"

"His source is Shaky Nichols's former bodyguard."

"Is Paxton his *only* source?"

"Yes."

"I would like to verify that," said Andie.

"Fine. You can ask Owens."

"Thank you," said Andie. "That's a start. But it may go deeper than that."

"How much deeper?" asked Beckham.

The ASAC spoke up, as they were moving to sensitive ground. "We may need to talk to inmate Paxton."

"I've told you he's our only source. Owens can verify it. Our word is not good enough for you?" he asked with a chuckle, though he wasn't at all kidding.

"Who is Paxton's source?" asked Andie.

"Paxton is his own source."

"You're certain of that?" asked Andie.

The state attorney threw up his hands. "Look, if you want to talk to an inmate at a Florida correctional facility, I can't stop you."

"We know," said Andie. "But we thought it was important enough to come here directly and put you on notice."

Beckham seemed to be taking it all in. Even though Andie had done her best not to bring the motivations of his office into question, it was clear that her words were not sitting well with the state attorney.

"Putting me on notice that your investigation might exonerate Imani and Shaky Nichols is one thing," said Beckham. "Suggesting that my chief prosecutor has a source other than Mr. Paxton, and that he's deliberately hiding that source from your investigation, is quite another."

"No accusations are being made here," said the ASAC. "Like Andie said: just putting you on notice of the situation."

Beckham looked in Andie's direction and held his gaze, as if he were indeed looking his "accuser" right in the eye. Finally, the state attorney rose. "Got it," he said. "I'm on notice."

The FBI agents rose and followed Beckham to the door. There were handshakes all around, but without smiles. No one, least of all Andie, was happy about the obvious tension between the FBI investigation and the Nichols trial. It bothered Andie that the state attorney was acting as though this was a silly turf war between the feds and the locals—that the FBI had stopped by his office just for grins, and that they somehow enjoyed making him squirm.

"Good luck with Mr. Paxton," said the state attorney. "He's a piece of work."

Andie thanked him, and they said goodbye. She and Greenberg found their way back to the elevator, and they rode down to the lobby, neither of them saying a word until they were outside the building.

"Thank you," said Andie as they followed the sidewalk to the parking lot.

"For what?"

"I was feeling pretty small after my presentation to the task force on piracy. It's nice to have your support."

"Don't worry about that. I call it 'task-force testosterone.' Anytime you put a bunch of cops from multiple agencies in one room, there's bound to be a couple of dicks who need to show the world how smart they are by cutting down someone else."

"Well, anyway. It's appreciated."

"No problem. See you back at the office."

They parted ways in the second row of the parking lot, Greenberg heading toward his car and Andie toward hers. Andie dug her keys from her purse, and as she unlocked the door, her cellphone vibrated with a text message. She glanced at it, and even though she didn't recognize the number, the message immediately caught her full attention.

its theo, the message read. The fact that there was no capitalization and no apostrophe in the word "it's" only made it more likely that it was him.

Another text bubble appeared on her screen:

when can I call u? its instant.

Andie surmised that the dreaded autocorrect had struck again. "Instant" probably should have been "important." Or "urgent." The protocol for random text messages from unknown numbers was to contact the IT experts. But if it was Theo, and if it was indeed "urgent," Andie didn't have time for protocol. Her thumbs went to work.

Call now, she texted back, if you can.

Andie got in her car, turned on the air-conditioning, and waited.

CHAPTER 43

Five o'clock Friday marked the end of the first week of trial. Jack and Imani went back to his office to debrief.

Jack's office was once the personal residence of a bona fide Miami pioneer. It dated back to the 1920s, ancient by Miami standards, built in the old Florida style with a coral-rock façade and a cozy covered porch that made you want to pull up a rocking chair. The previous occupant was the Freedom Institute, where Jack had worked as a young attorney fresh out of law school. Jack was well established in private practice when his mentor's unexpected death left the institute on the brink of financial collapse. Jack came up with a plan to save it, which meant buying the building. The Freedom Institute operated rent-free upstairs, run by Neil's daughter, Hannah Goldstein. Jack and his longtime assistant ran his practice downstairs. His personal office was in his favorite room in the entire house, the old dining room with the original hardwood floors of Dade County pine and a working fireplace that Jack used about once every five years and cleaned once every ten.

Jack entered his private office and flipped the light switch, but the ceiling lights didn't come on.

"Cool old house," said Imani. "But you might be interested to know that a lot of the offices they build these days come with electricity."

He'd heard the same thing from about a half dozen handymen, all of whom had told him it would be cheaper just to tear the house down and rebuild from the ground up. "I'll never leave this place."

Jack led her to the kitchen, which had been completely renovated—including electrical wiring—since Jack's days of bag lunches with Neil and his team. All that remained of the old décor was Neil's framed photograph of Bobby Kennedy on the wall. They sat at the table, and Jack started the conversation at the top of his checklist.

"Were you able to find your old passport?" he asked.

Jack had hoped that her passport would show no travel to the Caribbean prior to the death of Tyler McCormick, further undercutting the testimony of Shaky's former bodyguard.

"It's gone," said Imani.

Jack checked it off his list, though he wondered if it was truly "gone," or if she had strictly heeded his advice to find it only if it showed no travel to the Caribbean.

"Let's talk about Shaky," said Jack.

"What about Shaky?"

"I want to think like the prosecutor for a minute. Let's assume Shaky actually did tell his bodyguard he wanted to gibbet music pirates."

"Wanted to *what*?"

"Gibbet. It's the term for putting a pirate's corpse on display after hanging. I'd never heard it either until I read it in the *Boston Herald*'s coverage of Shannon Dwyer's murder. Anyway, let's even go so far as to say Tyler McCormick was the first music 'pirate' to be gibbeted on Shaky's order. Why did he stop at one?"

Imani looked confused. "Because it's murder?" she said, her response somewhere between a statement and a question.

"Yes," said Jack, jotting on his notepad. "But that raises two possibilities. One, it's murder, and it violated Shaky's sense of right and wrong. Or two, it's murder, and he was suddenly afraid of getting caught. What's another reason he might have stopped?"

"I don't know," said Imani. "Maybe there was no point to it."

"Pointless, how?"

"If killing pirates deterred music piracy, Shaky got more money from the sale of EML Records. After the sale went through, what was the point?"

"Except that the sale didn't close for almost six months after the murder of Tyler McCormick. A second murder with an explicit warning to pirates during that six-month period could have brought down piracy and benefited him financially. So that doesn't fly."

"Then I'm out of ideas."

"Let's think in terms of explanations that could implicate you," said Jack.

She seemed uncomfortable with the suggestion. "Like how?"

"Again, I'm thinking like the prosecutor here. I might argue that Shaky stopped because you knew about it, and you told him to stop."

"That's not what happened."

"Not saying it was. But right now, the prosecutor has testimony that you were the first person to say music pirates should be gibbeted, even if it was a joke. For all we know, he's fully aware that Tyler McCormick was stalking you, and he plans to spring that on Monday. Where does that lead him?"

"I don't know. Where?"

"A husband killed a man who was stalking his wife, or he had him killed, which is plausible. The two of you are left with a dead body on your hands. Instead of dumping the body in the Everglades, you implement the 'plan' you came up with—if only half-seriously—on that boat in the Caribbean. You gibbet the body, which becomes step one in a bigger plan to deter music piracy."

"But there's no step two."

"You and Shaky lost your nerve. It was one thing to gibbet Tyler McCormick to cover up the murder of a stalker. It's a very different thing to actually go out and murder someone just for pirating music."

"You make it sound so calculated."

"Not my first rodeo," said Jack.

Hannah knocked lightly on the doorframe and entered the kitchen. "Jack, I have that research you wanted."

Jack introduced Hannah to his client. Her work for the institute was separate from his practice, but he often called on her for trial support. After Paxton's testimony, he'd asked her to identify historical places in the Caribbean known for the gibbeting of pirates.

"If we can show you've never been to any of the places known for gibbeting," Jack told his client, "that gives us another angle to undercut Paxton's testimony."

Hannah took a seat at the table and reported her findings. "Keep in mind that before Parliament gave the British colonies the power to put pirates on trial, any pirates captured in the Caribbean had to be sent to London for trial and execution. Before 1700, the gibbeting of pirates was near the Tower of London on the Thames River. So even though this was prime territory for the likes of Captain Kidd, Jean Hamlin, Stede Bonnet, Tempest Rogers, Bartholomew Sharp, and Black Sam Bellamy, there aren't that many actual historical records of gibbeting in the Caribbean."

"That's helpful," said Jack. "That narrows the possible number of places that this alleged conversation about gibbeting could have occurred."

"One of the most famous spots is Port Royal in Jamaica," said Hannah. "Calico Jack Rackham and his entire crew were hanged at Gallows Point and their bodies were gibbeted at the entrance to the port."

"I've never been to Jamaica," said Imani.

"Good," said Jack. "What else you got, Hannah?"

"Right up there with Port Royal is the group execution of ten pirates in December 1718. That was in the Bahamas."

"I've been to the Bahamas," said Imani.

"When?" asked Jack.

"Long time ago. With Shaky."

"Before or after Tyler McCormick was murdered?" asked Jack.

"Before."

"Really, Imani? We've been talking all day about you and Shaky on a trip to the Caribbean. You're just now telling me about this trip to the Bahamas?"

"The Bahamas aren't in the Caribbean," she said. "They're in the west Atlantic."

It seemed like a technicality, but Jack had won plenty of cases on so-called technicalities. "Where in the Bahamas were you?"

"I don't know. They have hundreds of islands there."

Hannah interjected. "The mass hanging of 1718 was in Nassau."

"Were you on a boat?" Jack asked his client.

"Who goes to the Bahamas and doesn't go on a boat?"

"Was Paxton on this trip?"

"I don't remember," said Imani. "My bodyguard came along, so Shaky could have brought his, too."

Jack took a minute, then gave his honest assessment. "This is going to make it very hard to convince a jury that the conversation Paxton testified about could never have actually happened. It puts you and Shaky in a place famous for gibbeting of pirates before the murder of Tyler McCormick."

Jack stopped himself, then had a thought. "Wait a minute. Tyler McCormick was from the Bahamas."

"So?" asked Imani.

"Is that where you met him? Did you meet Tyler McCormick on this trip to the Bahamas?"

"Not that I remember," said Imani.

"Could there have been some encounter?"

"I don't know. I'm a celebrity. I meet people all the time. Maybe even say a couple of words to them. The whole encounter means nothing to me, but it means the world to the other person."

"Is that when the stalking started?" asked Jack. "After this trip?"

"Yes."

"Is it possible he followed you from the Bahamas to Miami?"

"The newspaper article said he was a student at Miami-Dade College at the time of his death. I don't know when he enrolled, but I guess it's not impossible that it was after I went to the Bahamas."

"Did he communicate with you from inside the United States or from the Bahamas?"

"I don't know. My security team tracked down the texts he sent. They all led to a burner."

Jack had to go back more than a decade to remember a criminal case that didn't somehow involve a disposable phone.

"Do you still have copies of the texts on your phone?"

"No. I deleted them a long time ago, and I've probably had ten phones since then. Why would we want copies of those messages anyway? You said it yourself: the fact that Tyler McCormick was stalking me only gives Shaky and me a stronger motive to get rid of him."

She had a point. But Jack was not ready to let go of this thread and see where it led.

"In the middle of your civil lawsuit with Shaky, I got an anonymous call. The tip was that if I wanted the case to go away, I should tell Shaky's lawyer that I was going to cross-examine Shaky about Tyler McCormick."

"I remember," said Imani. From her tone, it was clear she also recalled having lied to Jack about not knowing the name Tyler McCormick.

"I called Shaky's lawyer. That's when he dropped the case."

"This is old news, Jack. What's your point?"

"I never found out who the anonymous caller was."

"Isn't it clear that it was Paxton? He's the state's star witness."

"The voice was disguised with a mechanical device. Paxton couldn't do that from prison."

"Then who was it?" asked Imani.

"I'm guessing it's someone who knew Tyler McCormick was stalking you. Someone other than you and Shaky, I mean."

"Who would that be?"

"I don't know," said Jack. "But it feels like high time we find out."

CHAPTER 44

Theo missed his Friday evening flight from Heathrow. It was on purpose. He had to take care of things with Gigi before leaving the country.

"Stubborn as a mule with attitude is what my Uncle Cy would call you," said Theo.

They were at the Thistle Hotel in Heathrow Villages, near the airport, where a Tube ride from Bethnal Green and then a train to West Drayton had landed them. Two hours had passed since Andie's call now text message, to which Theo had replied, as soon as I can. Theo and Gigi were still in her room arguing about it. Theo was seated in a European-design ergonomic desk chair that was comfortable enough to sleep in, complete with adjustable headrest. Gigi was sitting on her bed, at the foot of the mattress, her shoes off and legs crisscrossed.

"I won't ring a total stranger and tell her everything I know about Judge," said Gigi. "I don't care if she is your friend."

"Andie is more than a 'friend.' She's my best friend's wife, the mother of my goddaughter, and an FBI agent. She can help you."

"If she's so helpful, why doesn't she help you?"

Good question. It wouldn't have helped matters to explain that his own dealings with the FBI's legal attaché in London had come up short of full protection. He'd lost Gigi's attention anyway. She was staring at something on her phone, and her face suddenly lit up with excitement.

"Oh my God. It's the Autumn Nation Series at Twickenham Stadium this weekend!"

"The what?"

"Rugby! It's not far from here."

"We're not going to a rugby match."

"I didn't say 'we.' You go. Leave me here with the key to the minibar."

"That's a great idea."

"Really?"

"Uh, no," he said, sounding like a parent.

"You're so mean."

Theo reached for the burner phone on the desk. Gigi wouldn't let him use hers to call anyone in law enforcement, so he'd purchased the burner specifically to call Andie. "I have to call her back tonight," he said.

"Go right ahead. I'm not stopping you."

"Don't you understand how important this is? A man was murdered in Miami, and the killer wrote 'goodbye girl' on his body. A woman was just murdered in Boston, and the killer wrote the same message. It can't be a coincidence that this Judge gave you the nickname 'Goodbye Girl.'"

"Who's to say it's *not* a coincidence?"

"Agent Henning, that's who," said Theo. "She's working on those cases. Just get on the phone and tell her everything you know about Judge. Andie can decide if it matters."

"Why do I have to do this? You can tell her about Judge."

"I don't know anything about him. You won't even tell me what he looks like."

"Fuck off, Theo."

Precious few people could say that to Theo, but he understood where she was coming from. "Are you afraid to tell me what he looks like?" he asked.

"No!"

"You don't have to be afraid."

"I'm not afraid of anyone or anything. Except you and your big mouth!"

"Me?"

"I showed you where Judge lived, and the cops showed up the next day. You told the cops, didn't you?"

Theo couldn't deny it.

"I knew it! If I tell you what he looks like, you'll tell someone else, then they'll tell someone. Next thing you know, my name is in the newspaper next to Judge's picture, Judge sees it, and I end up like that girl in Boston whose face has been all over the news and whose dead body is all over the internet."

It was the closest she'd come to connecting Judge directly to the "goodbye girl" killings. "Do you think he killed that girl in Boston?" asked Theo.

"I don't know! Okay? I don't know!"

Theo tried a softer approach. "I understand what you're dealing with. I really do. That's why I think it's best just to take me out of it. I want you to talk to Agent Henning. Maybe she can protect you. You help her with her investigation, and she can help you. Will you do that?"

She looked away, then back. "If I do, will you stop bugging me?"

He smiled a little. "I promise."

"Okay."

"You'll do it?"

"Maybe," she said.

It wasn't a yes, but it was better than the flat no he'd been getting all night. He dialed Andie's number on the burner. He knew it by heart. Andie wasn't listed by name in his cellphone contacts, so anytime Righley called her "Uncle Theo," it was Andie's number that popped up.

"Theo?" she answered. "Is everything all right?"

Theo had no idea if she knew about his new passport and the urgent need to get out of the UK, but he didn't waste time with his own predicament. He quickly told her about Gigi and what little he knew about her life with a man who called himself "Judge."

"At best, he's a sex trafficker," said Theo. "He may be a serial killer. His nickname for Gigi is 'Goodbye Girl.'"

There was a brief pause on the other end of the line, as Andie absorbed the significance of Theo's words. "Is that why you're calling from a burner phone?" she asked.

"One of the reasons," said Theo, still leaving himself out of it.

"Can I talk to her?" asked Andie.

"Hold on," he said, and then he lowered the cellphone. "Gigi? Will you talk to Agent Henning?"

She was still seated on the bed. She didn't respond. Theo held the phone out to her.

"Gigi? Please?"

It took a moment, but finally she breathed out a short huff of a breath and took the phone from him.

"I'm putting her on speaker," said Gigi. "I want you to hear this."

"Fine," said Theo.

"This is Gigi," she said.

Andie's voice came over the speaker. "Hi, Gigi. This is Agent Henning. You can call me Andie."

"Okay, Andie. Here's the deal. Get me out of here, and I'll tell you everything I know about Judge."

Theo couldn't hold his tongue. "Gigi, just talk to her."

"No. First, I get out of London. Then I talk."

"Where do you want to go?" asked Andie. Her tone was conversational and calm, like a trained hostage negotiator.

"With Theo. To Miami."

"That's not going to happen," said Theo.

"Then I don't talk."

Andie said something over the speaker, but Theo wasn't hearing it. He was tired of trying to convince Gigi to do the right thing, and his tone reflected it.

"Gigi, don't play games."

"I'm not playing."

"More people could die if you don't talk to Andie right now."

"Then she'd better move fast."

He knew she couldn't possibly mean what she was saying, but words were flying, and Theo fired right back. "Damn it, Gigi! Tell her what you know!"

"Get me out of here and I will!"

"You're being selfish!"

"You're a user!"

"You're acting like a spoiled child!"

"Well, it's about damn time, isn't it!"

Gigi jumped from the bed and ran toward the bathroom. Theo couldn't see her face, but he knew she was crying and, after reminding her so many times that she was just a kid, it hurt to think that he'd blown everything up with his own impatience in dealing with a child. Gigi stopped at the bathroom door, pivoted, and threw the phone at him. Theo ducked and the moment he did, it sounded as though a rock had hit the window, the open blinds rattling. But it wasn't the impact of the phone. A bullet punctured the headrest of the ergonomic chair in which, a split second earlier, Theo had been seated upright. The kill shot would have hit him squarely in the back of the head.

Gigi screamed, ran into the bathroom, and slammed the door. Theo dove to the floor, grabbed the lamp cord under the desk, and yanked the plug from the electrical socket. The hotel room went dark. The cellphone lay on the floor by the desk, still activated and glowing in the darkness. Andie's voice came over the speaker.

"Theo, what's happening?"

A second "rock" hit the hotel room window, the blinds rattled again, and the cellphone exploded into pieces. Theo had been warned about the skill of the Russian sniper on his heels, and he was witnessing her talents firsthand. But for the argument with Gigi and his sudden movement, his head, not the phone, would have exploded. He rolled across the carpeted floor and took cover on the other side of the bed, away from the window.

Gigi screamed from inside the bathroom. "Theo, what's happening?"

"Stay in the bathroom! Get down on the floor!"

There was a phone on the nightstand, but it was on the dangerous side of the bed. Theo didn't dare leave his place of cover.

"Tell me what's happening!" she shouted. "Is it Judge?"

The possibility had never occurred to Theo, but he quickly dismissed it.

"No," he answered. "This one's for me."

The line went dead on Andie's end. She immediately dialed back, but there was no answer. The last thing she'd heard was Theo yelling at Gigi, calling her a spoiled child.

"Mommy!"

It was Righley calling from her bedroom. *That was weird.*

"Just a sec, sweetie!"

Andie and her daughter were home alone on Key Biscayne. Jack had canceled "date night" to catch the last flight from Miami to the Bahamas for "business." It was just as well. She knew Tyler McCormick was from the Bahamas, so his coyness about a "business trip" seemed stupid, and her pretending not to know the actual reason for his trip seemed even stupider. It was all starting to feel like a charade, which made her feel like anything but having a "date night."

Andie dialed Theo a second time, but there was no answer. She dialed her ASAC as she walked from the kitchen to Righley's room. Maybe IT could get a location and determine if he needed help. Her call went to voicemail. She left a brief message—"Call me, it's very important"— and kept her phone with her as she entered the bedroom. Righley was peeking out from under the covers.

"I'm scared," said Righley.

From FBI agent to mommy, on a dime. "Of what, honey?"

"Pirates."

"Again?"

She peeled back the covers enough to reveal the rest of her face. "Is that why Daddy went to the Bahamas? To catch pirates?"

"No, honey."

Andie didn't go near the subject of pirate *killers*. She crossed the room, selected a chapter book from the shelf, and sat on the edge of Righley's bed.

"*Wimpy Diarrhea Kid*?" she said, using Righley's twist on the title. Such was the sense of humor a seven-year-old brought to a book.

"Yay!"

Andie was still worried about Theo. She needed to follow up again with her ASAC. "You get started," she said, handing the book to Righley. "I'll be back in five minutes."

"Aww, Mommy."

Andie's cell rang, ending the debate. It was her ASAC. She stepped out and took the call in the hallway. She was about to tell him about Theo, but he had news of his own.

"We got another victim," said Greenberg.

Andie felt chills. "Who?"

"Twenty-four-year-old Black male. Autopsy won't be till tomorrow, but preliminary indications are that he was the victim of ligature strangulation. Body was found chained to a harbor piling after a tip to the local media."

"What about the killer's signature?"

"It's there," said Greenberg, "'goodbye girl.'"

"Where's the crime scene?"

"Jamaica," he said. "A place called Port Royal. I'm told that, back in the day, it was a notorious place for the execution and gibbeting of pirates."

"This guy is not very subtle, is he?" said Andie.

"The task force coordinator in D.C. has already been in touch with the Jamaican Constabulary Force and INTERPOL. No question that this is within the purview of Operation Gibbet. You're approved for access to the crime scene in Port Royal and the autopsy in Kingston. I need you in the air as soon as possible."

Andie glanced through the open doorway to Righley's room. She looked worried, as if she almost seemed to know that the call was about pirates. A sleepover at her best friend's house would put her at ease and solve Andie's problem of what to do with Righley with Jack out of town.

"Sure," Andie said into the phone. "I'll make it work."

CHAPTER 45

The EC-155 multimission helicopter covered the 585 miles from Miami to Jamaica in about three hours, landing Andie in Kingston before midnight. Within minutes, she was aboard a harbor patrol boat with three officers from the Jamaican Constabulary Force, marine division. The vessel slowed to no-wake as they rounded the moonlit cliff at the entrance to the harbor. Beyond the enormous pile of boulders that had rolled down the hills and fallen into the sea over the millennium, the crime scene was aglow. It was a bright spot in the night, lit by portable light trees brought in by the JCF. The noisy generators that powered the lights hummed in the darkness.

Port Royal is a natural harbor on the southern coast of Jamaica, at the end of a ten-mile sand spit between Kingston Harbor and the Caribbean Sea. It was once the busiest trading center of the British West Indies, until a late-seventeenth-century earthquake swallowed two-thirds of the town, as if to foreshadow more seismic changes to come. The glory days of piracy ended early in the next century, with many of the marauders hanged and gibbeted at the port entrance.

Andie's boat stopped at the site of the first gibbeting in almost three hundred years.

At the center of the lighted crime scene was a tall concrete piling that projected from the warm Caribbean waters. Chained to the pole was the victim's body. The medical examiner's team was taking photographs and preparing to remove the corpse from its place of gruesome display. Unlike the Boston Harbor site, where Andie had found the body almost completely submerged, this latest victim was mostly above the waterline.

"We must be near low tide," said Andie.

"Just passed it," said the Jamaican officer.

Two other Jamaican Constabulary vessels were anchored closer to the piling. Scuba divers below the surface searched for any relevant evidence the killer may have left behind, intentionally or unintentionally. Andie's boat rafted up alongside the larger of the two JCF marine division boats. She was about to board when her cellphone rang. It was the Miami ASAC, Arnie Greenberg.

"Andie, I need you on a videoconference right now," he told her.

The conference was with an FBI computer forensics specialist in Miami and Ian Jeffries, an assistant commissioner of police of the JCF's operations and crime division. JCF forensic teams had recovered the victim's cellphone from his apartment in Kingston, and Jeffries had called upon the FBI to assist in the analysis of data collected. Andie joined the conference in progress. The three men appeared in small rectangular boxes on her screen, but the larger image was something Andie didn't recognize.

"What am I looking at?" asked Andie.

Greenberg responded, "It's a screenshot of a lengthy text message recovered from the victim's cellphone. We think the message was from the killer. The text message is gone, but the screenshot the victim took of it was still in his photos. It was taken roughly thirty-seven hours before the local news station received an anonymous call saying that a body could be found chained to a piling in the harbor."

"Same time lag between time of death and tip to the media as Mc-Cormick and Dwyer. But there was no text from the killer or screenshot in those cases."

"We can talk about why that might be," said Greenberg. "But first, read it."

The screenshot was all words, no images. Andie enlarged her LCD screen and read to herself:

Congratulations. You have been chosen at random from among this piracy website's many users to be entered into this week's Piracy Lotto. One lucky pirate will win this special prize.

"Ye and each of ye are adjudged and sentenced to be carried back to the place from whence you came, thence to the place of execution, and there within the flood marks to be hanged by the neck till you are dead, dead, dead, and the Lord, in His infinite wisdom have mercy upon your souls. After this ye, and each of ye shall be taken down and your bodies hung in chains, to be thrice washed by the rising tide. Pirates, be ye warned."

Andie stared at the screen a moment longer.

"Andie, did your screen freeze?" asked Greenberg. "You still there?"

Her reaction—stunned—had only made her look frozen.

"Still here," she said. "I have a lot of thoughts. But let me start with a question. Why wasn't the text message retrievable from the victim's phone or the cloud?"

The tech expert replied, "I'm still investigating, but the text message was sent automatically to the victim's phone when he visited a piracy website. Apparently, it contained some form of malware that caused it to self-destruct shortly after it was read. But this victim was able to preserve the substance of the message by taking a screenshot of it."

"So, it's possible that Shannon Dwyer and even Tyler McCormick got the same message," said Andie. "They just didn't have the presence of mind to take a screenshot. Is that a fair statement?"

"It is," the tech agent replied.

The wheels were turning quickly in Andie's head. "Has anyone done a Google search on some of these archaic-sounding words?"

"Not yet. We're only three minutes ahead of you on this," said Greenberg.

Andie did a quick search on her phone with the opening few words: "Ye and each of ye are adjudged and sentenced to be carried back to the place from whence you came."

"I got a hit," she told the group, scrolling through the webpage. "The exact language quoted in this text is from the sentencing of fifty-two pirates in April of 1722."

"Let's hope the killer doesn't have fifty-two victims in mind," said Greenberg.

"He definitely seems to be taking the other aspects of the sentence literally," said Andie.

"What do you mean?" asked Greenberg.

"Notice the pronouncement about the 'bodies hung in chains, to be thrice washed by the rising tide.' Three tides is about thirty-six hours. That's how much time our killer has let expire before making an anonymous call to the media and telling them there's a body to recover."

There was silence on the videoconference, as the grim observation sank in.

"Sounds like he's made himself judge, jury, and executioner," said Michael.

Judge. Andie's brief call with Theo was suddenly top of mind, but the next words out of her mouth were even more urgent.

"We need to notify the public we have a serial killer," said Andie. "And we have to tell them that anyone who visits a piracy website is at risk."

CHAPTER 46

The wind was perfect for a Saturday-morning sail. Jack left his Nassau hotel early, and by nine o'clock he was aboard a thirty-foot sailboat with a Bahamian charter captain named Eli. It was research, not recreation. Scores of online reviewers had given Eli five stars, not just for his sailing ability, but for his vast knowledge of local lore and obscure points of Bahamian history—including pirate history. Jack figured that if anyone could lead him to the exact site of the group execution of ten pirates in 1718, it would be Eli.

"People love pirate stories," said Eli.

"The way they love ghost stories, I guess," said Jack.

"It's different, mon. There's no baseball team named Pittsburgh Ghosts. Everyone love pirates."

Not everyone, thought Jack.

They were fifty yards offshore, cutting through waters of sun-sparkled turquoise. The beach stretched for miles in either direction, a seemingly endless pinkish-white ribbon of sand. It was deserted, save for a tiki bar, where a half-dozen recreational boaters relaxed to calypso music. The choice between light or dark rum appeared to be their only concern, never mind the fact that it was barely breakfast time. Jack took a seat on the portside rail near the cockpit. He was safely away from the beam, as the main sail was to starboard.

"There's the spot," said Eli, pointing toward shore.

Jack saw nothing to mark it as "the spot." "How do you know?"

"I don't, mon. That's just my best guess."

"Wait. You're guessing?"

"Wha'choo want, mon? A pirate map that says 'X mark the spot'?

There hardly no records of this sort of thing. We talkin' over three hundred years ago."

It wasn't the answer Jack had been hoping for. "Can I ask you a question, Eli?"

"Sure, mon. No extra charge."

"Let's say I have a friend who was on a boat some years ago. She's trying to remember every little detail about that boat trip. Who was on the boat with her. What kind of boat it was. Who the captain was. She needs to remember everything she possibly can."

"Must've been one important boat trip."

"It was. To help jog her memory, I want to take pictures of where she was when someone on that boat pointed out the exact spot where the bodies of those ten executed pirates were put on display in 1718."

Eli laughed. "That's a good one, mon. The exact spot. Ha! Anywhere the captain say it happened, that where it happened."

Jack's heart sank. "Got it," he said.

"Why you look so sad, mon? Is this not an excellent sail?"

"The best," said Jack.

"Yes, sir. The best. You be sure to give Captain Eli five stars on the internet."

Jack's gaze swept the endless beach. "You bet I will."

"You sure you want the short sail?" asked Eli. "I give you the long sail for jis' fifty dollars more."

The bright side was that finding the historic site of the mass gibbeting wasn't the main point of Jack's visit to the Bahamas. Not even close.

"Short sail," said Jack. "Got a meeting at noon I can't miss."

Eli had him back at the Nassau pier in plenty of time. Jack caught a taxi outside the marina and rode into the city.

"Over the hill, mon," said the driver.

Jack wasn't getting any younger, but the appellation seemed better suited for his father than for him. "You mean me?" he asked.

"No. Where you goin'. Literally, over the East Street Hill. Can be rough there."

It was starting to sound like one of those trips that Jack took only with Theo at his side. "So I've heard," said Jack.

The ride was uphill and then downhill, as promised, taking Jack well away from the glitz of Paradise Island, past the colonial mansions and estates along the coast, and into the hardscrabble neighborhoods of old clapboard houses and the occasional shack constructed from random timbers and sheets of corrugated steel. Basic white was not a popular house paint among residents "over the hill." Coats of bright yellow, blue, and every other hue in the rainbow made the old houses as colorful as the hibiscus flowers growing along the street. Even in the lowest-income areas, Bahamians took pride in their neighborhood and gardens.

The taxi stopped outside a one-story, teal-colored house. Jack checked the address and confirmed he was in the right place.

"Don't stay after dark," the driver told him advisedly. "Good people here. But the gangs . . . not good."

Jack thanked him, followed the stepping-stones to the front porch, and knocked on the screen door. An elderly woman answered. Jack knew from Tyler McCormick's obituary that her name was Ramona.

"Mrs. McCormick?" he said through the screen. "I'm Jack Swyteck. The lawyer from Miami who called to talk about your son."

"I told you I didn't want to talk to you."

"I was hoping I could change your mind."

"Why should I?"

"Because I want to help," said Jack. "I sincerely want to help find whoever it was who really killed your son. Because it was not my client."

She thought it over and then opened the door. Jack entered and followed her into the kitchen. She filled two glasses of iced tea and brought them to the table, where they sat opposite one another. Jack opened the conversation by talking about his client, keeping it light.

"Believe it or not, I hardly knew anything about Imani before she hired me to be her lawyer."

"Hmm. Which rock do you live under?" she asked.

"My wife had the same question."

Ramona smiled a little, which Jack saw as a good start. He continued.

"First time I met Imani was at a private concert," said Jack. "A very wealthy man on Miami Beach hired her to perform in his backyard. Most people aren't aware that big pop stars do those kind of private events."

"Oh, I'm well aware," she said.

"Are you?" Jack said, a little surprised.

"Sure," she said. "That's how Tyler first met Imani."

Jack's response was on a couple of seconds delay, as if Ramona's words didn't quite register. "Tyler was invited to one of Imani's private concerts?"

"No, no," she said, chuckling at the suggestion. "He worked it. Tyler was a bartender."

"When was this?"

She drew a breath, trying to recall. "Maybe five months or so before he died."

"Where was it?"

"Here in the Bahamas."

"In Nassau?"

"No, no," she said with the same chuckle. "This was very private. On somebody's private island. They had to take everyone over by boat."

By boat. From Nassau. Past the site of mass execution of pirates. *Any where the captain say it happened, that where it happened.*

"Do you know whose boat it was?"

"No."

Jack tried to remain focused, but it wasn't easy to tamp down the anger he was feeling toward his client. The lies were starting to pile up. From the very beginning, she'd lied about the big things, starting with when she'd told him she'd never heard the name Tyler McCormick. She'd lied about the little things, too, splitting hairs about the Bahamas being in the west Atlantic and not the Caribbean. It hardly seemed accidental that she'd neglected to tell him that she'd not only been to the Bahamas, but performed a private concert there; not only that she'd met Tyler McCormick there, but that he'd worked her exclusive event—and maybe even had been on the boat from Nassau with her.

"Do you know anyone else who worked that party?" asked Jack.

"Tyler's cousin worked it. I can get you his number, if it's important."

"Yes, thank you," said Jack. "It's very important."

CHAPTER 47

The South African lobster tails with drawn butter were delicious.

Vladimir Kava was in his private dining room with his son, trying to decide between a second bottle of the chardonnay or moving to a light red, perhaps the pinot noir. The flat-screen television on the wall was tuned to CNN International. The lead story was delivered by a London-based anchorwoman. The graphic on the green screen behind her appeared in bold letters, a jaw dropper:

DEATH SENTENCE FOR MUSIC PIRATES

"What the hell," said Kava, the words coming slowly, more of a reaction than a question. He raised the volume with the remote control.

"They are calling him the pirate killer," the anchorwoman said at the top of her broadcast. "His victims include a young woman from Boston, Massachusetts, and a young man from Kingston, Jamaica. Less than one hour ago, unconfirmed reports surfaced of a possible third victim near Chicago."

Kava suddenly felt a wave of indigestion. "Sergei, have you heard about this?"

"No, nothing."

On screen, the anchorwoman continued.

"The victims have two things in common. One, they visited one of the busiest music piracy websites on the internet. And two, their murders mimic the gruesome execution and what is called gibbeting of pirates that was commonplace three centuries ago. This bizarre crime spree has some people asking: 'Has the music industry finally found the nuclear weapon in the war against music piracy?' More on this story from Simon Cutter in Kingston, Jamaica."

Kava slammed his fist on the table. "Sergei, check our platform traffic!"

His son cracked open a lobster claw. "Now?"

"Never mind. I'll do it myself," he said angrily, and he dialed his chief technology officer on his cellphone. "I need data on our current traffic," Kava told his CTO.

"One minute, sir. I'll check with my team."

Kava waited with the phone pressed to his ear. The live news report from Jamaica detailed the killer's method—ligature strangulation and gibbeting—and then it was back to "Lydia in London," who promised "more on this story that is instilling fear around the globe."

Next up was a reporter in Times Square, who was targeting people at random for their reaction. The headline PIRATE KILLER was scrolling on the huge digital newswire behind him.

"Excuse me," the reporter said, thrusting a microphone into a group of five young women who were all wearing University of Wisconsin sweatshirts. "Have any of you heard about the pirate killer?"

One of them stepped forward, glancing one way and then the other, as if not sure whether to look at the reporter or at the camera. "Yeah, we all just saw. It's all over TikTok."

"Does something like this make you think twice about visiting a music piracy website?"

"Uh, *yeah*," she said, as if the question were stupid. "Who wants to end up with their giblets chained to a post?"

Giblets? Social media was, at bottom, the world's worst game of telephone.

"I need my numbers!" Kava shouted into the phone.

"I'm—I need a minute," the CTO said, stammering.

"Just give me the numbers!"

"Something's wrong. Traffic is down sixty-two percent in the last thirty minutes. It has to be a system error."

Kava nearly choked on his wine. "Is the system telling you there's an error?"

"No."

"Have we ever had a system error that caused a sixty-two-percent drop in traffic in thirty minutes?"

"Nothing like this ever before," the CTO said in a voice that quaked. "We're now at sixty-eight percent and still falling."

"We need to get control of this. I want you, me, and Sergei on a conference call in five minutes. Get advertising and marketing on it, as well. Somebody better have a plan."

"Yes, sir."

Kava ended the call and placed his phone on the table.

"How bad is it?"

"Beyond bad," he said. Before he could say more, his phone vibrated on the table with an incoming text message. He put on his reading glasses and read it to himself:

Feeling the pain yet?

The sender's number was unfamiliar, but another text quickly followed:

Want a reprieve for pirates?

Kava stared at the message. His son said something about the "pirate killer" story, but Kava wasn't listening. Another text message appeared in a third bubble:

You can stop the killing NOW.

His son spoke again, but Kava heard only noise. Whoever was texting him had the oligarch's full attention. Another message appeared.

Pay me $75 million. Instructions to follow.

"Dad, what is it?" Sergei asked, his voice too loud to be ignored.

Kava's mind was racing. Piracy websites were worthless without traffic. Pirate executions were bad for traffic. It had taken a quarter century, but someone had finally figured out a way to stop music piracy. Kava was pretty sure he knew who his blackmailer was.

"Sergei, you've been following the Nichols trial, haven't you?"

"Who hasn't been?"

"Remember the testimony of the investment banker who worked for Shaky Nichols when he was trying to sell EML Records?"

"Yes. What about him?"

"How much did he say Shaky Nichols lost on his stock options because of music piracy?"

"I believe it was seventy-five million dollars," said Sergei.

"Yes. I believe you're right," he said, and a plan was formulating in his mind as he spoke. "One other thing. Has our sniper finished her work in London?"

"I'm told there was a miss last night. She plans to try again, tonight."

"Tell her she *must* finish tonight."

"Why?"

"I need her in Miami immediately," said Kava. "There's more important work to be done."

CHAPTER 48

Jack was in his Nassau hotel room, seated in front of his laptop computer screen, minutes away from an emergency hearing by videoconference before Judge Cookson.

Jack had seen the news of a second victim in Jamaica and possibly a third in Chicago. In Jack's mind, they were really the killer's third and fourth victims, with Tyler McCormick the first. It was time to turn his detective work into a winning trial strategy for his client.

Saturday hearings were a rarity in the practice of law. But Jack had sold it to Judge Cookson's assistant by putting his credibility on the line and representing that "this could end the case." If Tyler McCormick's killer was still in action, Jack's client and her ex-husband couldn't possibly be the killers. Even though they were out on bail, the media hounded them everywhere they went. The prosecutor could obtain a conviction only by somehow connecting the defendants to an active serial killer over a span of twelve years—and there was no such evidence.

At 4:00 p.m., the computer screen came alive with Judge Cookson's image. The prosecutor and lawyers for each defendant appeared in smaller boxes to the side, along with a lawyer from the U.S. Department of Justice. The way Jack had framed the issues, the FBI and DOJ had a pivotal stake in the outcome of the hearing.

"Good afternoon, everyone," the judge began. "It is now halftime in the annual Florida-Tennessee football game, and I intend to finish this hearing before my alma mater receives the kickoff to start the second half. I fully appreciate that if the man who killed Tyler McCormick is still on the loose, murdering additional victims, this case should be dismissed. But Mr. Swyteck, what's the specific emergency?"

"Judge, it's a very simple request," said Jack. "We want the FBI to produce a witness on Monday morning to testify about the killer's signature."

"You're going to have to explain better than that," the judge said.

"Glad to," said Jack. "The testimony at trial has established that Mr. McCormick's body was recovered with a curious message written with a marker pen. 'Goodbye girl.' That 'signature,' so to speak, has never been explained. As it turns out, the same message appeared on another victim, Shannon Dwyer, whose body was recovered this week in Boston Harbor."

"What about the victims in the news today?" the judge asked. "Jamaica and possibly Chicago?"

"I don't know if the same signature was on those bodies. That's the point of this emergency hearing. I'm asking this court to issue a subpoena to the FBI, directing the bureau to produce a witness who is familiar with the investigation and who can tell us two things. First, does the same message—'goodbye girl'—appear on all four victims? Second, is it the *same* message. By that I mean, is the signature the same? Surely, the FBI has done expert analysis of the writing on Tyler McCormick and compared it to the subsequent victims. If they have concluded that it is written by the same person, that means we have one killer. Which means that the killer is not my client or her ex-husband."

Judge Cookson checked his watch, apparently keeping track of half-time in the big game.

"Thank you, Mr. Swyteck," said the judge. "Who would like to speak in opposition?"

The lawyer from the DOJ replied. "I would, Your Honor. Beverly Camp on behalf of the United States of America."

"Proceed," the judge said.

"Judge, we have a vicious serial killer on our hands. Mr. Swyteck seeks a court order that would force the FBI to reveal sensitive details of an active investigation. If this court orders the FBI to divulge non-public information in open court, it would jeopardize the efforts of the multijurisdictional task force, dozens of law enforcement officers who are working around the clock to stop this senseless killing spree. The public—specifically, young people in their twenties and even teenagers who are more likely to visit piracy websites—would be in grave danger."

Jack heard background noise over his computer speaker. It sounded like a college marching band, which only confirmed what the on-screen technology was already telling him: the noise was from the judge. Apparently, halftime was wrapping up. And so was the hearing.

"I'm going to grant Mr. Swyteck's motion," the judge said. "However, to address Ms. Camp's concerns, the hearing will be closed to the public and conducted in my chambers at nine a.m. Monday morning. The FBI's witness can testify without any concern that sensitive nonpublic information will be disclosed. We're adjourned," said the judge.

"But—"

Before the DOJ lawyer could say another word, and before Jack could thank the judge, the screen was black. The hearing was over.

"See you Monday," Jack told the other lawyers, and he logged out of the videoconference.

It was a big win, and Jack wanted to call his client to share the news. But he dialed his wife instead.

Andie had called Friday night and told him she was dropping off Righley for a sleepover and heading to Jamaica. The reason for her trip was confidential, but Jack could add two plus two, and he could only wonder if she was still in the Caribbean or had moved on to Chicago and the next possible victim. His call rang to Andie's voicemail. There was little he could say about his case, and little she could tell him about the investigation. He confined his message to Righley, whose best friend happened to be Hannah Goldstein's daughter. A weekend sleepover might have been an imposition on any other family, but Jack had done so much for the Freedom Institute that Hannah could be counted on for the extended favor.

"Just checking in," said Jack. "I'll call Hannah and check on Righley. Love you."

He hung up, and his cell immediately rang—too soon to be Andie returning his call. It was the prosecutor. Jack answered cordially, but Owens's response was not in kind.

"Smooth move, Swyteck."

"What does that mean?" asked Jack.

"You want to cross-examine an FBI witness familiar with the investigation? You'll get one. Hope you enjoy embarrassing your own wife on the witness stand. Have a good rest of your weekend."

The call ended before Jack could respond. Maybe Owens was bluffing, just blowing off steam. Jack went to his laptop and ran a few key words into a Google search: "FBI Agent Andrea Henning" and "pirate killer."

The large number of hits, most of them less than twelve hours old, only lent credence to Owens's bluff—if it was a bluff. Jack didn't dwell on it. He did what any good criminal defense lawyer would have done.

He put his personal life aside for the moment, and he phoned his client.

Theo was alone in a windowless room in the U.S. embassy. Gigi was in another room with the FBI's legal attaché.

It had been a circuitous route from their hotel room back into the city. Metro Police had been the first on the scene. It wasn't clear to Theo if they'd responded to Gigi's call to emergency from the bathroom on her cell, or if someone else had called. What was clear, however, was that Andie or her boss had phoned the FBI's legal attaché in London after her call with Theo had disconnected in mid-conversation. Madeline Coffey was fully briefed by the time Metro Police delivered Theo and Gigi to the embassy.

There was a knock on the door, and it opened. Theo was about to rise as Coffey entered, but she told him not to bother and pulled up a chair opposite him at the table.

"Did Gigi talk?" asked Theo.

"First off, her name is not Gigi. It's Kelly Oswald. She's young, but not as young as she looks. She turned eighteen three months ago."

"She was still underage when this creep she calls Judge took her in."

"That's true."

"What did she tell you about him?"

Coffey didn't answer. Theo pressed.

"His nickname for her was 'Goodbye Girl.' That's why I called Andie. Do you think he's connected to these other killings?"

She paused, seeming to measure her response. "Thank you for calling Agent Henning. It was the right thing to do."

"That doesn't answer my question," said Theo.

"I'm afraid I can't answer any of your questions."

"Why not?"

"It's complicated."

"Yeah, well, to you it's complicated. To me it's bullshit."

"You brought us helpful information. You're a tipster. That doesn't make you part of the investigative team or a member of the multijurisdictional task force."

"I'm just asking what she said."

"If she wanted you to know, she would have told you."

Her point had some merit, but it gave rise to a different concern. "She's not part of this, is she?"

"It depends on what you mean by 'this.'"

"These killings."

"She's not a suspect, if that's what you're asking."

That came as a relief. "When can I talk to her?"

"That's going to be difficult."

"Why?"

"She left almost an hour ago."

Theo sprang from his chair. "What the fuck?"

"It was her choice."

"I don't believe you."

"You're very lucky that sniper missed last night. Can you blame an eighteen-year-old girl for not wanting to hang around and see if the second time's a charm?"

Theo settled back into his chair. It was like losing a friend without a proper goodbye. But he understood. And he certainly couldn't blame her.

"What's going to happen to her?"

"She's eighteen," said Coffey. "It's up to her."

"Judge threatened to come back to London and kill her if she talked to the police."

"She made us aware of that threat."

"Are you protecting her?"

"In my humble opinion, you should be more worried about what's going to happen to you."

Theo read between the lines. "Telling you everything she knows about Judge took an incredible amount of courage."

"I agree," said Coffey.

"But you're not going to do a thing to protect her, are you?"

"She's not even a U.S. citizen. It's time for you to focus on protecting yourself."

"I don't operate that way."

"Then you have a choice," she said. "You can stay in London and dodge bullets from a sniper who could be anywhere. Or you can let us drive you back to Heathrow, and you can fly wherever you want to go."

"And where can I go that they won't eventually find me?"

No answer.

"Not much of a choice," said Theo.

"No. Not much of one."

Theo rose, put on his coat, and did his best impersonation of a character from *Downton Abbey*. "Cheerio, old chap."

"That's the worst British accent I've ever heard."

Theo smiled, left the room, and left the embassy. He knew Gigi's—Kelly's—cellphone number. He walked around the corner in search of a red booth.

A ndie saw the sunrise over Lake Michigan on Sunday.
    Rumors of another victim in the Chicago area had proven true. Andie had flown straight from Kingston to O'Hare. She'd spent the rest of the night at the floating crime scene in Monroe Harbor, battling the cold November winds off the lake, the lights of the Chicago skyline glistening in the dark, choppy waters. Andie presumed that, had it been summer, or at least milder autumn weather, someone might have spotted the gibbeted corpse chained to one of the harbor's nearly four hundred moorings. As was the pattern, it took another anonymous tip for police to discover the body, "thrice washed by the rising tide." Except this time there was a twist.

"I assume we're at high tide," said Andie.

"Nope. Low tide," said the marine patrol officer.

"But the victim is almost completely submerged. The killer's pattern has been to position the body so that it's submerged at high tide and exposed, at least partially, at low tide."

"The Great Lakes are considered nontidal. The difference between low tide and high tide is about five centimeters."

"Apparently, the killer didn't know that," said Andie, thinking aloud.

"Which means he's probably not from around here," said the officer.

"Not a local copycat," said Andie. "This is the real deal."

Chicago marked a break from the previous two locations, both historic sites of gibbeting for pirates of old. The killer seemed to be sending a message, which was exactly what Andie told the task force leader in her morning update by telephone.

"What's his message?" he asked.

"It can happen anywhere," said Andie. "There is no safe place for music pirates."

Her words foreshadowed the morning headline. News commentators struggled to find precedent for the widespread fears causing public disengagement with piracy websites. "Not since *The Interview*, when North Korea threatened terrorist attacks against movie theaters showing the 2014 comedy about a plot to assassinate Kim Jong Un, have we seen fear drive consumer choices in the entertainment industry."

Andie checked into a downtown hotel with time to shower and catch a couple hours of sleep before heading back to the crime scene. She was just entering her room when a call from the U.S. embassy in London lit up her phone. It was the legal attaché, Madeline Coffey.

"I emailed you the notes of my interview of Kelly Oswald. Did you get them?"

"Yes. I read them with interest."

"I should have a sketch in an hour," said Coffey.

"How soon can we release it? With a killer who waits thirty-six hours to tell us where to find the body, I'm not just afraid we'll have another victim. I'm afraid we already do, and just don't know it yet."

"I understand. But there's a snag," said Coffey.

Andie took a seat on the edge of the mattress. "What kind of snag?"

"I need approval from Washington before we can release the sketch."

"The task force leader is the unit chief for the National Center for the Analysis of Violent Crime. What other approval do you need?"

"DOJ. Office of enforcement operations."

Andie's response caught in her throat. "Are you saying our suspect is in the Witness Security Program?"

"We believe he is. Metro Police collected fingerprints from his last apartment in Bethnal Green. Nothing turned up in the INTERPOL database. We got a hit in ours, but the system blocked us. Obviously, only Washington can confirm."

Andie went to the window. She could see the harbor from her hotel room. "Not good," she said, putting it mildly. "Not good at all."

CHAPTER 49

Jack entered the criminal courthouse in time for the 9:00 a.m. hearing in Judge Cookson's chambers. His client was at his side. Diehard Imani fans had been waiting since 5:00 a.m., hoping to snag a coveted courtroom seat, which made Jack glad it wasn't his job to tell them that Monday's proceedings were closed to the public.

"Good morning, all," said Judge Cookson.

Given his seniority, Cookson's chambers were more spacious than most, but things were still a bit cramped. The judge was seated behind his formidable antique mahogany desk. A long, rectangular table projected out from the front of the desk, battle-scarred by staples and binder clips dragged across its once polished surface at countless previous hearings. Defense counsel and their clients were seated at the table to the judge's right; the prosecutor was across from them and to the judge's left. At the end of the table, facing the judge, was the DOJ lawyer.

"Counsel, has the FBI identified a witness to testify pursuant to my order?" the judge asked.

The DOJ lawyer replied, "Yes, Your Honor. I have been in contact with the unit chief for the National Center for the Analysis of Violent Crime, who is head of the joint task force known as Operation Gibbet. He confirmed that the questioned document unit in the FBI laboratory division is currently undertaking a comparative analysis of the 'goodbye girl' signature in the Tyler McCormick case to the 'goodbye girl' signature displayed in more recent cases."

"I assume the analysis is being done by an FBI handwriting expert," said the judge.

"Yes. Dr. Gerald Stone in Quantico, Virginia, is leading that analysis with his team."

"Will Dr. Stone be testifying today?"

"No, Your Honor. Dr. Stone's analysis is not yet finished. For obvious public safety reasons, the completion of his work is highly time sensitive. He is therefore unavailable so that he can continue with that work, full speed ahead."

"I've ordered that the FBI provide a witness to testify about the comparison. Who will that be?"

"A member of the Operation Gibbet task force has been selected to review the preliminary conclusions of Dr. Stone and to present that information to the court."

"Does this person have a name?" asked the judge, his patience waning.

The DOJ lawyer glanced at Jack, then back at the judge. Jack wasn't quite believing what he knew he was about to hear.

"FBI Agent Andrea Henning."

Jack was required to sit, but it took all his strength not to rise to object. "Judge, Agent Henning is my wife."

The judge took a breath. He seemed to have passed the point of irritation, but not with Jack.

"I know who she is. Former Governor Swyteck has glowed about his daughter-in-law several times in my presence."

"With the court's permission," said the prosecutor, "I will present Agent Henning's testimony by videoconference. She is currently in Chicago."

"I don't care if she's right here, hiding under the table," said the judge, his irritation quickly turning to anger. "Mr. Swyteck's wife is *not* testifying."

"Judge, with all due respect," said the prosecutor, "Mr. Swyteck demanded that a member of the task force testify as to the FBI's comparison of the 'goodbye girl' signature. So we have provided—"

"His wife," the judge said, cutting him off harshly.

"Which is—"

"Which is *baloney*," the judge said, cutting off Owens again. "I issued an order. The prosecution and the FBI don't like my order. You are now sending me a message: If I insist on enforcing my order, you are going to bring in Mr. Swyteck's wife to embarrass him, to embarrass herself, and to make a mockery of this proceeding. I resent that kind of games-manship, and I won't allow it."

"Judge, if you will just allow us to proceed, you will see this is on the up-and-up."

"Don't test me, Mr. Owens. Is Agent Henning an expert in hand-writing analysis?"

"She is not."

"Of course not," the judge said. "She's a pawn in this stunt, and some-one with a very small mind at the bureau has decided that it's all okay, because Agent Henning brought it on herself by marrying a criminal defense lawyer. That, as I said, is *baloney*. I can only imagine how she must feel."

Jack, too, could only imagine, and it was making him nauseous.

The judge continued, "Fifteen minutes from now, my bailiff is going to swear in an FBI handwriting expert as witness, and that witness will testify in compliance with my order. If that doesn't happen, I will hold Mr. Owens and the FBI in contempt. We're in recess."

"Judge, this is really—"

"Stop, Mr. Owens. You now have *less than* fifteen minutes to comply with my order. I suggest you go, and go quickly."

The lawyers on the prosecution's side of the table packed up their computers and other items, but Jack was the first one out the door, leav-ing his client at the table with Shaky's lawyer. "Go, and go quickly" seemed like good advice to Jack. He found an empty room at the end of the hallway and reached Andie on her cellphone.

"This is not cool, Jack."

"I am so sorry," he said into the phone. "Owens threatened to do this, but I thought it was a total bluff."

"Why did you not tell me?"

"Because I was *sure* it was a bluff," he said—though, truthfully, he was only "sure" in hindsight. "The thought of you testifying as a witness in this trial is ridiculous. You're doing important work. I didn't want you to have to deal with a bullshit distraction."

"Well, it wasn't a bluff, and now I have to deal with it."

"No, you don't. The judge shot it down. He ordered the FBI to produce a handwriting expert as witness."

Andie sighed so heavily that it crackled on the line. "This makes me more certain than ever that my solution is the only solution to this problem."

She was referring to the conversation at Cy's Place, but he was still in the dark. "I still don't know what 'solution' you're talking about."

She paused, as if trying to decide whether this was the time to go there. She decided it was not.

"Why are you doing this, Jack? Why are you demanding a witness from the task force?"

"If the handwriting is the same, that means there is one killer. One killer means my client didn't kill Tyler McCormick."

"You're not going to get that testimony," she said.

Jack hesitated. "What?"

"Jack, if the work of the task force showed that your client is innocent, do you think I would just zip my lip and let two innocent people go to jail?"

Jack wasn't sure how to respond. "I don't know."

"What do you mean, you don't know?"

"You have confidentiality obligations to the FBI investigation. I didn't want to ask you to breach any confidences and put you in a compromising position."

"So, instead, you allowed me to be blindsided by the prosecutor, who wants me to be the one to tell the judge that your theory doesn't fly? The signatures are not written by the same person. Shannon Dwyer's killer did not kill Tyler McCormick."

Jack fell silent. It was a whipsaw of disappointment. Not only had his trial strategy fallen flat, but he'd put Andie in an untenable position.

"I'm sorry. You have a right to be mad."

"Getting angry isn't going to solve the real problem here."

"What do you mean?"

There was silence, then she answered, "This isn't working anymore."

He wasn't sure what she meant, but his mind raced to what she could have meant, and it scared him. "This what? *What* isn't working?"

"This arrangement of you not telling me about your cases and me not telling you about my investigations. It doesn't work. It hasn't worked in a long time. Actually, it never has."

She was talking about the cardinal principle of their relationship—of their marriage. Jack swallowed hard. "So, what are you saying?"

Another sigh on the line. "Can we talk about this when I get back from Chicago?"

"No. You can't just throw out something like that and say we'll talk about it later. We need to talk now."

There was a knock on the door. It opened, and Shaky's lawyer poked her head into the room. "Sorry to interrupt. The judge is back. The FBI has a witness by videoconference."

"I need a minute," Jack told her.

"Judge Cookson is in no mood to give anyone a minute."

Jack took her point. He spoke into the phone. "Andie, I have to go back to court. But I want us to talk about this sooner, not later."

"Sure."

"I'm sorry, Andie. I love you."

"Bye, Jack," she said, and the call ended.

CHAPTER 50

Jack was the last one to return to Judge Cookson's chambers. He took the empty seat beside Imani.

"So glad you could join us, Mr. Swyteck," the judge said, arching an eyebrow.

"My apologies, Your Honor."

"Mr. Owens, I don't see a witness in the room. For your sake, I hope you have one queued up for appearance by videoconference."

"We do," said the prosecutor. "We have Dr. Gerald Stone, a senior forensic handwriting and forgery analyst with the FBI's questioned document unit in the laboratory division at Quantico, Virginia."

"Let's get him up on the flat-screen," the judge said.

The screen was on the wall facing the judge. The courtroom clerk brought up the witness remotely, and the bailiff administered the oath just as if they were in a courtroom. The judge greeted the witness with the aid of technology, and then he addressed the lawyers in chambers with him.

"Mr. Owens will question the witness first. Mr. Swyteck can then cross-examine. Please proceed."

"Thank you, Judge," said the prosecutor.

Owens remained in his seat as he questioned the witness, but he seemed well aware that his case was on the line. His opening questions established Dr. Stone's credentials and experience, which included everything from the examination of signatures on legal documents and professional sports memorabilia, to the analysis of handwritten messages from alleged kidnappers, terrorists, and serial killers. Like all FBI analysts, Stone's training as an expert witness was evident. Even though he was speaking to a camera, he seemed to be looking directly at the judge as he answered the prosecutor's questions.

"Dr. Stone, I want to ask you about the handwriting analysis you have been asked to perform for the multijurisdictional task force known as Operation Gibbet."

With the remote control, the prosecutor changed the image on the screen and brought up a side-by-side comparison of the two samples for all to see. Jack tried to fight his own skepticism, but it seemed that whoever had selected the photographs for comparison had deliberately chosen photographs that emphasized the dissimilarities.

"Are these the two samples you compared?" asked the prosecutor.

"Yes," said the witness.

"In general, what was the scientific basis for the comparative analysis?"

"Any handwriting comparison is based on two generally accepted principles. First, no two people write exactly alike. Second, while no single person writes exactly the same way twice, certain characteristics reoccur throughout a person's writing."

"How did you apply these principles to the two samples you were asked to compare?"

"The same way I would in any comparative analysis."

"Did the fact that your two samples were written on human skin, as opposed to a document, affect your analysis?"

"Yes. But to be precise, I was not looking at samples on skin. My comparison was based on photographs of the images from the investigative files."

"Did the fact that the bodies had been immersed in saltwater have any impact on your analysis?"

"Actually, the fact that the bodies had been submerged in water is the single most important factor influencing my analysis to date."

"In what way?"

"May I take control of the cursor on the screen?" the witness asked.

The judge allowed it, and Dr. Stone answered while using the cursor as a pointer.

"Mr. McCormick's sample is on the left. It reads 'goodbye girl.' However, you will note that the letter 'g' in the word 'girl' is smudged," he said, indicating with the cursor. "This is not surprising, given that the body was in water for more than thirty-six hours. Now, look at the sample on the right, which is from Ms. Dwyer. You see the same or very similar smudging in the same place: the letter 'g' is not as clear."

Jack looked closely. The expert's observation was valid.

With the prosecutor's click of the remote, the samples disappeared, and Dr. Stone returned on the flat-screen.

"What does that tell you, Dr. Stone?" the prosecutor asked.

"My conclusion is that these two messages, though similar, were written by two different people."

It was going exactly as Andie had told Jack it would. All Jack could do was listen, as the witness breathed life into the prosecutor's case.

"Why does it indicate two different people?" asked Owens.

"It makes no sense that the message would fade or smudge exactly in the same place twice. More likely, the later sample is a meticulous copy of the first."

"I see," said the prosecutor. "So, whoever wrote 'goodbye girl' on Ms. Dwyer's body was making a meticulous copy of the message found on Mr. McCormick's body. Is that what you're saying?"

"Yes. It is so meticulous that the copy even duplicates features that are not part of the original author's handwriting pattern, such as the smudges caused by water or other external factors."

"Thank you, Dr. Stone. I have no further questions."

The judge rocked back in his leather desk chair, stroking his chin, as if he'd already heard enough. Nonetheless, he looked at Jack and said, "Cross-examination, Mr. Swyteck?"

"Yes, Judge," said Jack, remaining in his seat. "So, we have a copycat. Is that your conclusion, Dr. Stone?"

"Yes. In plain English, that's one way to put it."

"Just to be clear: you are not testifying that we have two different killers, are you?"

"I have no opinion on that."

"Even if you're right, and two different people wrote the 'goodbye girl' samples, it doesn't necessarily follow that we have two different killers. Does it?"

He seemed to understand Jack's point, but he was too well trained to concede anything that didn't need to be conceded. "I have no opinion on that," he said.

"Dr. Stone, earlier in this trial, we heard testimony from Mr. Nichols's former bodyguard, a Mr. Paxton. He claims to have written 'goodbye girl' on Mr. McCormick's body. Are you aware of that?"

"I've been made aware," said the witness.

"Have you compared Mr. Paxton's handwriting to the handwriting in the McCormick photograph?"

It was a straightforward question, but answering it seemed to cause the witness some consternation. "I have not."

"Have you been asked to perform that analysis?"

Another pause. "I have not been asked."

It was as Jack had expected. "Has it occurred to you that no one asked because your analysis could prove that the state's star witness is a liar?"

"Objection," said Owens.

"Sustained," said the judge, all but groaning. "Mr. Swyteck, the point of this hearing was to determine whether the FBI investigation has confirmed that Mr. McCormick's killer is still on the loose and active. If anything, Dr. Stone's testimony suggests the opposite. I understand your efforts to salvage something from this hearing, but let's face facts. You stepped up to the plate, you swung for the fences, and you whiffed."

True enough, Jack was trying to salvage a bad situation, but the judge's words were unusually harsh. It was just a hunch on Jack's part, but Judge Cookson seemed to be under the impression that Jack had demanded testimony from an FBI witness only because he knew with absolute certainty that the testimony would confirm the existence of a single killer and eviscerate the prosecution's case. In other words, the judge had assumed that Jack's trial strategy was informed by pillow talk. It was the very thing Andie worried most about in the marriage of a law enforcement officer to a criminal defense lawyer, and it left Andie's words echoing in his ear.

This isn't working, Jack.

"I see no basis to dismiss the indictment," the judge said. "This case is going back before the jury at nine a.m. tomorrow. We're adjourned."

"Thank you, Your Honor," said Owens.

The lawyers packed up their computers and other items, and they exited to the hallway. The prosecutor and DOJ lawyer took the first elevator down to the ground-floor lobby. Defense counsel and their clients waited for the next one.

"That got us nowhere," said Shaky. "What happened, Swyteck? Did you get bad information from your wife?"

"I don't get *any* information from my wife," said Jack. His voice had an edge, fueled by both the judge's remarks and the bomb Andie had dropped on him.

A down elevator arrived. The defense team rode alone, lawyers and clients staring straight ahead at the chrome doors. Shaky's lawyer broke the silence.

"We need to discuss whether the defendants will take the stand when the time comes," she said.

"Too early to say," said Jack.

"Shaky doesn't want Imani to testify."

"Does that mean Shaky will not be testifying?" asked Jack.

"Shaky most definitely will testify," said Ellis. "It's critical that the jury hear him say he is innocent."

"Hold on," said Jack. "Are you proposing that Shaky testifies in his own defense, but my client does not?"

Shaky spoke up. "Imani will make a terrible witness."

"Fuck you, Shaky. I'll make a great witness."

"You cry over a bad album review," said Shaky. "How are you going to handle a prosecutor's cross-examination?"

"You get caught in a lie every time you open your mouth. How are *you* going to handle cross-examination?"

The elevator stopped.

"Quiet," said Jack.

The ex-spouses exchanged one last hateful glare, but when the elevator doors parted, their expressions were pleasant, like the flip of a light switch. They'd been through this drill before. The media was waiting in the lobby, and the joint defendants faced the onslaught of reporters, cameras, and microphones without the slightest hint of a break in solidarity. Weird, thought Jack, how looking happily divorced could be as much work as the illusion of a happy marriage.

"Mr. Swyteck, what happened at the closed hearing?" a reporter asked. "Are you happy, Imani?"

Similar questions followed. Jack ignored them and continued across the lobby, keeping Imani at his side. Shaky and his lawyer followed right behind. It took a while to reach the exit doors, and for Jack it seemed like forever. His singular focus was to get out of the building, break away from the crowd, and call Andie. The *whomp-whomp* of the revolving door ahead of them was a sign of slow but steady progress. Jack sent Imani through first, and he followed. Shaky was next, but before he could emerge on the other side, the revolving door came to an abrupt stop. At least four reporters had tried to jump into the single slot behind Shaky and jammed the door. Shaky was momentarily trapped inside the glass wedge, like a goldfish in a tiny bowl, waiting for the media to find its manners and unclog the exit.

Jack was right outside the door when the tempered glass exploded into a hailstorm of diamond-like pellets.

Shaky dropped like a stone—and then Jack saw the blood.

"Shooter!" somebody screamed, unleashing utter hysteria.

It was like a swift kick to an anthill, with people running in every direction, some in search of cover, and others just utterly confused. MDPD crowd-control officers had been positioned outside the courthouse from day one of the Imani Nichols trial. One of the officers immediately grabbed Imani, shouting for her to come with him.

Jack followed, shattered glass crunching beneath his feet, as the officer pushed and shoved through the hysteria. The winding path to safety was across the courthouse steps to another door marked "Employees Only." Jack caught a glimpse of the revolving door as they passed. The glass partition in front of Shaky had completely shattered. The glass behind him was intact but sprayed red with blood. Shaky was a lifeless heap with a grievous wound to the head.

"Oh my God!" Imani shrieked.

The MDPD officer's radio crackled with a transmission from another officer on the scene. Jack didn't understand the numeric police codes the officers shared, but he heard enough to understand what had happened.

"Sniper" was the operative word.

CHAPTER 51

Tower Bridge was aglow over the River Thames, with St. Paul's Cathedral in the distance. A perfectly positioned moon above made for an exceptional photo op.

Theo and Kelly, whom he formerly knew as Gigi, shared a bench in King's Stairs Gardens, a riverside park along the south bank. They were a short walk from the nearby remains of the fourteenth-century manor house of King Edward III and the adjacent conservation area named in His Majesty's honor. It was now a recreational green space with hundreds of mature oak, ash, cherry, sycamore, maple, and silver birch trees. They were well upriver from the Tower of London, but if Theo looked closely, he could spot it. Theo had called her cell from a phone booth after leaving the U.S. embassy. She'd told him to meet her there at 5:00 p.m.

"No sniper on the rooftops?" asked Kelly.

"No sniper," said Theo.

"For how long?"

The murder of Shaky Nichols had been front-page news worldwide. Reports of a sniper hardly seemed like a coincidence, and Theo had promptly reached out to Madeline Coffey at the U.S. embassy to get her view on a possible connection.

"The FBI's legal attaché obviously has sources I don't. There's no doubt in her mind that the sniper who was after me here, in London, just made a hit in Miami."

"Which is hardly any comfort at all," she said, scoffing. "How long is a plane ride from Miami back to Heathrow?"

"It doesn't work that way. Russian oligarchs don't send their hit men—or hit women—on killing sprees. After a hit, they lay low."

"How long?"

"The legat says at least a couple of weeks."

"What if they hire another hit man?"

Theo couldn't rule it out. "I lost four of the best years of my life in prison for something I didn't do. I'm not going to live my life in hiding."

She smiled a little. "I like that. That's how I want to live."

"Everybody thinks that. Until they have to do it. It's the hardest thing there is, you know? Trying to make up for lost time."

She seemed to relate, and it made Theo sad to think someone so young totally understood what he was saying.

His gaze drifted toward the river. A dinner-cruise boat filled with tourists passed, motoring downriver toward the bridge. "Why did you want to meet at this spot?" he asked.

"Judge took me here once."

"What for?"

"That's what I was wondering. Then he started talking."

"What about?"

She glanced at Theo, then toward the Tower of London across the river. "Pirates," she said. "Mostly pirate executions."

"What about them?"

"Right across the river is where they did it. Execution Dock, it's called. Pirates sentenced to death were paraded over London Bridge, past the Tower of London and toward Wapping. It was like a spectator sport. Streets were lined with tons of people, and the river was packed full of boats, all keen to see the execution. The prisoners were allowed one stop on the way to the gallows. It was at a pub called Turk's Head Inn. They got their last quart of ale."

"Judge told you this?"

"Yeah. He was obsessed with it. The execution dock was actually in the river. They would hang the pirate with a short rope, so that his neck wouldn't break. They wanted a slow death by strangulation, lots of suffering. The crowd would laugh watching them kick their feet and pee in their pants."

"Huh," he said, but his thoughts ran deeper. All those years on death row, he'd thought the electric chair was a shitty way to go.

"Captain Kidd was especially gross," she said. "The rope broke the first time, so they had to hang him twice. But here's the part Judge really liked. Execution Dock was built at the low-tide line. They would leave the dead body on display for three rising tides. The idea was to warn other pirates."

All of it sounded exactly like the previous week's media coverage of the modern-day pirate killer. "Did you tell all this to the legal attaché when you were with her in the embassy?" asked Theo.

"I did."

"Then what the hell's wrong with them? This guy's picture should be on every newscast. The whole world should be looking for him. Didn't you tell her what Judge looks like?"

"Yeah. They brought in an artist. We did a sketch."

"This makes no sense," said Theo, thinking about it. "I need your phone. I should call Jack."

She gave it to him, and Theo shot off a quick text: "It's Theo. Pick up when I call."

J ack was alone in his office when the call came.

Two minutes earlier, Imani had been with him, lawyer and client trying to make sense of the morning tragedy and sort out the implications for Imani's trial without her ex-husband. But for the "heads-up" text message, Jack never would have asked Imani to step out, and he would have let the call from an unknown number go to voicemail.

"Theo? Where are you?"

"Still in London."

"Why?"

"Didn't Andie tell you?"

The question caught Jack off-guard. "No."

"I was on the phone with her when I got shot at."

The first thing that popped into Jack's mind was that Andie had said nothing about this to him, which only put a finer point on their ongoing troubles. Jack led with his second thought: "Somebody shot at you?"

"Yeah. Now the FBI tells me it was the same sniper who took out Shaky."

It was a lot for Jack to process. "Wait—what?"

"Jack, listen to what I'm saying. Your best friend got shot at. I was on the phone with your wife when it happened. She didn't say anything to you?"

"No, she didn't."

"Dude, that's fucked up."

It was, and it triggered those words all over again. *This isn't working anymore.* But this wasn't the time to get into the Andie situation, even if Theo did have the counseling skills of a world-class bartender, better than most psychiatrists.

"That's a whole 'nother conversation," said Jack.

There was a knock on the door, and it opened. Jack's assistant took a half-step into the room.

"Judge Cookson's assistant just called," she said. "He wants you back in his chambers at two p.m. Lawyers only."

Jack checked the time. It was short.

"Theo, I gotta go," he said into the phone.

"Seriously?"

"The judge called. I barely have time to organize my thoughts and get to the courthouse. Can I call you back on this number?"

"Yeah, sure. What do you think the judge is gonna do?"

A fleet of possibilities sailed through Jack's mind. "Better question is, 'What should I ask him to do?'"

CHAPTER 52

The mood was somber in Judge Cookson's chambers.

The building's main entrance was still a crime scene, so the lawyers had entered through the chute on "Lucky Thirteenth Street," which connected the courthouse to the jail. Jack and Jennifer Ellis were on one side of the table. The prosecutor sat across from them. But it was Judge Cookson who seemed most subdued. The courthouse had been his home away from home for decades, and it was as if the murder had happened on his own front doorstep.

"First, let me express my condolences to you, Ms. Ellis, on the terrible tragedy that unfolded this morning."

"Thank you, Judge. Shaky Nichols was a good, *good* man."

Jack was silent, but for an instant, the back of his mind rattled with his own client's cries of "Pick-me girl!"

"Let's not overstate things," said the prosecutor.

"Mr. Owens, please," said the judge. "Innocent until proven guilty. Does that ring a bell?"

"I believe we proved his guilt beyond a reasonable doubt," said Owens. "We simply didn't get the opportunity to hear the jury's verdict."

"That's exactly what I want to discuss," the judge said. "I have not yet discharged the jurors. Let's say I call them back to the courthouse tomorrow. Does the state have additional evidence to present as to Imani Nichols? Or is it prepared to rest its case?"

"As I stated," said Owens, "we believe we have proven our case. In deference to the FBI investigation, we do not intend to call Dr. Stone as a witness. That state rests its case."

"Mr. Swyteck, let me put the question to you," said the judge. "If the jury comes back tomorrow, and the state rests its case, does your client intend to put on a defense?"

"Possibly," said Jack.

"Spoken like a true criminal defense lawyer," said Owens.

The judge grimaced. "I don't share Mr. Owens's sarcasm, but I do share his frustration. That's not a very helpful answer."

"My apologies," said Jack. "But this line of inquiry strikes me as entirely academic. It has been my position all along that my client was prejudiced by having to stand trial jointly with Shaky Nichols. It would certainly be prejudicial to force her to continue before a jury who is undoubtedly, and as we speak, watching one newscaster after another speculate as to the reasons for Shaky Nichols's murder."

"I understand your point," the judge said. "And it may well be that I have no choice but to declare a mistrial."

"There is one other option," said Jack.

"What would that be?" the judge asked.

"The state has rested its case. This court has the authority to end the trial right now and enter a judgment of acquittal."

The prosecutor groaned. "A judgment of acquittal is appropriate only if the court finds that the evidence is insufficient to warrant a conviction. Clearly this is a case that should go to the jury."

"Maybe it was as to Shaky Nichols," said Jack. "But not as to my client."

"Are you making a motion for a judgment of acquittal?" the judge asked.

Jack hadn't come to the courthouse on twenty minutes' notice with that intention. But sometimes a lawyer just had to go with the flow.

"Yes, I am, Your Honor. Count one charges second-degree murder. There is absolutely no evidence that Imani Nichols caused the death of Tyler McCormick. Count two charges mutilation of a corpse. The only evidence is the hearsay testimony of a convicted felon who claims that Shaky told him it was 'Imani's idea' to write the message 'goodbye girl' on the corpse."

"Judge, that's a gross distortion," said the prosecutor.

"But Mr. Swyteck has a point," said the judge. "If I declare a mistrial, we have to start all over again with the trial of Imani Nichols. But if I enter a judgment of acquittal, double jeopardy attaches. The case against her is over. Forever."

"And that's the correct result," said Jack.

"That would be a terrible result," said the prosecutor.

"I'm not surprised the lawyers disagree," said the judge. "I'm going to take this matter under advisement, but not for very long. I'm not forecasting anything. We may resume trial tomorrow. I may declare a mistrial. Or the case against Ms. Nichols may be over. I will call the lawyers with my decision tonight. Understood?"

"Yes, Your Honor," the lawyers replied.

The judge again conveyed his condolences. The lawyers gathered their items and exited to the hallway. The prosecutor made a beeline to the elevator. Shaky's lawyer mumbled something about hoping to get her bills paid by Shaky's estate. Jack's phone vibrated with an incoming text message. He read it on the glance.

it's tyler's cousin. u can call me on this number.

Jack froze. It was the same number Tyler's mother had given Jack in Nassau, when she'd told him that the cousin had worked alongside Tyler at Imani's private event in the Bahamas. Jack had tried it at least a dozen times with no response. Jack didn't want to miss this opportunity to fill in some important gaps in his client's memory of her trip to the Bahamas with Shaky.

Jack found a quiet place and returned the call.

CHAPTER 53

Brownsville was just outside the Miami city limits, a ten-minute drive north from Jack's office. It was also one of the largest enclaves of Bahamian Americans in the United States. Tyler McCormick's cousin was visiting friends there. Jack deemed their conversation important enough to make it face-to-face. He met Leon McCormick at a café called the Bahama Mama, "the bright purple building next to the pink one," as Leon had described it. Jack found him at one of the neon-yellow picnic tables outside. A cheerful waitress brought Leon a basket of golden brown conch fritters just as Jack joined him at the table.

"Thanks for reaching out," said Jack.

"Wasn't exactly on the top of my to-do list, mon. Not till Shaky got blown away." He pushed the basket more toward the middle of the table. "Fritter? They make the best here."

Jack took one. The homemade hot sauce was in a vintage Coca-Cola bottle on the table. Jack splashed some on and agreed the fritters were "the best." He hoped Leon's truth telling would continue.

"Did you know Shaky?"

"Not really. Tyler and me was on the boat with him. One dead Shaky makes two dead people from that boat trip. I ask myself, *Who's next?*"

"What made you call me?"

"My auntie said you was looking for me. I looked you up on the Google machine. You seem like a good place to start, so long as it don't cost me."

"No, this is a freebie. I just want to know what you know."

Leon selected another fritter and splashed on double the hot sauce, as if to show Jack how it was done. "What you wanna know?"

"Tell me about the boat."

"Big boat," he said, chewing.

"How big?"

"Biggest boat I ever seen. Almost a ship."

The waitress returned with two cold beers, which made Leon smile. "Thank you, sweetie. You take such good care of me."

"Don't you know it," she said, leaving with a wink and a smile.

Jack drank from his beer, the perfect remedy for the hot sauce. "When you say almost as big as a ship, do you mean a superyacht?"

"Super-duper yacht, mon."

"Whose superyacht was it?"

"I dunno. Some old dude. Russian."

"Do you remember his name?"

"Vladimir somethin' or other."

"Vladimir Kava?" asked Jack.

"Kava, yeah. Vladimir Kava. And his son, Fergie."

"Sergei?"

"Yeah, Sergei."

Jack made a mental note of yet another lie from his client. He couldn't recall if she'd ever come right out and said she'd never met Vladimir Kava, but she'd certainly conveyed that impression in the negotiations with the FBI about wearing a wire to the private event for Kava's granddaughter.

"Did you talk to Mr. Kava?"

"No, mon. Nobody gets close to that dude. I served the guests."

"So, you never saw Imani talk to him?"

"Imani, sure. Everybody wanna talk to Imani. She's the star."

"Other than the people we've talked about, do you remember who else was on Kava's boat?"

"No, mon. This is more than ten years ago."

"Think hard. Even if you don't remember names, is there anything you remember about the other people on the boat?"

Leon popped another fritter into his mouth, thinking, then swallowing.

"I remember there were a lot of girls."

"Girls? Or women?"

"Definitely girls. Like teenagers."

"Do you mean teenage girls who were fans of Imani?"

"Maybe they was fans. But that's not why they was on the boat."

Jack could read between the lines, but he needed Leon to spell it out. "Why were they there, Leon?"

"Shee-it, mon. Why you think?"

The picture was suddenly coming clearer to Jack. "Let me ask," he said. "And there's no way to ask this delicately. Was your cousin Tyler stalking Imani?"

"Stalking? Not really. Though, I guess some people might call it stalkin'."

"What do you call it?"

"Me? I call it blackmail, mon."

Jack paused. In the short period of time he'd known Imani, Tyler McCormick had gone from a nobody to her lover, to her stalker, to her blackmailer. It was suddenly clear why Leon had gone to a criminal defense lawyer instead of the police.

"I need to hear more about that," said Jack, and then his phone vibrated on the table. Jack checked the incoming number. It was from Judge Cookson's chambers.

Lawyers, in general, were terrible readers of tea leaves, and their guesses as to whether a quick ruling from a judge would be good news or bad news were mostly useless. Jack didn't even hazard a guess.

"I have to take this call," said Jack. He rose and stepped away from the table, finding a relatively private spot beside the lone open outdoor table, the one with the big splotch of bird poop on it. He kept one eye on the cousin to make sure he didn't leave, though that seemed unlikely as long as there were more fritters on the way.

"Jack Swyteck here," he said into the phone.

Owens and the judicial assistant were already on the line. "Please hold for Judge Cookson," the assistant said.

The wait was short.

"Counsel, I've made a decision," the judge said. "Having considered all admissible evidence in the light most favorable to the prosecution, it is the determination of this court that no reasonable jury could find beyond a reasonable doubt that the defendant, Imani Nichols, committed the crimes charged. The defendant's motion for judgment of acquittal is therefore granted on both counts."

The prosecutor was silent. Jack, too, was at a loss for words.

"The jury is hereby discharged, and the defendant is released from all conditions of bail," the judge added.

"Thank you, Judge," said the prosecutor. There was nothing else to say. The prosecution has no right to appeal a trial judge's entry of a judgment of acquittal, any more than it can appeal a jury verdict of not guilty.

Jack couldn't help wondering if evidence that Tyler McCormick was blackmailing his client would have forced a different result. Shame on the prosecution for not uncovering it.

"Thank you, Your Honor," said Jack, and the call ended.

Leon was still at the table, willing to talk, and the waitress had just delivered two more beers. Their conversation was not yet over, but the first thing Jack had to do was call his client. Jack dialed her number.

"Any news?" Imani asked, and Jack could hear the eagerness in her voice.

"Yes. I have some very good news," he said, glancing one more time in the direction of the victim's cousin. "Good news for you, that is."

CHAPTER 54

News of Judge Cookson's ruling went viral in a matter of hours.
Imani's publicity machine immediately sprang into action to
make *#ImaniInnocent* the number-one trending hashtag in the
world. By 8:00 p.m., a prerecorded video thanking fans for their "un-
dying love and support" had millions of views. It outpaced even "Baby
Shark Dance" for one night, thanks to shares by everyone from a Disney
child star with 289 million followers, to a fortysomething pop star who
tweeted, "She *Is* That Innocent!" Imani was booked solid on cable news
from 7:00 p.m. to midnight, hopping from one show to the next in brief,
remote interviews. By design, the appearances were without Jack. The
last thing Imani's handlers wanted was the lawyers and legal experts
breaking down the evidence against Imani. The idea was to get Imani
out there answering the questions that really mattered, like, "How excited are you to have this behind you?" and, "How soon till you start
recording your next album?"

There was one sobering asterisk to all of it: the pirate killer was still
out there. Jack woke Tuesday morning with that thought weighing on
his mind. And thoughts of Andie.

"When's Mommy coming home?" asked Righley.

Jack was standing at the kitchen sink, rinsing the breakfast dishes.
"I'm not sure. Maybe today."

Righley handed up her empty plate, puzzled. "She doesn't tell you
when she's coming home?"

It was a seven-year-old's twist on her uncle Theo's line. *That's fucked
up, Jack.*

"Mommy tells me what she can, honey. That's how it works."

Or doesn't.

They were out the door by 7:30 a.m. Jack dropped Righley at school and drove to the airport. His flight was to Jacksonville, where he rented a car and followed the tree-lined highways of rural northeast Florida into Union County. The destination was the town of Raiford, population 255, not counting inmates. He had business at Florida State Prison.

Just before noon, he found a space in the visitors' parking lot. Before getting out of the car, he tried Andie on her cell. It went straight to voicemail, so he left a message.

"Hey, it's me. I've been thinking about what you said—that it doesn't work anymore. But maybe it's just like everything else. It works some of the time, but not all the time. When it does work, it works magic." He paused, kind of regretting what he'd just said. "Okay, that was corny. What I'm trying to say is that sometimes it could be an advantage for an FBI agent to be married to a criminal defense lawyer. Anyway, this message is already going too long. Can we talk about it? Come home soon."

Jack put his phone away, climbed out of the car, and walked to the visitors' entrance, where he checked in with the corrections officer in the lobby.

"I'm here to see Douglas Paxton," said Jack, and he added the inmate number.

The guard checked the computer screen. "I see you were here last month for a deposition."

Jack showed him his Florida Bar card. "I'm an attorney."

"But are you *Paxton's* attorney?"

"Not yet."

"Then you need to go to general visitation and talk through the glass, like everybody else. The phones will be monitored."

"Here's the deal," said Jack. "Mr. Paxton has a parole hearing coming up soon. He should be represented by counsel. I've come to offer my services, free of charge. Tell him this is a one-time offer that I will revoke unless he meets with me today, before the close of visitation hours, and accepts in person."

"I'll convey the message," the guard said.

"Please do. I don't think FSP needs any more publicity about interfering with an inmate's right to counsel."

Jack was referring to FSP's long-running controversy over guards listening to phone conversations between lawyers and inmates who complained about prison conditions.

"Got it," said the guard. "But even if Paxton makes you his lawyer, it will be at least an hour before I can get him over here to meet with you."

Jack's day was wide open, having cleared his calendar for the trial that had ended unexpectedly. "I'll wait," he said.

"Suit yourself," said the guard.

Jack took a seat in the waiting area with a handful of other visitors. The television in the corner was tuned to a cable news station, but no one was watching. Jack kept himself busy by working from his laptop. An hour passed. Then another thirty minutes. Finally, around two o'clock, the guard came for him.

"You can see your client now, Swyteck."

Jack followed the guard down the corridor to an attorney-client conference room. Another guard unlocked the door. Jack entered, and the door closed behind him. Paxton was seated at a table, shackled and dressed in the FSP jumpsuit. His face was flushed and glistened with sweat, and his biceps were bulging even more than usual. Jack surmised that he'd come straight from the prison weight room. Two corrections officers were with him, one standing at the prisoner's side and the other at the exit.

"You two can leave," Jack told the officers.

"Buzz when you're done," the one at the door said. The two officers exited and closed the door, leaving Jack alone with his new client.

"So, you're gonna help me get parole?" asked Paxton.

Jack turned the wooden chair around and sat with his forearms resting on the chairback, facing him. "Maybe."

"You're my lawyer now. You have to help me."

"You're my client now. You have to stop feeding me bullshit."

Paxton smiled. "Is that what this is about? You want the real story?"

Jack didn't return the smile. "There's a serial killer out there who thinks people who listen to music without paying for it deserve to die."

"I can't do anything about that."

"I think you can. And, as your lawyer, I think that's your best shot at getting parole."

"I already cut a deal with the prosecutor for my testimony."

"No, you didn't. The prosecutor was telling the truth about that. He never promised you anything in exchange for your testimony. And now that the case has been dismissed with no convictions, I can assure you that he will give you exactly what he promised. Nothing."

The reality was setting in, and Paxton's anger was evident. "That motherfucker. You're my lawyer. Fix it."

"I'll try, but I need your help. And I need the truth. Tell me everything you know about the killer's signature, 'goodbye girl.' I'll put together a proposal to the FBI."

"For what?" he said, scoffing. "So I can get screwed again?"

"No. This time you have a lawyer negotiating for you. You'll have a promise in writing that the United States government will appear at your parole hearing and will fully acknowledge their gratitude for your cooperation and invaluable assistance to Operation Gibbet."

Paxton took a minute, mulling it over. Finally, he looked at Jack and said, "I screwed it up."

"Screwed what up?"

"The message. 'Goodbye girl.'"

"How did you screw up?"

"It's funny, but I thought you were going to catch onto it at trial. Remember when the prosecutor was asking me questions about that Johnny Depp movie?"

"Yes. The opening scene, where he finds the pirates who were hanged, and the sign by their bodies says, 'Pirates, Be Ye Warned.'"

"Right. And Owens started asking me questions about pirates in the movies versus pirates in real life."

"What does that have to do with you screwing up the message 'goodbye girl'?"

Paxton folded his arms across his chest, flashing his overdeveloped biceps. "The message wasn't supposed to be 'goodbye *girl.*'"

"What was it supposed to be?"

"Goodbye . . . in real life."

"As opposed to the virtual world," said Jack, following it.

"Right. In real life. But using the abbreviation that people type when they're texting: I-R-L: 'goodbye irl.'"

Jack suddenly recalled the testimony of the handwriting expert. "That's why the 'g' was smudged. You realized you screwed up and tried to rub it off before you chained Tyler's body to the piling."

"How'd you know that?"

"Doesn't matter. But this means the pirate killer is writing 'goodbye girl' on his new victims only because you screwed up. The prosecution and the FBI are right. He truly is a copycat."

"That's about the size of it."

"But why is he copying you? And who is he?"

Paxton leaned forward, resting his forearms on the tabletop. "Will the FBI help me at my parole hearing if I have an answer to that?"

"Do you have answers?"

"Nuh-uh. You want me to make something up?"

"No, I want real answers," said Jack. "In real life."

CHAPTER 55

Jack watched the sunset from an altitude of thirty thousand feet, and his flight from Jacksonville landed in Miami well after dark. The tail end of rush-hour traffic was flowing against him, out of downtown, as he drove toward home on Key Biscayne. Not until he was at the eighty-foot peak of the William Powell Bridge, surrounded by the moonlit bay, due south of where Andie and the Miami-Dade Police had recovered Tyler McCormick's body, did it hit him: he suddenly remembered where he had seen "irl" before.

At the end of the bridge, he steered into the parking lot at the Rusty Pelican restaurant and turned the car around. He drove to his office in record time, paying no mind to the speed limit.

"Bonnie?" he said as he entered the lobby. It was wishful thinking. Trying to find old trial exhibits without his trusted assistant was like drilling for oil without a geologist.

Jack went to the storage room behind the kitchen and switched on the light. This was where old trials, won and lost, went to die. Anything more than three years old was shipped off to a warehouse in Hialeah, but Jack wasn't looking for anything nearly that old. Luckily, Bonnie had made his task easy. She'd already boxed up and labeled all exhibits from the hearing before Judge Stevens in the case of *Nichols v. Nichols*.

Jack pulled the bankers box from the shelf, carried it into the kitchen, and placed it on the table. He found what he was looking for in a file marked "confidential."

His cellphone rang, piercing the silence, startling him so badly that he nearly dropped the file on the floor. It was Andie, so he answered.

"Hey, where are you?"

"I just landed," she said.

"Great. Righley is going to be so happy."

It was the kind of remark that, under normal circumstances, wouldn't have made him think twice. But things being what they were, he felt the need to clarify. "And I'm happy, too," he said, which only seemed to make things more awkward.

"Sounds like we're all happy," said Andie. "Is Righley there?"

"No, I'm not at home. I'm at the office."

"Who's with Righley?"

"Abuela."

She groaned. "Jack, really? Your grandmother is getting too old for that much responsibility. Her bedtime is an hour before Righley's."

"That's such an exaggeration."

"She ordered Righley *goat* milk instead of *oat* milk from Instacart."

Jack thought it was pretty awesome that his *abuela* even knew *how* to order groceries online, but he stopped himself. Thirty seconds into their first conversation in almost two days, and they were on the verge of an argument. Jack wondered if this was how it felt when "it's not working anymore."

"I won't be here long," he said. "I'll see you at home."

"See you at home," she said, and the call ended.

Jack put his phone away, cleared his head, and opened the confidential file from *Nichols v. Nichols.*

At the top of the file were the sixteen "apologies" that Imani had texted to Shaky when they were married. Judge Stevens had reviewed each one and found they had nothing to do with Shaky's allegations of "forced penetration" or other sexual misconduct. They were generic apologies for unspecified actions.

Jack dug deeper into the file, but the messages he wanted weren't there. Predictably, he had to call Bonnie at home after hours. As always, she picked up, no complaints. She even helped him describe what he was looking for.

"You found the sixteen messages Judge Stevens reviewed, right?"

"Yes," said Jack.

"You want the text messages that Shaky's lawyer couriered to the office on the Saturday before you left for London. The ones she only threatened to show the judge. The X-rated ones."

"Well, I wouldn't call them X-rated."

"No? Did you not read them when I told you to read them?"

"Bonnie, it was five o'clock in the morning. Theo had just called from London to tell me he was in jail. The case was on hold, so I skimmed the messages and told you to file them away."

"And to get a shot of penicillin. They're X-rated. Case closed."

"Okay, they're X-rated. Where are they now?"

"In the red file with three Xs on it. Duh."

Jack checked the box. "Got it. I'm surprised I missed it."

"I'm not."

"You're the best, Bonnie."

"Good night, Jack."

He smiled, thinking how lucky he was to have Bonnie, and then the smile faded. The relationship "worked" for him, but it suddenly had him wondering. Was that the measure of a healthy relationship? Whether it worked *for him*?

He pondered the question a moment longer, but the red file beckoned. He opened it and renewed his search, bearing in mind that Bonnie's sensibilities were more closely aligned with the Hays Production Code than the modern ratings system. Even so, his focus wasn't really on content. He was looking for the use of one little abbreviation in any of the message threads. And he found it. Multiple times.

irl

The context in which it was used wasn't clear at first, but by the fourth thread, Jack had the idea. A married couple is interested in sexual experimentation with someone outside the marriage. Naturally, they start slowly. Slowly wasn't the right word. "Virtually" was more like it. The couple goes to bed, does the things they normally do, but spices it up this time. The difference is the flat-screen television on the bedroom wall. They're not watching some pornographic film about the lonely housewife who needs the help of the shirtless stud next door to hang a picture in her bedroom. A live sex chat is in progress. The wonder of the internet has brought a sexy redhead from Bulgaria into their room who can talk and masturbate at the same time, speaking just enough English to tell Shaky how much she wants his cock.

I was OK with it on the internet, Imani had texted, to which Shaky had responded:

more than OK with it! was YOUR idea!

Some ambiguous version of the "smiley face" emoji followed, and then Imani's reply:

Should never have done this irl.

Jack stared at the printed message. *In real life.*

He continued through page after page of printed text messages. He found it again. And again. She used it so many times that the conclusion was inescapable.

irl was part of Imani's texting vocabulary.

Jack laid the file to the side. The kitchen was stone silent, which only seemed to amplify the clash of thoughts running through his head. Jack didn't have enough information about the task force investigations into the latest killings to know if his discovery was important or not. If it might help catch a serial killer. If it might save the next victim's life. But "in real life" seemed like a key component of any pirate killer's message, whether the victim was Tyler McCormick in Florida or Shannon Dwyer in Boston.

Steal in the virtual world; die in the real world.

goodbye irl.

The only question was, who should he talk to first? His wife? Or his client?

Jack stared at his phone on the table. It wasn't going to dial itself.

CHAPTER 56

Andie was on her cellphone when Jack's call came.

She loved Abuela, and she was already feeling lousy about having made an issue about her babysitting Righley. Not taking Jack's call only made her feel worse, but she was on the line with the ASAC in Miami, the head of the Operation Gibbet task force in Washington, and the FBI legal attaché in London, Madeline Coffey. Andie's autoreply shot him a quick text: Can't talk now.

"I heard back from Enforcement Operations," said Coffey.

Andie had been waiting since her Sunday-morning phone conversation with Coffey, when she'd learned that a match for Judge's fingerprints in the FBI database was "blocked."

"What was DOJ's response?" asked Andie.

"In a word, cautious," said Coffey. "Which is what you'd expect when a fingerprint search turns up a match in the Witness Security Program."

"When was this guy a witness?" asked the ASAC.

"He never was," said Coffey. "He qualified for protection as a Homeland Security asset."

"What kind of asset?" asked the ASAC.

"Kidnappings," said Coffey.

"So he was, what? A ransom mule? An informant?"

"He was kidnapper," said Coffey. "He specialized in extraction kidnappings."

The line was silent. The use of third parties to apprehend fugitives and other foreign targets to facilitate extradition to the United States was not openly discussed within the FBI.

Andie followed up. "Do you mean like the extraction kidnapping of Vladimir Kava's son in London last month?"

"I don't mean *like* it," said Coffey. "I mean that's the one, specifically, that got him into the program. It went sideways. Sergei Kava's driver helped set it up. He was murdered, presumably at the oligarch's direction."

"So was his accomplice, Amongus Sicario" said Andie. "My husband was on the phone with him when he was shot. No one has seen or heard from him since."

"Well," said Coffey, "about that . . ."

"And his body was never found," said Andie, the pieces of the puzzle coming together in her head.

Coffey continued, "Amongus Sicario was passionate about the war against online piracy. A founding member of Musicians Against Pirates. Over the years, he was quite an asset to the United States government. This wasn't his first extraction kidnapping. When Vladimir Kava took out the driver who coordinated his son's kidnapping, Sicario sought protection. He got it."

"He was never really shot," said Andie.

"No. That call to your husband was staged to explain his sudden disappearance. Kava apparently bought it. He sent his hit woman after Theo Knight, the other guy involved in the kidnapping, not Amongus Sicario."

"Except that Theo wasn't actually involved in the kidnapping," said Andie.

"He was, as far as Kava was concerned. And Theo Knight was the only remaining target once Sicario disappeared."

"But when he disappeared, he didn't just go away," said Andie. "Amongus Sicario is Judge."

"Looks that way."

"And Judge was a sex-trafficking pervert who had Kelly Oswald under his thumb long before he was accepted into the Witness Security Program," said Andie.

"Virtually everybody in witness protection is a criminal. There are mafia hit men under protection."

"But now he's a worse criminal than he ever was. Judge is the pirate killer."

"Unfortunately, it wouldn't be the first time a witness in the program used his protection to start a new life of crime," said the ASAC. "You're a new person. New name, new social, new passport, new background, no arrest or incarceration record to follow you around."

"We need to get out a BOLO," said Andie, meaning a "be on the lookout" notice.

"My only question is timing," said Coffey. "He has credit cards linked to his Witness Security identity. We're following the trail."

"Where does it lead?"

"Last usage was to buy gas this morning in Miami. Once we put out the BOLO, he'll stop using the cards. The question is, do we keep following the trail, or do we issue the BOLO?"

The question was for the head of the task force.

"I'm not holding the BOLO," said the unit chief. "We can't risk another victim. The public has the right to know who this guy is and to protect themselves. And we benefit from three million sets of eyes and ears on the ground."

"What about his cellphone?" asked Andie.

"His carrier is based in Dallas," said Coffey. "I've already contacted the U.S. attorney there. Her office should have a warrant for his phone records tonight. But that's another consideration with the BOLO. He'll stop using his phone once we issue it."

"I'm not waiting on the BOLO," said the chief, more firmly this time. "Henning, coordinate with local law enforcement. I want the name of everyone this guy knows in Miami."

"On it," said Andie.

"And get tech involved. This guy may be smart enough to stop using his cellphone after he sees the BOLO, but he might not know enough to dump it. See if we can pick up a signal and get a location on him."

"Roger that," said Andie.

"And let's activate SWAT," he told the ASAC, his voice more detached. "This one probably isn't going down easy."

CHAPTER 57

Amongus Sicario spent the evening on South Beach.

"Another rum and Coke?" his waitress asked.

He was at a sidewalk café on busy Ocean Drive. Warm breezes from the Atlantic made for a perfect November evening. A far cry from Lake Michigan, where he'd nearly frozen to death.

"Make it a double," he said.

It felt good to be back, but a return to Miami had not been in his plans. Halfway on the drive from Chicago to New Orleans, he'd heard the news about Shaky Nichols and, just like that, the road was leading him to south Florida. He couldn't attend Shaky's memorial service and risk being recognized, but he desperately wanted to be a fly on the wall. He would park across the street from the cemetery and wait for the hearse to arrive. Long lines of limousines would follow. One music executive after another would step out and proceed to the graveside. A few would be genuinely sad. Most would attend out of obligation. They all had something in common: every single one had taken a hard look at an aspiring young artist named Amongus Sicario and labeled him "unprofitable."

The waitress returned with his drink. He gave her a credit card, an American Express platinum, which he'd been able to get in his new name with the good credit history that came with his new identity.

"Anything else?"

"I'm good," he said.

She left him alone. He tasted his drink and then checked the time. It was almost too late to call Moscow, but what did he care? He owed Kava a follow-up call. It was about payback.

The music royalties he'd lost to piracy on Kava's platforms over the years were incalculable. The industry kept data on revenue lost to piracy, but it was based in large part on takedown requests, which skewed heavily in favor of the big-name artists who had the resources to monitor piracy websites and threaten legal action. Where did that leave an artist like Amongus Sicario? Unprotected. Uncounted. Unpaid. His music should have made him a millionaire many times over. Instead, his musical screed against capitalism had left him broke. His fans loved the "fuck corporate America" message, which in their minds meant "fuck the record labels who charge for music." Sure, Drake and Jay-Z got pirated, too. But at least *some* people paid for their music. *Nobody* paid for Amongus Sicario. Maybe people felt better saying they were sticking it to the record labels, but they were really sticking it to Amongus— and putting ever more money in the hands of the wealthiest pirates the world has ever known.

It was time Vladimir Kava paid his due.

Amongus dialed him on his cell. Kava answered. Amongus got straight to it.

"Get a pen and paper," he said. "I have the wire instructions."

"I'm not paying you a cent," said Kava.

"Bad mistake. Every dead pirate cuts your website traffic in half. I've already got my eye on the next one."

"There won't be a next victim."

"There will be if I don't get my money."

"Seventy-five million was Shaky's money, not yours. Though I do give you points for demanding the exact sum that Shaky lost on his stock options due to piracy. For a minute, I even considered the possibility that Shaky was my blackmailer. Until I realized it was you."

"You have no idea who I am."

"You haven't been online in the last twenty minutes, have you . . . Amongus Sicario?"

He wasn't sure how Kava had figured out it was him, but he could deal with it. What was a Russian oligarch going to do? Run to the U.S. attorney and say he was being extorted?

"There is no more Amongus Sicario,"

"That's funny. Because his face is all over the internet. The FBI just issued a BOLO."

Amongus was left speechless.

"Goodbye, Amongus. Or should I say, 'goodbye girl.' Whatever that was supposed to mean."

The line went silent. Kava was gone.

Amongus quickly googled his own name—his old name—on his cellphone. The results hit him like a tsunami. Ironically, it was what he had once dreamed about: a simple name search yielding countless hits from virtually every corner of the worldwide web. This was a nightmare.

BE ON THE LOOKOUT FOR A NEW TOP TEN FUGITIVE the headline read. Below it was his photograph with the caption, "Amongus Sicario, formerly known as Ronaldo Concepcion, also goes by the name Derek Brown and the nickname 'Judge.'"

Derek Brown was his witness protection name. Ronaldo Concepcion was the name his mother had given him. The name he'd taken to prison with him. His name before he became Amongus Sicario. It had been a very long time since anyone had called him Ronaldo. More than a decade. The last person, in fact, had been Imani.

They were on a trip to the Bahamas. Imani had taken a look at his passport, which was under his old name. She'd made fun and called him *Rr*ronaldo the rest of the trip, trilling the "r" in a very affected accent. Shaky had also been on that trip. They were on Kava's boat. It was the same trip on which Amongus—*Rr*ronaldo—had brought up the Johnny Depp movie and pointed out the spot in Nassau where ten pirates were hanged and gibbeted in real life.

Imani told the FBI.

The thought hit him with as much force as the BOLO.

Judge Cookson had dismissed all charges against her, so her cooperation with the FBI was without risk. She could say what she wanted about the trip to the Bahamas—the trip that no one was *ever* supposed to talk about. Amongus had brought up the movie. Amongus had pointed out the site of execution. It was Amongus who'd said they should try it on music pirates. Imani had thought he was joking.

It was no joke.

Amongus squeezed the wedge of lime into his rum and Coke and drank until only the ice remained in his glass. A plan was forming in his head.

Imani lived nearby. Practically within walking distance from Ocean Drive. She owed him. The executions in Boston Harbor and Jamaica had done her a favor. If the charges had not been dismissed, surely Swyteck would have told the jury that Shaky and Imani were innocent, that it was the "pirate killer" who'd killed Tyler McCormick. Yes, Imani owed him big-time. Most of all, she owed him an explanation. Why did she have to tell the FBI about the Bahamas trip? Why did she throw him under the bus?

Why shouldn't he make her pay for it?

Amongus rose from his table and started walking north, toward the island residences of the rich, the famously rich, and, in Imani's case, the rich *and* famous.

CHAPTER 58

Jack rang the bell and looked straight into the security camera outside Imani's front door. Her voice came over the intercom. "Jack, what's up?"

"I have to talk to you," he said.

"Now is not a good time," she said, her voice crackling over the speaker.

"This can't wait. It's very important."

He waited. A minute passed. Finally, he heard the deadbolt turn. The door opened revealing Imani dressed in a bathrobe.

"Really not a good time," she said.

Less than twenty-four hours. It was a new record in Jack's experience—the time it took for a client to fall out of love with the lawyer who'd kept them out of prison.

"I'll be quick," he said, and Imani led him to the kitchen. She stood on the chef's side of the counter with arms folded. Jack sat on the barstool. The discreet undercabinet lighting gave the room a soft glow.

"Don't take this personally," she said, "but I'm putting the last few months of my life completely behind me. You're a big part of that world."

"I didn't come over to hang out."

"I know exactly why you came."

Jack wondered how she could possibly know—unless it was her way of telling him it was about time he figured it out. "You do?"

"Yes. I get it. After all that's happened, you must have something to get off your chest. So, say it now. You have the floor," she said with a wave of her arm.

Jack paused to collect his thoughts. He wasn't sure where to start, so he went all the way back to the beginning.

"How hard did Vladimir Kava have to push you to start the 'go pirate' campaign?"

She laughed nervously. "What?"

"Nobody benefited more from it than him."

"That doesn't mean I was doing it *for* him."

"I didn't say you were doing him a favor," Jack said. "I assume he was blackmailing you. The same way Tyler McCormick did."

More nervous laughter. "Jack, you are way off."

Jack leveled his gaze. "I spoke to Tyler McCormick's cousin. They both worked that trip you and Shaky took to the Bahamas on Kava's boat. I know Tyler tried to blackmail you. Maybe he had pictures of Shaky having sex with underage girls. I'm guessing you knew about it. Maybe you even participated in it. In real life. *Irl.*"

The façade of denial withered away. "I was barely twenty years old, Jack. No longer young enough for Shaky. Of course, in his mind it was all *my* idea. I *forced* him."

She was picking up where the civil case had left off: Who was the "victim" in their twisted relationship? Jack reminded himself that he was dealing with a pop star—a trained performer who knew how to push an audience's buttons.

"I read the text messages between you and Shaky," he said. "You knew exactly what you were getting into. You would have done a private concert for Jeffrey Epstein, as long as the money and the girls were there. And you would stop at nothing to keep it quiet. I don't feel sorry for you."

Some people might have been defensive. Imani drew on her street toughness. "That's a shame, Jack. I actually liked you."

"We were never friends."

"No, we weren't. But it's still a shame. A damn shame you know too much."

The pocket door to the dining room slid open. The dining room was dark, but there was enough kitchen light to illuminate the man in the doorway.

Jack took a good look at his face, and it was immediately clear why no one had ever found the body of Amongus Sicario.

"You were never shot," said Jack.

Amongus raised a pistol and pointed it straight at Jack. "Have you not seen the BOLO?"

Jack hadn't. He looked at Imani.

"I should have realized this so much sooner," said Jack.

"Realized what?"

"You and Shaky were actually the perfect match."

CHAPTER 59

Andie was on South Beach, waiting in a parked car, a block away from the FBI communications van on South. Her longtime partner was with her in the passenger seat. It was Andie and Grace Kennedy who, as much younger agents, had joined the search for and recovery of Tyler McCormick's body in Biscayne Bay.

Andie checked in with the ASAC for an update. He was with the tech crew in the FBI communication van.

"What's the Stingray telling us?" she asked.

The Stingray was a mobilized tracking system that could roam through target areas and "trick" a cellphone into thinking it was connecting to a cell tower when, in reality, the user was revealing a more precise location than the FBI could obtain through triangulation based on actual cell towers.

The ASAC replied by radio. "Signal is stationary. SWAT is on site."

Andie had traveled with tactical teams in past operations, and a crystal-clear image came to mind. To maintain the element of surprise, a box truck rather than the big, black Suburban, the usual FBI vehicle of choice, was parked on the street. Inside were six members of FBI SWAT from the Miami field office, sitting shoulder to shoulder, three to a side. The team leader sat nearest to the steel barn-style doors. The team was dressed in full SWAT regalia with Kevlar helmets, flak jackets, and night-vision goggles. Five were armed with M-16 rifles and .45 caliber pistols. The sixth, a sniper, touted a .308 sniper rifle. The compartment was silent, save for the steady hum of the air conditioner that kept them from roasting. Each agent was deep in thought, recounting the plan, calming the nerves, trying to bring that pulse rate down to the optimum firing level of sixty-to-seventy beats per minute. Any higher rate was a marksman's liability. It wasn't just the bad guys who killed more efficiently with cold blood.

"Are they at yellow?" asked Andie. Andie didn't live and work beneath the SWAT rainbow, but she knew that yellow was code for the final position of cover and concealment. Green was the assault, the moment of life and death, literally.

"Yes. But not for much longer."

Andie's cell rang. It was the tech agent in Dallas, and Andie assumed it was about the cellphone records. She muted her radio and took the call.

"What do we have?" she said into her phone.

"The last call on his cellphone was tonight, 7:58 p.m."

"Who did he call?"

"You're not going to believe this. Imani Nichols."

Andie froze. She suddenly had reservations about the SWAT launch. She put the Dallas agent on hold and got the ASAC back on the radio.

"Hold SWAT at yellow!"

"Too late," said the ASAC, and Andie heard the count of the tactical team leader in the background, which was playing on speaker inside the communications van. He was speaking through his bone mic from the point of breach—the door that was about to be battered down.

"We're at three, two, one . . ."

Radio squelch followed. Andie braced herself for the crack of gunfire, but she heard only the shouts of SWAT agents on the move.

"Down, down! Get down on the floor!"

There was a crackling over the radio and more shouting. Finally, there was silence.

"What's happening?" asked Andie.

"Nothing," said the ASAC.

"What?"

"Where are they?"

"Golden Sands Motel. Room 402. Nothing there but the subject's cellphone. He was smart enough to leave it there and leave it turned on so the signal would draw us there, after he was long gone."

Andie started the engine. Tires squealed as she pulled a quick U-turn and headed toward the islands.

"Divert SWAT to Imani Nichols's residence," she shouted into her phone. "I'm heading there now!"

CHAPTER 60

The gun wasn't literally to Jack's head, but a squeeze of the trigger by a cold-blooded serial killer was all that stood between life and a bullet in his brain. Amongus was standing at one of the short ends of the rectangular kitchen counter, with Imani to his left and Jack to his right, on opposite sides.

"First problem we have to solve is this," said Amongus. "One of you has to go. I don't need two hostages. Imani, tell me why it should be you."

"Uh, because I'm *Imani*?" she said, adding the lilt of a question to emphasize how obvious the answer was.

Amongus shook his head. "Doesn't cut it here. Son of a former governor. Husband to an FBI agent. In terms of hostage value, that's kind of a wash. At least in Miami."

"I can't believe we're having this conversation," she said.

"*You* can't?" said Jack.

"Shut up, counselor," said Amongus. "It's Imani's turn to make her case. You'll get yours. Tell me, Imani. Why should I keep you?"

He was acting like a judge. Judge and executioner.

Imani turned on her powers of persuasion. "Amongus, we go way back. We started MAP together."

"Yeah, I started it because piracy was killing me. You started it because it made you popular with other artists. And when the going got tough, you got out."

"You can't trust Swyteck," she said. "You can trust me."

"Oh, really?" he said with skepticism.

"At any point, I could have thrown everyone under the bus and saved myself. I didn't. I could have told the FBI that Tyler McCormick was such a dumb fuck that he tried to extort me, Shaky, *and Kava*. I could have told them that when Tyler McCormick came to our house to collect his extortion money, Kava's hit man was waiting for him. He left the dead body for Shaky and me to deal with. Swyteck knows all of this."

Jack didn't, but it made sense. Forcing Shaky and Imani to dispose of the body made them complicit.

"You didn't keep quiet about Kava out of loyalty to anyone," said Amongus. "You did it out of fear."

"The point is I am loyal to *you*. I could have told the FBI that you came up with the idea of killing pirates. I never did."

"How do I know you didn't?"

"Look at the BOLO! It says, 'Also goes by the nickname Judge.' Where did they get that, Amongus? Not from me! Who called you 'Judge'?"

Amongus fell silent, and Jack could practically hear the wheels turning in his evil mind. Jack didn't know who called him Judge, but it was clear that this judge had made a decision.

"Imani, we need rope," said Amongus. "In a pinch, an extension cord will do."

CHAPTER 61

Andie flashed her badge to the security guard at the entrance to Star Island and put him under strict orders not to notify any residents of the FBI's arrival.

"My lips are sealed," he said, dragging a finger across his lip to emphasize the point.

Imani's waterfront estate was at the tip of the island. It was not lost on Andie or Grace that, had it been daylight, they could have seen all the way to Isola di Lolando, where Tyler McCormick's body had been recovered.

Andie stopped the car two houses away from the wrought-iron entrance gate to Imani's driveway. They were in the shadows, beneath the sprawling limbs of a leafy banyan tree, outside the glow of the nearest streetlamp. Andie called her ASAC.

"Where is SWAT?"

"Stuck in traffic. Head-on collision on the causeway. Lanes blocked in both directions. I may have to call for a boat to pick us up for a water approach."

"How long will that take?"

"I don't know. Sit tight."

The call ended. Andie slapped the steering wheel in frustration. "Sit tight? Seriously?"

"Worst case, we can call in MDPD's SWAT," said Grace.

The idea had some appeal. Andie had worked with them before. But before taking that step, she wanted a clearer picture of the situation.

"Try the Kingfish," she said. "Let's see if we get a signal from the house."

The Kingfish operated like a Stingray, but it was handheld and could literally pinpoint a cellphone to a specific room. Grace switched on the device, and in a minute the results flashed on the screen.

"Two cellphones are pulsing," Grace said, and she stated the first number.

"That's Imani's phone," said Andie, recognizing it from the Dallas cellphone record data.

Grace read the second number aloud, and Andie's heart skipped a beat.

"That's Jack's cell," she said. Andie immediately opened the car door, but Grace reached across the console and grabbed her by the arm, stopping her.

"We have to wait for SWAT."

"That's my husband in there, Grace. You can sit here by yourself and wait for SWAT or you can back me up. What's it gonna be?"

They locked eyes for a moment in the shadows.

"I'm not going to break down the front door like a one-woman SWAT team," said Andie. "We make one pass around the house, check things out. And then we call the team. Deal?"

Grace was thinking it over. "Deal," she said finally.

They did a quick firearms check and then climbed out of the car, careful to close the doors without making a sound. Andie quietly popped the trunk, and they put on their Kevlar protective gear, each checking the other to leave no room for error.

"Ready?" asked Andie.

"Ready," said Grace.

Andie had been straight with her partner about her intentions, but the two agents had worked together so long that they both understood the reality.

The "deal" could change at any moment.

"Let's do it."

CHAPTER 62

Jack placed his hands behind his back, as the pirate killer directed. Imani's search of the kitchen junk drawer had turned up a six-foot extension cord.

"Tie it nice and tight," said Amongus.

Imani complied. Amongus checked her work, yanking the cord so hard that it nearly broke the skin on Jack's wrists.

"Good to go," said Amongus.

"Go where?" asked Jack. "Walk the plank?"

Amongus slapped the side of Jack's head with the butt of his pistol. A trickle of blood ran toward the corner of his eye.

"Just leave him here," said Imani. "He has a kid. You don't have to kill him."

"If we leave him here, the police will know you're helping me."

"I'm your hostage, not your helper."

"You crossed that line a long time ago," said Amongus.

"That's a lie!" said Imani.

"Let's ask the lawyer what he thinks," said Amongus. "How 'bout it, Swyteck? Hostage or helper?"

Jack didn't answer.

"Let me add one more fact to your legal analysis, counselor. When's the first time you heard the name Tyler McCormick?"

Jack didn't want to play this game, but he didn't need another blow to the head. "It was during the civil lawsuit. I got an anonymous phone call. Someone speaking through a voice altering device."

Amongus repeated the message: "'Tell Shaky's lawyer that if he reopens the hearing, you'll call Shaky back to the witness stand and ask him about Tyler McCormick.'"

"That was you?"

"As if your client didn't know," said Amongus.

"I *didn't* know," said Imani.

"Who else *could* it have been?" said Amongus. "The way I see it, we've been rowing in the same direction for a long time, Imani. Starting in your civil lawsuit with Shaky. And it just kept right on going in the criminal trial, where the return of the pirate killer could have been your best defense. Lots of reasons for the cops to think you and me were working side by side from the very beginning," he said, and then he looked at Jack. "Right, Swyteck?"

Jack was silent. Amongus pressed the muzzle of his pistol to Jack's forehead.

"I said, 'Right, Swyteck?'"

"Right," said Jack.

"Let's go," said Amongus. "Out the front door."

At gunpoint, Jack walked down the hallway with Imani at his side. Amongus was behind them. Imani's car keys were hanging on a hook in the foyer. Amongus grabbed them. Imani opened the front door, and they stepped out into the night. Amongus popped the trunk of Imani's Mercedes, which was parked in the driveway.

"Get in," he told Jack, and almost immediately there was another voice in the darkness.

"FBI, freeze!"

Amongus wheeled and fired three quick shots in the direction from which the voice had come. Imani screamed, and Jack dove to the pavement, taking her with him. Two return rounds popped from somewhere in the darkness. Amongus left Jack and Imani where they lay, hurried around the rear bumper to the driver's side door, and flung it open.

"Freeze!" Jack heard again.

It came from the passenger side, but this time the voice was familiar. Jack couldn't see Andie, but the next sound was unmistakable.

A shot rang out at very close range.

From his position of cover on the driveway, Jack caught a glimpse of the action in the driver's side mirror, which unfolded as if in slow motion. The angle was such that he could see into the sedan as the gunman's head snapped back, unleashing a crimson spray across the interior. His gun flew from his hand and landed in the driveway. His body tumbled backward, like a rag doll, and landed on the pavement. His lifeless eyes were in Jack's direct line of sight, as if the two men were staring at each other beneath the chassis from just a few feet away.

"Jack, are you hurt?"

It was Andie's voice.

"I'm fine," said Jack.

"Me, too," said Imani.

"*You* are under arrest!" Andie told her. "Stay down!"

Andie hurried to her partner, who was still down on the lawn, just off the driveway.

"Hang on," Jack heard her say, pleading. "Just hang on, *Grace*."

EPILOGUE

J ack was at Andie's side late into the night, seated and waiting outside the surgical suite at Jackson Memorial Hospital. Agent Kennedy's husband was with them, and they had the added comfort of
knowing that there was no better place for a gunshot victim to land than
the Ryder Trauma Center at Jackson. Andie's partner had presented
with a non-life-threatening gunshot wound to the leg, and the surgery
went well. "She'll be on crutches for a while," the surgeon told them,
"but she'll be fine."

"Fine" was not the prognosis for Imani.

Her initial social media strategy was predictable: Imani was a hero
who had convinced Amongus Sicario to spare Jack's life. That narrative was actually gaining traction for a day or two—until the first
victim came forward. A twenty-eight-year-old woman from Australia
felt that she owed it to her two daughters to expose the abuse she had
suffered as a sixteen-year-old girl on Vladimir Kava's superyacht, at the
hands of Shaky Nichols. Imani's messaging strategy quickly pivoted
from hero to "victim," claiming that the pop star knew nothing about
her husband's sex crimes. Naturally, the media swarmed around Jack
for information.

"Say one word about me, and I'll have you disbarred," Imani warned
him. Jack had refused to sign Imani's NDA as part of the engagement,
so a bar complaint or defamation suit were the only threats she could
make to silence her former attorney. Bar rules are not a muzzle, however,
and truth is a defense to any defamation suit. Jack could have jumped
into the national chatter with both feet, but he chose not to. He simply
gave up the phone number for Tyler McCormick's cousin.

"Call him," he told the media. "And be sure to taste the conch fritters."

Imani's "victim" messaging quickly backfired. Fans and followers peeled away by the millions. Imani's "go pirate" campaign had a new twist: "Cancel Imani."

Whether she would face criminal charges was unclear. Double jeopardy prevented the state attorney from bringing charges against Imani for any involvement in the murder of Tyler McCormick, even if his status as blackmailer was a previously unknown fact. Charges for covering up the sex crimes of her husband were part of the national chatter, but even the state attorney had to admit that it might be too late to bring those charges under the statute of limitations. It left many people feeling unsatisfied.

It was early December, following what Righley decided would be an annual holiday cookie-baking party at her house. Jack and Andie were in their kitchen, cleaning up what looked like the aftermath of *Cupcake Wars: Nuclear Edition*. Jack wasn't sure what had triggered it, but Andie suddenly wanted to sort out how the dust had settled.

"So, she gets away with it?" said Andie.

"Depends on what you mean by 'it,'" said Jack.

"Having threesomes with her husband and underage girls. Conspiring to murder the blackmailer who threatened to expose their crime. And then mutilating the corpse to make it look like the work of a deranged pirate killer."

"The only thing we know for certain is that Imani refused to pay a blackmailer who threatened to make it public that her husband had sex with underage girls. Once she knew, she should have done something about it. Instead, she helped her husband hide his crimes."

Andie squeezed the last of the dishwasher soap into the dispenser. "That's it? In your mind she's guilty of being a pick-me girl?"

"No. A pick-me girl throws other women under the bus to curry favor with men. Covering up your husband's sexual violation of underage girls is an actual crime."

"Conspiracy to commit murder is also an actual crime."

"If there's evidence to provide it beyond a reasonable doubt."

"How big does the mountain of evidence need to be, Jack?"

"Kava's hit man killed Tyler McCormick because he wasn't just black-mailing Shaky and Imani, but Vladimir Kava, as well. He left it to Shaky to dispose of the body. Shaky was probably in on the murder before it happened. Maybe, after the fact, Imani was actually happy her blackmailer was dead. But as awful as Imani's conduct was, I've seen no evidence that she actually conspired and agreed *in advance* that Tyler McCormick should be strangled to death."

"Oh my God, Jack. This only convinces me more: my solution is the only solution."

She was referring to the "solution" that she had come up with on her own, and that she couldn't discuss with Jack until the conflict between his trial and her investigation abated. It seemed that time had arrived.

"What's your solution?" asked Jack.

Andie paused, setting up her delivery, as if she were announcing this year's Oscar winner for Best Picture.

"I want you to stop doing criminal defense work," she said.

It sailed right over Jack's head. "Huh?"

"Hear me out. Fighting crime is the essence of what I do as an FBI agent. I don't have a choice about being averse to the criminal bar."

"Criminal *defense* bar," said Jack, a distinction he'd drawn at least a thousand times in their marriage.

"Right. My point is, you do both criminal and civil cases. Only one of those is averse to law enforcement. The choice is obvious: stop doing criminal defense work."

Jack was incredulous. "That's your solution?"

"Yes."

"How can you expect me to do that?"

"What do you mean, 'how can I expect it'? Women make these sacri-fices all the time. I have friends—top-notch law enforcement officers—who gave up their careers entirely because it was the best thing for their families. I'm not asking you to give up your entire legal career. Just an aspect of it."

"An aspect? What if I asked you to give up undercover work? That's just an 'aspect' of your career, but it's what you enjoy most."

"I would do it if that would solve our problems. But it wouldn't."

Jack took a breath. "There has to be a better solution."

"There's not. This case proved it. I haven't even begun to tell you the problems your trial created for me and my role in Operation Gibbet."

"I was doing my job."

"I'm not just talking about doing our jobs," she said, pleading. "I'm talking about *us*. This stupid rule that I don't talk to you about my active investigations and you don't talk to me about your cases is killing us. Wouldn't it be nice to be able to talk to your wife about something that's going on at work without worrying that your client might end up in jail? Wouldn't it be nice if I could vent to my husband without worrying that I was exposing an FBI weakness to the entire criminal bar?"

"Criminal defense bar."

"Stop it. I'm being serious. Think about the questions I just asked you. Don't you sometimes feel like there's something missing between us?"

He could see in her eyes that she was speaking out of love. But even without that, her words landed with more force than she could have possibly realized. It was the "fog" he'd been feeling for some time, even before the Imani Nichols case—the sense that something was indeed missing in their relationship, and his inability to pinpoint exactly what it was.

Andie closed the dishwasher door and started the machine. The motorized spray hissed like white noise in the fog.

"So," she said, her expression as serious as Jack had ever seen. "You'll think about it?"

Theo took a taxi to Heathrow for the Friday afternoon flight to Miami. Kelly was standing at the curb outside the terminal. She had a carry-on bag with her. They'd already said their goodbyes in Bethnal Green. Or so Theo had thought.

"What are you doing here?" asked Theo.

"I have a flight to Miami. What are you doing here?"

Theo simply groaned.

"No way!" she said, shoving him so hard that she nearly knocked him off the curb. "You're going to Miami, too?"

Theo groaned again. "I'm not buying you a ticket to Miami."

"You don't have to. I already bought one."

"With what money?"

"Did you know the FBI offered a fifty-thousand-dollar reward for information leading to the capture of the pirate killer, dead or alive? Guess who gets it?"

That actually made him smile. "I'm happy for you. But you're not coming to Miami with me."

He started away from the curb. Kelly walked with him through the sliding double doors and into the terminal. "I didn't say I was going *with you*."

"Don't split hairs. You're on the plane. I'm on the plane."

"But we're not *together*. You're not in first class, are you?"

Theo stopped short. "Don't tell me you blew a chunk of your reward money on a first-class ticket."

She let him fret for a moment, then smiled. "No, I'm not that stupid."

"Thank God," he said, and they continued walking through the terminal.

"But see?" she said, tagging after him. "There are a million ways for me to blow through this money if I don't have a big brother to look after me."

"Kelly, I'm not your big brother."

"We don't have to put a label on it. What I'm saying is, you got a pot of money when they let you out of prison, right? Your friend the lawyer settled that lawsuit for keeping you in jail while you were innocent."

She seemed to know everything about him. "Do you live on Google?"

"You turned that money into Cy's Place," she said. "You didn't waste it. Now I got all this reward money. I can blow it. Or I could learn from you."

"I'm definitely not a role model."

"But you could be my boss," she said, and then she leaned her head against his shoulder, adding a cheesy smile. "My very benevolent boss."

"Where do you get these words?"

"I'm a woman of means."

"You're eighteen. Barely a woman. I can't hire a teenager to work in my club."

"Yes, you can, as long as I don't serve alcohol. I googled it."

Theo stopped. There were a couple of open spots on the long, bench-style seating near baggage check-in. He and Kelly squeezed in between two people who did absolutely nothing to make room for them.

"I can't let you come," said Theo.

"It's not your decision."

Theo was trying to have a serious conversation, but the guy to his left was watching the newest Tom Cruise movie, no earbuds, the sound blasting for the entire terminal to hear. The quality was so poor, Theo could tell instantly that someone had literally gone into the theater, filmed the entire movie on a cellphone, and posted it on the web for others to watch on their phones.

"You know that's illegal, right?" said Theo.

"Sue me," the guy said.

Less than a week since the demise of Amongus Sicario, and it was as if there had never been a pirate killer.

Theo rose, and Kelly walked with him to the security checkpoint. They took their place at the end of the long, winding line.

"You're really coming to Miami," he said, resigning himself to it.

"I really am," she said, and then she poked a finger at his ribs. "Come on, admit it. You're glad I'm coming."

His gaze drifted toward the front of the line. A girl about Kelly's age was having a hard time getting her carry-on through the X-ray machine. From the looks of things, she'd crammed everything she owned into that bag. She was with some guy, but he was as helpful as dirt. For whatever reason—maybe it had something to do with his mother's too-short life, or maybe it was just the young woman standing right beside him—Theo was suddenly thinking of the "blokes" he'd seen in the East End selling passports out of convenience stores. He wondered what this girl's story was. He *worried* what her creepy boyfriend's story might be.

He lifted Kelly's bag onto the conveyor belt. "I know this great little place in Miami," he said.

"What kind of place?" asked Kelly.

"Best pancakes ever."

She smiled. "Oh, I *seriously* doubt that."

ACKNOWLEDGMENTS

This year marks the thirtieth anniversary of the publication of the first Jack Swyteck novel, *The Pardon* (1994). Jack was a young, idealistic criminal defense lawyer who defended death row inmates. His father was the law-and-order governor of Florida who signed a death warrant for a man Jack believed was innocent. The courtroom drama and father-son differences wrapped up nicely, and it wasn't my intention to launch a series. Over the next several years came a steady flow of letters and emails from readers asking, "What ever happened to Jack?" Five books later, Jack returned in *Beyond Suspicion* (2002), along with his sidekick Theo Knight. *Goodbye Girl* is Swyteck number nineteen, with more to come.

During his thirty-year run, Jack has been fortunate to have the same publisher (HarperCollins) and the support of my literary agents, the late Artie Pine and his son, Richard, who have been Swyteck fans almost as long as I have. Rick Horgan edited *The Pardon*, starting with a thirty-five-page letter in which he set forth the "five essential elements" of suspense, explained in excruciating detail how my first draft of *The Pardon* failed on all five counts, and then, mercifully, laid out a plan to fix it. Carolyn Marino gets credit for really launching "the series," editing fourteen Swyteck novels, including the winner of the Harper Lee Prize, *Gone Again* (2016). My current editor, Sarah Stein, entered with *Twenty* (2021), which many longtime fans regard as a favorite.

I'm also happy to report that *Goodbye Girl* continues the long tradition of "character auctions" in the Swyteck series. Starting with *Beyond Suspicion* (2002), the tradition of naming a character in a Jack Swyteck novel after the highest bidder at a charity auction has raised well over

$100,000 for so many wonderful causes, from cancer research to pre-school education. Mark Greenberg loaned the name of his brother, Arnie Greenberg, to Andie Henning's boss in *Goodbye Girl*, all for the benefit of the Broward Public Library Foundation. My "beta readers" have changed over the years, but they are an essential part of the team. My thanks to Judy Russell and Ann Carlson for doing their best to clean up the typos. Any remaining mistakes are my own.

Finally, as if Jack's debut weren't enough for one year, I married the love of my life just a few months before publication date of *The Pardon*. Happy thirtieth anniversary, Tiffany. To borrow a favorite phrase of our third child, you made 1994 and every year since "the best ever."

ABOUT THE AUTHOR

JAMES GRIPPANDO is a *New York Times* bestselling author of suspense and the winner of the Harper Lee Prize for Legal Fiction. *Goodbye Girl* is his thirty-first novel. He lives in south Florida, where he is a trial lawyer and teaches Law and Literature at the University of Miami School of Law.